The Secret Bureau:
The Bloodied Girl
(Vol. 3)

Charles Félix Henri Rabou

The Secret Bureau:
The Bloodied Girl
(Vol. 3)

translated, annotated and introduced by
Nina Cooper

A Black Coat Press Book

Acknowledgements: Thanks to Charles Griggs for his reviews of all drafts and his helpful critique of each. Thanks to the Henneveux Family for their loyal support, as well as to Daniel Auliac for his always invaluable help.

Visit our website at www.blackcoatpress.com

TABLE OF CONTENTS

Introduction

The first volume of the saga of the Secret Bureau (in French: *Le Cabinet Noir*) was first published in Belgium by A. Lebègue in 1859 in a truncated version; the complete edition was then released in France in five small volumes by L. de Potter in 1856. Its sequels, *The Brothers of Death* (*Les Frères de la Mort*) and *The Bloodied Girl* (*La Fille Sanglante*), followed in 1857, and the story eventually concluded in *Le Marquis de Lupiano*, released in 1858.

Volume I of *The Secret Bureau* starts with the son of E.T.A. Hoffmann, the author of the celebrated *Tales*, Frantz Hoffman, a medical student in Paris, who agrees to help a man seemingly risen from the dead, François-Maximilian Kormer, a.k.a. the Marquis de Lupiano, to publish his memoirs which include the history of the Secret Bureau. The Marquis takes part in all the episodes of the story, but changes names frequently, using the various aliases of Monsieur Lelourd, Colqhoum, Marquis Vincente de Samaniego, Marquis de Saint-Just, etc., but always retaining and elaborating on his evil designs, plots, and influence.

At the beginning, *The Secret Bureau* mostly tells the story of the Hulet family, for centuries the custodians of the French Government's spy system. This secret system, called in English the "Secret Bureau," opens and examines all domestic and foreign correspondence, including those written in code. The secret position is inherited, going from father to eldest son when the latter reaches his majority. If the son is not fit, stupid, or irresponsible, he will be imprisoned, killed, or, if he refuses to assume his inherited position, he will be watched throughout his entire life, never allowed to succeed in whatever he may attempt.

When nearing his majority, Henri Hulet, whose principal characteristic is ambition, has contracted a relationship with the daughter of a rich friend of Hulet the elder. It is advantageous and a love match. Hulet the elder refuses to give his permission, but without any reason, except that their fatal inherited burden would, by that match, draw a new family into the Hulet fate.

To try to avoid his mysterious fate, the details of which he has not yet been told, Hulet junior enters the priesthood, rises in the hierarchy, is punished because of his pride, ambition, and inordinate severity, and sent back to his monastery, hidden as if he didn't exist. But when the Revolution of 1789 begins, he is defrocked, enters political life, and marries his former intended fiancée, now a nun who has forsaken her vows. He rises in political life to become part of the Convention Assembly that decided the fate of King Louis XVI. He casts the deciding vote at the Convention for the death of the King. During the Reign of Terror, both he and his father are imprisoned. After the death of his father, who is taken to the guillotine in his place, Henri Hulet is released and leaves public life, retiring to the country.

During his time in the country, he is a model father and useful medical practitioner. Hospitality given during a storm to a passing couple leads to the kidnapping of one of his sons and, finally, to his being summoned to the office of Joseph Fouché, who had recommended the death of Louis XVI, without a vote. Fouché is now the head of Napoleon's secret police. He is aware of the function of Hulet's father, and wants to enlist the younger Hulet in the same service for the government he now represents. He has a file in the handwriting of Hulet's father detailing the secret history of the Hulet family, beginning more than a hundred years before. He places Hulet in a private room and gives him a key to the file and leaves him to read his family history.

The saga then returns to the Hulet story some ten years later, when Henri Hulet is now the head of the Secret Bureau. A chance encounter in Napoleon's office antechamber with another petitioner, whose description matches that of the Marquis de Lupiano, again casts him into the disasters awaiting him.

Volume 2, *The Brothers of Death*, continues the Hulet family history and reintroduces the Marquis de Lupiano into the story. When it opens, Rabou tells a short tale of a young man who, for a small mistake, is mustered out of Napoleon's army. He tries to commit suicide, but is deterred by a stranger and is inducted into a secret society. Then he fights bravely out of uniform with the military. He is again inducted into the military, rescues a rich young woman, whom he has seen and admires, from a burning building, is offered her hand in marriage, but refuses, even though he loves her. When commanded by the Emperor, he marries her, but on his wedding night he receives a note which causes him to commit suicide. The stranger he met was, of course, the infamous Marquis de Lupiano, who has now organized a group called the "Brothers of Death," whose members commit suicide by lottery.

In the third volume of the saga, *The Bloodied Girl*, Rabou finally answers to some of the reader's questions, as he had promised to do in the first volume. He also solves some of the mysteries we encountered in the two previous volumes. At the end of *The Brothers of Death*, Rabou had revealed the identity of the author of the *Memoirs of the Secret Bureau*, now identified as a man called Carbonneau. He had also identified the editor who is now interested in publishing the remainder of Carbonneau's secret history. The editor wants to find the missing volumes which followed the previous two. He and a psychologist friend have been told that the remainder of the documents might be in Germany, where young Frantz Hoffmann returned after completing his medical studies in Paris. At the end of *The Brothers of Death*, the two men were contemplating going there to search for them.

Most importantly, in this volume, Rabou draws together some of the earlier plot threads involving not only Henri Hulet but also the Maltese man, Gregorio Matiphous, both of whom, at the end of *The Brothers of Death*, were working for the Secret Bureau. He also reintroduces, and reintegrates into the plot, Matiphous' enemies from the two previous volumes, including the Marquis de Samaniego, a.k.a. the Marquis de Lupiano, as well as Henri Hulet's ubiquitous nemesis, the man who once stole his infant son under the identity of Rempailleux. Finally, Rabou also brings back Herminie Daliron, Georgiana's confident from Volume I.

As an employee of the Secret Bureau stationed in Italy, Matiphous has discovered that two of his former acquaintances are now colleagues and have forgotten the valuable help he gave them in England in the past. With his skill as a surgeon, Matiphous kept the criminal Broughton alive after he had supposedly died from hanging. He was also instrumental in releasing a man named Fauntleroy from Newgate Prison, where they had met. Broughton the boxer, and Fauntleroy, alias the Prince of Asturias, are now corresponding by letter about a counterfeit scheme they are operating. Broughton, in his letters, sheds light on what happened at the lighthouse of Bell Rock in Scotland after Matiphous left.

Rabou must now answer several pending questions:

1. How was it that Kitty Ketch, who was last seen supposedly thrown from the top of the Bell Rock lighthouse into a raging sea, was later seen by the unfortunate Mademoiselle de Limeuil in Italy? Escorted on the arm of a Scottish nobleman, her husband, Kitty pretended not to recognize Madame de Limeuil, but was indirectly the cause of her death.

2. What use will Gregorio Matiphous make of the information concerning the counterfeiting ring of Broughton and Fauntleroy?

3. Where and how, if he does, will the editor find the missing documents concerning the history of the Secret Bureau?

4. Who is the eponymous "bloodied girl," and what role will she play?

5. Why has Rempailleux come back into the plot, and where has he been?

But, as Rabou himself said to his readers in the first volume:

In the vast and arduous development of what could be called an immense imbroglio, in which strangeness and mystery must be one of the principal elements of interest, will it be too much to ask patience from those who would really like to follow the line of deduction? The explanation for everything will always finally be given. Could they also be asked to pay attention to the creation of multiple incidents of the plot that must be disentangled, and to call to memory some facts already related at a much earlier point that often will be echoed or finally resolved?

Now, read on...

Nina Cooper

PREFACE[1]

For several years, when attending somewhat aristocratic funerals, it rarely happened that we failed to notice, among the mourners, a man whose unusual appearance intrigued us a great deal. Tall, seemingly more than sixty years-old, he always wore the most correct attire: a black suit, a white tie, linen gloves. To that, it must be added that his pale complexion, his sunken cheeks, his somber eyes and his excessive thinness made him the most tomb-like personality it was possible to imagine.

On leaving the church, whatever the length of the journey, and whatever the weather, no one slipped away sooner than he from the dead man's group. Not joining the intimate friends or the family, he was always the first, and the most in a hurry, to get into one of the official mourning carriages forming the cortege. We eventually noticed something else: in the more modest convoys where mourners followed the hearse on foot, we never noticed the presence of that lugubrious individual. We inquired about him in vain. Few people had noticed him, and in the small number who had paid attention to his strange regular attendance or his strange appearance, no one knew him.

One day, upon leaving the Père Lachaise,[2] by chance we found ourselves seated next to him in one of the carriages that

---

[1] In this "Preface," Rabou uses the editorial "we," since the source of the information supposedly comes from an anonymous publisher. The editorial "we," also called the "royal we," is used by writers, editors, etc., to avoid being too specific.

[2] The largest cemetery in Paris located n the 20th arrondissement. It takes its name from the confessor to Louis XIV, Père François de la Chaise (1624–1709) and was opened on 21 May 1804.

had brought us, and which, following the usual practice, was supposed to take us back to our domiciles. Believing that the right opportunity had come to question this living puzzle, we struck up a conversation by pointing out to him that, on more than one occasion, in a similar circumstance, we had the pleasure of encountering him. That attention that we showed him didn't seem to please him, and as if he wanted to teach us a lesson about indiscretion, he responded dryly:

"I wouldn't know how to be present without emotion at the funeral services of a friend. I always bring memories and preoccupations there, which hardly allow me to notice the faces around me."

We're going to see about that, I said to myself.

Asking that sentimental grave-digger some details about the private life of the dead man, we weren't long in being sure that the man to whom he had come to render our last respects, was in every way a stranger and unknown to him. That being true then, was he a gentleman who followed the dead as an amateur, as there are, on the sidewalks of Paris, *gentlemen who follow women*? But if so, how could this unusual taste be explained? Was he a man fulfilling a vow? Was he dominated by some kind of notion about devotion to the dead? Was he, in a Christian way, trying to remind himself constantly about the thought of death? Or, perhaps, was he a vampire?

We could have spent a lot more time going over these diverse suppositions if, suddenly breaking off the conversation, the inexplicable personage had not, almost without a transition, put us onto the subject of politics. At the end of several sentences, he had found a way to show himself as a most exalted Republican.

This time, we were sure of the fact. A man who, without any preparation, without knowing us, began to tell us his extreme political opinions, could be nothing other than a police informer. To make death the business of the police, that refinement seemed monstrous to us! What's more, as we responded with only extreme reserve, probably realizing that he had been found out in every way, our questioner didn't seem

14

to need to prolong the encounter. Past the Rue de la Roquette, as soon as the carriage arrived at the Place de la Bastille, he had it stopped and left us saying goodbye with a rather noticeable coldness.

Some weeks later, we were in the waiting room of our doctor, waiting for the end of a consultation begun before our arrival, when we suddenly saw the same pall-bearer who had given us so much to think about come out. We had every reason to believe that he recognized us, because, turning around immediately, he went back into the doctor's consulting room, probably advising him to be discreet in case we asked some questions about him.

"Pardon me, Monsieur," he said to us, when coming back shortly thereafter, "for prolonging your wait, but I had a question I needed to ask the doctor about his prescription."

Then he took leave with unusual courtesy and left the office.

The doctor, who was also our friend, seeing us enter, began to laugh and said to us:

"So you know Defunctis?"

"That man who left here is named Defunctis? That's probably a nickname, which he earned by his mania for following funeral corteges?"

"No, not really," the doctor replied. "That's actually his name, and if you doubt it, you can refer to the *Almanach Royal* of 1789.You will find his father listed there under that name among the Commissioners of the Châtelet."[3]

"Let's say, then, that his affiliation with the police no longer surprises me; him being the son of a Commissioner of the Châtelet, he has followed his father's business."

"Defunctis affiliated with the police!" the doctor exclaimed. "The poor man! He has conspired against all the governments for the past thirty years, and he has spent a good

---

[3] Court and police headquarters in Paris begun in 870, moved, restored, or enlarged, in 1130, 1190, 1506,1657, 1684 and demolished after the Revolution of 1789.

third of that time in jail as a political prisoner. That was his true mania; the other bizarre behavior that struck you only resulted from it."

After we had told the doctor about our multiple encounters with his lugubrious patient, he said, laughing:

"That's very true. He follows funeral corteges; but have you noticed that he never follows them on foot?"

"Well!" we said with a bit of impatience, "whether a first- or a second-class burial, does it seem any more pleasant to you?"

"No," said the doctor, laughing even louder, "but the idea is really original. Because of that, I would be very annoyed if that unfortunate man found a persecutor in you. Contrary to the suggestion he came to give me not to say anything to you, I'm going to tell you everything, since a secret, already divulged in part to a gentleman, is a great deal safer in his hands when it's told him in its entirety, and when it's careful to be placed under the safeguard of his integrity."

Our curiosity thus excited, the doctor continued:

"I must start by telling you that this poor devil, whose ardent political preoccupations could certainly have deranged his brain a little, has, in addition, suffered for some years from a chronic stomach illness. That explains his cadaverous appearance, and it's evidently in jails, where he's made repetitive long stays, that he must have contracted that annoying affliction."

"But first of all," we asked, interrupting him, "a chronic stomach illness... What do you mean by that?"

"Gastralgia is a neurosis of the intestines or of the stomach, where, in addition, the exact location is rarely found. Involving, in a more or less serious way, the digestive functions, most of the time that type of proteiform disease remains rebellious against all remedies. To relieve the sick person, when we want to treat him without charlatanism, we can seldom advise anything except a mild and limited diet, clean air, travel, moderate exercise, on foot or on horseback, or a carriage outing, but most of all, avoiding all strong emotional excitement.

From this, it is concluded that the case of our good Defunctis could very well be incurable, the least acts of exertion causing him constant irritation."

"Yes, then, in order to cure him, one would have no other method except to proclaim the Republic; but that doesn't explain to us his unusual habit of following funeral processions."

"Pardon me," the doctor answered, "but moving about either on foot, on horseback, or in a carriage, could have an excellent effect on our sick man. The first time I gave him that advice, he said to me: 'Doctor, you are advising that very casually. A carriage, a horse, those are the remedies of rich people. But do you think that a Brutus[4] like me, ruined in the service of his convictions, has the means to rent carriages by the hour to lounge around daily in the Bois de Boulogne?'"

"The Devil!" we said, struck by sudden enlightenment. "I now understand his method, although it is very unusual and rather bizarre."

"Without a doubt," said the doctor, "but you have to admit that it is ingenious. Funeral arrangements have good berlines,[5] comfortable and with good suspensions. And for two or three hours, every day, to arrange to take a free carriage ride, isn't so unskillful. Only, to think up such an idea, and most of all, to practice it for so long and with so much perseverance, it's my opinion that a little crack in the brain of our patient might be necessary."

With that explanation from the doctor, about which, in addition, we promised absolute discretion, our balloon had, in a single moment, been deflated. We were dealing with neither a police agent, an ascetic Christian, or a vampire. In a very middle-class way, we had run into an unusual man who, dis-

---

[4] Allusion to Defunctis' efforts to overthrow the government, just as Brutus thought that, by killing Caesar, he would save Rome from dictatorship.

[5] A make of expensive, luxurious, and popular carriages built in Germany.

daining the ease of the omnibus, had, at the expense of the mourning families, resolved the problem of a cheap outing.

Several months passed without our having otherwise thought about the unusual Monsieur Defunctis, when, last July 27, at the Montparnasse Cemetery, as we had just made a pilgrimage to a beloved tomb as was our custom, turning into a pathway, we found ourselves face to face with him. He was holding in his hand two wreaths of green leaves mingled with *immortelles*[6] and, in addition to his usual formal funeral attire, he wore a large crepe band on his hat. We had never before seen him so haggard and as gaunt, which made us think that his illness had become more serious.

"Monsieur," he said to us, "I hastened to meet you in order to give you my thanks. The doctor didn't leave me ignorant of the fact that he thought it prudent to be candid with you. But at the same time he reassured me, confirming to me that I could count on total discretion on your part."

"But, Monsieur, that discretion has very little merit," we replied. "What interest could I have in frustrating you in a.... hygienic practice that has taken nothing that isn't perfectly innocent?"

"As you put it very well, Monsieur; I harm no one. I try to associate myself as unobtrusively as possible into the mourning family group, and, at the same time, I take care of the needs of my health that, unfortunately, give me increasing and considerable worry. But my action has something bizarre about it. It could become fodder for an amusing story and when certain people are ready to lose twenty friends for a good joke, couldn't a poor unknown person like me be easily destroyed for the pleasure of telling about an eccentricity?"

"Monsieur," we replied, "if the recommendations of our friend, the doctor, hadn't been all-powerful for me, with a man like you, whose misfortunes, unshakeable and disinterested convictions he told me about, my conscience would always

---

[6] Several varieties of long-lasting flowers placed on graves.

have made me show myself perfectly in agreement and sympathy."

Great nervous susceptibility on the part of our questioner could be explained just by the single fact of his illness. Thus we noticed that we had made tears come into his eyes.

"Thank you, Monsieur," he told us, shaking our hand. "Your words do me good and I needed to hear them in a day so full of sad memories for me."

"You have someone who is dear to you here?" we asked.

"Yes, Monsieur, today is a gloomy anniversary for me: July 27, 1816, but also July 27, 1830![7] When Providence has permitted the crime, it also arranges the expiation."

Seeing that we had not understood him, despite the deep emotion which this remembrance seemed to bring forth, Defunctis added:

"Come with me, Monsieur, to see the tomb that I came to visit. You are not one of us, as I couldn't help but notice during our first encounter, but you have a good heart, and whatever their political affiliations, generous men never refuse to be interested in victims."

We walked for some distance and, in one of the side paths of the cemetery, there appeared a small mound surmounted by a truncated column, a monument raised in 1848 to the Sergeants of La Rochelle. Stopping in front of a modest tomb, ornamented with some flowers and granted in perpetuity,[8] Defunctis said:

"It's here, Monsieur. Read."

---

[7] Allusion to the period following the Bourbon Restoration in France: 1815-1830, when events and anger among French citizens moved from an attempt to establish a constitutional monarchy based on the British system to, finally, the restoration of the House of Bourbon.

[8] Burial sites in France are granted for a limited time and may be rented for 10, 30, or 50 years. If grave sites are abandoned, the contents are boxed, tagged and moved to an ossuary in the Père Lachaise in Paris.

We read the following epitaph:

JEAN-FRANÇOIS CARBONNEAU,
Died for Liberty - July 27, 1816
Exhumed by the cares of his family and friends
March 7, 1840

"Carbonneau," we said, "wasn't he one of the three pa-triots of 1816? Tolleron, Plaignier and Carbonneau?"[9]

"Ah! You know their names!" exclaimed Defunctis with a gesture of pride and joy. "Yes, Monsieur, three unfortunate men who, by police machination, even before proofs of their claimed conspiracy could be presented, were sent to the scaf-fold as being guilty of the crime of *lèse majesté*. Carbonneau

---

[9] The Affair of the Patriots of 1816 happened during the reign of King. Louis XVIII. Tolleron, a 30 years-old carver, Carbonneau, a 34 years-old, clerk, and Pleignier, a boot-maker, joined a society called The Patriots of 1816, the pur-pose of which was to overthrow the Bourbons. The Minister of Police, Élie Decazes, was regularly informed about the activi-ties of the Patriots and decided to use them to bolster the fail-ing Monarchy in the eyes of the public. He used an agent named Schlestein to manipulate and incite the three men to-wards a more radical opposition. On April 25, Schlestein vir-tually gave them the blueprint of a plot to blow up the palace of the Tuileries, where the King resided. The next day, Tolleron, Carbonneau and Plaintiff were arrested, along with 25 other people. On June 27, a trial was held at the Court of Assizes of Paris. Twenty sentences were handed down: eight persons were sentenced to deportation; eight to six, eight and ten years of detention; Tolleron, Carbonneau and Plaignier were condemned to death. All appeals were dismissed. On July 27, the three were guillotined. After the execution, the bodies were buried in the Sainte-Catherine cemetery then transferred to the new Montparnasse cemetery, opened in 1824.

was my friend. He had a heart of gold and died like Cato.[10] Ever since his remains were returned to his family, never has a July 27 passed that I haven't come to place a remembrance here."

That said, Defunctis attached his two wreaths to the tomb, then reverted to a brusque and commanding tone:

"I need to be alone," he said to us.

We went some steps away and then we saw him kneel, and for some minutes, his bald head uncovered, he prayed fervently. When he had again rejoined us, he continued:

"Pardon me, Monsieur, for having sent you aside, but I was afraid that it would be hard for you to kneel, following my example, on that tomb of an executed man."

"It was only a moment ago that you judged me a better man when you told me that in good hearts, there is always sympathy for victims. Besides, the Patriots of 1816 were a great deal less strangers to me than you seem to believe, and Monsieur Carbonneau is mentioned in a book for which I am the publisher."

"Really?" said Defunctis with admiration. "What is that book?"

"*The Secret Bureau,* and on that subject, I even have some information to ask you."

"At your service!" my questioner answered.

"In your long battle with the government of the Monarchy, did you ever know a political prisoner named Carbonneau, but not the same man who perished on the scaffold along with Plaignier and Tolleron?"

---

[10] Rabou does not specify if he means Cato The Elder (The Censor) (234-149 BC) or The Younger (95-46 BC), his great grandson. From the context, he must mean The Younger, who fought against Caesar and the Triumvirate, in a vain attempt to preserve the Roman Republic. As a last holdout, after the war had been lost, Cato the Younger evacuated all his remaining supporters who would leave, then committed suicide.

"Yes, I actually did! I met him in prison. That one was a man who had a somewhat deranged mind."

"And do you know if, when he died, he left some manuscripts?"

"That might be. His folly was to believe himself obsessed by a specter who forced him every night to write what he dictated."

"That's the one," we continued. "Well, those numerous manuscripts, the results of that madness—would you know to whom he might have left them?"

"Perhaps," said Defunctis. "Before being taken to Charenton,[11] where he died. Charbonneau lives on the Rue Neuve-Guillemin, in a little furnished hotel run by a former mistress of Saint-Just[12] who always was devoted to the Republicans. It is very possible that the manuscripts of her former tenant have remained in her possession. Would you like for me to find out?"

"You would render me a real service if you did," we responded.

And, leaving our address with him, we left.

Four days later, he came to see us, carrying an enormous bundle of papers.

"Here are the manuscripts," he told us as he entered. "But I arrived just in time. The poor woman owed some rent to her landlord, who had everything she owned sold. I took it upon myself to acquire what I'm bringing you, for thirteen francs, twenty-five centimes. Do you think that was paying too much?"

---

[11] Lunatic asylum founded in Paris in 1645 by the Brothers of Charity. Today it is called Esquirol Hospital, named after its 19th century director, Jean-Etienne Esquirol.

[12] Louis-Antoine-de Saint-Just (1767-1794), youngest deputy elected to the National Assembly, one of the leaders of the First Republic, he headed the movement to execute Louis XVI and authored the radical Constitution of 1793. His execution and that of Robespierre ended the Reign of Terror.

"Not at all!" we answered, after having untied the bundle and found ten or twelve continuations of the incomplete manuscript whose publication we were forced to interrupt. "There is a very different accounting to make between us. For me, these documents have a value of a thousand francs, at the least. I had some reason to believe that I might find them in Germany, and to go there to look for them, would have cost me at least five hundred francs for the trip. Instead of thirteen francs twenty-five centimes, it's then fifteen hundred francs that I'm going to pay you."

We could never make Defunctis understand that this calculation was serious, and he stubbornly insisted on seeing the value given to his discovery as disguised charity. Insisting on receiving only the expenses he had disbursed, he nevertheless waned to take it upon himself to find the woman who had become Carbonneau's heir, in order to give her the sum we intended to pay him. For himself, he was satisfied with only being given a copy of the book when it would be published.

The very day it was put on sale, we went to the Rue des Boulangers, a rather ugly street in the Saint-Victor neighborhood, where the man we were indebted to lived. As we didn't remember the exact number of the house where he lived, we asked a coal woman who was knitting, seated in front of her shop:

"Monsieur Defunctis, please?"

"There, across the street," she answered.

And on the other side of the street, supported by two chairs and occupying half of a dark alley, we saw a coffin. On the mortuary cloth there had been placed a small branch of flowers in a jam jar, a small benediction of the poor improvised by the charity of a neighbor. We were seized with a sad presentiment. We approached a group of men with beards and pointed hats, who were stationed in front of the house.

"Is Monsieur Defunctis...?" I asked with hesitation

"Present!" one of those we had asked responded, motioning with his hand to the coffin.

The hearse arrived shortly thereafter, which was not exactly that of indigents. In a moment, all the inhabitants of the street were at their doors or their windows. In the middle of a double row of poor men, who removed their hats with respect, while the women made the sign of the cross, the convoy, which hardly resembled those that Defunctis had usually followed, slowly took the road toward the church of Saint-Étienne-du-Mont. After a modest service, we gathered at the Montparnasse cemetery. Seeing his place prepared in the communal grave plot, we asked one of the workmen:

"What! Is he to be buried there?"

"And where else would you suppose?" he answered. "Lamennais is right there."[13]:

Hardly consoled by that argument, the next day we went to the Hôtel de Ville[14] where we bought a place in perpetuity. Some weeks later, we took part in the exhumation and saw the body placed in a tomb that we had ordered from one of the local marble workers. The cost, in all, came to a little less than a thousand francs. Our conscience telling us we had gained something from the price that we had assigned to the manuscript, we sent five hundred seventeen francs to the Mayor of the 12th Arrondissement.

Such was the way in which we entered into possession of the remainder of *The Secret Bureau*. Now we will again take up the publication.

---

[13] Hugues-Félicité-Robert de Lamennais (1782-1854), Catholic priest, philosopher, political theorist, at odds with the Vatican, for many years, he finally broke with the Church in 1833 and in 1834 published *Words of a Believer*, denouncing the social order as a conspiracy of kings and priests against the people. He was buried in the communal grave of the Père Lachaise without religious rites.

[14] City Hall.

PART I: BRITANNICUS THE BLACK

I. A Female Suitor

Many things were revealed to Matiphous by the voluminous letter that had just passed under the eyes of the reader. First of all, it had explained to him the sad end of his colleague, the Jew Ephraim, who had gone insane at the news of Napoleon's coronation. In his dementia, that poor man, by throwing himself on Broughton, had thought he was behaving as Brutus. But this time a Caesar, dealing a strong blow with his fist, had gotten the best of his assassin. Next, Matiphous learned the new obligations that he had to that murderer. It wasn't enough that, after owing his life to him, Broughton had begun by stealing his mistress. That man had gotten satisfaction by throwing on him the suspicion of a double crime, one that the miserable man had himself committed; the other one of which there was no certainty and which, in fact, had existed only in his imagination. Under the blow of that infamous denunciation, without his fortunate hurry to leave the lighthouse, not only would the unfortunate man from Malta had had to contend with British Justice, but at the same time he would have faced the daggers of the *Grand Firmament*.[15] And what had kept him from perishing from a frightful death?

So, in the first feeling of indignation that the revelation of all those evil deeds had caused him, Matiphous thought of writing to England to reveal the presence of the man that he had shielded from justice. At the same time, he would have alerted the English government to that counterfeiting enterprise created by the misguided ways of the Marquis de Samaniego. But to throw the former boxer into the hands of

---

[15] See *The Brothers of Death*, p. 232.

Jack Ketch was to shield him from the eagerness of Mistress Aston, and, everything considered, to let him become the husband of that shrew appeared a vengeance with a much better taste.[16] From then on, for Matiphous, it wasn't enough to leave everything to chance for that glorious marriage. To push it forward, to make it inevitable, such was his intention. For several days, his mind had already been occupied in pursuing that result when the emergence of the most fortunate unexpected event seemed to promise him its approaching and entire realization.

And by the letter of Monsieur de Limeuil, who after the catastrophe at Bell Rock, verified the presence of Kitty Ketch in Rome, as well as by the letter of Fauntleroy, who, later, said he had also been found with her, it was superabundantly proved that girl had survived her terrible accident. How she had survived an almost certain death and how she had, following that, continued her life, that's what's now advisable to explain.

It will be recalled that, when climbing onto the platform of the tower, Kitty was enveloped in a large Scottish cloak. Matiphous had advised her not to let the wind get inside it. Once she was launched into space, the North Wind, on the contrary, made its way freely under that cloak to form a parachute, by means of which Mistress Broughton was immediately deposited rather softly, and then held for several minutes, on the surface of the water. At the same moment, not far from the place where she had landed, a fishing boat was passing by. Having seen a human form launched from the top of the tower, the owner of the boat hurried to maneuver toward that object. And if, when he became aware of the idiot's work, Matiphous' emotion had left him his self-control to look down into the sea, where he was persuaded that Kitty had found her doom, he would have seen, still on the horizon, the sails of the little boat which, after having picked up Kitty, whom they

---

[16] Rabou reminds the reader of the dictum: "Vengeance is a dish best eaten cold."

mistook for a shipwreck victim who had only fainted, carried her away, perfectly alive.

Because of the bad weather that was then beginning, not only could the boat in which Kitty had found asylum not reach Bell Rock, but it wasn't even possible to reach the coast of Arbroath. Pushed throughout the night by a furious wind, it was only the following day that it reached the port of Peterhead, a little village of the County of Aberdeen, situated at a considerable distance from the point from which it started.

Once she had regained consciousness, Kitty was, to be sure, questioned with great curiosity concerning the circumstances of the events which had brought her so near death. But she had undergone in herself something like that moral revolution that mythology in the past has attributed to the jump into the sea from Lefkada.[17] Without exactly having forgotten Broughton, her adored one, she had come to see him such as he was, and found that corpulent man who, unworthily, had left her exposed to the fury of the man from Malta, ignoble. In addition, without talking about the terrible tragedy through which she had just passed, it must be remembered that the poor girl had gone from love to marriage, and, as the poets say, it isn't too often that marriage continues to wear the blindfold of Love.

Instead of saying then who she was, and of showing some desire to get back to Arbroath to rejoin her husband,

---

[17] Greek island located in the Ionian Sea on the west coast of Greece, a.k.a. Leucas, Leucadia, Lefkas and Leukas. This is a reference to the myth of Aphrodite, who, disguised as an old crone, was ferried free of charge from Lesbos to the continent by an ugly, old boatman, Phaon. In gratitude she gave him an ointment which would make him young and handsome. Sappho, the poetess, fell in love with him, but finally, spurned by Phaon, she threw herself into the sea at Lefkada, to see if the fall would cure her of her love for Phaon, or if she would drown. She drowned. (That Sappho committed suicide is contested by some modern scholars.)

Mistress Broughton, who had found that she had some money with her, took up residence incognito in an inn. There, while getting over her terrible ordeal, she consulted with herself, considered the new hand that fate had dealt her, and following her new mental outlook, decided to embark on a new path in life.

In the inn where she was staying, there lodged an old Laird,[18] or Scottish gentleman. Some business had temporarily taken him from the solitude of a venerable manor in the depth of the Orkneys, where he normally lived. The mortal boredom that he, like all the Highlanders, endured in a city, far from his cherished isles, made him more than accessible to tender fascinations. To see Kitty was to fall in love with her, and without any other ceremony, he proposed to her and asked her to follow him to his castle, where he had often regretted not having some companion of her kind; this could have been considered on the part of the Scottish gentleman as a somewhat extraordinary procedure, if it had to be judged from the point of view of our measured and thoughtful civilization. But for such a man, who remained close to nature, who had spent his life in one of the most isolated corners of the Highlands, that suddenness of desire and of decision had absolutely nothing that should surprise us. And in the lifestyle that, even today, distinguishes the north of Scotland, it can find its justification. Laid out in its entirety, it must also be admitted, with the most imprudent abandon, that this arrangement offered to Kitty wasn't accepted by her with nearly the same abandon and lack of reflection. She had informed herself through the people at the inn. She had learned that her new suitor was well situated in terms of lands as well as fortune. Next, she had found that the name of Stuart was, in addition, rather well known in the Three Kingdoms,[19] and, in the person of the old Laird, bore all its glorious significance. In fact, the over-enthusiastic lord was

---

[18] Rabou uses the Scottish term for Lord when referring to Kitty's new husband.

[19] England, Ireland and Scotland.

publically recognized as one of the products of that marvelous zeal that, in 1745, the Jacobite ladies showed around the pretender Charles-Edward, when he came to attempt in Scotland that perilous restoration attempt that the disaster of Culloden[20] ended so deplorably.

Not being able to boast such high birth, Jack Ketch's daughter had at least wanted to neutralize the scent of adventure which unfortunately had been attached to her the situation in which she had been encountered, and her adventure at Bell Rock. She did not, to tell the truth, exploit it too clumsily. She made her old suitor believe that, destined to a marriage against which her heart revolted, she had herself jumped from the top of the lighthouse and had tried to find in death a refuge against that abhorred union.

The naïve Scot then acted as a protector and friend, adding modestly that, with the age and the physique of a man born around 1746, he could scarcely hope to reconcile the young and attractive lady with the frightful idea of marriage. For Kitty, on the contrary, in the suitor whose research, disparaging to her, she, at all costs, had wanted to thwart, it was a lot less the negation of physical advantages than the complete absence of those moral qualities which are, above all, the feudal contractual rights of the man arrived at his maturity. In short, by a strange reversal of the usual course of things, confidence and true love were on the side of the old man, while on the side of young woman, everything was intrigue and calculation; so they were not slow in coming to a marvelous understanding and, less than a week after their encounter, Sir Edward Stuart's conquest was installed in the chateau he in-

---

[20] Battle of Culloden. Queen Anne, last of the Stuarts, died in 1714. The British throne by the Act of Settlement was given to the House of Hanover and resulted in the Jacobite rebellion of 1745. The Battle of Culloden, with terrible loses to the Jacobites, was the last battle of the uprising to restore Charles-Edward and the Stuarts to the throne.

habited on the island of Mainland, the largest of the Orkneys, some leagues from Kirkwall, the principal city of the County.

In that tête-à-tête which, in some way, could be said to have taken place at the top of the world, it became very difficult for a man as much in love as Sir Edward Stuart to maintain the distance of that paternal protectorate to which he had appeared to agree at the beginning of his acquaintance with Kitty. In good condition, and having by the rough activity of his country existence kept the infirmities of old age at a distance, despite his fifty-eight years, he still felt himself vigorously alive, and sometimes showed himself a little more tender than what was called for. But Kitty was careful not to seem overly indulgent toward his overtures. Just like Broughton, her glorious husband, after some reflection, she had only a very relative faith in the solidity of a union blessed by an irregular Gretna Green marriage.[21] Having a project in mind, she consequently didn't want to seem to melt her coldness, except at the moment when, exasperated by the resistance and the constant presence of his loved object, her host's ardors had decidedly taken their course toward the holy denouement of their marriage.

The pretended certainty that her family would never want her to depart from the so-called project of marriage, against which she had supposedly fought right up until death, was an excellent reason not to have her parents intervene in its conclusion. Besides, it's well known that, once drawn into a youthful folly, old people sink their teeth into it. Kitty MacLeod, then, one fine morning, became Lady Stuart, a fitting example of the very level of civilization at which the Caledonian Archipelago had arrived. Since nothing was known of the bride's family—none of whom had attended the nuptial benediction—, from a far-away echo of the catastrophe at Bell-Rock, gossip had spread that the old Laird had picked her up in the middle of the waves. His vassals, who still believed in the Sea Monk, The Girl with the Green Hands, a.k.a. the

---

[21] See *The Brothers of Death*, p. 392.

Liambdearg,[22] and other assorted Green Women, persuaded themselves that Kitty was a Mermaid, or a Siren, and they never saw her pass by without frightened curiosity.

In a country where a road and a tree are a curiosity, where eternal fog saddens the naked and solitary flat sand, constantly battered by an enraged sea, where, during winter days, the sun shows its reddish disc at eleven a.m. and which, before three o'clock in the afternoon, has gone down to the horizon, it's understandable that Kitty didn't patiently endure her exile very long, and that she wasn't long in maneuvering into *absenteeism,* as the English say when they speak of that natural inclination which causes the great proprietors of those desolate parts to lease their lands and migrate towards gentler climes.

A destination for the pretty bride wasn't difficult to find. In the Cardinal of York, Priest of Ostia Antica, of Velletri and Frascati, Vice-Chancellor of the Roman Church, Archpriest of the Vatican Basilica, Dean of the Sacred College and more, younger brother of the Pretender to the Throne of England, Charles Edward, Sir Edward Stuart had in Rome a natural uncle, immensely rich and eighty-two years old. There was, therefore, no good reason as to why he hadn't yet dared to take steps to guarantee that succession. What's more, the mortal remains of the Pretender, Charles Edward, who'd died in 1778, reposed at Frascati.[23] Wasn't it equally strange that the

---

[22] "Red Bloodsucker," also known as Ly Erg, a ghostly warrior of Scottish origin that haunts the Highlands. His right hand is said to be stained with bright red blood.

[23] Charles Edward Stuart died in Rome on 31 January 1788, aged 68, of a stroke. He was first buried in the Frascati Cathedral, where his brother Henry Benedict Stuart was bishop. At Henry's death in 1807, Charles's remains (except his heart) were moved to the crypt of Saint Peter's Basilica in the Vatican, where they were laid to rest next to those of his brother and his father. His mother is also buried in Saint Peter's Basilica. His heart, however, remained in Frascati Cathedral, where

idea of a pious pilgrimage to his sepulture had not yet come to the mind of a man who had the distinguished honor to be his son?

Thus attacked, the old husband, who, in many other things was the very humble executor of the will of his young wife, hadn't been able to resist very long. Despite his attachment to the country where he was born, and where he had spent the major part of his life, he decided on a trip to Italy for the purpose of satisfying the interest and the duty which had been so strongly exposed to him.

In Rome, Kitty Ketch encountered Madame de Limeuil and, without suspicion, killed her with one of her looks. There also she crossed Fauntleroy's path. At that time, as he had been in the past, he became for her a man easy to manipulate. In addition, she found in him one of her adorers from *La Fénice.* [24] As Laird Stuart, her respectable husband, didn't occupy in her heart the place Broughton had occupied there, she remembered the ardent attentions that that former suitor had rendered to her in the past, another reason to welcome him. And, well! Without the pretty lady's preoccupations with the Cardinal of York, the old Laird could have run some danger.

Moreover, despite all the ways in which the beautiful petitioner tried to enlist him in the matter of the succession, the Cardinal of York greeted the two spouses very coldly, and, sometime after their arrival in Rome, he gave up his soul to God without leaving anything to them in his will. A long time in the past, his will had been made in favor of George III, King of England, who, for several years, had paid him a pension of four thousand pounds sterling. Thus frustrated in that hope, with the terror that the approaching necessity of a return to the Orkneys inspired in her, Kitty found the inspiration for a

---

it is contained in a small urn beneath the floor under a monument.

[24] *Teatro La Fenice* is an opera house in Venice, one of the most famous and renowned landmarks in the history of Italian theatre.

new bit of high political intrigue. And the old Laird, thanks to the increasingly absolute control that his wife had over him, let himself be led about with an unparalleled amiability, like the most obedient of dummies.

At that time, there resided in Florence the Countess of Albany, widow of Charles Edward. It seemed to Kitty that, with such a close relationship to the Stuarts, a Jacobite resurrection ought to encounter the most avid welcome. It was therefore resolved that they would go and visit her in Tuscany. In a solemn conference where the comedy of human affairs had never seemed more grotesque day, the daughter of Jack Ketch seriously proposed to the widow of the last of the Stuarts that she recognize as claimant to the throne of England and Scotland the old Laird of Mainland. This first step taken, it would then be necessary to contact the Emperor Napoleon, who, in his furious hatred against the British, would not hesitate to encourage an armed attack on the coast of Scotland, and God knows what effects under his protection such a manifestation might produce.

With a thousand reasons, Kitty put forward the worst of her burlesque imagination. First of all, the Countess of Albany had lived in a relationship full of bitterness with the Claimant to the throne, her husband, from whom she had finally separated, and she ostensibly received a pension from England. Next, since the death of Charles Edward, she had been publically the wife of the tragic poet Vittorio Alfieri[25] who had communicated to her the exaltation of his Republican ideas. At the time Kitty came to suggest the restoration of the Stuart crown, she had contracted a third morganatic marriage with a French painter.[26] All her ambition was then reduced to making

---

[25] (1749-1803), Italian dramatist and poet, considered the "founder" of Italian tragedy.

[26] Rabou uses the idiom *marriage de la main gauche*, i.e. a morganatic marriage, or "left-handed marriage," a marriage between people of unequal social rank, which prevents the passage of the one's titles and privileges to the spouse and any

her house the rendezvous of the artists who lived in, or passed through, Florence. Assuredly, no one was less than she disposed to intervene in the manipulation of dynastic affairs in which she would have had to take a passionate interest.

The only result of her interview with Kitty was that, after having brought up public interest of the highest order, as a result of that strange drift into which conversation is often drawn, they began to talk about music. The old Laird revealed that his wife possessed a magnificent contralto voice. The Countess of Albany immediately invited Kitty to a concert she was to give some days later, asking her if she would be willing to sing.

After having escaped the terrible menace of the Camp of Boulogne,[27] England was once again saved from the projects which the powerful political genius of Kitty Ketch was plotting against it. Wasn't it, in fact, a very formidable scheme which consisted of throwing onto the English soil as a legitimate Claimant to the Throne, a dubious heir of that line who, for the last twenty-five years, had lived in obscurity and ended his life in exile? If she'd been a little less ignorant of European affairs, the daughter of Jack Ketch would have known that, even for the direct descendants of James II, many things had been settled by the Revolution of 1688.[28] While assuming, right at the last moment, the title of King of England, the poor cardinal in whose person the House of the Stuarts had just been extinguished, modestly wrote on his currency: *Henricus nonus angliae rex Dei gratia sed non voluntate hominum.*

---

children born of said marriage; it is thus named because the spouse of superior social rank gives his left instead of his right hand.

[27] A military camp established by Napoleon in 1803, until 1805. This was where he assembled his Army for a planned invasion of Britain that never took place.

[28] A.k.a. the Glorious Revolution, the overthrow of King James II of England (James VII of Scotland) by a union of English Parliamentarians with William III, Prince of Orange.

(Henri IX, King of England by the grace of God, but not by the will of Man.)

Let us add, however, that, when it's a question of making one of their wishes triumph, so many women are powerfully helped by their instinct, and that Kitty's idea, if she hadn't thought about it, would have had some sort of foundation. In fact, in reading *The Memorial of Saint-Helena*,[29] the following words are found in the mouth of the Emperor:

If, in my time, and in the circumstances into which the English Ministers had plunged England, there had yet been found some young Stuart, brave, enterprising, capable, at the height of the century, he would have set sail for Ireland, carrying modern doctrines. And there would without a doubt have been seen the spectacle of the Stuarts regenerated, dispossessing in their turn the Brunswicks.

But the Stuart Kitty wanted to use was only Stuart of the left hand. He wasn't young, hadn't been an entrepreneur except for the stupidity of his most deplorable marriage, and, in the end, would have found himself the son-in-law of Jack Ketch, the notorious London hangman. From that position, the distance to the English crown remained somewhat difficult to cross, and all that resulted from that high political aim was that Kitty would sing.

II. Matiphous' Accounts

The mystical success soon obtained at the reception of the Countess of Albany by our late female Pretender, was incomparably superior to that of her unfortunate intrusion into the domain of politics. By that peaceful triumph, better than by her fabulous research into English descent, she was temporarily protected from the harsh necessity that she had wanted

---

[29] *The Memorial of Saint Helena* is a collection of memories of Napoleon written down and edited by Emmanuel, Comte de Las Cases, as a result of their almost daily conversations during the former's exile on Saint Helena.

to avoid, that of returning to exile in the Orkneys. Because of the invitations that came from everywhere to the husband of the beautiful virtuoso, he agreed to spend the end of the winter with her in Florence. Despite his position as a British subject, with the highest recommendations, an exceptional visitor's permit had been given to him. From that point, sought after for all the reunions where, apart from her talent as a singer, the great name of her husband gave her an entrance, for a long time the daughter or Jack Ketch no longer saw on her horizon anything but a continual enchantment of pleasure, of gallant praise, and parties. She didn't know, the imprudent one, that a serpent was going to slide under that bouquet of flowers.

That "serpent" was Gregorio Matiphous. Lady Stuart had been in Florence for several weeks without his having been aware of it in any way. Because of the requirements of social position, as well as by taste, the man from Malta saw very few people of high society. No occasion had then arisen for him to encounter his beautiful enemy in the salons. But one evening, at the Cocomero Theatre in Florence, where there was a concert followed by a ball to benefit the poor, the emotion of the man from Malta can be imagined, when, in an incomparable costume, standing near a piano which was going to accompany a solo piece of the *Serva Padrona,*[30] Kitty Ketch appeared before him, splendidly and decidedly resurrected.

For that strange girl, that evening was a veritable triumph. The Grand Duchess had honored the evening with her presence, and she was the first to commence the applause, which shook the hall three times. When the singer had finished her piece, the ball began. There was a rush to see who would have the good fortune to dance with her, and never had a beauty seen herself so surrounded. The more the success of that woman, to whom he had sworn so much hatred, grew, so did Matiphous' desire to trouble her success and her joy. In short, and for the present, to make himself known to her, seemed to

---

[30] *Serva Padrona (Servant Turned Mistress),* an opera buffa by Giovanni Battista Pergolesi (1710-1736).

him a sufficient feast of trouble. Making his way through the crowd of well-wishers obsessed with the queen of that party, he confronted her, saying softly:

"Lady Stuart, would please permit the most humble of the unknown to place at your feet the expression of his strongest and most ardent admiration?"

On hearing that voice and recognizing the features which, for her, were so full of threatening memories, the triumphant woman could verify the truth of that famous saying: *The Tarpeian Rock is close to the Capitol.*[31] The instant before, she'd been drunk with congratulations and homages; now, she suddenly saw herself in the claws of a vulture who, with one blow of his wing, could reverse all the foundation of her happiness. A deadly pallor appeared on her face, which, fortunately could be attributed to the excessive heat of the room and to the many intoxicating emotions which she had felt.

Astonished at the sudden emotion that his appearance had just produced, Matiphous felt a movement of pity, and if, appealing to his generosity, his victim had taken a conciliatory attitude toward him, perhaps, under a sense of forgiveness, he would have allowed himself to waver and be disarmed. But Kitty's intention was very different. Almost immediately, she recovered from her first astonishment; then, she began by quickly throwing her dangerous enemy off-guard, opening under his eyes a long and intimate conversation with Fauntleroy from whom she asked advice about the state of affairs.

The next day, he, the clumsiest negotiator possible, came to finish destroying everything by presenting himself at the lodgings of the man from Malta, in order to give him a kind of ultimatum, the terms of which must have been decided during the conference of the previous night.

Far from humbling herself under the menace of danger where her star had flung her, the daughter of Jack Ketch asked her adversary proudly what his intentions were exactly, and if

---

[31] Meaning that "one's fall from grace can come swiftly."

he wanted war or peace? If it was peace, she would gladly shake hands and nothing in her behavior would show that she had kept any remembrance of the past. If, on the contrary, Matiphous decided to take a hostile attitude towards her, he must not at all think that his surveillance was an exaggerated worry. After all, his own indiscretions could be seriously brought to light, while the wife of Lord Stuart was retrenched in a high social position from which the first bit of gossip would not shake her.

To that haughty declaration, Fauntleroy thought it proper to add his own, saying that he would add the weight of his own statements and testimony to what Kitty had said. He insinuated that he could carry knightly behavior right to making himself the armed champion of her quarrel. Then, only when he had exhausted all his commentaries, he returned to a more peaceful order of ideas.

"To sum thing up," he finished, "all of us, such as you, Lady Stuart, and I, find ourselves to have vulnerable sides. And without arguing about knowing which one of us has the most to lose in making public a regrettable past, arrived as we have to a happy situation of fortune, believe me, let's not make a spectacle of ourselves."

That said, Fauntleroy went away, very confident of the success of his ambassadorship, since Matiphous had listened to him with an air of agreement almost without interruption. It seemed to him that the man from Malta had all the appearances of a man very strongly impressed by the unexpected strength of his argument. However, in his estimate of Matiphous' guarded attitude, Kitty's envoy was far from the truth. During all the preceding night, the vindictive character had not stopped thinking of his encounter at the soirée, and it wasn't his former griefs against his triumphant fiancée which had come most strongly to his mind. The revelations which he had gained from the correspondence of Broughton and Fauntleroy were for him a fresher and bloodier wound. And to see Lady Stuart call on one of those men and authorize his presumptuous pretention of becoming Broughton's successor, only seemed like a new injury to him. At that point, confounding in the same thought his hatred for each of the members of that evil trio, he promised himself that he would spread his justice equally. And when Fauntleroy had just provoked him by insolent threats, already the design of that shared vengeance began to appear clearly in his mind. From there, a calm disdain that Fauntleroy had taken for fear, and clever dissimulation masking the success of his project, turned into one more opportunity.

To begin with, Matiphous wrote to Paris, to Minister Fouché, saying that he knew an important depository of political documents concerning the tranquility of France and that of several European States, was stored in a lighthouse off the coast of Scotland, of which, the Minister might remember, he had once been the guardian in the past. To indicate the precise and present location of that depository was impossible for him, since to conceal it from all searches, they changed its place constantly. But with the map of the lighthouse that he enclosed with his letter, in that narrow enclosure where it was easy to enter with a disguise, some clever agents could easily supplement his insufficient information. Matiphous ended his letter by advising that the expedition should be carried out with the most extreme urgency, given the fact that several secret associations interested in possessing these precious documents planned to steal them in the near future.

As the correspondence of Broughton and Fauntleroy proved, nothing had yet been decided relative to when they would go to Bell Rock. There was every reason to hope that, with that warning given to the French police, the two associates could be dispossessed of that revolutionary inheritance on which they were building so much hope.

But, whatever the time of their excursion, the man from Malta was busy arranging other things for them in the person of Mistress Aston.[32] She would be an embarrassing traveling companion, and, in addition, a complication to that project of

---

[32] See *The Brothers of Death*, p. 390.

marriage caressed by the tavern owner, which he had promised himself to bring to its realization.

Still in possession of that wickedly clever letter in which Jack Ketch's daughter had made him decide in the past to save Broughton, he managed to forge her handwriting very passably. Then, under the name of Lady Stuart, he sent to the former owner of *The Bottle and the Magpie,* a note the remarkable cleverness of which the reader will recognize:

Florence, 2 February 1808,
Dear Aunt (the daughter of Jack Ketch had supposedly written),

Since I am writing you this letter, it is enough to tell you that the accident by which I found myself separated from Broughton didn't have the disastrous results that had, at first, been supposed. I am now in Florence, enjoying perfect health, and a very happy change that, in any event, will interest you, has even come into my life. Gossip has reached me that, in the event of Broughton becoming a widower, you had a wish to take him for a husband. That's not an idea that anyone can disapprove of. And it can't be denied that Broughton has everything necessary to make a woman happy. I will go further and strongly suggest that you persist in your project, because this is what is happening to me today, and which will help a great deal. Married in Gretna Green, where you must know registrations are kept rather casually, I never thought of myself as Mistress Broughton, except in the measure that was convenient for me. Now, despite the attachment and the esteem that I have for a former friend, it is much less proper for me to consider our marriage as binding,, since today, in a manner a great deal more definitive, circumstances have made me the wife of a Laird immensely rich, who bears one of the most noble names in England. You can therefore, dear aunt, without fear of finding me in your way, carry forward resolutely your first idea. I am even in a position to send you some information which appears to me to be useful for your success.

Just between us, and without disparaging your qualities, I don't think Broughton is very disposed to become your husband. The disagreement that he had in the past with the law, which could still cause him some misunderstanding regarding the validity of his first marriage, all of that makes him more meticulous and fearful. I suspect him of thinking of leaving England and of preferring celibacy a great deal more than marriage. Follow carefully what he's doing and you will find that he proposes to take a trip to Scotland a short time from now, exactly where he took me at the time of my accident. Now, where does that attraction he feels for that savage country come from? That's because in a lighthouse situated off the coast, some miles from the little port of Arbroath, he knows about a treasure that, for a long time, he has thought about appropriating. And I admit to you, frankly, that it was not with any other intention that our trip was made.

Once he has put his hands on that rich fortune, you can count on the fact that he will no longer be available to you. He will move over to the continent, and you can say goodbye to your marriage to him. I must also tell you that, needing a second person in the rather difficult task of getting out the goods, instead of coming to you, as would have been very natural, he has written to a man named Fauntleroy, who, after being involved in a counterfeiting business, was almost on the point of passing into the hands of my father.

If I'm not mistaken, a short time from now, you will get wind of the arrival of that nice confident. I believe you would embarrass both of them if, while pretending not to know about their projected visit to the Bell Rock lighthouse, willingly or by force, you went along on the trip. As for me, I know very well that, in your place, I wouldn't miss it for the world.

Dear Aunt, you have always been so good to me, that, in case you decide to follow these gentlemen to Scotland, I dare ask you for a small favor. For the peace of my future, I would like, and you will understand why, that the folly of my first marriage, as nullified as it might be, left no trace after it. You have, like me, some interest in that, and you, who know so

41

many clever people, could surely arrange for a page of the register from Gretna Green to be torn out by mistake, couldn't you? If this little infringement doesn't seem too difficult to bring about, arranged by your care, you would make me over-joyed with your kindness by sending me here, in a well-sealed envelope, that very same page that had "wings" and that would give me true pleasure to read again with my eyes.

It is useless, Dear Aunt, to advise the most absolute se-crecy about what I'm writing here to a careful and clever woman like you. In the position in which I am placed, I must not make enemies. Broughton, as well as Fauntleroy, could behave terribly toward me if, in whatever way it might be, they came to learn that I am in correspondence with you, and that I contributed to exposing them.

While waiting for the pleasure of your reply, I am forever and as in the past, your very loving and very affectionate,

Kitty Stuart.

P. S. My address in Florence is: Palais Peruzzi, in Via San-Sebastiono.

Scarcely three weeks after having sent that perfidious epistle, Matiphous received the agreeable reassurance that his project had received from the French government all the coop-eration for which he had hoped. It must even be added that that certainty came to him in a rather pleasant form. Minister Fouché, for being well-served, paid with a generosity that had become proverbial. In that circumstance, he sent the man from Malta a draft for a thousand *écus* to be drawn on the secret police funds, and, at the same time, told him the importance he attached to his information, and the merit of the accuracy he had found there.

Thus certain that Broughton and Fauntleroy were going to encounter a painful deception, Matiphous found that the best game to play was to precipitate the realization of that re-sult as soon as possible. Consequently, one morning he went to Fauntleroy's residence and had the following conversation with him.

After having pointed out to Lady Stuart's confident that she should be relieved and that he had no plans whatsoever to take any action vis-à-vis her, he hypocritically added:

"Now, as chances of hostility between us appear less and less probable, perhaps, my dear Fauntleroy, if you promise me to be discreet, I could tell you something in confidence about a fortune, in order to definitely reestablish friendly rapports and trust between us. After all, former companions in captivity ought not to let relations be altered so easily between them."

As Fauntleroy remained rather cool to that overture, the man from Malta appeared to not notice that glacial attitude, knowing very well that, shortly thereafter, his confidences would be welcomed with much less indifference.

"I certainly plan to tell you about that fortune," he continued, "but, first, with the atmosphere of coolness that you thought proper to create between us, can I absolutely count on your discretion?"

Fauntleroy's excuses and protestations had all the warmth that could be expected from a man already intrigued and who would have despaired to see the conversation remain where it was.

Appearing to give as payment for the pleasant words he had provoked, Matiphous continued:

"I have to tell you that, at Bell Rock, I had a bizarre character as a colleague. A demagogue by temperament and profession, he aspired to nothing less than to revolutionize the world. Affiliated in every country with all the centers and persons promoting chaos, he kept the immense and detestable product of his wild revolutionary imaginings locked up in a red briefcase, that he furthermore hid with the greatest care. As a result, he was a very dangerous man, and twenty times I thought of denouncing him to the government."

"That would have been a bad role to play!" Fauntleroy remarked.

"Indeed, so I did nothing about it, and that miserable lunatic was still living peacefully at Bell Rock when I left the lighthouse."

43

"But," said Fauntleroy, "I don't see any relationship between that man and the fortune you mentioned."

"Don't you understand? That fortune was in his briefcase, for which all the police of every country would have paid considerable sums, and if I hadn't left the lighthouse, the ownership of those astonishing archives would naturally have come to me, my unfortunate colleague having, it seems, been suddenly struck dead without having been able to dispose of it."

"Since you didn't, someone else must have put their hands on that briefcase."

"Impossible. No one except me suspected its importance. Besides, it was carefully kept out of sight of the profane, being moved from hiding place to hiding place for more security."

"So, you think that it can still be found in the lighthouse today?"

"I have no doubt of it, and if I had had a resolute man to help me, I would have been master of that precious depository a long time ago."

"Pfft!" said Fauntleroy, "that might incurring a lot of trouble for a collection of junk and dreams."

"Oh, not at all. There must be a lot of worthwhile information among those papers! Besides, what danger is there in appropriating them? With a little cleverness and a partner to assist me, who knows the location intimately, I am sure of success."

During that conversation, Fauntleroy's thoughts were easy to divine. Sitting, as he did, between two opportunities, which one would he choose? Would he choose Matiphous, who really had the most chance of succeeding, or Broughton, who had talked to him first? Let's say that, to his honor, and after a very short hesitation, he decided to pick Broughton, his long-term associate. Consequently, one might have thought that he would have answered with a peremptory refusal to help. But he was more cunning. If he refused outright, Matiphous could go elsewhere and soon find an accomplice. On the contrary, by asking him for several days to think about the offer, the man from Malta would be paralyzed and Fauntleroy would have time to inform Broughton of the danger of following too closely the letter that as to bring about the denouement of this affair.

You can be sure that, the next day, on opening a very frightened short note that Fauntleroy had written to the boxer, Matiphous had the luxury of enjoying his surveillance, because even before opening said letter, he already knew its contents. So, three days later, going to Fauntleroy's domicile, he was told that the aforementioned Fauntleroy had gone away on a trip. But he had been told nothing that he didn't already know in advance. His earlier visit had had precisely the goal of bringing about such departure. The obedient puppet, Broughton's associate, was now on the road, following the hoax prepared for him as a foretaste of other bitterness. There now remained for Matiphous only to learn the effects of the forged letter that he had sent to Mistress Aston.

After some delay, obviously necessary, the answer that he was looking for every day finally arrived. It goes without saying that that letter, quickly intercepted, reached Matiphous' hands without Kitty, whose address it carried, getting the least wind of its arrival.

London, 29 February 1808,
Dear Niece (wrote the former hostess of *The Bottle and Magpie*),

How pleased your letter made me and what joy was to learn that, instead of being drowned in the waves of the sea, you have become a Lady! There's how the calculations of that monster Matiphous are thwarted. And he thought he was avenging himself! It's true that, believing in your final end, I had some ideas about Broughton. Age approaching, you don't want to be alone. There are interests in common with a man, and you think about having company in your old age. As much as it's necessary to believe in a certain amiability in that man since such a charming girl as my Kitty fell in love with him, I am entirely of your opinion; he is not the husband that you

45

need. Having found a better one, you were perfectly right in taking him and in dumping that fat Falstaff who will suit an old broken-down frigate like me very well.

Well! Does your fortune allow you to have police at your beck and call since you seem to know so many things which have since been shown to be as you told me? The fact is that the gentleman in question seemed as if he wanted to refuse marriage; the fact is that he spoke of having to make a trip to Scotland; the fact is that the other hypocrite, Fauntleroy, has suddenly returned to join him, and I, having talked of being part of the trip, was asked very politely not to take that trouble. But I let them leave, followed their trail, saw them embark on a boat to go to the lighthouse, and I was there to meet them the moment they returned. It seemed the treasure wasn't in their hands, since on returning their faces were as long as an aune.[33] Probably they needed to pass their bad temper on to someone, since they looked at me as if they wanted me to leave, because I was there as they landed. They constantly whispered together in sentences where I caught the name Matiphous, as if he might get to the treasure before them.

All that was marvelous, but I didn't let myself be scared away and I said to Broughton that I wasn't one of those women who can be led around by the nose, and that I wanted to settle it once and for all. As he refused, citing the fact that in England they hang bigamists, and that he didn't want to undergo the same ceremony twice, I may amaze you in telling you that I made him believe that you and your new husband had found ways to make the page validating your first marriage disappear from the register at Gretna Green. And I added that I was sure of that, having sent a man I trusted to do the same job, and he had found that sheet was not in the register, and therefore there was no more reason to dawdle. And if he didn't go along, I prepared to call on Jack Ketch. Hearing my threats, Fauntleroy took my side and he agreed that, since that register page had been destroyed, it was ridiculous for

---

[33] Old measurement for cloth.

Broughton to refuse happiness, and he suggested finishing everything by stopping in Gretna Green, which was on our way back to London. But me, I said I would wait until our return to London, and that my friend, the Chaplain of Newgate, knowing about the false death of Broughton, would be able to marry him under his real name, that would be more valid than the villainous Scottish name of MacLeod.

From that point on, I didn't leave my couple of thieves, who certainly seemed to want to escape me, and I led them on a leash right up to London, where the marriage took place yesterday. After having submitted to it as if to an act of violence, Broughton will have to learn the value of a wife like me, or, in the name of God! he will know that I am his wife and not a weak and languishing woman, as you behaved toward him.

You can then, dear Kitty, be tranquil; everything is going well, and as you wanted I am sending you the paper in question so that you can yourself throw it into the fire with your pretty white hands. I don't see anything more to harm you in society, except your father's profession. But, although I didn't tell Fauntleroy that I had corresponded with you, and that I knew that you were in Florence, I spoke to him in such a way as to let him understand the danger of ever confiding with any person, living or dead, from our family. When I laid that out to him, he understood what I meant, seeing that he was working with Broughton on a certain counterfeiting of bills in a way that he almost got himself hanged and that I knew all about it.

Here both of us are bound in the ties of marriage, and I don't need to recommend to you to be pleasant toward your husband, because, you see, dear Kitty, gentleness is the great virtue of women. That's the best way to hold their husbands.

This is a very long letter. I am as in the past, and can never stop talking to you. As for you, my Kitty, I hope you will keep me informed of the affairs in your household and write sometimes to her who calls herself for life, your very affectionate aunt.

Mrs. Broughton
Born: Henriette Aston

III. Moth to the Flame

Broughton, now definitely shackled to his loving tavern keeper, Kitty's safety compromised by the theft of that document certifying her double marriage now in his hands, Fauntleroy having made the voyage to Scotland pointless by going there only to find disappointment, all that was a rather beautiful result for the grudge of the man from Malta. But not stopping there, in a rather pleasant spot, he was preparing for the Broughton company another truly staggering blow, by proposing to suddenly dry up the source of their illegal and lucrative industry.

In addition to taking the role of informant, somewhat repugnant to his conscience, Matiphous, a gourmet of vengeance, found that, by turning in the two associates to the British government, he would not have enough of a direct hand in their fate. During Fauntleroy's absence, to go to the engraver, to terrify that man by the threat of police intervention, and to face him with the necessity of withdrawing his help to the others, appeared to promise a result just as certain, and at the same time, more personal and more refined. Consequently, the day after Mistress Aston's letter came to him, Matiphous arrived at the house of the artist whom he had promised himself to take away from his two enemies.

When Fauntleroy had described the engraver as a most difficult man to meet, he had truly not slandered him. It's useful to know that, in Florence, the "civetta," or the owl hunt, has its fanatics, just as pole fishing has in Paris. Going back to remote antiquity, and having in the past the honor of being the delight of Dante Alighieri and of Machiavelli, that sport, according to the knowledgeable M. Valery,[34] is practiced in the

---

[34] Note from the Author: *Italie confortable, in-12.* M. Valery, Tourist Manual, 1841.

following way: Minerva's Bird[35] is attached to a post with a string about three feet long. The bird has been trained to make certain jumps and certain bows which attract other birds. The hunter has provided himself with little sticks coated with glue, as well as with an instrument placed in a tube that imitates the song of the red-chested bird.[36] As soon as he sees or hears some of them, he puts the sticks in place and whistles. The birds, deceived by the sound, approach, and, curious about the movements of the owl, to better study him, they light on the shiny sticks where they remain glued down.

Passionate about that interesting exercise, Hans Krafft the engraver literally devoted two-thirds of his life to it. Thus, unless there was a beating rain or work at the end of which was his next day's bread, it was almost impossible to find him in his shop. To go join him in the place where he set up his glue sticks would have been useless, or even dangerous, because when he saw you in the distance coming toward him, his strong and animated pantomime would have warned you to stay at a distance. And if, despite his signals, you persisted in your approach, God knows with what treatment, the least trouble brought to his owl's maneuver, you would have been threatened. In the evening, at the Hébé Café, where dominos crowned the day, there was the same reception and the same absorption of his whole being. Who, in fact, does not know the terrible responsibility in which one places himself vis-à-vis his partner, for the least distraction coming to glide into the difficult gestation of a four player game!

Thus, Matiphous was on his third visit without having even seen the face of the engraver. But he didn't get discouraged. Far from that, he had rather himself conspired to make Hans Krafft invisible, because here's what happened. The first day he presented himself at the artist's shop, the man from

---

[35] Roman goddess of wisdom, war, art and commerce. Her traditional companion is the owl.

[36] Rouge-Gorge (Red-Throat): name given to several types of birds that have red chests.

Malta had already been shown that the daughter, a proud Italian beauty, who, by the air of majestic dignity in her features and in her manners, effectively demonstrated that severity of principles and character with which Fauntleroy had credited her in presenting her as an obstacle to the freedom of his communications with Hans Krafft. Although surprised in the middle of the most humble housekeeping chores, in the embarrassing situation which the paternal derangement made a necessity, she had greeted the visitor with the self-possession and airs of a duchess. And, while talking to him, she had fixed on him big melancholy, velvet eyes so full of sweet promises that, for the rest of the day, Matiphous dwelled on the memory of that look. During the third visit, the beautiful eyes of the Italian girl continued their fascination. Matiphous had completely changed his reasons for coming to see Hans Krafft.

"I would like to get married," he told himself, alluding to a matrimonial thought with which we have seen him preoccupied before, "and I have found that, under the adverse effects of the wicked secrets that weigh on my life, to introduce myself into an irreproachable family isn't the act of an honest man. But, everything considered, this worthy artist, who counterfeits Bank of England bills, and by his disorders, compromises his future and that of his daughter, can't he, without being lowered in social status, take me for his son-in-law? As for the young woman, despite her haughty look, and while embodying the strong woman of the Scriptures,[37] she participates, whatever she may be, in the shame that her father amasses under their name. Daughter of a counterfeiter, or wife of an opener of letters, in my opinion, it's all the same for her. Except, however, that the employee of the Secret Bureau brings her comfort, while the incorrigible laziness of the miserable author of her days, seems to condemn her to poverty at the same time as celibacy."

Put that way, Matiphous didn't need to be concerned any more with turning the engraver away from his collaboration

---

[37] Allusion to Proverbs 31.

with Fauntleroy and Broughton. It benefitted him, on the contrary, to let him get more and more embroiled in that wicked industry in order to establish between them a perfect level of indignity and social disapproval. In the meantime, he would study the character of the young girl. If he found her definitely according to his heart, he would resolutely offer her his hand without his conscience, it seemed to him, reproaching him in the least.

The next day, reflection having only confirmed his thoughts, Matiphous returned to the home of the engraver, who—an extraordinary occurrence!—was at home. Just as Matiphous entered the workshop, he saw the artist make a rapid movement to hide what he was working on, that showed him that his prospective *dear father-in-law* must have been at work for the account of the Broughton Company, and that discovery could only satisfy him. He talked about an important work that he came to order, forced the artist, who didn't defend himself very much, to receive a payment in advance for the order, but at the same time declared loudly his claim to be served with the shortest delay possible. On leaving, he said:

"I know, Monsieur Krafft, that your reputation for scrupulous care is nothing less than established. You will then allow me to come here often in order for you to remember me."

That wasn't too clumsy a way to get a foothold in the household.

Matiphous kept his threat to visit frequently to watch over his order, and, as he expected, he almost never found the fanatic amateur of the *civetta* at work. Put in the necessity of always furnishing excuses for his absence, Mademoiselle Krafft soon exhausted her imagination. Having come to receive Matiphous on a footing of the greatest familiarity, and thanks to the presence of a cousin, habitually a companion of her solitude, who served to break the tête-à-tête, she could, without inconvenience, allow the visitor rather long stays. She at last shared her condemnation of her father's activities, then was slowly led to open the unpleasant secrets that his conduct had caused her. From that point, between her and the man from Malta, there was a beginning of confidence, quite proper to favor matrimonial projects that were then in play. Shortly afterward, the time came when the visits of the secret suitor dispensed with a pretext. For two poor recluses, whose life flowed eternally deprived of pleasure, must it not, in fact, have become a precious diversion? So, from day to day, Matiphous found himself given a friendlier welcome.

Soon, while keeping the most extreme distance, Matiphous received the permission to render some services to the girl, and was given permission to present her with some of those gallant bouquets that are so common in Florence that the nice name of *city of flowers* had remained attached to it. What's more, the man from Malta took care not to show any difference between the two young relatives. But the further he went, the more he remained convinced that the eyes that at first had told him so many things, were the mirror of a privileged soul with whom he could associate his life in all confidence.

In that union of which, from moment to moment, Matiphous caressed the thought with more satisfaction, there was revealed in addition an unexpected convenience, which was truly to strongly strike his imagination. One day, he found the two cousins looking at a lithograph recently published in London. He recognized the arresting subject immediately. Under the title of *The Hamburg Ossuary,* that engraving represented the famous collection of skeletons that, in the past, the Marquis de Samaniego had put on exhibit in London and which he then had buried in Westminster in what he claimed was his family's tomb.

As Matiphous didn't find it useful to make it known that he had lived in England, he acted as if he didn't know what the engraving under his eyes represented, and he was astonished to see two young girls look with sympathy at such a lugubrious subject.

"That's because for us," Hans Krafft's daughter explained, "it has the interest of a family souvenir."

"A family souvenir?" asked Matiphous, astonished.

"Yes, the unfortunate men represented here were members of a secret society. Surprised in the place of their reunion, they were walled up on the cruel order of the magistrates and condemned to die of hunger. Now, their leader was one of our ancestors who, like my father, bore the name of Krafft and was also an engraver in Hamburg."

"So, among those sad relics, there is one of your ancestors?"

"No," answered Mademoiselle Krafft. "Through the cleverness and the devotion of his daughter, he was able to leave Hamburg before that catastrophe and go abroad. After his death, his daughter came back to Europe, where she married another Krafft, her cousin, who was also an artist in Lubeck. It's from that branch of the family that my father, marrying a Florentine woman, mingled the Italian blood, from which descends your humble servant."

"But what you haven't been told," added the young relative of Mademoiselle Krafft, "is that we have here a portrait of that charming girl who was the guardian angel of her father. With almost the same hair color, she resembles so perfectly my cousin that we never use her baptismal name and never call her anything but Christiana, the name of our ancestor from Hamburg."

To tell the truth, the portrait that was a moment later shown to Matiphous reproduced in a striking manner the traits of the living Christiana. But of all he learned, the man from Malta was still most strongly impressed with another similarity, because looking closely at the engraving that that had brought about all that commentary, there was no doubt that it was the photograph of an office of letter openers, and in that position, the ancestor of his would-be fiancée had had the same profession because of which, a moment before, he had thought himself unworthy to aspire to her hand. Thus, the woman whom he felt inclined to make his life's companion, was to him as if approved and guaranteed by the marvelous resemblance with a woman who was said to have been a model of filial devotion. Providence had permitted that, in his thought of marriage, he had justly come to the one family that, in another time, had equally secretly practiced the violation of correspondence. So, unusually encouraged in his plan, Matiphous didn't believe he should put off much longer its execution. The following day, he took it on himself to question his intended, and having found in her the disposition he had hoped, nothing more remained for him to do but to obtain the consent of the father.

One morning, when rain was coming down in torrents, since he couldn't think about hunting with owls, Hans Krafft could obviously be expected to be at home. The man from Malta went to his workshop and happily started the conversation.

"Dear Monsieur," he said, "I want to possess a work made by you, but since I am wasting my time, instead of the work which you haven't made for me, I will dare ask you for another one which I know is *already made*. If you agree to that, I will gladly make the exchange."

"What's that?" asked the artist, a thousand leagues from understanding what his questioner meant.

"Yes," Matiphous continued, "in addition to the very remarkable pieces that come from your chisel, you are the *author* of a charming girl. Supposing that you agreed to give her to me as compensation, I would tell you that I have in advance consulted with her and that she put no obstacle to your releasing yourself in that fashion."

"Well, well," said Hans Krafft, completely astonished. "You're asking me for my daughter in marriage?"

"You couldn't translate my thought any clearer, and to justify the audacity of my claim, I can tell you that, on the positive side, I believe I am not a poor party myself. I bring to the marriage, fifteen thousand pounds of income at the present. As for my personal qualities, it is most of all up to your lovely daughter to be concerned about them, and I have hopes that they please her."

While Matiphous was speaking, the engraver had gone to the window so as to consider the state of the sky.

"The weather is the same everywhere," he said with disappointment, "and we're going to have this rain all day."

Then, he came back and sat down, adding:

"So you want to get married... You're not like Monsieur de Rebundus, whom no woman suited?"

To understand this question, the reader has to know another bizarre thing about Hans Krafft that Fauntleroy didn't know, because otherwise, he would have mentioned it to Broughton at the time he enumerated all the things that had irritated him in his relations with that man.

Gifted with a rare talent for narration, and like his fellow countryman, Hoffmann, who flourished at the same time, remarkable by the fantastic turn of his imagination, Hans Krafft liked to tell stories. But instead of writing them down, he improvised them. And, as if contradiction were a muse for him, he never felt himself more in form than when he could impose himself on a listener and recount the story which came to his mind in the most unexpected and inconvenient way. So, almost always, when someone came to discuss something serious with him, unless the man with whom he had business was insistent, he would begin by answering him with one of his *Thousand and One Nights*-like tales, and thus subject his patience to a more or less prolonged test.

For that unusual man, a son-in-law who presented himself, especially on a rainy day in which he felt himself absolutely nailed to the lodgings, would become too obviously a martyr for him not to hasten to take advantage of the opportunity. For the request that Matiphous had just made, he therefore answered, as has been seen, by introducing this totally unexpected mention of Monsieur de Rebundus into the conversation.

Joining in with into the joke, the man from Malta said:

"I don't know this Monsieur de Rebundus, whom no woman suited. For my part, I know that I have found one who suits me very well."

"Rebundus," the engraver replied, "was one of the most unusual characters, and, since according to all appearances, we are going to have this damned weather until tomorrow, I must tell you some of his adventures."

In his position as a petitioner, Matiphous was not able to appear uninterested in listening to his putative the father-in-law's tale:

"Christiana," shouted Hans Krafft, "quickly, bring a bottle of Carmignano wine from that priest in Fiezzole."[38]

Then, he lit a pipe from which he blew large puffs of smoke which soon formed a thick narcotic fog around him. In the middle of that cloud, with the air of a man calling on inspiration, he walked up and down until Christiana came to place on the table two glasses and the wine he had asked for.

A resigned victim, Matiphous waited without saying a word for what might be called *the subject of the story*. But before leaving, Christiana, with a charming smile, sent him a token of comfort for the cruel test he was going to have to go through. During this time, Hans Krafft had gathered his thoughts and began thusly:

IV. The Story of Monsieur de Rebundus

"About twenty years ago, the odd behavior of Monsieur Charles de Rebundus was the subject of all conversations in the city of Magdeburg. At the time I'm speaking of, Monsieur de Rebundus was no older than thirty-three, but to see the premature deep wrinkles that unknown worries had creased on his forehead, you would have thought him about forty. What's more, tall, well-built, with an open and attractive face, he

---

[38] Note from the Author: In Florence the greatest lords sell the wines of their vineyard wholesale at the entrance to their palace at a *paul* (55 centimes) the measure.

could still pass for a very handsome cavalier, if it were not for a certain way he had of walking with his arms held tightly to his sides, as if he were always afraid of taking up too much space. This always gave his stature something strange and unnatural. As for his moral qualities, he was generally thought to have intelligence and honesty. But, in any case, a merit he incontestably had was a round and liquid fortune of twenty-thousand pounds of income left to him by his father, Monsieur Maximilien de Rebundus, which he had very honestly earned in the practice of medicine. It is therefore easy to understand that Monsieur de Rebundus had become the target of all the mothers who had, at that time, daughters to marry. They overwhelmed him with all sorts of polite attentions in view of robbing him of his celibacy.

"However, if, at the time of this story, girls, unless they had a considerable dowry, hadn't begun to be somewhat difficult to marry, it is doubtful that Monsieur Rebundus would have seen himself so eagerly sought after. The least that can be expected, when admitting a man into a family, is to have some general information about his past. Now, although it was impossible to state the least precise fact against Monsieur de Rebundus' morality, it still was no less true that during a rather long period of his existence, there reigned a kind of thick fog that one would have liked to pierce. In a word, that was the weak side which seemed to lay itself open to wickedness.

"At nineteen years-old, Monsieur Charles de Rebundus had left Magdeburg, his native city, to attend the University of Iena to begin his medical studies and, following that, prepare for the doctorate. At his departure, he had promised his mother who, embracing him and inundating him with her tears, that two weeks wouldn't go by before he sent her news, and he was to return to Magdeburg to spend his vacation at the end of the academic year. But during that mortal year, not one letter from him came to the paternal household, and, according the most exact and rigorous information, it was clearly established that young Charles de Rebundus had never appeared in Iena. Not only did vacation time, which was to bring him back, pass by without his return, but during twelve years, still expecting him, his mother moved heaven and earth to learn what had become of him. At the end, eaten away by sorrow, the poor lady descended to the tomb, where she was soon followed by her husband. The Rebundus family then extinct, those not directly in line for inheritance were temporarily put in possession of the estate, and no one in Magdeburg thought any longer about the young student, until one beautiful morning, exactly thirteen years after his departure, news of his sudden return created astonishment among his fellow citizens.

"The fact of his return was already surprising, but to believe the different versions which were circulating, it had taken place in the most unusual circumstances. It was in fact confirmed that, one evening, after curfew sounded, Monsieur Charles de Rebundus had suddenly appeared in the paternal house. The doors of that house had remained closed and the old concierge, who had inhabited it alone since the death of his former masters, had not been alerted to the presence of the returned man by the sound of the bell or the door knocker.

"Appearing thus unexpectedly, Monsieur de Rebundus showed himself with an extremely pale and sad face and, although afterwards he finally recovered a reasonable amount of weight, at the moment of his arrival, he was seen in such a state of thinness and of weakness that to take him for a walking skeleton would have seemed a kind of flattery, his appearance then being rather that of a pure spirit.

"After being reassured that his young master was positively himself, the old concierge did the work of a trusted valet and helped him to bed, but, at that moment, what must have been the stupefaction of the zealous servant when he recognized that the clothes that Monsieur de Rebundus had just taken off were the same ones that he had been wearing the day of his sad departure!

"Finally, between his knee-britches and his shirt, which had become the color of saffron, Monsieur de Rebundus carried a leather belt which held the sum he had been given by his parents for the time of his absence. A fact prodigiously curious, that sum, the monetary identity of which could be easily verified, comprised as it was of pieces of gold with the effigy of a sovereign who had ceased to reign, was found almost intact, only a few pieces having been used.

"It would be difficult to be sure that everything in that very elaborate account was perfectly, rigorously, exact, so much more so because different accounts sprang from the heirs of the man who had returned, and did not willingly pardon him the hard necessity in which they found themselves to return his wealth to him. But in the long disappearance, as in the unexpected return of the absent man, there was certainly something of the extraordinary, and public curiosity really had the right to be disturbed by him.

"From Monsieur de Rebundus' side, it appeared that no information was forthcoming. Not only did he seem not to give explanations, but he seemed decided to greet with very bad grace every attempt to break into the reserve into which he had retrenched. To all those who had attempted to obtain some enlightenment, he had dryly answered *that he had traveled* without any other explanation about the countries he would have visited, and any other circumstances of his long wanderings. Moreover, the opportunity to ask him questions was rare, because he almost constantly lived in the country, and when, something extraordinary, he came to the town, his existence there continued to be completely cheerless and withdrawn. However, after some months of that solitary life, that dark humor to which Monsieur de Rebundus seemed to have desperately embraced, it seemed, ceased to dominate him, and he came back to live in Magdeburg.

"There, he was at first accessible to a small number of friends. Then, when he was sure that the inquisitive curiosity with which, from the first moments of his return, he had seen himself confronted, had died down a little, he finally came to terms with the shadows in which he had shrouded himself, and little by little attended some gatherings. It was then that several mothers, finding in him a man of gentle and good manners, despite the mysteries of his life, and considering the fortune that he was known to possess, simultaneously had the thought of wanting him as a son-in-law.

"What's more, apparently tired of his isolated existence, Monsieur de Rebundus didn't find himself repelled by the idea of marriage. As a result, in a few weeks from various directions, several proposals, more or less acceptable, were positively presented. Among other contenders there was the daughter of a Legation Councilor, whose beauty was striking. She seemed to have the best chance of attracting his attention and the affair, after some negotiations, was led to that point of maturity when a meeting with the father of the young girl could be arranged. In such cases, the mothers are always in a hurry to show off their daughters' talents. In his youth, Monsieur de Rebundus had been a singer and, at one time, he was thought to have one of the most beautiful tenor voices then in Magdeburg. The Councilor thought it would then please him to know that his daughter was a first-rate harpsichord player.

"However, to the great astonishment of the audience, the young virtuoso called to justify that praise, not only did not seem to make any impression on Monsieur de Rebundus, but during the time that his would-be fiancée, with the true self-assurance of a master, executed a concerto riddled with difficulties, instead of being in ecstasy with the rest of the audience, Monsieur de Rebundus couldn't keep from showing some scarcely hidden signs of impatience. The effect of such behavior was easy to see, not to mention the general indignation which greeted it. However, despite the lack of taste shown in the circumstances by Monsieur de Rebundus, he nonetheless, with twenty thousand pounds of income, remained an eligible bachelor. The wife of the Councilor didn't want to break off relations with him on the spot. In addition, deciding not to find him guilty, at the last extremity, she considered that in music, perhaps not impressed with her daughter's *tour de force*, he might have enjoyed melody and expression more.

"Speaking then to her daughter, who had left the harpsichord rather angrily when she had seen the negative effect that her talent had made on her possible fiancé, she said:

" 'Stephanie, I suspect that the gentleman doesn't at all like pieces filled with music notes, in which he seems to be a connoisseur. But you should show him that you are equally capable of playing in a simpler style.'

"And she began to tap the first measures to start her daughter on her way.

" 'B flat!' exclaimed Monsieur Charles de Rebundus, jumping at that word as if the armchair in which he was seated had been set on fire, or that the point of a milliner's needle had pierced the upholstery.

" 'Yes, Monsieur,' replied the mother, who took the movement of her future son-in-law as a sign of enthusiasm. 'That adorable sonata in B Flat that you know by heart as well as I do.'

" 'Your servant, Madame!' the fantastic character then said, picking up his gloves and his hat. 'On my honor, a tone well chosen!' he added, speaking to himself as he reached the door and left without any other explanation.

"He left those in the drawing room in a state of astonishment that can well be imagined, each one persuaded that the unfortunate man had just fallen prey to a fit of madness.

"That story didn't miss being passed around, and probably the secret wound in Monsieur Charles de Rebundus' heart had been opened again by that unusual incident, because he again became invisible, and there was no longer a question of him marrying.

"However, during the following summer, having had rather often the opportunity while hunting to meet a gentleman who was his neighbor, he developed little by little some familiarity with him, and even decided to visit him from time to time. That gentleman had a daughter, and whatever had been said about him, Monsieur de Rebundus had always appeared to him to have such perfectly good sense that he did his best to search for a means of making him his son-in-law.

"In the presence of a young woman, well brought up and completely pleasant, the strange man didn't exhibit the resistance that might have been supposed. Soon his visits be-

61

came rather frequent, and one might have believed him to be on the verge of proposing. One day, he was seated in the drawing room of his would-be future mother-in-law, chatting with her in a very good humor, without anything suggesting that a storm was about to break. Suddenly the sharp and shrill sound from a music box was heard from a neighboring room. The *serinette*, or *turlutaine*,[39] never claimed to be an instrument very agreeable to the ear, but it has never been said to make people fall into a faint; when the violin is badly played, it sounds like a *chanterelle*,[40] and most of all like a harmonica. Nevertheless, in that particular case, it produced a surprising emotion. Standing up, Monsieur de Rebundus, in great confusion, asked in agony *what it was that he was hearing*

" 'Be reassured, Monsieur,' said the mother of his intended. 'My daughter is not at all a musician.' (In that, she believed she was saying the right thing, because, since what had happened at the home of the Councilor, Monsieur de Rebundus was reputed to have a horror of the musical arts.) 'All of Clara's talent,' continued the prudent lady, 'consists in very great patience in training her canaries.'

" 'Thank you for that information!' replied Monsieur de Rebundus, rising from his chair with as much emotion and impetuosity as he had shown on another occasion, He then exclaimed: '*From the small to the large, there is only a difference in size and volume.*'

"And after he had stated that bizarre axiom with a profound air, worthy of Monsieur de La Palice,[41] he left the house

---

[39] A music box used to train birds to sing.

[40] Common name of various species of birds of the *phasianides* family. The female partridge sound is used to call male birds.

[41] Jacques de La Palice (or de la Palisse) (1470-1525), nobleman and military officer who fought under several French kings in the Italian wars. La Palice gave his name to the *Lapalissade*, a comical truism or tautology, originating from his epitaph, which read, "*Ci-gît le Seigneur de La Palice; s'il*

and no insistence or explanation could make him decide to set foot there again.

"After this, it was obvious to everyone that Monsieur de Rebundus' head was decidedly cracked. All that they could agree on was that his alienation was intermittent, leaving him in possession of his wits at rather long lucid intervals. But experience was there to say that the most unexpected and most indifferent circumstance could start another attack. And something worth being stated: when it has often been observed that using music can be helpful in the treatment of mental disorders, it was found that, in the subject in question, it appeared on the contrary to be the agent of causing the appearance of the sickness. It goes without saying that, following such an outburst, twice repeated, Monsieur Charles de Rebundus was declared decidedly unable to *light the torch of Hymen.*[42] More deeply than ever rejected into celibacy, he again began to devote himself to solitude. It appeared that henceforth no influence could draw him away from the empire of his dark thoughts.

"However, it happened that, sometime later, walking in the area around a chateau near his domain, Monsieur de Rebundus found himself in the path of a dashing amazon, who, mounted on a white mare, rode it with as much grace as ability. As that great equestrian competence drew the attention of the walker, he was led to notice that the valiant rider was one of the most exciting beauties that he had ever encountered. Then, that was all that happened; he let her pass as one of those pleasant images that, at the same instant, blossoms and vanishes—the illusion of a dream. Hardly was the beautiful horsewoman out of sight than Monsieur de Rebundus began to think of something else and no longer recalled her. But, sud-

---

n'était pas mort, il ferait encore envie." (Here lies the Seigneur de La Palice; if he weren't dead, he would still be envied.) The last words were misread as "*...il serait encore en vie*" (he would still be alive).

[42] i.e.: get married, Hymen being the Greek god of marriage.

denly, loud cries of distress drew the walker out of his reverie. He turned around quickly and saw his graceful apparition carried away, her horse out of control. The two horsemen who were her escorts, whom she had very far outdistanced, were not near enough to come to her aid. Monsieur de Rebundus didn't hesitate a moment. The spirited animal was coming straight at him. As alert as courageous, like a veritable hero of a novel, he seized the bridle with a firm hand and managed to pull the mare up short. He had the good fortune, at the price of a sprained wrist, to snatch the adorable young woman from imminent peril. Not at all faint, and jumping nimbly to the ground, the lady, together with her escorts, who by then had rejoined her, began to express her gratitude to her savior. But still like a hero of a novel, modest and discreet, Monsieur de Rebundus shrank from her thanks, and it was impossible to get him to stay.

"However, that adventure could not stop there. The next day, a doctor was examining the wounded arm when a servant came to tell the solitary man that a young lady, accompanied by an old man, who seemed to be her father, notwithstanding all contrary instructions, was insisting upon seeing him. Suspecting whom that could be, Monsieur de Rebundus gave orders that they be asked to wait in the drawing room and he went there himself shortly thereafter. He found the beautiful horsewoman had, in fact, come with her father to ask news of him and to thank him for his help.

"The debut of the pretty visitor was as pleasant as unusual. Pretending to quarrel with him instead of saying words of gratitude to him, she stated:

" 'It may seem proper to you, Monsieur, to save the lives of people, and then remove yourself afterward so that they cannot get to you to say a single word of thanks; but you will learn that, when I have something in my heart, I have to say it. I would then have come here alone if my father, present here, had refused to accompany me. And I would have, if necessary, laid siege to your home in order to be able to tell you straight out the gratitude that I feel towards you.'

"The man spoken to in that way had to answer that compliment, whose initiative, by which an insignificant service had been recompensed, made him very happy and proud. The conversation continued for some time with a tone of good humor and gallantry. Obliged to give in to the friendly entreaties made to him, Monsieur de Rebundus, when he separated from the beautiful woman who was in his debt, had promised to visit her soon in the chateau where she lived.

"Monsieur de Rebundus carried out that promise some days afterward. Now, it has to be explained that, a widow for some years, the amazon was entirely mistress of her hand and had a considerable fortune to her name. The reception that she gave her savior was so cordial and so attentive that she triumphed yet again over his intentions of absolute seclusion. To the first visit, there followed some other encounters in which the open and very friendly reception of the beautiful chatelaine soon banished all formality. The acquaintance thus developed, and Monsieur de Rebundus must have noticed that, from day to day, he was more welcome. Soon things were at the point that, unless he was the least intelligent of men, he had to recognize that his quest, in case he decided to declare himself, would be enthusiastically accepted.

"Either because of timidity, or need not to declare himself only after mature thought, Monsieur de Rebundus took a rather long time before manifesting his intentions; so much so that it was the season for leaving the country before he opened his mouth about that marriage that could be settled with a word. However, far from changing anything of the sweet intimacy into which our temporizer had little by little let himself be drawn, the stay in the city only confirmed his feelings. He regularly visited the town house of the friendly chatelaine, where he was sure to receive the most affectionate welcome.

"During a cold December evening, he arrived in a most happy mood. His hesitation had finally ended and he had decided to propose. Chance was in his favor; nothing came to trouble the *tête-à-tête* with which he was favored, and his heart was expanding with all the tenderness that he had amassed for a long time, when colder and colder air invaded the room. The beautiful widow noticed that, because of the on-going conversation, they had let the fire in the fireplace almost go out. Not wanting to be interrupted by a servant, who would have brought endless conversation to an interview full of interest, the young widow took charge of rebuilding the fire with her beautiful hands. It was only a matter of reassembling the dispersed materials. Then, when the dying embers were brought together again, she asked her suitor, seated across from her on the other side of the fireplace:

" 'Would you please pass me the bellows?'

" 'The bellows!' he answered in a dark and monomaniacal voice.

"The widow, somewhat astonished by his tragic and solemn accent, replied:

" 'Yes, the bellows that are hanging up near you.'

" 'Ah! Madame,' exclaimed Monsieur de Rebundus, covering his face with his hands, 'Could I believe that you too... Well,' he added, 'there are fatal destinies...'

"And rushing out of the drawing room, where he had entered in a very different mood, he had already gone down the stairs and closed the door to the street behind him, before, stupefied by this action, the amazon had the time to say a word to stop him.

"After the unimaginable indiscretion which she had just witnessed, the charming widow, who, at first, had refused to believe the wicked gossip surrounding Monsieur de Rebundus, was forced to lend credence to it. And when he decided on taking some steps in view of re-establishing their relationship, everything between them nevertheless remained irreparable. What security would she have in fact in uniting her life with that of a man with a kind of sensitivity so that one couldn't do things in certain ways without immediately causing him to go into a nervous frenzy? But it wasn't necessary at all for her to use firmness or resistance with Monsieur de Rebundus. He had completely called off the marriage that he had for a moment projected, and had no thought of again setting foot in that house from which we saw him make such a strange exit. But in that circumstance, he no longer behaved in his usual way. Instead of throwing himself into a retreat, as he usually did after each of his seizures, on the contrary, he showed himself in society more than ever before, in order to meet the ingrate toward whom he believed he had so much to complain, and to have the daily opportunity to defy her.

"Now, in that new way of managing his existence, and because of his marked enthusiasm determined to appear at all the gatherings to which he was invited, here's what happened one fine day.

"A celebration was taking place at the home of the principal magistrate of the city. Monsieur de Rebundus had arrived late, and as there was a large crowd in all the rooms, not being able to get into the room set aside for the dance, he had decided to sit down in a boudoir where, by mirrors reflecting each other, he could glimpse at a distance the room in which the dance was being held. The crowd, however, hid the view of the dancers, and only visible to him were the diamonds, the flowers, and the ribbons ornamenting the dresses of the women. It created for him the illusion of an animated and living flower bed which, at moments, when there was a breeze, mingled all its sparkle and all its colors. But beyond the glittering atmosphere of that enchantment, seated like decorative plants against a wall, on tiers of golden velvet, and dressed in the richest finery, he saw other women who, although reduced to the role of spectators, had not yet lost all their youth and beauty. One face struck him among the others, remarkable by her elegance, her features and the splendor of her gaze. And although the rays of warm light that darted from her beautiful eyes came to him only pale and weakened at a great distance from where Monsieur de Rebundus was seated, he seemed nevertheless to feel their brightness in his heart, and he became very moved.

"Drawn by an unknown charm, Monsieur de Rebundus wanted to see that enchantress closer, and, after having left the sofa where he was sitting, with patient and clever maneuvering, he came to the salon where he had first seen her. But during the time it had taken him to make his way across the crowd, the beautiful star had disappeared. He found only a frightful old woman coiffed with a ridiculous turban of nightmare orange, which shaded an ugly nose expanding like a cork as it leaves a bottle, and with little gray, mocking eyes looking at him.

" 'The Devil! The Sibyl!' exclaimed Monsieur de Rebundus upon recognizing the Councilor whose daughter he was supposed to marry, and he quickly turned his back.

"It was well he had made that rapid conversion, because, just behind him, giving her arm to the master of the house who had danced with her, there was the charming young woman that he had been looking for. He only had time to throw himself respectfully to one side in order to let her pass. But on seeing him, the woman with the flaming eyes stayed where she was and gave him a glance that was of such penetrating sweetness that he thought his heart would break with emotion and happiness. At the same time, in a completely melodious voice, which it seemed to Monsieur de Rebundus that he recognized the enchanting timber, the beautiful unknown woman said to him:

" '*B flat.* Does he no longer recognize *B natural*?'

"At those words, Monsieur de Rebundus' emotion knew no bounds. His eyes were covered with a cloud. It seemed that his knees gave way under him and he had only time to cry out:

" 'Oh! Heaven!'

"And he fainted."

V. The Story of Monsieur de Rebundus (cont'd)

"Some weeks later, in the usually very gloomy daily activities in the house of Charles de Rebundus, there was unusual animation: windows shining with lights, comings and goings of the domestic staff, appearing to be busy, the freshness of the livery, their white gloves, and the bud in their boutonniere, and, finally, at the door a great crowd of people in carriages. All that seemed to indicate an extraordinary event. And, in fact, a great revolution had occurred in the life of the solitary man. That same morning, he had just been married!

"Considering the prodigious obstacles that the new spouse had put in the way if such a denouement, one might well wonder who was the clever young woman that had learned to triumph over his bizarre behavior to halt his irresolution. But to what could this miracle be reasonably attributed if it wasn't to the lady at the ball, the one whose strange words had made Monsieur de Rebundus faint? But that lady—who was she? Where and how had he known her? By the words she had spoken to him, it was obvious that they had met each other before. And if Monsieur de Rebundus knew her, how did it happen that, having had time to examine her face, he didn't at first recognize it, and that she needed to make him hear her voice in order for him to remember her?

"All these questions and many other obscure things in this story surely merit an answer and an explanation. But everything will be brought to light by Monsieur de Rebundus himself, because, at his wedding dinner, at dessert, when one of the guests, following a custom not yet out of fashion started to toast to the health of the spouses, he asked that they all kindly listen to him. He began to speak in the following terms:

" 'Dear friends, well-beloved relatives, and honorable fellow citizens! Since the day after an absence of thirteen years—an unlucky number!—I reappeared among you, I must suppose that some of my actions must have seemed extraordinary to you. I even know that, relative to my mental state, some unfortunate rumors have been repeated. Thank God, I was misjudged. In the middle of the misfortunes and strange events which my live has passed through, Heaven has at least been gracious in conserving me my healthy reasoning and the free exercise of my faculties. If, therefore, from time to time, there has been something unusual in my behavior, which surprised you, thanks to the happy event that unites us today, I find myself finally able to give the most detailed explanations, and, I dare say, the most satisfactory ones.

" 'In order to bring to your minds a perfect justification of the unusual things that may have scandalized you, I have only to tell you my story. It is up to you to see if, during a half-hour, you will give me the precious honor of your attention...'

"That short exhortation having been followed by a unanimous murmur of willing agreement, all the chairs were heard to be moved, because each one, as if in the presence of a clergyman who had just taken the pulpit, arranged himself to listen comfortably. Encouraged by the signs of general curiosity, and by the deep silence that soon came about, Monsieur de Rebundus continued thus:

" 'I don't know in all of Germany a more agreeable town than the little city of Halberstadt. The day when I was traveling from Magdeburg to the University of Iena, I happened to go through that pleasant city. Its liveliness was supplemented by the preparations for two feasts that were to take place the next day. They were getting ready to celebrate the birth of Breyhahn, that Bacchus of the North to whom we owe the invention of beer,[43] and, on the same day, following the repair of the grand organ of the Church of Notre-Dame Church, the delivery of that magnificent instrument. For the richness of the sound, the brilliance and the variety of sounds, there is nothing in Europe to compare with the organ of the Cathedral of Freiburg, or that of the Abbey of Weingarten.

" 'Delaying my trip for a day or two without inconvenience, I let myself easily be persuaded by the hostess of the *Golden Lamb* to stay at her inn in order to attend the double ceremony. Having then become, until the next day, a citizen of Halberstadt, after having supped at the *table d'hôte* and going to the stable to reassure myself that my horse had been suffi-

---

[43] Halberstadt has given birth to two celebrities: the poet Johann Wilhelm Ludwig Gleim (1719-1803) and Kurt (or Court) Breyhahn, a brewer who, in 1626, allegedly invented a new type of beer now bearing its name.

ciently provided with oats and bedding, I went out for a moment to visit the city and to see some of its monuments.

" 'It was the end of August and, at that time of the year, night fell at a rather early hour. The sun had just descended to the horizon at that very moment I arrived at the Old-Market Square. The Church of Notre-Dame was situated not far from there. Near the main door of that edifice, an unusual spectacle awaited me. Their necks stretched, their eyes looking up to Heaven, more than five hundred assembled people seemed to be watching an object in space. Beginning to look up like the others, I had the advantage of stating that I saw absolutely nothing. I then approached a group where there was holding forth one of those all-knowing people who never miss being where there is a crowd. I heard him affirm in a knowledgably tone that the *thing* could be explained as the most natural thing in the world, the refraction of the sun's rays into a cloud. An old woman, who didn't seem to favor that explanation, shouted that *such an apparition* was an infallible announcement of some misfortune.

" 'After having listened for some time to that conversation, I finally understood that the emotion of that great group of people, of which I was a witness, had been caused by the fact that two white monks, who had been seen together, had risen into the sky after having floated for an instant over the city. The miracle was sworn to by the greatest number, while some clever ones maintained that two statues of Saint Peter and of Saint Paul, situated on the platform of the Church reflected each other, and an optical illusion in the setting clouds must have produced that illusion. That explanation seemed the most plausible.

" 'I then left all the people there who, after having watched and commented a great deal, began to disperse. And continuing my adventurous promenade, I soon found myself in a somewhat deserted area near the ramparts. From that spot, in the last rays of twilight, I stopped for some time to enjoy the magnificent vista of the Spiegelberge.[44] When I resumed my walk, night had already fallen and there were deep shadows over the city.

" 'As I passed near a pavilion situated behind the wall of a vast garden, my ear was suddenly struck by the sound of a harp that resonated under a learned and practiced hand. Almost at the same moment, the voice of a woman, in a sad but deeply penetrating accent, began to sing a simple song, accompanying herself in *arpeggios* intermingled with improvisations, which showed consummate talent in the player. Naturally, I had to listen to that concert, and, as it continued for some time, I finally was so very delighted in the heavenly harmony that, the player going on to a tune that I had myself sometimes sung, I couldn't keep myself from interrupting at a repetition and of singing the last couplet.

" 'As soon as I was heard, the attention of the musician, as can well be imagined, became fixed on me. By the light of the lamp that lit her bedroom, I very distinctly saw her shadow outlined on the venetian blind which she approached. She remained at that place until I had finished the couplet that I had allowed myself to steal from her. Noticing that she had immediately gone away, and that a rather long silence had followed, I had some suspicion that what I had done had displeased her. Persuaded that this commencement of an adventure had to rest there, I was going to retire, when I saw the silhouette reappear behind the venetian blind. At the same time, it seemed to me that a ribbon passed through the slats of the blind, descended the length of the wall and soon was so close that I could reach it. Without my saying so, my hurry to seize that mysterious token can be understood. The hand holding it released it without resistance as soon as mine held it. A paper was attached to the end of the ribbon. I unfolded it rapidly and wanted to read it, because something was written on it. But the location was too dark. Besides, the window behind the blind had now closed. That seemed to make me understand that I had nothing

---

[44] A small elevation of 180m above sea level near Halberstadt.

more to expect. Curious, as can be believed, to know the contents of that mysterious message, I hastened to return to my inn. Without even giving myself time to go up to my room, I entered the travelers' lounge. There, taking out my precious paper, I read there what follows:

" '*If you have as compassionate a heart as you have a beautiful voice, you will not refuse to come to the aid of a girl who has persuaded herself that Heaven led you under her windows this evening in order to save her. I am young; I am thought to be agreeable, and I enjoy an independent income, which the man who will become my husband may immediately acquire. If you decide to risk* everything *to help me escape, come tomorrow to the reception of the organ of Notre-Dame organ. At the church exit, stop near the font, near the first pillar to the right of the nave, and have the ribbon that accompanies this note around your neck. Later in the day, if you pass under my window, more detailed explanations will be provided to you.*

" 'Then, as a nice piece of flattery, a postscript added:

" '*I really thought I sang that song well, but you sing it much better than I do.*

" 'What was I to think of that note? Was it a hoax? If, on the contrary, the adventure was serious, was it wise and prudent to follow up on it? Those word: *If you have decided to risk* everything *to help me,* seemed to mean that my cooperation could create some danger for me. Wouldn't it be better to continue my trip calmly than embark on an adventure, an enterprise for which it was impossible for me to calculate the outcome? On the other hand, however, if all the moral perfections of the woman who wrote to me were equal to her admirable musical talent, if in addition, as she said, she was young, beautiful, and rich, wasn't this an excellent opportunity offered to me, and, even at the price of some perils to confront, should I hesitate to take advantage of my good fortune?

" 'Besides, I had until the next day to decide. I could therefore take time to reflect, and, while waiting for the time to act, it would be easy for me, with some cleverly collected information, to clarify my position, and make myself at least able to measure the consequences of my participation. In such circumstances, no one better than the mistress of an inn seemed to me to be usefully interrogated. Going then to see the innkeeper of the *Golden Lamb,* I tried to learn from her the identity of the owner of the pavilion near where I had stopped. In addition, I gave her a somewhat exact description of the area so that she couldn't misunderstand the habitation which I intended to ask about.

" ' — Ah, my dear Monsieur, that worthy lady said to me, you didn't take your walk toward the place with the best reputation in the city. It's not good to find yourself at night in the vicinity of Baron de Hostrub's dwelling. Very strange stories are told about that house!

" ' — The Baron de Hostrub? I repeated, in order to fix that name in my memory.

" ' — Yes, Monsieur, the hostess continued. The Baron de Hostrub, a sort of hell hole whose depth no one has ever measured.

" ' — And where does he come from, that famous villain? I asked.

" ' — I don't know exactly, but there is unusual gossip about him. They say he works with forbidden sciences; that he is a man wanting to know about more than a Christian and a creature of God should. Where he comes from, how he lives, no one can say, because it's useless to try to find out. For twenty leagues around, there is no man who had heard of him before he arrived, and I think it would be rather hard to tell you the country that sent him to us.

" ' — If, however, I answered, there is nothing more serious to reproach with, I don't see why there is so much bad talk about him. There are people, according to the precept of the wise man, who like to keep their life hidden.

" ' — As for that, you could say that he hides it marvelously well, since during the day, he never shows himself out of doors, and when he comes out at night, it's in a carriage that few people would like to meet on the road.

" ' — And what is that frightening vehicle like?

" ' — Once a week, the hostess continued, lowering her voice to take on that mysterious accent that one is instinctively led to use when recounting frightening or supernatural facts, on a dark night, on a Friday, he always goes out in a black carriage pulled by black horses with black lackeys, driven at a speed so fast that it would be impossible for even the best mounted horseman to follow him; that vehicle, however, or so they say, makes no sound on the pavement.

" ' — That is something unusual, I answered, without, however, giving very much credence to that detail. But this bizarre person, does he live alone? Doesn't he have some family with him?

" '— That's another story, the hostess answered. For some time, behind the window whose blinds are never opened, there can be heard the sound of a harp and singing in such a doleful and sad voice, that it would, or so they say, break your heart. Perhaps you heard it this evening and that caused you to notice the house?

" '— Me? No! I exclaimed.

" 'It seemed to me that the way in which I came in contact with the young virtuoso should be kept secret.

" ' — But does anyone know anything about this mysterious musician? I asked, feeling that I had arrived at the heart of the matter.

" ' — Nothing, she answered. Everything around that man is ruin and shadows!

" 'It was rather natural, at this stage, to ask how it was that civil authorities didn't try to penetrate that obscurity. To the observation I made in that sense I received the following:

" '— The magistrates! the hostess of the *Golden Lamb* exclaimed disdainfully. Have them look into that? Instead, they prefer tormenting a poor innkeeper about a register that is not up to date, or about the quality of the wines she has in her cellar, or about the price of the inn's services, instead of trying to learn about what such a man may be. And under the pretext that he doesn't harm anyone, they let him lead his shadowy existence. Besides, she continued, making the gesture of counting out money, I'm sure he has a way of dealing with these magistrates…

" 'Seeing that I had put the worthy lady on a chapter which would never dry up, and besides, having gathered all the information that I could expect, I seized upon a pretext to break off the conversation, and tell her that her last words had been rather unwise. After which, taking a candle and the key to my room, I wished her a good night and I retired.

" 'At first, I had some trouble going to sleep. The decision I had to make was nearly at hand; the details which my hostess had furnished me had given me something to think about. I finally went to sleep and was awakened by the sound of loud ringing bells and beating drums going through the streets, telling the civilian guard to gather at their ordinary place of assembly. Having gotten out of bed immediately, I regretted very much having only my traveling clothes. Without having, at that time, considered the manner in which I would appear vis-à-vis the woman who would see me at the Church, I would have liked, if I could, to seem well-dressed. But I had sent my bags ahead and had kept only the clothes that I wore on the road, so I had to be satisfied with that. At least I gave my hair and the small necessities of my grooming all the attention which I could. And the moment came to know if I would wear the beautiful sky blue ribbon that I had been asked to wear around my neck. Understanding that showing it didn't commit me to anything yet, and that my freedom remained no less intact, I placed the recognition sign around my shoulder, and left shortly afterward.

" 'I walked toward the old Breyhahn house, located near the Old Market Square. It could be recognized by a copper plate placed above the door upon which one could read the birth and death date of the inventor of the German beer, with some verses in his honor. At that particular time, the proprietors of a brewery called the *Garden of Harmony* occupied that old and respectable dwelling, and had in some way decorated it. From its foundation to its roof, it was ornamented with garlands of hops intermingled with flowers that gave it a very festive look. Music ahead of them, preceded by their banners, the corporation of brewers and that of the barrel-makers came to line up around the square, one side of which was already occupied by the civilian guard.

" 'Then, the Mayor, having mounted the platform set up for that purpose, pronounced a very long and boring speech, concerning the esteem due to the useful arts, followed by a cantata sung with some spirit, but the verses of which were perfectly flat, like all cantata verses. Finally, they crowned the bust of Breyhahn, which was set in the middle of the platform. That ceremony, combined with the absorption of an immense number of tankards of beer consumed during the day and during part of the following night, made up all there was of the festival, and, in good conscience, was it worth the trouble to delay my trip to take part in such a paltry festival?

" 'The delivery of the Notre-Dame organ, in which I had a particular interest, promised to be more interesting, since for thirty leagues around, all the organists had come to play the beautiful instrument and to display their talent at the same time. However, it was understandable that I didn't give my full attention, without feeling distracted, to the fugues that they played marvelously. In fact, while they were spreading out waves of harmony, I was involuntarily drawn to search among all the women's faces within reach of my line of vision for the one that would best show me the image that I had formed in advance of my unknown woman. But I was wasting my effort; I didn't find anything that approached my ideal. I was therefore somewhat discouraged in my search, when a

77

serious incident focused my interest exclusively on the musical solemnity that had just finished.

" 'The man to whom the reparation of the Notre-Dame organ had been entrusted, Gregoire Kleng, was not only a very talented worker and organ maker, but a true artist who, after having traveled throughout Europe, had returned to his country with the wonderful invention of the pedal keyboard.[45] He was so intent on the perfection of the work with which he had been entrusted that, most of the time, he put his own money into it, so that, after the immense work accomplished, having scarcely any other fortune but his reputation, he was naturally very protective of it, as can easily be understood. The work that he had executed on the Notre-Dame organ was extensive. Before it, the wind was distributed into the pipes by twenty bellows and it took no fewer than ten men to maneuver them. In addition, the keys were so hard to press down that it took the strength of all the fingers, reducing the speed of the play. And, finally, the organist had had no keyboard under his feet. When the connoisseurs found that Kleng, by simplifying the mechanism of the bellows, had reduced them by half so well that two men were enough to make them function, their admiration became apparent. Then, what a joy for the players to feel keyboards under their fingers as soft to the touch as that of a harpsichord! As for using the pedal keyboard, they then could use the bass, the use of both hands remaining free for the top. It is also accurate to say that several of the former pipes, under that man's hands, had acquired a sound much superior to what they had formerly had, and by adding several others, he had added a great deal to the richness of the instrument. Thus, Kleng received from the tribune above the compliments of the commissioners charged with examining his work, while in the Church below there were long bouts of coughing.'

---

[45] Historically, the organ of the Church of Halberstadt was built in 1361 by a priest named Fabri, and indeed repaired and improved by Gregoire Kleng—but in 1495!

" 'Pardon me for interrupting,' said a gracious lady present at the wedding dinner of Monsieur de Rebundus, who had followed with interest like everyone the development of his story, 'but I don't understand why the coughs that day in the Church served to confirm Kleng's great success. It would seem, on the contrary, that they would contribute to disturbing him.'

" 'That's because you don't know a custom which I, in fact, should have told you about,' Monsieur de Rebundus replied. 'In a church, the respect due to the location does not allow applause, as in a concert. The custom is then, when a piece has pleased the public, to testify one's satisfaction by greeting it with a little kindly cough. Upon hearing it and understanding that the harsh sound is the same as applause, the heart of the artist is as joyful as if he had heard clapping of hands.'

"The lady having apologized for her ignorance and thanked him for his explanation, Monsieur de Rebundus continued:

" 'There remained, for trying out the instrument in all its details, a pipe reserved for the end, considering that it was thought by amateurs to be not only the most harmonious of all the pipes of the organ, but also superior to all the other pipes of the same type which could be found in organs throughout the world. This pipe had the sound of the human voice and was thus named because it was played in such a way that it did imitate the sound of a man singing. However, nothing is rarer than this pipe successfully arriving at a perfectly complete imitation. Now, in the organ of Notre-Dame of Halberstadt, it was known that such unusual perfection had been achieved, and that one would have sworn that he had heard a bass voice, a tenor, or a soprano singing. The inhabitants of Halberstadt were as proud of their *human voice* as the people of Strasbourg of their *Munster* [46] or the people of Frankfurt of their

---

[46] *Das Liebfrauenmünster*, i.e.: Cathedral.

Römer [47] or city hall. The organist never plays this pipe except at the greatest festivals or the days of great feasts. In a special meeting of the Council of the city, Kleng had been instructed not to touch that divine creation said to be a masterpiece that couldn't be imitated, and not having any need of repairs, it could only be harmed by being tinkered with. For his part, Kleng, although he had absolute faith in his ability, was not annoyed with being thus officially discharged from the restoration of that pipe which, being in a form completely different from that which he ordinarily worked on, would perhaps have presented great difficulties, if it had been a question of his reworking what his predecessor had crafted. Kleng had therefore by necessity followed the very easy instruction to do nothing. He hadn't even displaced the pipes to remove the dust, in order to avoid any type of responsibility.

" 'The moment had finally come to have the adored pipes heard; the organist seated at the keyboard, pressed the note and immediately all the people of Halberstadt became quiet. But what had happened? The organist stopped, then began again, then stopped again. And finally, since nothing is so quick as the spread of bad news, there began to spread throughout the church the gossip that something was wrong with the *human voice* and the pipe no longer spoke!

" 'The fault couldn't be Kleng's, who, once again, had strictly kept to the orders that he had received. But expect a superstition, troubled in being carried out, to have common sense and moderation! As the unfortunate craftsman was most naturally the one to blame, there was immediately an inexpressible outburst against him. Shouted at in the most violent manner, he could convince no one of his innocence and was everywhere overwhelmed with curses. Hoping that his talent could get him out of this bad situation, he then committed a grave error by deciding to work on and modify something in the mute pipes to give them speech again. However, it was the

---

[47] Medieval building in the Altstadt of Frankfurt and one of the city's most important landmarks.

wrong moment to go beyond the terms which the City Council in its deliberation had established. Whatever the fanatics could say about it, there was the presumption of his participation in the misfortune. So, after some fruitless efforts to remedy the evil, the sad workman was obliged to declare he was powerless.

" 'There arose a veritable riot against the poor man and there were almost acts of violence committed against him. The anger of the crowd hadn't calmed very much until it was known that the Council was present at the reception and had just deliberated on the spot. Gregoire Kleng was enjoined to put things right within three days, or, if not, all the rigors of the law would be used against him.

"Not being a citizen of Halberstadt, I couldn't take the event as seriously. Following this unpleasant incident, the crowd, with emotion difficult to describe, drifted away. Almost alone, remaining cool-headed, I went to place myself on lookout at the spot pointed out to me the evening before and I looked everywhere. It was useless; I didn't notice that any lady honored me with any significant, or even particular, attention. However, the church was slowly emptying. Judging that, for the moment, I shouldn't any longer hope for my unknown lady to be revealed, I gave up my search and retired.

" 'Nothing is as dangerous as the attraction of those adventurous decisions to which one arrives down a gentle slope, degree by degree. The situation that one would certainly have backed away from, if it had been a matter of immediately responding, one finally accepts, so imperceptibly, one is led step by step into it. Thus, my first instinct had been not to follow up on my epistolary intrigue; but having a long road ahead of me before arriving at the denouement, at each step that I made toward the danger, I told myself that there would always be time to go back and thus, little by little, I committed myself.

" 'It was in virtue of that reasoning that having gone to the Church of Notre-Dame, I was still drawn to adventure and went to the area around Baron de Hostrub's house in order to get the *more detailed explanations* promised me in the beautiful virtuoso's note. However, I should have known that the situation was beginning to become very serious. I already understood that the purpose of that meeting was to communicate to me instructions to help the young woman to *escape* from her present situation. And once the dangers, that had vaguely been presented to me, would be revealed, would I have the good grace to recoil before that enterprise in order to decline it? But, dear listeners, I have to admit my weakness to you. Having, at that time, an opinion of my good looks as being passably advantageous, I was curious to know the opinion of the careful person who, before putting herself definitely in my care, seemed to put the restriction that my face did not displease her. To that kind of coquetry, add the lack of prudence natural to youth, its taste for the extraordinary and unknown, perhaps a little the influence of my star of destiny, and you can understand why, contrary to all prudence, at three o'clock in the afternoon, I found myself in the dangerous vicinity where my adventure had begun the evening before; that is to say, near the elegant pavilion under the window and facing the blind that I was expecting, from one instant to the next, to open to let me contemplate the face of my charming unknown woman.

" 'However, that didn't happen; nothing moved. I waited patiently for a quarter of an hour; but as there was no movement, I finally had to admit the modest supposition that my face had displeased her. Halfway saddened by that failure, halfway glad not to have to go any further in an affair that might cause me very serious difficulties, I was about to leave, when, suddenly, I heard a brilliant prelude. The harp began to accompany a recitative which, the evening before, a voice had carefully pronounced the words. In this, she was not imitating the opera singers that one would gladly think were paid to leave nothing out of the verses they were singing. However, at first, I didn't pay careful attention to the verses with the music, supposing that they didn't make any more sense than ordinarily the poetry of a *libretto* does.

" 'As for me, I thought it rather unusual to take the time to sing to me that should be given to tell me more important information. Nevertheless, as the same words were constantly repeated, despite my distraction, I heard some of them, and considering that they might have some rapport with the situation which had at first escaped me, I put more effort in understanding what they meant. Then I caught very distinctly the following sentences:

" '*Monsieur, I have seen you... I cannot write to you. I can only sing. But if to take me away from my cruel martyrdom, it pleased you to attempt, a few steps from you, you will see a door. An hour before midnight, this evening, I will come down there. I will have put the cohort of my Argus*[48] *to sleep. I have confidence in you. Where you go, I will go.*

" 'Obviously, I was a fool not to have at first understood. Feeling herself closely watched, the beautiful musician had thought of an ingenious way to get to me the instructions I had come to look for. In those eight verses, good enough, it has to be admitted, as verses for a meeting, was everything I needed to know. Evidently, I had pleased her. She hadn't been able to send me a letter, but with her recitative, one that probably wouldn't arouse the suspicions of those watching her, she had alerted me that at eleven o'clock that evening, she would be at the door that I saw. And counting on my loyalty, she had decided to flee with me. Explained by the letter of the evening before, that musical suggestion had all the desired clarification. I should have had all the explanations necessary. But that was not all that had to be understood. It was necessary that the intention of the person sending the verses had also been understood, because setting her couplets in every pitch, she had repeated them four or five times, as much to be sure that it had gone to where it had been sent, as to receive the answer that it naturally demanded. Was this a situation in which to hesitate and fall back into cold prudence? I had come; I was counted

---

[48] In Greek mythology, a giant with a hundred eyes who was set to guard Io with whom Zeus had fallen in love.

on; and the woman I had already recognized as a musical talent of the first order, by the ability she had just shown, giving me unimpeachable testimony of her spiritual frame of mind—how could such an enchantress be resisted!

" 'The recitative was still going on and was even taking on a movement that seemed to indicate impatience. I was afraid of appearing to be a man devoid of any intelligence if I didn't finally admit that I had understood her. Taking advantage of a moment of repetition, without having too much calculated the extent of my commitment, I also answered in music with this ill-fated verse:

" '*Until this evening! Until this evening! I will come without fail!*

" 'Just the response for which she had certainly been waited, because I had no sooner sung it, than the harp was quiet. Almost at the same moment, the window in front of the blind closed with a great noise, which was probably meant to tell me: *We have understood each other. Now, leave for fear of drawing attention.* But I didn't need that prudent advice, since I had just seen an object that was enough to put me to flight. Drawn, I could believe, by the music that those like him are reputed to like a great deal, a green lizard of the largest species, darting his flaming eyes at me, had stopped below the window of the beautiful captive. Now, every species of reptile being an object of horror and disgust for me, I didn't try to stay in the area where I had just arrived. On his side, the hideous oviparous didn't seem otherwise in a hurry to make my acquaintance. Seeing that he had drawn my attention, following his instinct, he climbed up the wall and hurried to hide in a crevice where he disappeared. So, like two brave fellows in a comedy, we had mutually frightened each other. But not making it a matter of ego to remain master of the field of battle, I hurriedly ceded the field to him and left quickly.

" 'Recovered from that ridiculous emotion and finding myself alone, face-to-face with the serious engagement I had just made, I wasn't without finding matters for rather serious reflections. But the die was cast; I had promised, and an honorable man is nothing but his word, especially to a woman. Trying then to see the bright side of my situation, I repeated to myself several times that reassuring sentence of my unknown woman. *I will have put the cohort of my Argus to sleep,* and managed to persuade myself that there was, in that assurance, a sufficient guarantee of security against all the dangers what could threaten me.

" 'One other influence in addition contributed to consolidate my confidence and my courage. Supper was served at five o'clock at the *Golden Lamb.* Almost at that time I went to seat myself at the *table d'hôte*, if only as a diversion for my thoughts. The food at that inn was, in general, quite acceptable, but that day, in celebration of the double festival, the cook had wanted to distinguish himself, and the worthy hostess herself had ordered that they bring out the best wines from her cellar, declaring that she proposed to toast her guests with only the best. Lending myself with very good grace to that joyful threat, under the warm influence of Rhine wine, I wasn't long in feeling in all my being a more rapid flow of blood and life. All my faculties were increased and made me conscious of a power of action and will superior to what I ordinarily possessed.

" 'In that happy disposition, I no longer had any doubt of the success of my perilous intention. Impatience and irritable eagerness to carry it out began to take the place of my preceding lukewarm resolution. Nevertheless, it was necessary to remain calm and wait for the appointed hour, and, in addition, think about preparations for my departure, the moment for which was henceforth imperatively set. So, as soon as I had left the table, I asked my hostess to please draw up my bill, announcing my intention to start on the road during the evening and resisting all the well-meaning invitations made to me to prolong my sojourn in Halberstadt.

" 'I then ordered a stable boy to have my horse saddled at exactly 10:30 p.m. Having thought about it, I judged that I should not acquire another horse for the companion of my

85

flight, and I thought even less of procuring a post chaise.[49] In addition to the fact that there was not enough time for these arrangements, I was afraid that, in doing that, I would reveal my secret enterprise and set on my tracks the terrible Baron de Hostrub, who would begin pursuit as soon as his prisoner had eloped. As I was acting the part of a wandering knight, my beautiful, unknown woman, like the beautiful chatelaines or princesses from the stories, snatched from the hands of en-chanters, would do me the kindness of mounting behind me until we had gotten enough ahead to be a little more comforta-ble and travel in a more usual way.

" 'All my arrangements thus made, I had several hours to spare. In order to spend them pleasantly and without letting the cold hand of wisdom put its hand on me, I invited those who were guests at the table of the *Golden Lamb*, with whom I had developed some familiarity, to come with me to the *Gar-den of Harmony,* that I was told would be the rendezvous that evening for the whole city. There we would empty several steins of beer in honor of Breyhahn, and then drink a glass of punch to our short acquaintance and in the hope of seeing our-selves again more than once in the short pilgrimage of life. I will not stop here to paint for you, my dear listeners, the pro-digious animation of the tableau we witnessed once we had, with great difficulty, found a table where we sat down in the garden of the brasserie. As I had been told, all of Halberstadt crowded in that celebrated place. From moment to moment, there arrived entire families, including servants, water span-iels, and the breast-feeding infant that had to be brought along, since there was no one left at the house to look after him.

" 'In the middle of that laughing, smoking, chatting, humming crowd, and most of all, making gigantic libations to the divinity of the place, there circulated strolling musicians, going from place to place to take their nomadic harmony, beg-gars, second-hand merchants, and most of all Jews, a mer-chandising and industrious race that, on the day of the last

---

[49] A fast, closed carriage popular in the 18th century.

judgment in the Valley of Josaphat[50] will still be seen in the middle of the crowd, busy hawking good bargains for their last scarf or opera glasses.

" 'Soon, night, my accomplice, silently descended on the celebrating city, and tried to put an end to all the Bacchanals. But there was no question of that for me, and, on my word, the beautiful dreamer in the robe of black satin sprinkled with stars, was going to find out what she was dealing with! The façade of the former dwelling of Brayhahn was only waiting for her first shadows to substitute for the garlands of green that decorated it in the morning, the splendid night garlands of illuminations in colored glass. And while the bright lights of the lanterns played about in the trees from which they were suspended and went to the deepest of the groves to chase away the shadows, the Roman candles lit by the artillery men of the civil guard, ran to carry their empire right to the heavens. As for my guests and I, we didn't hesitate to bring our contingency to that conspiracy of light, by means of a blue flame of a huge bowl of punch served to us.

" 'As it threw its bluish lights all around, I noticed a person who had just sat down at a table near ours, just become vacant, who immediately attracted my strong attention. He was accompanied by a still young woman on whom it appeared that he had strongly placed the weight of conjugal authority in the least gentle and tempered way. She looked at me with tears in her eyes and spoke a few rare words only in

---

[50] a Biblical place mentioned by name in Joel 3:2 and Joel 3:12: "I will gather together all nations, and will bring them down into the valley of Josaphat; then I will enter into judgment with them there, on behalf of my people and for My inheritance Israel, whom they have scattered among the nations and they have divided up My land; Let the nations be roused; Let the nations be aroused And come up to the Valley of Jehoshaphat, for there I will sit to judge all the nations on every side." This location is also referred to as the Valley of Decision.

trembling, to which he hardly deigned to reply. Near them was seated a child about ten, the living portrait of his mother, and like her, the object of the brutal remarks of the despot who criticized the way he sat on his chair, and her on the way she drank her beer, and above all the terrible crime the child committed in letting his hat fall on the floor.

" ' — That's fine! Ruin a new hat! said the bully. As if I had the means to buy another one!

" 'The mother picked up the hat, wiped it off carefully, remarking that it had fallen on a well-swept spot where it couldn't have picked up much dust. Then placing it again on the child's head, she said:

" ' — It's all right, but try not to put your father in a bad mood and behave like a big boy.

" 'A rather long silence followed, during which time I considered the face of that man which, despite the harsh bitterness of his manners, had something that interested me. His eyes were piercing and lively, his face honest and thoughtful, and his forehead, although lacking a little in hair, had beauty, since it could be supposed that it was with battles of thoughts that he had lost his crown.

" 'Noticing the attention I seemed to be paying them, the woman appeared to worry about it, because she glanced at me with a look full of anxiety. Leaning near her husband, she said some words to him in a low voice full of emotion. Then he, in response, replied loudly:

" ' — What does that matter to me! Am I not here under the protection of the magistrates? It's only in three days that I can be hanged; until then, no one has the right to look at me the wrong way, and I can be here just like anyone else, drinking beer and smoking my pipe.

" 'And at the same time, he drank the contents of a big glass that he had in front of him in one gulp and blew out several puffs of tobacco smoke. He disappeared with his family for several moments in the cloud of smoke that rose around him. That fear that his wife had manifested to see him the object of some insult, that delay of three days that he gave himself before something bad happened to him, and something hard to explain by which one recognizes people one has never seen, made me suspect that I had, before me, the unfortunate Gregoire Kleng, whom, jumping to a conclusion without facts, the people of Halberstadt had accused of the damage done to *their human voice* and to whom, one will recall, the gentlemen of the City Council had in fact given him three days to repair it.

" 'What's more, my doubt was soon ended, since some minutes later, another person stopped in front of the table where the man whose identity I believed I had guessed was seated. He asked him in a very polite way if he wasn't Gregoire Kleng, the famous inventor of the pedal keyboard?

" ' — Myself, at your service, the artist responded.

" 'During the exchange of the question and the answer, I had glanced at the face of the new arrival, and as much as I felt myself favorably disposed toward the organ-maker, I experienced repulsion for his questioner from the first glance I gave him. Just to look at him, however, he seemed made to inspire a totally different feeling. He had an imposing presence, was dressed in very good taste, and demonstrated as much ease as urbanity. But considered closely, one wasn't slow to catch something false and sinister in his face. And there was a certain derisiveness that gave his features, otherwise handsome and regular, an indescribable expression of moral ugliness. Covered by thick eyebrows that came together at the beginning of the nose, his eyes seemed to throw out fatal lights, and in the sound of his voice, as penetrating as the low notes of a harmonica, there was a marked neuralgic vibration, at the same time unpleasant to the ear and disquieting to the spirit.

" 'Gregoire Kleng having avowed his identity, his questioner spoke again, asking him if there could be any way to have a word with him in private.

" ' — You see, replied the organ-maker, pointing to his child and his wife, that I am here with my family. But tomorrow, you will find me all day in my workshop.

" ' — Yes, but it's this evening and at this moment that I must speak to you, answered the sinister person, and it will be of great interest to you.

" ' — I wouldn't be able to do that, answered the artist, without being moved by that insistent manner of asking him for an audience, and besides, this is not a very convenient place nor the time to talk business.

" ' — That depends, the unknown man answered. If Madame would permit me to take you for a moment to the place where I was sitting an instant ago, we will find a bottle of Tokay wine there, to open, and a small provision of excellent Oriental tobacco to fill our pipes.

" ' — Thank you for your honesty, replied Kleng, but I will not leave my wife alone in the middle of people who would perhaps take advantage of my absence to abuse her.

" 'And on saying that, he threw his glance in my direction.

" ' — You are not aware, perhaps, he then added, that the good bourgeois of Halberstadt accuse me of having put two notes from the pipes of their Notre-Dame organ in my pocket, and I had to use all my conjugal authority for the poor creature that you suggest that I leave here, to decide to follow me into this garden where she thought I ran the risk of being eaten alive.

" ' — I don't insist, said the man with black eyebrows, but you will perhaps regret not having listened me, because it is exactly about the trouble that happened to you that I have an important revelation to make to you.

" 'Kleng looked at him as if to reassure himself that he wasn't telling him a fib.

" ' — Yes, my dear Monsieur, it's about your business of this morning, and nothing else that I want to talk to you, continued the persevering person in a persuasive, truthful voice.

" ' — Speak lower, the artist then said. I have decided on a way.

" 'At the same time, he called a waiter of the establishment, paid his bill, then stood up.

" ' — If you will wait for me a moment, he added, I will take Betty and my child back home. After that, I will be with you.

" ' — I'll see you soon, then, answered the officious unknown man.

" 'Pointing out to him a table situated some distance away, right under a statue of Diana the Huntress, he added:

" ' — You will find me there.

" 'Then, having taken his leave of Madame Kleng, he left.

" 'Either because she didn't like to see her husband thus led away, or because the man her husband had agreed to come join had produced on the wife of the artist an impression like mine, she appeared to want to make some resistance to the arrangement he had just made. But with a commanding gesture, after arranging her coat on her shoulders, Kleng silenced her, and, after having given me, before he left, a last and hardly welcoming glance, taking the arm of his sad companion and his child by the hand, he went toward the door of the garden which he soon went through.

" 'After a few minutes, I saw him return and go sit down with his new acquaintance. And I admit that I wasn't without some curiosity to know the tenor of the communication that was going to be made to him. But at the distance I was from the two chatting, far from being able to seize something of their conversation, I could hardly see their faces. I therefore stopped taking notice of them, and returning to my guests, that I had greatly neglected in following the attention that I had given to the episode that I have just recounted, I found that they had almost emptied the bowl of punch, which, combined with the Rhine wine I had at supper, and the beer that we hadn't drunk sparingly, had lifted them quietly into dream land. I appreciated that happy result, because it favored perfectly the intention I had of slipping away quietly in order to avoid explanations and, perhaps, the annoying goodwill that would make those good friends of one day accompany me.

" 'Having consulted my watch, seeing that it was time to think of my rendezvous, I rose, saying that I would be absent only for a moment. Then, after having paid what I might owe, I took the road back to my inn, where I had another bill to settle.

" 'In looking over the bill presented to me, I saw with edification that the very generous feast given by the hostess had, in fact, been charged to my bill. *Wine opened has to be drunk; wine drunk has to be paid for*, as the saying goes. I therefore made no comment relative to the manner of economy the good lady had found to treat us so magnificently, and I paid without saying a word. My horse had been saddled and had its bridle on, and needed nothing more than my valise which I myself secured on its back. And promising that I would never stay anywhere else if I ever returned to Halberstadt, and acquitting myself as well with the valets as I had done with the hostess by distributing a generous tip to them, I mounted my horse and left the *Golden Lamb* with the inhabitants persuaded that, in several minutes, I was going to be traveling on the road to Iena.

" 'All the population was concentrated in the *Garden of Harmony* or in several dance halls from which came the faraway sounds of wind instruments and tambourines. I therefore went through the city without seeing a living soul and, several minutes later, I set foot near the place where I was expected.

" 'After having tied my horse some distance away in order to approach the house without any noise, I went toward the door where I was supposed to be met. I had calculated my time and my distance so accurately that I was not fifty feet away when the clocks of the city began to ring and formed a concert which, for several minutes, continued in various tones. The weather, that evening, was very overcast. There was a great deal of obscurity where I was, and I could barely see the habitation of Baron Hostrub, only as a black mass in whose windows no light appeared. But soon, from the side where the door toward which I was walking was situated, I saw a shining ray produced as if coming from a lantern. Coming near that terrestrial lighthouse, I was expecting to finally meet the woman whose face I was very impatient to see. But, judge my astonishment when, in the place of a young and beautiful girl, I saw only a strange little creature created only to frighten me. It wasn't a dwarf, that is to say one of those deformed creatures with short legs and a monstrous head, such as it's not rare to encounter in these regions. On the contrary, it was a miniature old man, very sprightly still, despite his wrinkled and decrepit features, and he was perfectly proportioned in his small height. As clothing, he wore a cap with plumes on top, an apricot-colored doublet with green braiding, britches of the same color, and boots of fawn-colored leather, almost as we see the pages and troubadours of comedy represented on the stage. What I had taken to be a lantern was the phosphorescent light of a huge firefly surmounting a stick that he held in his right hand which threw out light so bright that it illuminated everything.

" 'He came towards me, as soon as he saw me and said to me, in a broken, but nevertheless piercing voice:

" ' — My mistress sent me ahead to ask you to be patient. The narcotic that she used to get rid of the *dueña* who guards her didn't take effect as soon as she had thought. But the old dragon won't be long in going to sleep. While waiting, for fear that you might be seen by someone, my mistress asks that you please come in and wait for her in her study where she will join you as soon as she can.

" 'I had no confidence in that debut to my adventure. My unknown lady's servant had something too strange for me not to remember the unusual things the hostess of the *Golden Lamb* had told me. Suspicious, therefore, that the supernatural and sorcery were at the bottom of everything I was seeing, I quickly refused the invitation, answering that I could wait very well outside. The thought immediately came to me to get myself out of the dangers that I foresaw by fleeing, but seeing my hesitation, the damned little man directed toward me the light that came from his firefly. I received such a glare that, struck with a kind of vertigo, I felt myself drawn, unable to make any resistance, to the opposite side of the one I wanted to take. I was drawn in such a way that it soon made me go through the entrance to the house and took me in front of an ebony door covered with magnificent sculptures, probably the one opening into the room where he had proposed stationing me earlier.

" 'At that moment, another disagreeable incident made me regret the lack of prudence I had shown in coming at such an hour, to such a place. Suddenly, I heard the sound of the gallop of a horse in the distance. Thinking that it could be mine that someone was stealing, I said so with anxiety in order to run after the thief.

" ' — Bah! said my wicked conductor, don't let that worry you. My mistress has taken care to have two chestnut horses brought to the city gate. They will serve for your flight with her, and if you lose something by the theft that's just occurred, she is rich enough to have you reimbursed.

" 'I was going to say that it was not proper for me to receive any reimbursement from her, that I wanted my horse back, and that I wanted absolutely to go after the one that belonged to me, but the ebony door had already turned on its hinges and the fascination of the phosphorescent insect continued to operate on me.

" 'I soon found myself in the middle of a vast gallery lit by the rays of gigantic *cincindelas*.[51] Insects decidedly seemed to be the method of lighting adopted in that fatal house.

" 'Having led me where he wished, the little man said:

" ' — Amuse yourself by looking at the curious things in this room. I'm going to report to my mistress, who will be here in a moment.

" 'Saying this, without waiting for my answer, he disappeared.' "

---

[51] Commonly known as common tiger beetles, they are generally brightly colored and metallic beetles, often with some sort of patterning of ivory or cream-colored markings.

VI. The Story of Monsieur de Rebundus (cont'd)

" 'Nothing interested me less than to be occupied with curiosities. I had only one thought: to find myself outside that infernal dwelling. Then', as soon as I was alone, I ran to the door in order to take advantage of the absence of the traitor who had led me there. But as I approached to turn the key, the figures of men and animals which filled the panels, on the inside as well as on the outside, appeared to come alive. The faces made horrible grimaces at me, their mouths opened and showed me gnashing, menacing teeth; others yawned wide enough to dislocate their jaw, and with a well-known contagious effect, forced me to imitate them. Then, as my desire to escape was stronger than my astonishment and my fear, I made a movement to pick up the key. It went back into itself, re-entering the keyhole, level with the lock, as a tortoise hides his head in his shell. Giving itself a double turn, it made me see that I was caught in a trap and that every means of evasion had been taken from me.

" 'Worried more than ever about my situation, I began to look around for an exit, which naturally gave me the opportunity to better consider the general aspect of the place and its furnishings. I was soon convinced that, the door locked, no way of salvation was open to me. All the length of that gallery, getting daylight from above and having no windows, there were huge armoires filled with shells, minerals, and all kinds of vegetable and animal products impaled, dried, or preserved in jars of spirits ranged along the wall. At the extreme end of that kind of natural history museum, facing directly opposite the door, there was an immense clock in an enclosure of ironwood incrusted with gold, almost resembling, but in a more considerable dimension, the shape of those sarcophagus where the mummies of Egypt slept enclosed. On both sides of that beautiful work of clock-making, there were raised two vast bookshelves filled with volumes decorated with gold clasps and bound in Morocco leather of the most excellent taste.

95

" 'A desk of sandalwood stood in the middle of the room, enriched with exquisite carvings of pure gold which were reproduced on a chair made of the same material, made to go with the desk. The rest of the room was filled with a terrestrial globe, a celestial globe of great volume, an electric machine, an astrolabe, instruments dealing with optics, physics, and mathematics, beakers, flasks, an alembic, in short, all the amenities of the richest and most complete science laboratory.

" 'In considering the furnishings of that gallery, which actually showed that its proprietor had a great taste for natural things, and showed no indication of his dealing in cabalistic studies, I began to be somewhat reassured and to explain the animation with which, a moment ago, the carvings on the door had seemed to me to be gifted, as an illusion produced by fear. I told myself that probably in this sanctuary I would have less to fear than I had at first supposed. Men devoted to the culture of the sciences are rarely cruel. I still had to explain to myself the unusual personality of the little servant, but, after all, nature that has its caprices, and could very well be manipulated to produce that *homunculus*. Therefore, it wasn't astonishing that the master of the house, who seemed to take pleasure in drawing public attention, which spread a scent of the miraculous over all his existence, would have wanted to make one of them part of his household. There is nothing more natural than to imagine his betraying the Baron for the benefit of a young and unhappy mistress who had drawn him into her interests. Looked at in that way, the danger that I could foresee was brought back to ordinary proportions. I promised myself I would have the necessary resolution to face it when, suddenly, the door to the gallery opened quickly.

" ' — We are lost, the little man cried out, running about with a frightened expression. The Baron that we thought would be absent a much longer time, has just returned and is walking toward this gallery. He usually works an hour or two before going to bed. If he finds you here, that will be the end of you!

" ' — But wouldn't I have time to slip away through the door? I asked in a somewhat emotional voice, which was certainly permitted, having been greeted with such a comment.

" ' — Impossible, exclaimed the *homonculus*. He is on our heels, and our only recourse is to hide you somewhere.

" ' — I won't hide, I said proudly. If your Baron threatens my life, I will defend myself.

" ' — But what about my mistress' life? And my own, Monsieur? the little servant said, in anguish. Would you want to endanger them both? Without considering the fact that you yourself would never be able to overcome such a dangerous enemy! Ah! he said, as if he had suddenly had an idea. Come this way! We are saved!

" 'And pulling on my coat tails, he led me toward the end of the gallery. I went along with it, because, finally, what could happen to me worse than the treatment with which I was threatened? Climbing slowly the length of the ornaments on the enclosure of the huge clock, the odious little man opened a lateral door, and showed me a great, empty interior.

" '— You will be perfectly safe here, he told me, able to breathe and even able to see the Baron comfortably. He will never suspect that you are there. The only the inconvenience is staying on your knees, but that will only be for no more than two hours, the time that a guard spends standing in his sentry box. Get in! I hear him coming!

" 'I had only half-way decided to make use of that bizarre resource, and had very incomplete confidence in my officious liberator. But pushing me with a hand whose vigor was out of all proportion to his frail body, he shouted:

" '— Get in!

" 'He then pronounced a horrible swear word, and forced me into that terrible sheath, closing the door after me before I knew it and sealing my imprisonment by attaching two very solid hooks.

" 'At that moment, I realized that I was the victim of deceitful infamy, because the wicked little man had no sooner seen me encaged than he let out a long burst of laughter that

97

rang throughout the gallery. At the same moment, the *cincindelas*, shutting off their light, plunged me into the most profound darkness.

" 'It is only in a very incomplete way that I can make you understand what I experienced at the bottom of that box as soon as I was enclosed there. Assuredly, nothing equivalent has ever been done to a human existence. It was already a cruel thing to see oneself thus hermetically sealed in a clock. But how can I describe my agony when I began to be aware that I was becoming *the clock itself*, and, in some way, that noisy machine was embodied in me.

" 'My head being, at first, the siege of a horrible revolution, it seemed to me that in the center of it was installed a device of wheels and gears that began to function with a din as deafening to my ears as the sound of a fulling mill[52] or that of the interior of a pump action shotgun. The major spring was in my breast, right at the place of the heart. Like a serpent rolling up into itself, to the warm and regular activity of circulation there was substituted the inert and jerky development of its steel spiral, a pitiable parody of the spontaneous movement of the vital force. It seemed to me that, behind my neck, had been attached a long steel rod ending with a weight. At the same moment, I began to feel along the backbone the monotonous coming and going of the pendulum that had become my pulse.

" 'But that physical degradation and that miserable and ridiculous descent to the condition of a machine was nothing. A very different ravage had taken place in my moral being; I no longer thought, or, to put it better, a single and unique idea still lived in me, to know time and the fractions into which it could be divided so well that to any question that I could be asked, to any word addressed to me, I would no longer know how to answer except: eleven hours twenty-five minutes—eleven hours twenty -six minutes—twenty-seven minutes—twenty-eight minutes, and so on, until there was a complete rotation of the second hand. The movement of the hand in-

---

[52]Ancient mill used to clean and beat cloth in water.

tended to mark successively the numerals having become the only manifestation of my intelligence, the knowledge of *the present hour* remained the only concept in my possession.

" 'Fortunately, that violent situation didn't last long, since, at the end of several minutes, it struck eleven thirty, and after the shudder of the impact of the chimes, which functioned inside of me, I, like all the rest, made a movement so brusque that the pendulum stopped and the frightful phenomenon stopped. Life in me again took on its usual course. At the same time, the door of the gallery opened and the *cincidelas* began to shine again with the greatest brilliance. Accompanying the terrible little old man, by whom I had been so dreadfully duped, I saw a tall man who, after taking off the dark-colored overcoat he was wearing, sat down in the chair placed in front of the desk. Evidently, he was the master of the lodgings—the terrible Baron de Hostrub. I no longer had to search for the cause of the instinctive repulsion I had felt toward the unknown man who, three-quarters of an hour earlier in the *Garden of Harmony*, had approached the organ-maker. In the person who had just entered, I recognized that odious individual. As soon as he was seated, he motioned to the little man to bring him a book from one of the bookshelves that he pointed to with his finger. That order quickly carried out, he began to leaf through the volume as if searching for a passage. After having found the place he desired, he left it open in front of him and then speaking to the executor of his commands:

" ' — Anything new during my absence? he asked casually.

" ' — Indeed, there is much new to report, answered the little monster, jumping with one bound onto his master's desk, where he squatted down as do tailors, and seemed in that posture an ink blotter or a carved ink stand.

" ' — Well! Speak, Migrelin; I'm listening, the Baron said, with an air of curiosity.

" ' — Without me, answered Migrelin (and let it be said in passing that I found that his name was perfectly appropriate to his nature and his height),[53] your pupil Alberta would, right now, have taken the key to the fields with a dandy whom she met somehow, and would be getting ready to accompany him in his flight.

" " — Is that how you guard her? shouted the Baron angrily, and are those the services you render me?

" ' — On the contrary, it's because I keep good watch that I discovered the whole plot, and you can see that I was right when I advised you this morning not to give her permission to leave to attend the ceremony at the Church of Notre-Dame, because, to all appearances, once she was outside, you would never have seen her return.

" ' — But, even so, since I took your advice, where was she able to make contact with the insolent person who wanted to kidnap her?

" ' — Women, when they get into their heads not to remain somewhere, always have the way to make contact with someone, Migrelin answered in a knowing tone. 'To tell you where and how she met her accomplice, is not at all possible for me, and total *mandragore* [54]that I am, I don't flatter myself that I can divine the abilities a female mind is capable of! However that may be, having heard that dear person make a great noise with her harp this afternoon, and having seen at the same time a young man prowling around the house, I took the shape of a lizard and slid under the boudoir window that opens onto the street that you unwisely left open.

" ' — Tomorrow that window will change place and will look out onto the garden, said the Baron, as if it were a question of merely moving a piece of furniture.

---

[53] In French, the name suggests someone small and rachitic (*maigrelet*).

[54] *Mandragore* (or mandrake), because of the shape of their roots which often resembles human figures, have long been associated with magic and alchemy, and connected to the creation of *homonculi*, miniature, fully formed humans.

" ' — Good precaution! said the malicious little old man, but which has certainly come a little late.

" ' — Enough of your opinions, answered the Baron. Finish your report.

" ' — Well, to sum it up in two words, continued Migrelin, listening as much as I could, I heard that the beautiful one was giving a rendezvous in music this evening to the officious person. The evening having come, and your charming pupil waiting for the time in her bedroom, without seeming to do anything, I locked her door. After that, going to the savior, I pretended to have been sent by the one he came to get. Then, having drawn him here, I enclosed him in the clock, where you can dispose of him at your will.

" 'If I was cruelly disappointed by learning of the trap I had fallen into, and if I started to shiver at the thought of the treatment that the terrible Baron was reserving for me, hurled against me in curses, I nevertheless felt great relief not to have been fooled by her to whom I had devoted myself. Then, since in desperate situations one holds on to the lightest glimmers of hope, I counted a little on her to get me out of the bad situation where I found myself. But I didn't carry these thoughts very far, because changing subjects, the two questioners began to hold a conversation that, even in the middle of my perplexing situation, greatly excited my curiosity.

" ' — Now, another chapter, said Migrelin. When that clock strikes three o'clock, it will mark thirteen years that I have been in your service to carry out every order that it would please you to give me. And you know our contract: at the end of thirteen years, you have sworn to be mine, body and soul, unless someone else is found to take up your bargain and pass on the same conditions to be your servant with another contract.

" ' — But why not renew this lease with me? the Baron asked with an engaging air.

" ' — Not at all, if you please, Migrelin responded. Either you will be mine, or I will enter the service of someone else; it would bore me to always have the same master. At the end of thirteen years, we know each other by heart. And we know each other's faults too perfectly to endure each other any longer.

" ' — All right, Monsieur Logician, said the Baron with disdain. It will be as agreed, and someone is going to come whom I count on passing you to.

" ' — Should I go find this future master to bring him here? asked Migrelin.

" ' — Yes, go meet him, answered the Baron, because when he left me, he had nothing more to do except to return to his house to tell his wife that some business forced him to be absent. And now, he should be very near here, if he isn't already at the door.

" ' — I will run to open the door for him, answered the little man, jumping off the desk where he had taken a seat.

" 'And he left the same moment.

" 'Two minutes had not gone by when, conducted by Migrelin, I saw enter the guest they were expecting. And, dear readers, if you will please recall what happened at the *Garden of Harmony,* you will be as little astonished as I myself was on recognizing the one who entered: Gregoire Kleng, the organ-maker, with whom Baron de Hostrub had been in such a hurry to have an interview.

" 'Going to meet him, the master of the lodging complimented him on his promptness; then, having asked him to be seated, and having himself returned to his chair, he said:

" ' — We have no time to waste; I will come to the subject. I promised you, my dear artist, to let you know the cause of the damage that manifested itself in the Notre-Dame organ, and which is such as to make you incur the most rigorous treatment from the citizens of Halberstadt.

" ' — Ah! Their justice, I'm hardly worried about that, Kleng answered sadly. They will do with me whatever they like, but what concerns me is my compromised reputation, my name threatened with remaining stained.

" ' — Well, I have exactly the remedy for that misfortune, continued the Baron. And here, he added, pointing to the volume opened in front of him, is what shows you the way out of that trouble. But before everything, I must know if I'm doing business with a meticulous mind full of stupid prejudices or with an independent and resolute spirit.

" ' — I don't lack either courage or will, answered Kleng, and if you have nothing to ask me contrary to the integrity and sentiment of a good Christian...

" ' — You can very well understand, my dear Monsieur Kleng, interrupted the Baron, that in order to possess certain notions that place me in a sphere superior to that of other men, I have had to undertake persevering studies of a somewhat ardent nature. I have worked night and day for twenty years of my life to delve into those mysteries. And I will frankly admit to you that, during that long and absorbing research, I scarcely busied myself with knowing if monks were chanting morning prayers and if I was really sure of the path to paradise.

" ' — That means that you are somewhat of a heretic, the organ-maker then said.

" '— Have your read Paracelsus?[55] the Baron de Hostrub asked, without bothering to answer that insinuation.

" ' — I? No, answered the organ-make. I know only one book in the world; that's the *Traité de la fabrication des orgues*[56] by Dom Bedos, a learned French Monk from the Saint-Maur Congregation, three volumes in-folio.

" ' — And in that work, asked the Baron, is there anywhere a mention of the *mandragores*?

" ' — What! responded Kleng, that villainous plant with a yellow flower for which I was given a herb tea for a tumor

---

[55] Paracelsus (1493-1541), Swiss physician, alchemist and astrologer of the German Renaissance, a pioneer in several aspects of the medical revolution of the Renaissance, also a prophet whose *Prognostications* were studied by Rosicrucians in the late 16th and 17th centuries.

[56] *The Art of Making Organs* (1766-70) by Benedictine monk François Lamathe Dom Bedos de Celles de Salelles (1709-1779). .

that had appeared on my left leg, and which purged me in such a harsh way?

" ' — No, replied the Baron. I'm talking about the *mandragores,* spirits of the earth that Paracelsus shows the way to invoke, and which procure, when one knows how to become their masters, science, riches, honor, power, and everything.

" ' — Dom Bedos spoke of nothing similar, answered the honest organ-maker, but he added after thinking about it, and lowering his voice: Would that unusual little man who opened the door for me be, by chance, one of those you are talking about?

" ' — Exactly, the Baron replied, and I'm going to have you get better acquainted with him. Migrelin, he said at the same time in a commanding voice, approach!

"The organ-maker didn't seem too eager to make that acquaintance, because he quickly moved backward, without, however, leaving his seat, when he saw the *mandragore* jump to the desk and seat himself there as we saw before.

" ' — Explain to the gentleman the manner in which we are together, and tell him your talents, said the Baron.

" ' — As for my talents, responded Migrelin, the list isn't very long; I know how to do everything. As for the rest, not lacking in intelligence, I believe that I can learn easily.

" ' — So, you would know how to make an organ? questioned Kleng, and you claim you understand the methods of its fabrication?

" ' — But, of course, replied Migrelin, I think I am as clever at that as at everything else. And Gregoire Kleng that you are, I believe that I can show you a thing or two.

" ' — We'll see about that, retorted the organ-maker, piqued by that presumptuousness.

" 'And, immediately, like an old professor examining a student before according him a degree, he began to put forth to the little old man the most difficult problems of his art and tried to confuse him with questions. But the Migrelin knew his material completely, and soon it was he who took the offensive and at last embarrassed the professor, which sometimes happens in other exams without the recipient being a great intellect.

Seeing that he was dealing with a hard jouster, Kleng thought at least to make use of his defeat.

" ' — Since you know so much, he said to the *mandragore*, and you are so clever, would you please tell me what makes the two *human voice* pipes in the Notre-Dame organ no longer speak?

" 'The malicious Migrelin replied:

" ' — Without a doubt, that comes from the fact that they no longer make any sound.

" ' — Yes, but what is the reason that keeps them from making sounds? the organ-maker insisted.

" ' — The reason, said Migrelin in the same malicious way, comes from the fact that they have lost their *voice*.

" ' — Ah! You're joking, replied Kleng with bad temper, but you don't actually know anymore than I do about that subject.

" ' — You are wrong, the Baron said, again entering the conversation. Migrelin and I are perfectly able to resolve your problem, but in return you must be a little friendlier to us.

" ' — What must I do? asked the organ-maker, made impatient by those long circumlocutions.

" ' — Migrelin, said the Baron, speaking to his *mandragore*, I am now telling you to reveal to Master Gregoire the terms which bind us together. Read him a little of our contract.

" 'Migrelin, taking from his pocket a little shagreen[57]book, fastened with precious stones, took from it a note written on parchment from which hung two seals, one of black wax and the other of green wax, his and that of the Baron; then reading aloud:

---

[57] Shagreen – rough, untanned skin from rays, sharks or dog-fish.

" ' — *In front of those present, I engage myself for thirteen full and consecutive years to remain in the service of the very high and very powerful Lord Fortuné Sigismond, Baron de Hostrub, and to obey him in all encounters and in all commands. And from his side, the before named Lord and Baron, at the end of thirteen years, promises to be the valet, I becoming the master, unless, however, he finds a substitute to take up his contract under the same conditions as above. Made by both in good faith, the twenty-ninth day of the month of August of the jubilant, cabalistic, free mason, and climacteric leap year*, and we have signed: *Baron de Hostrub* and *Migrelin* and affixed our seals.

" 'The reading of that unusual document finished, the Baron asked:

" ' — Well! What say you about that, Master Gregoire?

" 'Shaking his head, the organ maker replied:

" ' — I say that appears enormously like a pact with the Devil, and I don't have any wish to be a substitute in that contract. That is probably what you meant by being *friendly*?

" ' — You're right, answered the Baron. Before sending away Migrelin, that I recommend to you as an excellent servant, I would have preferred that it was you, rather than someone else, who took advantage of this opportunity.

" '— And I, said Kleng, would just as soon leave that opportunity to someone else. And if that is all you have to propose to me, he added, rising, I believe I would do well to leave.

" ' — But think, then, Master Gregoire, the Baron said, in thirteen years, you could, like me, find someone to put in your place, and, in succeeding you, set you free.

" ' — Thank you very much, said the organ-maker, but I don't have any taste for such complicated business.

" ' — So, you are going to put yourself at the mercy of the people of Halberstadt, who will put you in prison, hang you perhaps, because when it's a question of their *human voices,* they don't know either right or justice?

" ' — Well! At least I will die a good Christian, said the artist, not seeming, however, as quick to leave as before.

" ' — But your wife, your child, will be reduced to poverty and they will perhaps treat them worse.

" ' — If that's a cross that Heaven sends me, it has to be accepted, Kleng replied.

" ' — And your fame as a great artist, the Baron continued perfidiously, what will happen to that when all the biographies will read: Gregoire Kleng, a famous organ-maker and inventor of the pedal clavier, merited his great reputation so little that, having once disarranged two notes in one of the pipes of the Notre-Dame organ in Halberstadt, he wasn't able to see clearly into that blunder and preferred to let himself be hanged rather than have the mind to repair it.

" ' — Don't tempt me like this, said the unhappy organ-maker in despair. To think that anyone could be slandered like that; it's enough to drive one insane.

" — 'And nevertheless, that will be the truth, answered the tempter, because, in fact, there are two pipes that must be made to *speak*, and as talented as you are, you don't know how to manage that.

" ' — Me, I am only a man, responded Kleng, but if there's some sorcery in all that...

" '—Exactly, said the Baron. For a magician, it takes a magician and a half, and it's only by supernatural powers that supernatural powers can be dominated and vanquished.

" ' — But, then, supposing that I sign that contract, and in thirteen years I can't find a substitute, what will happen to me? asked the organ-maker, whose resolution was quite evidently shaken.

" ' — You will serve me, answered Migrelin, just as I would have served you.

" ' — But what does that service consist of ? Kleng demanded, wanting to know where he was going.

" ' — Ah! You are asking me too much, my boy, Migrelin said. Accept or don't accept.

" ' — In that case, let me leave, said the sad artist. I am sure that at the bottom of all this, it's the salvation of my soul that's in play.

" ' — As you like, my Lord, said Migrelin, getting down from his place to conduct him out, when he saw him go toward the door of the gallery.

" 'But that wasn't the end of it for the Baron, and, seeing his man about to escape him, he thought he should try one last effort.

" ' — Listen, my dear Monsieur Gregoire, he said to the artist, you are probably under some illusion and you are persuading yourself that, by some stratagem of your art, you will manage to bring about the restoration that is demanded of you. Well! Consider everything. I'm going to read you the passage from this old chronicle which has to do with the Notre-Dame organ. And after that, you will tell me if you can reasonably keep some hope of getting out of your difficult situation by yourself.

" 'Gregoire Kleng was too curious to refuse to know the revelation offered to him, and not to give it all his attention. He retraced his steps and sat down again beside the Baron. Picking up the volume opened in front of him, the Baron began reading in these terms:

" ' — And in that same place in Halberstadt and in that same year, there took place a very important event which was a very great sensation. The monastery of the Dominicans had, in that place, been struck by lightning from Heaven and reduced to cinders, without there remaining the least vestige of the buildings, nor of those who inhabited them. This was regarded as a just chastisement for misbehaviors of all kinds committed in that dwelling, where an extreme laxity of morals had been introduced, and where no one ever went to the choir to say the offices. Time was spent in laughing, in singing, in festivities, day and night. And the Devil having debauched all those monks, the power that he took over them that led them astray from the ways of salvation, was pleasant. Instead of taking them straight into Hell, as he could have done, he preferred to take them into the workshop of an artist who was at that time busy constructing the beautiful organs of the Church of Notre-Dame. In his absence, he deviously put, one by one, all those Dominicans into the pipes, creating the phenomenon now known as the *human voice*, telling them: « You didn't like to go to the choir to say vespers and compline,[58] well, you will now sing, my little monks, whether you want to or not. » And it is in fact those monks who are heard in the *human voice* of the organs of Notre-Dame. It is then not astonishing that there is found nowhere in the entire world, a pipe where the singing of men is so well imitated.

" ' — Certainly not; that's not astonishing, said Kleng, interrupting. Who could fight against the Devil and do as good work as he?

" ' — You, me, all those who have Migrelin to help them. Accept putting yourself in my place, and you will see how the job demanded of you will be done in a flash.

" ' — But how did it happen that those two damned pipes, because that's certainly the word, have lost their *voice*? asked the artist, without responding to the new entreaty of the Baron.

" ' — There is nothing easier to explain, answered the Baron. Do you know the color of the Dominicans' clothing?

" ' — White, said Kleng.

" ' — Now, what was seen yesterday floating above the city?

" '— Two white monks, according to what was reported.

" ' — Alright! Now listen to the rest of the chronicle: « But the Devil hadn't done such a good job as he had at first thought, since, seeing that he had not conducted the Dominicans directly to Hell, he took pity on them and decided that the organ in which they were imprisoned had served as purgatory

---

[58] A service of evening prayers forming part of the Divine Office of the Western Christian Church, traditionally said (or chanted) before retiring for the night.

for them. After having lived there for a certain number of years, more or less, according to the magnitude of their sins, they would find themselves thus purified by that penitence and would return into celestial glory. »

" ' — That explains everything! said the organ-maker, clapping his hands. The white monks that were seen yesterday going through the air, that was two of those Dominicans who, having served their time, left their pipes empty and went away to Heaven.

" ' — Exactly, replied the Baron. And tell me, my dear artist, a little of what you can make of that.

" ' — Oh! Nothing without a doubt, said Kleng, and I see very well that I am a lost man.

" ' — Say rather a saved man, responded the tempter. You have only to say the word and with the help of our dear Migrelin....

" 'At that moment, I no longer heard anything. The odious little old man, while the Baron and the organ-maker were debating, had noticed that the pendulum had stopped functioning, and as he was in every way an exact and faithful servant, he had perched himself on the library ladder and had opened the crystal circle of gold which covered the clock dial and had begun to reset the machine. As he put the key into the lock on the face of the clock, it seemed to me that it penetrated my eyes, and I felt in all my nerves the winding of the noisy transfer to all the springs. Once again, the mechanical life absorbed mine and that living lethargy was better than the terrible vision which served as an alarm clock.

" 'At first, it seemed to me that a resounding voice shouted at me: « Get out, Monsieur, get out! » and at the same time, a strong arm seized mine, drawing me outside the clock, and threw me down on the gallery floor.

" 'However, the bright light of the *cincindelas* which had lit the room before had been replaced by a reddish light produced by a blazing fire on which there was a bubbling bronze caldron. Mounted on a stool with an immense spatula in his hand, Migrelin was majestically stirring the contents which cracked and rumbled under the heat of the fire. From the silver filets that the *mandragore* let flow from his spatula from time to time, lifting them from the surface of the liquid, as if to test the degree of its fluidity, it was clear that was a metal being smelted.

" 'Having probably triumphed over his scruples, Gregoire Kleng seemed to be watching that hellish cuisine with worried attention. His pale visage scarcely reflecting the incandescent material above which he was silently leaning, he seemed to be a spirit from the abyss witnessing preparation for the torture of a damned.

" 'Suddenly Migrelin shouted:

" ' — More alum,[59] Master, more alum! The metal is boiling and about to overflow.

" 'At the same moment, I felt myself inundated with fetid water poured in waves over my head and in which my whole body floated. At the same time, the metal contents in the caldron escaped, bubbling down the edges. Like burning lava from a volcano leaving a long train of fire, it flowed toward me, taking as it approached the form of a serpent, its mouth open, threatening to swallow me whole. I wanted to cry out with a terrible suspicion. I wondered if, instead of being under the empire of a dream, I had not been delivered to the grip of a disastrous reality and was a victim of the most odious of enchantments. Going, with despair, more deeply into that thought, from moment to moment I found new reasons to confirm it.

" 'Hadn't the organ-maker already been strongly shaken in his Christian resistance when I could no longer hear his conversation with the Baron? If the tempter had finally seduced him, wasn't it by promising he would be able to execute

---

[59] Alum is both a specific chemical compound and a class of chemical compounds. The specific compound is the hydrated potassium aluminum sulfate (potassium alum); it has a wide range of uses: purification of drinking water, stop bleeding in minor cuts, flame retardant, etc.

work above human capability? Finding at the same time an opportunity to revenge himself on me, hadn't the miserable sorcerer made use of me, living material, for his abominable experiments? Then that serpent of fire, by which I vaguely remembered having been swallowed, was without a doubt a magic instrument to make of me what the Devil had made of the monks. That infernal precaution to inundate me with a solution of alum before the contents of the caldron had boiled over, could be explained by the need to make me impenetrable to the action of the boiling hot metal, because I read some-where that, with the aid of that substance, charlatans and jug-glers made themselves fireproof and were able to handle melt-ed lead and red hot bars.

" 'Nevertheless, to have to become an organ pipe was at the same time, so fatal and so burlesque that I still couldn't believe it. Despite all the clarity of my logic and of my memory, I expected to wake up any instant and be delivered from that terrible enchantment against which I was fighting. But suddenly I heard below me a terrible noise, like that of a hurricane let loose; at the same time, a whirlwind pushed by the bellows, that had just been put in movement, rushing into the narrow pipe where I was held, penetrated me from head to foot and agitated me with a metallic vibration that, at each insertion of air, drew from me a long cry of distress. How then could I doubt my transmutation when my ear, trained to ana-lyze the unique sound I was putting out, made me distinguish in that tone, the seventh note of the scale and when, soon after that, more careful attention allowed me to recognize that the note was lowered by a half tone. Recognizing that, I was then no more Charles de Rebundus; I was not even a man, animat-ed and living, any more. I was only a simple sound, a fugitive vibration—in a word, a *B flat*!

" 'Moreover, that kind of trial by wind which was appar-ently only a first trial of the resonance of my voice, didn't last a long time, and the bellows, soon ceasing to torment me, eve-rything around me became tranquil again. But within that calm wherein I lived, what sad thoughts didn't I find bombarding me? To think that, in the flower of my age, I was separated from the entire world, condemned to the shadows, to inaction, to solitude, to hear nothing for distraction except the periodic return of the torture which I had just undergone, and to tell myself that all manifestations of life in me were henceforth limited to the sad complaint that torture without an example and without a name would draw from me, wasn't that enough to drive me insane?

" 'I would have liked to lose more than reason, and I called for death with all my wishes. But after a day, as well as I could estimate it, passed in my terrible sequestration, I had to renounce that sad recourse, because I found that the charm placed on me left only completely entire the use of hearing and the voice. All the functions of physical existence were impossible to combine with the situation in which I had been placed, and were suspended by a magic power that had in some way metalized me. Could I, at least, count on one consolation? Since other unfortunate people endured a similar fate, wouldn't the sad pleasure of exchanging my complaints with them be permitted to me? To know if I could hold onto that hope, trying to make myself heard by the one of those unfortunate ones who inhabited the pipe nearest the one where I myself was enclosed: « Brother, suffering as I am, do you hear me? » But no voice responded to mine, and I heard only the echo of my words being lost in the arches of the church, making the vaults in the distance resound with a gloomy and pitiful *hou! hou!*

" 'I can't say what I would have become if there had been no soothing to my misfortune, because the thought of man being finished, how could it, in pleasure and in suffering, rise from the depths of the infinity. But at the moment I was thinking the least about that, I heard the murmur of a voice come to me; judge if I listened to it. First of all, I recognized some Latin sentences, and soon from their meaning which was broken into almost equal intervals of *versets* and into *oremus,* I judged that it was the souls of the condemned monks saying their breviary, and from the moment that this sound came to me for the first time, I never missed hearing their prayers devotedly recited each day at the same hour. I judged that they were in that way expiating, often having repeatedly missed going to the choir and making up for the time they had so scandalously spent in debauchery and in orgies.

" 'At that pious exercise of penitence, in addition to the advantage of having, by the daily return of its practice, a way of measuring time, that otherwise the division would soon have been abolished for me, I had the benefit of a fortunate inspiration, to know that of asking the consolations of pray and to raise my soul toward God. I call myself a very good Christian and know that, into whatever abyss he one fallen, one must not cease hoping. In addition, another softening was to be brought to my sad situation.

" 'The day after the day my captivity began, I heard stomping around me, followed by blows from a hammer and filing, indicating that men were working in my vicinity. The touch of a body that they seemed to place beside me soon penetrated me with a soft warmth, and almost immediately after that, I heard the sound of wind rushing through, and a voice that it tormented as I myself had been tormented, beginning to sing a *B natural*, so that I had to believe that another unfortunate person had been sacrificed to the need to save the reputation of the *human voice* that the return of the two monks to Heaven had left vacant.

" 'It was perhaps a feeling that does little honor to human nature, but the thought of not being alone to suffer, caused me great joy and it seemed to me that my misfortune had been cut in half by the sharing that I foresaw. After that, my somewhat egotistical satisfaction was excusable, because it can't be denied that in the cruel position to which I was reduced, the happiness of having near me someone to whom I could communicate my thoughts and have hear my complaints, was an immense gift. I therefore hurried to get in touch with my companion in misfortune, who, after having sung at the harsh solicitation of the bellows and the clavier, still gave out long sighs and pitiable moans.

" ' — You are not alone here, I said with interest. Some-one beside you is also deprived of liberty. If you hear me, an-swer me.

' ' — Yes, I hear you, a woman replied in an infinitely sad voice, but I am ashamed to answer you, because you must detest me.

" ' — And why should I detest you? I replied in the kind-liest of tones possible for me. I don't know you.

" ' — Oh, yes, in fact, you do know me, said my sad companion, because it's because of me that you are here.

" ' — Great God! I then exclaimed. Would you be the lady that I wanted to deliver from the hands of the terrible Baron de Hostrub?

" ' — Alas! Yes, Monsieur, was the answer. And please believe that the thought of becoming the cause of what hap-pened to you is what, in my misfortune, makes me the most regret.

" ' — Why blame yourself for what is instead the result of the fatality of my star? It is only your infamous tutor that I must attack. But how did it happen that he also sacrificed you?

" ' — It is only that, Monsieur, that can make me forgive myself in my own eyes. I am sharing your fate because the Baron, thinking to cause me great displeasure, began yester-day to recount to me with satanic joy the treatment he had made you undergo. Then when I told him that he wouldn't carry his crime any further with impunity; the first time I was free, I would denounce him to the magistrates. Knowing that I was a woman to carry out my threat, and the artist needing a second victim that he didn't know where to find, my tutor gave me to him and I was put as well as you into the enchant-ed pipe.

" ' — You can see very well, Mademoiselle, I replied, that we have nothing to reproach ourselves for, since, if you were the cause of my misfortune, I, in my turn, have caused yours. But clarify a doubt for me. That Gregoire Kleng who, at first, had seemed such an honest man and who, I thought,

115

would not listen to the proposition of the Baron, did he at last let himself be tempted and sign a pact with the *mandragore*?

" ' — I have reason to believe so, answered the ward of the Baron de Hostrub, because when my tutor led me into the gallery, the usual theater of his magic operations, it seemed to me that the artist acted as the master of the odious little monster, who suddenly locked me in my bedroom at the time I was supposed to go down to you. Besides, she added, Gregoire Kleng was a maniac about his art, and when it's a question for an artist to save his reputation, it's easy to make him succumb to temptation.

" ' — You will perhaps find my curiosity very indiscreet, I then said, but I can't understand how a person as well-born as you are could have found herself in some relationship with a monster like the Baron?

" ' — My father, I was answered, without being involved with the spirits of darkness, was very curious to know supernatural secrets and he began to study astrology and to search for the *philosopher's stone*. Having been introduced to the infamous Hostrub, who passed himself off as an adept at those sciences, he became little by little linked with him in a very close friendship. At his death, he believed that he couldn't put the guardianship of my person and the administration of the considerable wealth he left to me in better hands. Thus my master, the Baron, behaved like most of the tutors of young and rich heiresses. He fell in love with his pupil and wanted to marry me. As I felt a natural repulsion for him, and as I refused to give him my hand, he took me to Hungary, where I was born, and where my properties are located. Establishing himself in that city where the magistrates are easy to do business with, he kept me prisoner in the house that you know, trying to break my will, sometimes by his gallantry and kindness, sometimes by using his sorcery and the harshest treatment. My patience was at an end when you, under my window, having heard me sing...

The amiable speaker couldn't say any more, her speech having been suddenly cut off by a mass of air thrown across our conversation that penetrated us right down to the marrow of our bones and forced us to give out all the *B flats* and the *B naturals* the organist demanded of us as he was seated at his clavier to play the Divine Office.[60]

" 'Our task finished, another kind of torture almost as terrible as the first one, was revealed to us. After the organist had ceased making the *human voice* pipes, of which we were an integral part, speak, and when the register [61]passing under the pipes had sheltered us from the attack of the bellows, we found we had the rebound of the tempest that it raised in the other parts of the organ. Then it seemed that the church was shaken right down to its foundations by the thunder of the thirty-two feet and the stop pedal. Deafened by the heart-rending cries of the *trumpets* and the *crumhorns*, by the muffled roll of the *bourdons*, by the blaring of the *nazard,* by the loud sound of the *cornets* and the *clairons,* and the sharp notes of the *doublets,* of the *fourniture* and of the *larigot,* we would have thought ourselves in the middle of the sea on a vessel furiously beaten by the waves and the winds. We experienced a little release from the terrible emotion thrown into all our nervous system by the riot of the unchained instruments, at a moment when the mellow sound of flutes, married to the melancholy accents of the oboes, gave us something like the memory of the naïve joys of country life; but thinking then of the beautiful blue sky, of the brilliant sun, the green of the prairies, and the shady tops of the tall woods that we must never again contemplate, we began to cry bitterly.

" 'Near that terrible din that was renewed every Sunday and Feast Days, and the daily prayers that we were forced to make, our life,' continued Monsieur de Rebundus, 'flowed by rather peacefully. During the long years that we spent in cap-

---

[60] Liturgy of the Hours (*opus dei),* canonical hours *(Breviary),* set of prayers marking the hours of each day, sanctifying the day with prayers.

[61] Rabou here uses the names of various organ stops: *bourdons, nazard, doublette, fourniture, larigot*, etc.

tivity, we were not as absolutely unhappy as it might be supposed. Without speaking of the force of habit that always somewhat dulls the most poignant sadness, a strong attachment for one another that we had developed as a result of the sweet familiarity of our eternal *tête-à-tête* contributed a great deal to give us less to complain about, and if we were suffering in the present, a great confidence in God, the hope of freedom, that never abandoned us, and that of being one day more completely united, sweetened the bitterness of that chalice, from which we found consolation in drinking from the same cup. There is something it will be difficult to believe: my amiable companion, in the middle of such a sad situation, still had kept a great depth of gaiety that was natural to her. When she found me discouraged and near despair, she would say to me:

" ' — My dear B Natural, you don't like me very much if you want to increase my suffering even more by the thought that you cannot endure yours.

" 'Naturally, I always answered that my heart was completely hers, but that continuation of our sad situation, for which the end couldn't be foreseen, was finally triumphing over my constancy and my resignation.

" ' — Come now, come now, she answered me, have more courage and faith in the future! Perhaps, without our knowing it, we are nearing the moment of our deliverance. And to cheer you up, I'm going to tell you one of my beautiful stories that, in your opinion, I tell so well.

" 'And, in fact, with a richness of imagination which sometimes made me compare her to the Sultaness Scheherazade of the *Thousand and One Nights,* she improvised for me marvelous stories filling weeks, months, and right up to entire years, without their interest being diminished for a moment. And so the time flowed by.

" 'But I hadn't yet reached the depth of my misery; a last test, the cruelest of all, remained for me to endure. One day, under the spell of one of those charming stories, I was waiting for the denouement with childish impatience, when there was an unusual noise in the cell of the story-teller. She suddenly stopped talking, and several moments later, I felt the evaporation of that soft warmth revealing the presence of a living and animated being on the side where my pipe was next to hers. The natural supposition that came to mind was that the enchantment of my companion in misfortune had ended and that she had re-entered life. Certainly that separation was sad; however, as it was combined with the legitimate hope that, set free, she that I had just lost would be occupied with my deliverance. I endured that blow with some patience, expecting every day, in one way or another, to hear from her, explaining the rather long delay her devotion made me endure, by the great difficulties opposing her from the supernatural powers, under which I was still placed.

" 'But when I knew that more than three months had gone by without any attempt by her to get in touch with me, all illusion began to abandon me. Then I blamed my careless friend with having behaved like so many other women who don't know what it is to have a memory, and that she, as soon as she was free, had completely forgotten me. Then to my misfortune were added horrible tortures of the heart, and I can say, in that last period of my captivity, I had the feeling of despair like that, in the bosom of their eternal pain, those condemned by the justice of God must experience.

" 'Nevertheless, the hour of my deliverance arrived and during the night of the 29th to the 30th of August of the year in which you saw me reappear in my native land, my dear listeners, exactly thirteen years from the day and moment I was fatally tied to the Halberstadt organ, I found myself lifted by an unknown force that delivered me from my envelope of metal. And without understanding the way in which the journey took place, I found myself transported to Magdeburg, into one of the bedrooms of my father's house where, with the exception of the old concierge who had remained its guardian, I had the sadness to no longer find anyone of those I had left.

" 'Now, is it necessary to explain to you any of my unusual behavior? My very changed health and a long established habit of solitude which made me for some time unable to endure the contact of others, at first confined me to the retreat where I spent the first part of my return to life. When I felt myself strong enough to fulfill some of the duties of society, was it astonishing that the least circumstances that could remind me of sadness of my captivity caused me extreme nervous irritation? And could I hear the tone B flat, or hear the sound of a canary, which is actually only a small organ, and think only of a bellows, the agent of the cruelest and the longest of my suffering, without undergoing the most painful emotion?

" 'And if those bizarre characteristics which I could be asked to explain, are in this way justified, perhaps it would be more difficult to explain the ease with which I entered into all the marriage propositions made to me. After all, I could be told: « You gave yourself heart and soul to a woman filled with perfections, and although appearances were against her, before believing yourself completely free of your engagement, you should have been certain of her infidelity and her abandon. Now the circumstance that brings us together here is witness enough that you didn't acquire it, since you have today become her husband and by that event in possession of the most perfect happiness. »

" 'That objection is certainly well worth the trouble to take into account and if the patience of those listening to me is not at an end, I propose to satisfy them in a few words.'

"Monsieur de Rebundus' guests having protested that they listened to his story with as much interest as astonishment, and having asked him to continue, here's the way he finished his speech:

" 'Once I had been set free, although I thought I had a great deal to complain about the woman whose lack of memory I deplored, I still gathered all the information about her that I could. At first I researched in Halberstadt the numerous facts that I naturally expected to find there. Not feeling that I had the courage to return to that fatal city, I had some information cleverly gathered there. Here is what was revealed to me:

" 'At the time I reported the deliverance of my companion in misfortune, Gregoire Kleng was dead, and although
there was some bad gossip about him, dating from the moment
that he came to repair the damage done to the Notre-Dame
organ, he died in a very Christian manner, after having received absolution from his confessor, and was generally
mourned, given the beauty of his genius. What's more, Baron
de Hostrub, since my disappearance, had continued to live in
Halberstadt as a good gentleman and to his reputation of caba-
list was substituted that of a man very learned in the natural
sciences, which finally brought him great fame. But the very
day of my recovering liberty, a great noise was heard in his
house. He had not appeared since that moment. And it was
noticed with astonishment that, during the night he disappeared, all the trees and all the plants in his garden had died
and had been burned right down to the roots, as if struck with
fire from Heaven. Putting together the various circumstances,
here are the conclusions I drew:

" 'At the moment I had been condemned to become *B
flat*, the bargain between the *mandragore* and the Baron still
had an hour or two to run. It was, in fact, due to that wicked
man that I had been enchanted.

" 'Seeing that the first pipe which he needed had been
given to him, Gregoire Kleng had signed the pact with the
mandragore. When, the next day, the Baron offered him his
ward, whom he was afraid would denounce him, to be a *B
Natural*, it was by the command of his new master that the
wicked little spirit of the earth had her imprisoned in the metal.

" 'Gregoire Kleng having died before the expiration of
the thirteen years, the charm governing his account was immediately broken. That explains why the Baron's pupil had
recovered her liberty before me. But the organ-maker, dying in
a state of grace, was subtly taken from the *mandragore*'s
hands. Seeing himself thus frustrated for payment of his services, he turned to the Baron as having furnished him a bad
slave, and when thirteen years had gone by, at the end of the

contract for which he alone was responsible, the sorcerer was carried away, I don't know where, the final denouement that had been the cause of my freedom.

" 'Nevertheless, none of all that told me what had become of the woman who, despite my projects of marriage, and all my effort to forget her, I never stopped for a moment adoring. My ruined health and ego, not to seem to be running after her, didn't permit me to go immediately to Hungary. I had a very exhaustive search made by letters. I was answered that the person about whom I wanted information had in fact considerable property in that country, but that her tutor, with whom she had left one fine day, more than ten years before, had sent back news of her death and, dating from that period, she had not been heard from in any way.

" 'That vague response that I myself knew was badly informed, not being of a nature to satisfy me, I finally decided to leave to go to the city of Pesth, knowing more and more each day that I couldn't hope for any happiness in this life if, faithful or unfaithful, I didn't find my lover. Judge then my emotion when, one evening at a ball, I found myself face to face with her, and when with her sweet voice that made me faint she asked me how it was possible *that B flat didn't recognize B natural.* Nothing, however, was easier to explain, because, if the unusual circumstances of our meeting are recalled, it will be remembered that I had never seen her face, and it was not one of the least bizarre things of our star to have loved each other passionately, and to have spent nearly thirteen years side by side, never leaving each other for a minute, without, however, ever having seen each other.

" 'After the first emotional moment, followed by our recognizing each other, I asked for an explanation, and it was given to me as satisfactorily as I could wish. Like me, transported by an unknown force to the place where she was born, which was without a doubt a law of the liberating force, Alberta—for such is her name—found that her relatives had taken possession of all her wealth. In order not to have to make restitution, as she had had the lack of forethought to recount what had happened to her, they had taken the position that she was mad and had her shut away in a sanatorium, so that, while I was accusing her of forgetting me, the unfortunate woman was enduring a second captivity. Being less cruel than the first one, it was nonetheless a very cruel and very unusual perseverance of an inexorable destiny. However, not having lost courage, she was able, by means of some friends who took an interest in her fate, to prove the injustice of her detention, and took advantage of the first moments of her release to file a lawsuit against her persecutors to restore the fortune which they had taken from her. It's known the time and care lawsuits require; it was only after several months that a judgment was rendered. It declared the plaintiff discharged of all suspicion of mental alienation, put her back in possession of her great wealth, that she made it her happiness to bring me as dowry.'

" 'But then,' said the lady who had once before had interrupted Monsieur de Rebundus, 'if during the time Madame was debating with the law, you had married, of which it was a question more than one time, what regrets for both of you!'

" 'Impossible,' replied the married woman. 'I knew that Monsieur de Rebundus was looking for me in spite of the care my good relatives had at first taken to have me passed off as a lunatic. And keeping myself abreast of all his inquiries, if I had seen some serious danger of an engagement that he was on the point of taking, I would have immediately written to him and asked him to wait for me. And I certainly believe,' she added shrewdly 'that he would in fact have waited for me.'

" 'If I would have waited for you!' exclaimed Monsieur de Rebundus. 'For years! For centuries! From the moment I was sure of your heart, but it was still very cruel of you to have left me in such great ignorance of your destiny.'

" 'My idea was to come and surprise you,' replied the new Madame de Rebundus. 'Are you now angry that all happiness has come to you at once?'

" 'In fact, my dear listeners,' said Monsieur de Rebundus, rising from the table, finishing his story, 'my happiness is today so great that I can scarcely believe it. But I beg you, if I have been under an illusion, in a dream, don't make any noise around me, for fear of waking me.'

"The suggestion was scarcely followed, because as soon as the guests had left the banquet room to step into the drawing rooms, while still conversing about the prodigious circumstances of that story, joyous music began to sound and announced the opening of a magnificent ball, to which every important person in the city of Magdeburg had been invited. Everyone was of the opinion that it was impossible to be more gracious and to do the honors of a festivity better than Madame de Rebundus.

"From that moment, her house became the meeting place for all celebrations. At the same time, all the unfortunate were generously cared for.

"Several days after his marriage Monsieur de Rebundus was present with his wife, in the Saint-Maurice Church. Not only did he not seem disagreeably moved by the sound of the organ, but the one executing it, being a very talented player, he seemed to take great pleasure in hearing it. Naturally he was asked to account for the way in which he had come to dominate the invincible aversion that he must have kept for an instrument by means of which he had suffered so much.

" 'The organ did me much harm,' answered Monsieur de Rebundus, 'but I owe having become the husband of my wife to it; the happiness that it brought me has absolved all the past. Peace has been made between us; I am no longer angry with it.' "

Now, let's pay justice to the fantastic imagination of Hans Krafft; his stories, if they were long, were not boring. And despite the impatience certainly permitted to Matiphous in that situation, the sacrifice of listening to the story of Monsieur de Rebundus right to the end hadn't been as painful to him as might have been thought. Nevertheless, as soon as Hans Krafft had stopped talking, he called him back to the question and asked him not to forget the subject about which he had come.

"Ah! Very good, my dear fellow," the engraver said. "You are a candidate for my daughter's hand. Then I will ask you the usual questions. Your profession, please?"

"Veterinary at the stables of the Grand Duchess!"

"An honorable position, and one which promises that, if we happen to break our legs, they will be set without its costing us anything...Your family?"

"That's what I would call negative. Never having known my parents, I owe only myself for the little that I am."

"Then we are sure," Hans Kraft said gaily, "of never having a lawsuit with that parentage. What dowry do you think I should give my daughter?"

"None, I don't think I need one."

"Good! And you will see that things continue that way?"

"Dowries are made for sons-in-law, and when the sons-in-law don't claim them?"

"They are fools or insolent!" said the engraver, getting excited. "Because you see, my little man, that I understand very well what you think. Hans Krafft, you tell yourself, is a lazy man who, instead of working to establish his daughter, spends his life chasing little birds. But understand, little Monsieur, that if he sets to work, Hans Krafft, in fewer than two weeks, will be able to give his daughter a dowry. Until then, you will, if you please, be patient. In the meantime, we will get to know each other better, and if the business comes to an end, at least no one will be humiliated."

It was useless for Matiphous to protest against that fit of paternal ego that he found greatly uncalled for. The engraver was intractable in his claim not to be outdone in generosity. And at the moment, the favorable solution that could be seen had to remain suspended until the time when Hans Krafft had finished the work that he promised to pursue with great activity. Obviously, it was a question of that bank note plate that Fauntleroy was waiting for with so much impatience, on which, until then, the careless artist hadn't worked on except in a desultory way.

VII. He who has drunk will drink.[62]

We are going to return to Britannicus, that Negro that Matiphous took charge of after the Prince Bevillacqua catastrophe. His new master had too much praise for his services not to have had him follow him to Florence when he was sent there. Good at everything and joining to the most diverse aptitudes energy without parallel, the only thing that boy found to change in his situation was that he didn't have enough to do. Working for Prince Bevillacqua, we have seen him combining the functions of *valet de chambre*, those of usher of the wheel of Fortune in the lottery office, and those of master of ceremonies and of upholsterer -decorator of the *Grand Firmament*. Passed into Matiphous' service, by imitating the surgery that he saw him perform, he had also picked up medicine and had become a dentist-pedicurist, two professions, notwithstanding the distance of one pole from the other, frequently came together in the same hand.

In Florence, while continuing his services devoted to human suffering, under the pretext that the sojourn in Paris had taught him beautiful manners, he also had the triumphant idea of making himself a master of dancing and a teacher of deportment! In addition, he undertook to give violin lessons and fencing lessons. Passing himself off as a ladies' man, in his Creole jargon he had composed and had printed a little treatise on *The Art of Seducing Ladies.* Summing up, his claim was to continue on the path of the famous Chevalier de Saint-George,[63] a tropical example whose memory he had constantly

---

[62] "A leopard can't change his spots."

[63] Joseph Bologne, Chevalier de Saint-Georges (1745-1799) was a champion fencer, virtuoso violinist, and conductor of the leading symphony orchestra in Paris. Born in Guadeloupe, he was the son of George Bologne de Saint-Georges, a wealthy planter, and Nanon, his African slave. During the French Revolution, Saint-Georges was colonel of the Légion St.-Georges, the first all-black regiment in Europe, fighting on

in his mouth, and whose name he never pronounced without taking off his hat in respect. His somewhat burlesque originality wasn't slow in giving him rather great popularity. His master didn't always see without impatience the large crowd of people of all kinds which the encyclopedic knowledge of that sort of dark Figaro [64] attracted to his door.

Among the visitors, Matiphous had noticed a man having one of those faces that, once encountered, remain forever engraved on the memory. A large face, black, flat hair, an olive complexion, eyes slanted and narrowed like a Chinese, a crushed nose and excessively high cheek bones, everything about that man showed him to be a most outstanding example of the Tartar race. Usually he wore a red tie, an ample blue redingote buttoned right up to the neck, riding boots and carried a riding crop. Each time he came to see Britannicus, he had infinitely long conversations with him.

Matiphous was finally curious to know what that entire parley was about and he asked Britannicus who was the inopportune man with the sinister expression with whom he was so often obsessed.

"Master doesn't know Tamerlane?" replied Britannicus, as if that name said everything.

The name just seemed unusual to Matiphous, and on his request to be a little more clearly informed, the black man

---

the side of the Republic. Today, Saint-Georges is best remembered as the first classical composer of African ancestry.

[64]Character invented by playwright Pierre-Augustin Caron de Beaumarchais (1732-1799) who appears in *The Barber of Seville* (1775), *The Marriage of Figaro* (1778) and *The Guilty Mother* (1792). Figaro is a Spaniard from Seville, lively, sentimental, enthusiastic, insolent, popular and sympathetic, sometimes pathetic and dramatic. He is usually the witness and the catalyst of the story, the lover, the matchmaker, the talker, the twirling servant, but also the clumsy fool, the provocative fellow, and finally the resigned valet.

explained that Tamerlane was a kind of Franconi,[65] the first subject of an equestrian troop whose acts were then very sought after. To that he added that the amiable expression of the horseman seemed to have installed him in the fancy of a great lady and that, not knowing how to give a conclusion to those kindly dispositions, he had come to consult with him, Britannicus, concerning the way to succeed in the tender interest of which he thought himself the object.

Finding very amusing the naïveté of that suitor who took his black servant so seriously and turned over to him the handling of his love affairs, Matiphous wanted to know the name of that inflammable lady with whom it was a matter of coming to terms. But Britannicus was discreet and respectfully defended the secret that his master wanted to penetrate. That resistance could only sharpen Matiphous' curiosity. As a consequence, that same evening, he thought of going to the Maria-Novella Theater where the equestrian troop was performing. He promised himself, by following the direction of the horseman's glances to discover the hardly scrupulous beauty who was thinking of honoring him with her favors. It also has to be said, in addition, that he wasn't without a certain presentiment that he had guessed the secret that was haggled over.

When he entered the locale of the spectacle, the first face that Matiphous saw was that of his intimate enemy, Lady Stuart, in a box very much in view. She was accompanied by the old Laird, her husband. That encounter had just confirmed the vague suspicion that Matiphous had had at first when remembering the incredible enthusiasm of Kitty Ketch for the boxer Broughton. However, that view was almost immediately con-

---

[65] Antonio Franconi (1738-1836), famous Italian equestrian who started as a juggler and wandering physician, then arranged bullfights in Lyon and Bordeaux. In 1783, he associated with the English horse rider Philip Astley who had opened a riding school in Paris and founded an equestrian theater named Cirque Olympique, which acquired an impressive reputation.

tradicted, because, shortly afterwards, a magnificent bouquet in his hands, Fauntleroy entered the box. At that, Matiphous learned of his return to Florence, and he could see the very enthusiastic and friendly way in which the gallantry of the newcomer was received. There was scarcely any way to misunderstand the scene. Following up on the tender projects that he had formerly outlined in Rome, Broughton's associate was working at becoming his successor, and his intention didn't seem in such a bad way to being realized.

But suddenly there was a great blare of trumpets; three salvos of applause rang out, and in the artist whose entry was accorded so much favor, Matiphous recognized Britannicus' client, *The Great, The Stupendous, The Marvelous,* as the Italians say in their hyperbolic language, *Signor Tamerlane!*

Right up to the moment that Tamerlane had appeared in the spotlight, Lady Stuart, who was not bothered in any way by the presence of her old husband, dozing in a husbandly way at the back of the box, seemed to be all ears, listening to the evidently very animated speech Fauntleroy was addressing to her; but as soon as the horseman's act began, the beautiful spectator's absorption became so complete that Matiphous could believe himself at that famous combat of boxers where he had met the deceitful Kitty for the first time. There was the same breathless attention paid to Signor Tamerlane, the same frenetic applause, the same symptoms, in a word, of the most passionate admiration.

So there was no more doubt for the man from Malta. When the horseman had finished his *tours de force*, at the moment he made his farewell salute, he turned toward Kitty's box, and his hand placed over his heart, seeming to thank the public for its applause, he addressed to the beautiful lady an unequivocal declaration of his feelings. The response wasn't slow in being returned. Kitty Ketch was holding in her hands the flowers that Fauntleroy had just offered her. Without paying any attention to the presence of the donor, she threw the bouquet to her protégé, an act which a great number of the female spectators imitated, so many that around the equestrian

129

artist mounted a kind of perfumed litter that two boys from the theater had difficulty removing. The switch from Broughton the boxer to Tamerlane the equestrian, as Matiphous had already suspected, was so logical that, truly, with the certainty that he had just obtained, it didn't cause him any great emotion. While flirting with Fauntleroy, whom she needed to manipulate, Kitty had a kind of peculiar fascination for skill and a strong physique. It seemed that, by the peculiarity of the choice, where she had returned despite the chance social elevation, she had in store a vengeance for her former suitor rather than mere humiliation.

But Matiphous didn't arrive at this discovery by logic. Feeling the former wound to his ego opened, he said to himself:

"It is then written: that woman will be accessible to everything and everyone, and that only I, having sacrificed my honor for her, would never have been considered."

His engagement to the engraver's daughter was an obstacle to his setting up competition between the two men who, in different degrees, had, for the moment, a part of his former fiancée's favor. But at least, he wanted to have the pleasure of troubling the security of those despicable amours. Remembering the page torn from the Gretna Green marriage register that, until then, had remained in his hands without being used, he rushed to his apartment and placed that compromising piece of evidence in his wallet. Afterward, he went to the foreigner's casino, where he was almost sure of encountering Fauntleroy after the performance. Finding him there, in fact, he went straight to him and, without any other preamble, said:

"Ah, what kind of a man are you? You are told about a serious business which cannot be delayed, and that's the exact moment that you choose to go away and disappear for a month!"

Caught unprepared, Fauntleroy excused himself by talking about some pressing business that had suddenly required his presence in Holland.

"In Holland? I would rather have thought that it was in Scotland that you went."

"Why in Scotland?" said Fauntleroy, pretending to be astonished.

"Because I myself was there and I would swear that I saw you there."

"Don't tell me that. After I returned, I asked about you, and you had not left Florence."

"Since you put it that way, I will be more precise and go so far as to tell you the company you were with when I saw you."

"Really, that would be clever!"

"But of course," said Matiphous, cleverly using the information that he had extracted from Mistress Aston's letter. "I wasn't too ill advised to have found myself at one of the windows of a little hotel that has a view of the Arbroath harbor, precisely at the time when, returning from Bell Rock, you got back to land, accompanied by that ex-boxer, Broughton."

At Broughton's name, a wave of redness spread over his associate's face. Although caught in his lie, Fauntleroy believed he should still retrench himself in a vague denial.

"Do I need to give more precise details?" Matiphous continued. "You were met at the dock by the respectable Mistress Aston. Let it be said in passing that you weren't delighted to see her."

"But if that were true," Fauntleroy asked, trying to retake the offensive, "you yourself—why did you go to Scotland?"

"Me? I'm not hiding it. Your hesitation to accept my offer, and soon afterward, your sudden departure, made me fear an underhanded trick. Without losing a moment, I got on your trail. Only, as I went directly to the lighthouse and didn't have to make a detour to London to pick up the respectable Mr. Broughton. Everything was finished, and the precious briefcase secure, two days before you stuck your nose into Bell Rock."

"One thing in all that is true," Fauntleroy replied bitterly. "It is that you had carried out, by some of your men, the removal that you pretended to want us to take care of together. As for my trip and yours, those are two fables that you want to put forth to excuse a hardly honorable action that, on your part, doesn't surprise me very much."

"Terribly incredulous as you are," Matiphous answered, seizing that opening to get to the real object of the meeting, "do you need a written proof of my presence in Scotland? Here, look at this!"

On saying that, he drew from his wallet the marriage certificate of Miss Ketch and Broughton. The man from Malta had correctly judged that he would find a most eager accomplice in the one he wanted to use to let Kitty know of the existence of the paper that had fallen into his hands, because, cutting short the question of the trip to Scotland, Fauntleroy quickly asked:

"This paper—what are you thinking of doing with it? Why did you appropriate it? Do you want to break the sworn peace?"

"Me? Not at all," Matiphous replied. "My thought, on the contrary, is to use that lucky find to put my rapport with Lady Stuart on a totally different footing. Broughton was the obstacle between her and me. Now that she is finished with him, I count very much on reviving our former engagements. And don't you think that in returning this paper to her, which must be important to her, I recommend myself rather strongly to her interest?"

"I'm not saying that Lady Stuart should remain insensible to a generous act, but to the object that has disappeared, one infinitely more respectable has been substituted. And that is what you seem to forget."

"Who? That old husband?" Matiphous said disdainfully. "It certainly isn't to him that a woman, who, after all, must know me, would want to sacrifice all the future and all the tranquility of her life."

"You do, Monsieur, what you please," Fauntleroy said drily, "but in my opinion, indifference and forgetfulness between Lady Stuart and you is the most prudent procedure."

That said, he started to break off an interview, where every word, to tell the truth, had been like a thorn to him. Matiphous let him leave, but, as if he had thought of something, he said, running after him:

"At least, keep my secret. Knowing that in my hands this paper would be a mortal worry for Lady Stuart, and until the time when I will be able to be in a position to return it to her, I totally count on your discretion."

After having said his piece, he believed he could release the puppet whose strings he had manipulated for a quarter of an hour, sure that the next day, at the latest, the alarm would have been given to Kitty.

Some days passed, and having arranged the pleasure of throwing terror into the enemy camp, Matiphous was no longer concerned with knowing the results of his malicious revelation. His thought of vengeance had been only a momentary triumph, and he soon gave himself entirely to taking care of his forthcoming marriage. He no longer worried about anything, except the way in which Hans Krafft would keep his word and hastened to complete the work on which his daughter's dowry was the mortgage.

The conduct of the engraver was exemplary. He hadn't had the smallest fall back into his bad habits and remained constantly employed in his workshop, so well that one evening Matiphous' fiancée could tell him that her father was on the point of finishing the plate that he had to deliver the next day.

The day that followed that pleasant news, the man from Malta was at his future father-in-law's house at an early hour. But in the coldness and the lack of attention in the greeting of his would-be fiancée, he could fear that some new and unexpected complication had come up.

"My father is here," the young girl said. "He needs to talk to you."

And immediately taking Matiphous into the workshop, she seemed to intend to remain there as a third party during that interview, which seemed to mean that it had to have a certain solemnity.

"Ah! Ah! It's you, Monsieur my son-in-law," said the engraver, without looking up from what he was working on, which consisted of preparing the birdlime for the hunt with owls.

"That's a good sign," said Matiphous, who had not noticed any disquieting nuance in the tone of that comment.

At the same time, he glanced at his fiancée, but he encountered only a cold scrutiny and no affectionate expression tempered the severity.

"Yes," the engraver answered, "my work is delivered and the dowry is ready; now, take a seat and let's talk."

Before sitting down, the man from Malta wanted to bring forward a chair for Christiana. She motioned him that she preferred to remain standing, and, at the same time, with a commanding gesture, she seemed to tell him to pay attention. Matiphous wasn't left long in doubt about what was going to follow, because Hans Krafft continued:

"Dear Monsieur, you didn't tell us that you had made a sojourn in England, mostly in London."

In itself, that attack could have extreme gravity, but the ironic tone in which it had been said, added to the very unusual reception by his fiancée, gave Matiphous still more to think about. He responded:

"Monsieur, before going any further, just one question: the work that you had really wanted to work on with such laudable activity in view of providing a dowry for Mademoiselle, your daughter, wouldn't it be an Englishman named Fauntleroy who asked you for it?"

"English, Russian, or Italian, what does it matter?" replied the engraver.

"Really a lot, I think. You seem to be interested in where I have lived in England. I myself would like to know if you are acquainted with some Englishmen."

"Apparently to see," Hans Krafft answered rather sharply, "if you should continue your claims, which could be verified?"

"There is not a single question," Matiphous replied with dignity, "however little it may seem useful to ask me, which I am not able to answer; but still it is good to know the people by whom you have been informed."

"Truth is all the same, Monsieur," replied the engraver sententiously, "and a mouth through which it passes can't make it other than what it is."

"Pardon me, it can be said and at the same time distorted, but condemning me in advance with the worst reports which could have been made about me, I insist on knowing if the Englishman Fauntleroy is, or is not, one of your acquaintances."

"Well! No," answered the engraver, "I don't know what you mean about your Englishman Fauntleroy!"

"Very well," replied Matiphous, the engraver's lie having made him more than ever defiant. "Speak; I'm listening."

"I was saying that you didn't tell us about your very long stay in London. The fact omitted, perhaps, without indiscretion, I ask you what profession you had there."

"I was a surgeon, as I am in Florence."

"And you have never had any other profession?"

Matiphous glanced at his fiancée. The kind of feverous anxiety that he discovered on her face while she awaited his response left him no doubt that the indiscretions had already been presented.

"Oh, yes I did," he then answered firmly. "I was for a short time the assistant to the hangman."

"You see!" said Hans Krafft, addressing his daughter, who, without saying anything motioned him to continue.

"And," continued the engraver, "while you were practicing that pleasant profession, you didn't have any disagreeable adventure?"

"On the contrary," answered Matiphous, very sure that complete frankness couldn't make his position any worse. "In London, like a criminal I was branded with a hot iron."

"Wicked man!" shouted Hans Krafft. "How dare you ask for my daughter's hand!"

"Because everything that you have insisted on making me admit is only relatively true."

"But, Monsieur, are you denying or are you admitting?" Christiana asked sharply, leaving her role as an observer, into which, until that moment, she had entrenched herself.

"I am admitting, Mademoiselle, but at the same time I am explaining. I agreed to be the assistant of the hangman for one day, but in devotion to science and in view of performing an experiment by means of which I was rather fortunate to save the life of a condemned man. Branded, I also had the misfortune to be, but not by condemnation of justice. A man made me submit to that atrocious vengeance, precisely because his long series of crimes had been revealed by me."

"It doesn't make any difference, Monsieur," answered the engraver, "your explanations don't leave you without reproach. You don't come into an honest family with such a background, and you will stay a bachelor."

"For several years," Matiphous replied, "that thought of eternal celibacy had also been mine. Since then, I have had other ideas, and the motives for this change I will tell you alone, if you will allow me to."

"It's me, most of all, Monsieur," Christiana then said, "that your information concerns; to justify yourself to my father would be insufficient."

"That's evident," the engraver replied rashly, mindlessly. "Speak, Monsieur, we are listening to you."

"Well, since you force me to, I will tell you, Monsieur, that notwithstanding the sad recollection of my past, if I came to knock on your door, it was because there I had discovered a compromised name. I thought I could associate mine with it."

"Here! A blackened name!" shouted the engraver, and he rose emotionally.

"Father, be calm," said Christiana, throwing herself in front of him.

"One word, Monsieur," Matiphous said tranquilly, "and you will understand me. Do you here deny that some type of relationship exists between you and that Englishman, whose name I told you, and that you know very well, despite all your denials?"

"Do I have to answer to you?" responded Hans Krafft, with visible embarrassment.

"But, father," asked Christiana, "that gentleman that Monsieur has mentioned with so much insistence, do you in fact know him?"

"Known or unknown to me, what difference does it make?"

"A great deal," replied Matiphous, "because if that man, whom you know, does illegal work, for which I have reason to believe you are an accomplice, I will be the one who will break off thinking of allying myself with you."

"Leave here, you miserable man!" shouted the engraver. "Everything is over between us."

"Calm yourself, Monsieur," said Matiphous, rising, "because I have done nothing here but defend myself, and whatever happens, the secret which concerns us won't be spread around. Everything then rests in the hands of Mademoiselle. Now maybe she will understand that a stain fallen on a name, if it is always a misfortune, may sometimes not be a crime. And in case she still deigns to accept my continuing to see her, you couldn't seriously, Monsieur Krafft, want to reverse that kindness. After having been the real link between her and me, it would be very bad grace of you to want to disunite what you have brought together."

That said, he bowed and left.

VIII. Venezzia

La Bottegone is a café situated in the Duomo Square,[66] frequented by the high society of Florence and somewhat re-

---

[66] Square in front of the Duomo Cathedral in Florence.

sembles our own Café Tortoni.[67] After leaving the engraver's workshop, Matiphous hurried to go to that Square. Fauntleroy usually had lunch there and he was counting on him for an explanation. He had separated from his fiancée the evening before on the best of terms, and the next day, going to deliver his work, precisely following a conversation that Hans Krafft must have had with Broughton's associate, he had been greeted in the way just seen. How could it be doubted that Fauntleroy was the author of the indiscretions that had caused such a regrettable change?

At the moment Matiphous entered the café, and before he could locate the man he was looking for, he was accosted by a man he knew, a kind of short story writer by profession, for whom everything was an event.

"Have you heard the gossip going around?" that man asked him mysteriously. "This morning, before dawn, Lady Stuart left Florence."

"No, I don't know anything about that," replied the man from Malta. "And why that brusque departure?"

"An adventure at the masked ball, and something rather scandalous, it seems."

"I haven't heard anything about it," Matiphous then said, cutting short a conservation that, some other time, might have piqued his curiosity.

That said, he went to sit at a table adjacent to that occupied by Fauntleroy.

"If I remember correctly, Monsieur," he said to him in a low voice, "we had agreed on a kind of truce between us. We were both supposed to guard the secrets from our past."

"No doubt," replied Fauntleroy. "And in that peace treaty a third person was included, who, still more than us, as a woman, had a right to expect its frank and loyal execution."

---

[67] Parisian cafe that was very successful in the 19th century. Its successive owners, of Italian origins, were ice-cream makers and turned it into a luxury establishment open to all.

"This peace treaty, are you accusing me of having broken it?"

"Me, no. But this lack of faith that I don't personally reproach you with, you have, it appears, been guilty of it vis-à-vis Lady Stuart. This morning, as she was getting into the carriage to leave Florence, she slipped a note to me in which she accused you of having organized an infamous trap for her."

"A trap!" Matiphous quickly interrupted. "And of what kind? Since our encounter at the Foreigners' Casino, I haven't even thought about Lady Stuart's existence. I only knew of her departure two minutes ago, and I haven't yet made use of that compromising paper that I spoke to you about."

"Tell someone else that, my dear fellow. The injury you have done to a woman of whom I have the honor of being the friend, I can't tell you in detail, but Lady Stuart is counting on me for her revenge, and that revenge she will have."

"You mean that *she has had*," retorted Matiphous, strongly emphasizing the change of tense.

"Oh! It's just the beginning of her vengeance!" said Fauntleroy.

"Monsieur," the man from Malta continued, strongly emphasizing his words, "I have just left the shop of Hans Krafft, the engraver, a man you know?"

"No doubt, and a man, if my information is correct, whose daughter you propose to marry?"

"Perhaps, but before aspiring to that good fortune, I have a harsh duty to perform, that is to shut the mouth of a man who prides himself on knowing my background."

"And how, if you please, do you propose to put a padlock on people's mouths?"

"I will say to that man that he is a cowardly slanderer and that I am ready to prove it to him with weapons in my hand."

"So you say!" said Fauntleroy in an accent whose insolence it would be difficult to describe.

"I am saying that, in two hours, I will have the honor of expecting you at the Parco delle Cascine [68] where I will be with my pistols. I suggest that you have yours with you and to all appearances, one of us will not come back."

Fauntleroy shrugged and, pretending to pick up a newspaper, replied:

"Come now, does anyone fight with a man like you?"

"At some other time," Matiphous said, "I could be amused by your airs of ridiculous fatuity, but I repeat that I will have your life, or you will have mine, and that's my firm intention."

"I don't see too much interest in executing you," Fauntleroy said in the same tone of disdain, and for letting you execute me, an order from a Court of Law, you understand, would first be necessary."

Fauntleroy had in front of him a cup of boiling coffee that had just been poured for him.

"Monsieur the counterfeiter," said the man from Malta, whispering to him, "do you prefer that, to avenge myself for your slanders, I denounce you and your worthy friend Broughton to the Bank of England?"

And at the same time, he threw in Fauntleroy's face the contents of the cup, which drenched the other man's suit and shirt. Hearing Fauntleroy's cry of rage, employees ran to intercede in the brawl which seemed imminent.

"This is nothing, Messieurs, this is nothing," said Matiphous in a tone of perfect serenity. "The gentleman was drinking his coffee. I was clumsy and pushed his shoulder. Now," he said, in a tone to be heard only by Fauntleroy, "I will be waiting for you where you know. Otherwise, tomorrow I will write to London."

Immediately leaving the café and thinking of the rendezvous that he hoped he had made inevitable, Matiphous didn't dwell very long on that denunciation of Lady Stuart that

---

[68] Note from the Author: park where the high society of Florence stroll, like the Bois de Boulogne in Paris.

seemed to provoked the indiscretions of his adversary and that nothing could even in any way explain to him. He went to see an Infantry Lieutenant, and asked him to please serve as his witness. Considering that role in all its consequences, the officer wanted first to know the reason for the quarrel in order to judge if the situation was really serious enough to require an urgent need to be settled by weapons. But Matiphous explained to him that the affair was of such a nature that it couldn't be confided, even to the one who helped the combatants. His only mission would be to witness that his opponent had been shot off out of duty.

After a little difficulty, the officer, seeing the man from Malta was decided, if need be, to do without his help, finally accepted the charge of second, in the terms proposed to him. The two hours set by Matiphous had hardly expired than, together, they arrived at the place set for the rendezvous.

If it was in Matiphous' destiny to never follow through with a marriage, as witnessed by the daughter of the Gozzo fisherman, then later by the daughter of Jack Ketch, and now the daughter of Hans Krafft, it equally seemed that a duel for him was a difficult desire to satisfy. After two hours spent waiting at the Parco delle Cascine, he had to return to the city without having seen his adversary appear. We may recall that, a little time before, he had met a similar disappointment at the Bois de Boulogne.

To find out what to make of Fauntleroy's behavior, Matiphous went to his domicile, and there he learned that, about two hours before, the Englishman had ordered post horses and left hurriedly. However, Fauntleroy wasn't a man to flee an encounter, and at another time, we have seen him bravely become the opponent of the Marquis de Samaniego. His sudden departure had, then, some other explanation than fear. And that explanation, at first foreseen by Matiphous, was soon confirmed. Having, in fact, returned to the engraver's workshop, a traveler had come in a post-chaise to pick up the father and the girl. Nothing was more obvious than that. Fearing his secret had been divulged, the counterfeiter must have understood their common danger. Therefore, with the engraver, his accomplice, and before anything could happen, they had arranged to leave Florence together, taking with them, willingly or by force, the sad Christiana.

The first thought of the man from Malta, thus separated from his fiancée, was to go after the fugitives, but what direction should his pursuit take? Nothing indicated the direction his enemies had taken, and he could only choose his path blindly. Besides, he was not at the end of the incidents and emotions which filled that day for him. As he approached his lodgings, he saw a large number of people assembled. When he had gone through that crowd, up to a stretcher carried by four black penitents, he recognized on the stretcher Britannicus lying motionless, giving no signs of life. As soon as Matiphous appeared, while they were occupied with transporting the Negro inside the house, one of the penitents broke away from his brothers. Pulling back his capuchin, he showed the man from Malta one of the most aristocratic faces in Florence, since, in that city, under the name *Brotherhood of Mercy*, there was an unusual institution about which we will be permitted to say a word in passing.

Founded about the middle of the thirteenth century, during the terrible plagues that ravaged Italy, that pious association, as a learned traveler explains, "*is one of the institutions particular to Catholicism, and that only it can organize or ordain. Its members, among whom are found the greatest lords, who can be only simple brothers and are excluded from a high positions in the brotherhood, devote themselves to caring for the wounded and transporting them to the hospital, where they continue to care for them. Sometimes, you see coming from the most brilliant circles one of the brothers alerted to some accident by the ringing of the Duomo bell. At that appeal to charity, he hurries to dress in his religious costume, a kind of black robe with a hood, a monastic costume that hides the inequality of ranks and to which a chaplet is suspended. That man of high society, born in the center of life's pleasures, seizes for himself one of the ends of the stretcher, walks slowly across the city streets, carrying his suffering brother, and he passes without regret from the palace to the hospital.*"

The distinguished person who, obedient to the vows of that association, has just put his hand on Britannicus' transportation, explained that, a half-hour earlier, the poor devil had been found in a side street, stretched out on the pavement, and having beside him a cudgel that apparently had been used to put him in the pitiful state he was in. Greater details could only be expected from the wounded man himself. But only all the care that his master could hasten to give him would bring him out of his state of unconsciousness. In his weakness, it was impossible to obtain the least word from him.

Taking up the trail immediately, the police soon managed to gather some information. They knew that Britannicus had been seen in the company of Tamerlane, and they seemed to be quarreling. Then, the same day, without meeting his appointment with the director of the equestrian troop, the horseman had disappeared. He was suspected of having committed that act of violence against Britannicus. They equally knew that, the evening before, during the masked ball given at the Pergola Theater, a woman in a domino mask had hurriedly left a box where she had spent a quarter of an hour in a *tête-à-tête* with an unknown man, also masked, and that, before leaving the room, she had been seized with a violent attack of nerves.

When taking off her mask to get some air, it was discovered that the unknown person was Lady Stuart, who, following the scandal, had left Florence in the morning. But that was all the information the police found. And since Britannicus had a violent fever, accompanied by delirium, and had not yet recovered the use of speech or of his faculties, information about that shady affair couldn't be constructively followed.

After that, work at the Secret Bureau, which had already told him so many things, enlightened Matiphous. And if on the side of Kitty and Britannicus, his long-time curiosity still couldn't be satisfied in the way most important to him, it suddenly shed sinister light for him. Taking seriously her title as

Ruler, the Grand Duchess required that all the administrators of the departments that formerly made up the three departments of the Grand Duchy of Tuscany correspond directly with her. But, on the other hand, the Director General of the police, stationed in Florence, reporting more immediately to the French police minister Fouché, had been ordered to secretly look into all the correspondence in which it was supposed there might be some important information, and send a copy of it to France.

Having that work in his functions, about eight days after the departure of his fiancée, Matiphous unsealed a voluminous report from the Prefect of the Mediterranean Department, whose seat was in Livorno. Soon the reader will understand the reason that we are going to reproduce all the contents of that administrative document:

Livorno, April 1st, 1808
Madame la Grande Duchesse,
The City of Livorno has, for a long time, reported to the different authorities to which the administrations of said city has been entrusted, the situation in a neighborhood called Venezzia *as being constantly a menace to public tranquility. Taking as its name "Little Venice" because of the many canals which crisscross it, that quarter, thanks to its configuration and its type of circulation, at the same that it offers convenience for the interior transport of merchandise, on the other hand, has the inconvenience of a complicated and difficult access. From that situation comes the fact that, from time immemorial, it has been the rendezvous and refuge of all those who could fear some dispute with the police. Packed into that narrow space, its swarm of beggars, vagabonds and ex-convicts would already give it the make-up of one of those unwholesome gatherings that were, in the past, called* Cour des Miracles,[69] *if, in addition to its aforementioned disorderly*

---

[69] One of the poorest and most notorious slums of 17th century Paris slums. The name came from the fact that those who had

elements, its proximity to the port didn't add the special dan-
ger of a entirely different population dealing in contraband
and deserters deposited by the various foreign navies that
come to do business in Livorno.

Made up of a choice, and I dare say, the very essence of
a cosmopolitan group of criminals skimmed from every sur-
face of the Earth, these wretched men, by their audacity and
their determination, have the upper hand in Venezzia and have
been, for a long time, the terror of the law-abiding and work-
ing segments of the population. They had reigned for a long
time in that quarter when, some days ago, with the arrival of a
stranger, about whom I will shortly give you more details,
things have reached the point where a decisive repression, to
be carried out on the largest scale, will seem to you, no doubt
as it is to me, Madame la Grande Duchesse, to have become a
necessity.

That stranger, who calls himself Salvador Arbib, on the
very day of his arrival, went to the Commissariat General of
the police and presented for inspection a passport given to
him at the beginning of 1806 by the police authority of Bom-
bay. On that passport, he is identified as an Armenian mer-
chant, and, in a review of the visas that were affixed in it, it
was found that, at different times and in different places, the
man had successively visited Lahore, Herat, Tehran, Mecca,
Jerusalem, Damascus, Smyrna, Constantinople, Belgravia,
Vienna, Milan, and, finally, Livorno, which, for the moment,
marked the end of that immense peregrination.

That man's frail exterior made it difficult to understand
how he could have endured the fatigue of such a long journey
made across the Earth. His face was deeply furrowed with
wrinkles, but, in reality, he showed no signs of age. And his
bulky Armenian costume opened up the idea, which gained
more credence after he'd been seen arriving without baggage

---

faked being ill or crippled while begging during the day were
miraculously "cured" when they returned to their usual health
in that slum.

and without servants, despite exterior signs of wealth, that he was the Wandering Jew himself—or so the population believed. To which, however, it was objected that the Wandering Jew had never dared approach Jerusalem. In addition, very remarkably clean-shaven, the new arrival lacked in that way the most essential part of the description of the character about whom the legends say that never had there been a man with such a beard.

Whatever else could be said about Salvador Arbib, one fact was certain: that he had a line of credit open to the limit of a million and a half with the banker Micholetti. What's more, at the end of a few days, we saw a heavily-loaded schooner arrive at the port. After having unloaded, at the address selected by this new Croesus, a rich cargo of Cashmere wool, Ostrich plumes, fantasies from India and China, and cloth from the Orient, the ship immediately sailed back out to sea. To justify his Armenian merchant status, as soon as that cargo was unloaded, Salvador Arbib, with the permission of the municipal authority, set up a splendidly decorated tent in the oriental style at the Pisa thoroughfare and there he began to sell his merchandise. But what right away caused a great rumor is that, according to all experts, his articles were sold at fifty, sixty, and often seventy-five percent below the market prices. What's more, the salesmen employed in this unusual market place had all been selected exclusively among the convicts, whom the prison administration allows to work in the city. Clothed in their prison uniform, but immediately ready to greet the public with extreme politeness, the men, through whose hands objects of great value passed, were in themselves a curious spectacle. However, at Salvador Arbib's bazaar, even the fabulous bargains that that man was proudly offering were still not enough to draw a great number of customers.

Informed in all the details about this peculiar way of doing business, I had already foreseen a situation that must be called to the attention of the authorities, when, on the one hand, the Jews, who form a considerable part of the population, and, on the other hand, several well-known merchants

146

came to ask me to intervene and put an end to the depreciation of articles from the Orient, which seemed to have been premeditated by that stranger.

Ordered to appear before me, Salvador Arbib expressed himself very well and had all the manners of a well-bred man. It seemed that he couldn't be more astonished at having been called to account for the manner in which he sold merchandise. I could never make him understand that the law had foreseen the case where, by fraudulent dealings, a seller would try to bring down the usual price of merchandise.

"Very well," he kept saying "for those who use those fraudulent means, or those only suspected of that; but me, where am I doing that? I open a shop. I sell my stock there at a price which I find reasonable. Who can find fault in that?"

At the moment I left him, as I was suggesting that he should think about it and come back the next day and bring me his answer, he replied:

"From here until tomorrow, all cause for disagreement between us will have disappeared."

In fact, that evening, I was told that the tent of the Armenian had just been set on fire and, aided by his strange salesmen, he opposed using any help against the flames that came to him from all sides. In fewer than two hours, everything was destroyed, and the man who had set the fire had the presumption to send me news about it in a note.

The next morning, there was a kind of unrest among the lower class people in the city. Several reports to the police claimed that money had been spread around. I then found it useful to make sure of the location of a man whose activities had been suspicious, if not beyond reason. But the turbulent man had already taken refuge in the heart of Venezzia, and when agents of authority tried to begin a search, they were met with threats. Following some assaults, they had, for that day, to give up executing their arrest warrant.

The next day, there was a different reaction; no resistance and violent opposition, but everywhere, as the police passed by, doors were closed, to such an extent that the quarter, ordinarily so animated, had for several hours the look of a city devastated by the plague. It was impossible for the people I sent to arrest the accused, to find where he was hiding, or obtain the least information.

The evening of the same day, a rumor came to me that, at a tumultuous assembly that had taken place by the light of torches under a huge hangar used to store merchandise, Salvador Arbib had proclaimed himself Duke of Venezzia, and the next day, in fact, there was spread throughout Livorno a proclamation and the regulations with which the new dignitary would govern his Duchy. Then, when some detachments of the marine guard tried to put down so much audacity, they found the entry to the canals barricaded and closed with chains. From the adjacent houses some shots were fired that wounded several men, so that an all-out siege seemed necessary to deal with that ridiculous and audacious usurper.

During the day of March 31st, arrangements were made and a vigorous attack carried out, so that all the disorder was finally suppressed. But toward the evening, a man came forward to me, saying that he offered me the means of taking Salvador Arbib into custody, without resistance, at an agreed upon price and, as a condition that he remain in my hands as a hostage, this traitor gave precise information for reaching the retreat of the chief of the insurrection. But Arbib was missed by only a few minutes in the place that had been revealed to me.

However, that police raid was not absolutely without results, because, while the house where the so-called Duke of Venezzia had installed himself in a truly royal fashion was being thoroughly searched, they found a door to a newly-walled-up cave, which was naturally suspicious. That door was immediately opened, and the explorers found themselves confronting a rather strange spectacle. Myself, on their report, I had the curiosity to go and see it for myself. Imagine this, Madame la Grande Duchesse: a vast cave all hung with black curtains, laid out like a chapel of rest, lit by tomb lights. In the middle, stretched out ceremonially, there reposed the body of

148

a still young man, that of an old man, and that of a beautiful young girl, all three frozen in death. Dressed in their clothing, each of those unfortunates had around his shoulders a little steel chain covered in bronze, to which was attached writings on ebony wood.

On the writing attached to the shoulder of the young man could be read: "The bank will rejoice at this," *and, in fact, in his right hand, my men discovered shortly afterwards an engraved plate for bills issued by the Bank of England, that certainly could sustain the minutest comparison with the original that should be in London.*

On the writing hanging from the shoulder of the old man, on one side was the image of an owl, and on the other side the following words could be read: "The birds rejoice," *and in the dead man's hands there were hunting instruments, as if to show that, during his life, he had been a dangerous persecutor of the flying gents.*

Finally, on the writing attached to the shoulder of the young girl, was written: "Beatrix Cenci: sed casta inviolata et in patrem, pietatis numquam redi vivum exemplar." *(Beatrix Cenci, chaste, pure and a model of piety such as will never be seen again.) In the dead girl's right hand was a palm, while in her left hand was a little delicately sculpted ivory box on the cover of which was written:* "Powder from Java."

Finally, on the side of the door facing the inside of the cave could be read, in white letters on a black background: "A sequel to the Hamburg Ossuary."

I will not undertake, Madame la Grande Duchesse, the kind of archeological work, the object of which would be to discover the meaning of these different inscriptions that I have had the honor of putting before your eyes. I leave that honor to the police, who have seized and taken control of it. Just the mention of Java Powder *implies the idea of a crime. Javanese poisons have always had appalling fame.*

What remains for me to tell you is that, in the night that followed the escape of Salvador Arbib, as midnight struck, one of those flares used as communication between sailors explod-

149

ed from the top of Mont Nero. Some strollers on the Ardenza promenade, from which there is a view of the sea, saw a light in the distance, followed by a cannon shot. Since the night was magnificent, it couldn't be the call of a vessel in distress, and everything leads me to believe that this was one last gesture of insolence by the so-called Duke of Venezzia. Probably sent to reach the vessel with which the flare from Mount Nero had put him in contact, it sent us his farewell salute.

Since his departure, everything in Venezzia has somewhat returned to normal, but following this report, perhaps you would find it useful, Madame la Grand Duchesse, to invest me with some extraordinary powers that would allow me to fully implement the rule of law where, for such a long time, it has been ignored.

I have the honor to be with deep respect, etc., etc.

IX. Painter's Studio for Rent

During the month of February, 1813, that is to say five years after the events reported in the preceding chapter, the concierge of a building of mediocre appearance, located on the Rue Royale-Saint-Antoine,[70] was asked to kindly show a potential tenant an artist's studio which a sign outside indicated that it was *for rent* in that house. It was evening, and in a man with blonde hair, wearing glasses, and draped in an ample military coat, the concierge, not seeing a client who wouldn't come back, observed that it was very late and that was not exactly the proper hour to look for an apartment. However, as the would-be tenant insisted, and as the lodging in question had remained a long time vacant, the concierge decided to interrupt the reading of his newspaper and to undertake the walk of ninety-seven steps from which he had at first recoiled.

---

[70] Today's rue de Birague, in the 4th arrondissement (renamed in 1864).

Shown into a kind of attic, lit only by a window called a *snuff box,*[71] the renter seemed rather disposed to take it, only he seemed to doubt that all the furniture that he intended to put there could easily fit. As a consequence, he asked the concierge to get him a folding tape measure so that he could take some measurements. Seeing the attic likely to be rented, and the unknown man being safely left alone in a place that had only, as is commonly said, the bare four walls, the concierge hurried to go down to get what he had been asked for.

Soon after that inconvenient witness had left, the would-be tenant ran to a kind of deep, dark cavity that was difficult to notice in a room situated exactly under the roof, and which the architect had left open in several places. From that hiding place, he took out a rather heavy object, but under the heavy coat of dust and spider webs, its nature was not easy to make out. That object rapidly placed under his coat, it goes without saying that he didn't wait for the return of the concierge. As he met him midway on the stairs, coming up as he was going down, he told him that it was beginning to be too dark for him to take measures, and that, the next morning, without fail, he would return.

The following day, the would-be tenant did not reappear, but the attic immediately found another client. The new applicant was a woman approaching, if she hadn't already past, middle-age. With a rather pleasant face, she had something careless about her dress and, far from hiding a regrettable absence of distinction, the extreme care of her make-up rather served to point it out.

When she had visited the attic, the tenant, while finding several things to alter, thought she could, nevertheless, fit things in and to begin with, she would like to put down a deposit. But the concierge remarked that, before settling anything, his duty was to take down some information.

---

[71] A skylight.

"If you want to know if I will pay," the artist said quickly, "would you like a payment in advance? Do you require two?"

The concierge then began a somewhat roundabout sentence, the meaning of which was that, in a quiet house, notwithstanding the solvency of a *single woman,* one would also like to know their way of making a living.

"Monsieur le Concierge," said the renter after having gazed at her questioner's face, "do you know that you have a remarkable face? One of those that one would pay to have the pleasure of painting. As for how I conduct myself, you really don't have to worry about that. I am telling you so that you can strictly control it; I will never be available to anyone. If I retire into your pigeon roost, it's to finish a painting that I intent to enter in the next Exposition, and also with the intention of getting away from one of the most irksome persecutions."

"You are being persecuted, Madame?"

"Yes. In the house where I live, there is an old monkey of an owner who, under one pretext or another, is always snooping around my studio. The other day, by way of his porter, he sent me the most extravagant proposals, that I laughed at. That means that, if you ask information from one or the other, they will tell you a thousand horrors about me. That's their tactic to prevent me from renting elsewhere. You, on the contrary, seem to be a respectable man, and if I need to, I am sure that I can count on your protection."

"Oh! As far as that's concerned," said the concierge, "Madame can have no worry."

"Then it's agreed," said the artist, "no later than this afternoon, I will arrive here with all my packsaddle of tools. I will give you twenty-five francs a month to do my housekeeping, and after your portrait, I will really have to paint that of *Madame* so they can be hung together."

The good faith deposit offered to the concierge was one of the most honorable. The woman was ready to pay two months in advance; he had the prospect of seeing himself painted, and in a portrait opposite that of his wife, and in addition, he would have the housekeeping to do; that was a mass of seductions to put in default the most total prudence. It was therefore agreed that the artist, who stated that her name was Madame Lebois, would, if it was convenient for him, move in during the day.

In fact, about three o'clock in the afternoon, Madame Dubois arrived with rather modest painting tools: an easel, three chairs, a box of paints and some sketches. As for the remainder of her furniture, it was supposed to follow the next day. Like a woman who has no time to lose, after having instructed the concierge not to let anyone in to see her, whoever it might be, the artist prepared her *palette* and shut herself up in the attic. As soon as the door was closed, she hurried to explore the hiding place that the man with glasses and overcoat had visited before her, but found nothing there. She seemed to show a rather strong disappointment. After having minutely checked the smallest nooks, she took an open letter out of her bosom, and after she had re-read it, she said to herself:

"It really is here."

And she began to search the room again. When it became clearly obvious to her that her investigations were useless, she went down to see the concierge. She asked about the previous tenant, but the man she questioned had not known her predecessor and could not answer her questions. Then Madame Lebois left.

The next day, she came back again to the artist studio and searched for a long time, but still as vain. Then she was never seen again. Since she had definitely not paid the rent in advance, and all the furniture she had left behind was worth, at the most, fifty francs, the concierge finally accepted the fact that he might have been dealing with a fraudster.

The real name of that strange artist, and the reason for her interest and actions, the reader will learn later, but right now, we can say that the mysterious man who had come before her was none other than Gregorio Matiphous. Five years before, we had left him in Florence. In a few words, during that interval, here's how he used his time.

Seeing the report the Mediterranean Prefect addressed to the Grande Duchesse, he was in no doubt that the three bodies left behind in the Venezzia cave, the writing and the emblems that accompanied those sad remains, were those of Fauntleroy, Hans Krafft and his daughter. As for the Armenian merchant, his description and his bizarre acts were enough to reveal in him one of the familiar avatars of the Marquis de Samaniego; his famous ossuary of Hamburg had been mentioned before by that famous mystery man, and had expressly been used in the unusual funerals discovered after his departure.

But under that gloomy apparatus, how many other questions there were! How could the fugitives have been in contact with the so-called "Salvador Arbib"? What part had he played in their end, that everything showed had been violent? Did he act only as the one who had arranged their funeral after the fact, or was he, in fact, their murderer? And Christiana in particular, what role had she played in that dark drama where she, at the same time, might have been a Beatrice Cenci, the most famous of parricides, and yet an incomparable model of filial piety?[72]

All those obscure things agitated Matiphous' emotions and it became too much for him not to go to Livorno to look into them. With the information that he himself could bring to the investigation, it seemed to him impossible that it would not soon sift out the truth.

However, before starting out, he wished that Britannicus' condition allowed him to question him because what had been

---

[72] (1577-1599) young Roman noblewoman who murdered her father, Count Francesco Cenci. The subsequent, lurid, murder trial in Rome gave rise to an enduring legend about her. She was beheaded for the crime in 1599. Her life inspired *The Cenci*, an 1819 tragedy by Percy Bysshe Shelley, and the 1971 opera *Beatrix Cenci* by Alberto Ginastera to a Spanish libretto by the composer and William Shand.

done to that unfortunate man, the brusque departure of Lady Stuart, and the trap of which she claimed to have been the victim, comprised as many mysteries equally made to stir his curiosity. And then, it must be said, when going to attack that dangerous person who, after having in isolation deceived the British Government, had actually now dared to start a revolt against the all- powerful Imperial Government, Matiphous did not hide the peril to himself. That man, as he had done after his departure from London, had perhaps left behind in Venezzia some henchmen with whom he might have to contend. Considering everything, to go to Livorno was therefore a serious step, and he should not take it without giving it serious thought.

However, while human prudence deliberates, God disposes. One morning, a letter came to the Director of Police in Florence, and with that letter, which he was told to share with Matiphous, the order was given for the latter to go to Paris in all haste. Instead, then, of deciding to go to Livorno after having taken only the time to provide for the care demanded by Britannicus, the man from Malta started for France. After having made contact with the Minister of Police to receive his instructions, he was immediately sent to Bayonne, where a highly confidential mission had been arranged for him.

At that time, Napoleon had decided on a plan to be rid of the Bourbons in Spain and to replace them with a Prince of his own family. Foreseeing that, for the success of that substitution, cleverness rather than force would be more effective, in view of the correspondence that he would have to intercept, the Emperor, who thought about everything, had ordered that an intelligent and trustworthy letter-opener should be attached to the cabinet of his secretary. The Minister of Police had then remembered the valuable depot of archives, the existence of which, a short time before, Matiphous had revealed to him, and, prejudiced in his favor, he hurriedly recommended him.

Matiphous had then been present and was a small part of the diplomatic drama that developed shortly afterward and ended in the captivity of the old King Charles IV at Fontainebleau and that of his son at Valençay. [73]

But the effect of the good opinion he had given of his aptitude for secret missions didn't end there for Fouché's protégé. After King Joseph had been enthroned, he was tasked with organizing, for the benefit of the new Spanish kingdom, a Secret Bureau modeled after that which existed in France. The functions as Director that Hulet had filled in Paris, Matiphous would fill in Madrid.

It was only in that city that he could be rejoined by Britannicus, whose convalescence had been excessively long and difficult. The explanation that the boy was then able to give relative to his unfortunate affair in Florence was found to be very little in accord with the idea that his master had formed about it. To hear the Negro tell it, the real cause of Lady Stuart's departure would have been the jealousy of her old husband, after an officious indiscretion had circulated about the intrigue she had started with the equestrian artist, Tamerlane. Far from being the would-be murderer of Britannicus, they had separated on the best of terms. Tamerlane hadn't suddenly left Florence, except to follow the steps of the beautiful conquest who was escaping him.

---

[73] Economic troubles, rumors about the Queen having an affair and the King's own ineptitude, forced King Charles IV of Spain to abdicate on 19 March 1808, in favor of his son, Ferdinand VII. Having appealed to Napoleon for help, Charles and Ferdinand were summoned before the Emperor in Bayonne in April. Napoleon forced them both to abdicate, declared the Bourbon dynasty deposed, and installed his brother, Joseph Bonaparte, as King Joseph I. The ex-King and his wife were held captive in France, first at Compiègne, then in Marseille. After the collapse of the regime installed by Napoleon, Ferdinand VII was restored to the throne. Charles IV drifted about Europe until 1812, when he finally settled in Rome. He passed away on 20 January 1819.

As for the violence done to his person, the Negro didn't know if he should attribute it to Lord Stuart, punishing him in that way for the interest he had shown towards the projects of Tamerlane, or to the terrible envy of a dentist, a part of whose clientele he had stolen.

In the end, Matiphous didn't put any great importance into delving into the value of those very late explanations. At that moment, he began to treat rather lightly all these things that were in the past, and in the middle of the upward flight that his fortune had taken, the impression of the events that, at another time, would have affected him strongly, was becoming, day by day, less and less important. Even the loss of his presumptive fiancée, the daughter of Hans Krafft, was far from having left a significant mark on his life, as might have been supposed. The rapid change that he had been forced to make at the first moments of his sadness, had prevented it from weighing too heavily on his heart. In the urgent and multiple occupations, he had found great resources for distraction and forgetfulness.

Besides, the sad way his last loves had ended had finally given him a very disenchanted morality. In thinking about the sad way in which all the women who, until then, with different titles, had had access into his heart, he had come to regard himself as a kind of vampire, or the fatal man who, just by his powerful presence, had the sad ability to sow death around him. At that point, he decided to flee all serious engagements. He was very careful to avoid any encounters that could bring tempests into his life, living in Spain, the classic country for adventures, for three years, from 1808 to 1811, leading the calmest and most unified of lives. In his existence, this was a kind of fallow period, which didn't furnish the smallest chapter to glean.

Unfortunately for him, in the first months of 1811, following an altercation that he had with Don Pablo de Arriba, the minister of the general police, over service matters, he had been forced to leave his functions in Spain and return to France to pick up in the Secret Bureau the post that he had

157

previously occupied before his departure for Florence. But upon his return to Paris, he encountered hardly welcoming attitudes among his former colleagues. His mission to Bayonne, and the kind of good fortune that had followed it, had made some envious, and those had taken a wicked pleasure in humiliating him about his disappointment.

As for Hulet who, as will be remembered, lived in eternal antagonism with the Minister of Police, seeing in Matiphous a protégé of this rival power, he had developed a secret aversion to him. Once he had seen him back in his department, he never stopped making him feel the heavy weight of his authority. Badly viewed by his superior, condemned to bitter or cold relations with the other employees, not having been, when he was Chief of service in Madrid, used to obeying, Matiphous had necessarily become disgusted with his functions. With the goal of freeing himself from a position that, from day to day, had become more insupportable, after two years patiently plotting everyday to escape, he had finally decided on the suspicious and mysterious scheme in which we have just seen him become involved.

The result that he was hoping for was not, however, immediate, because, a year later, we find him still occupying his same position in the Secret Bureau, without his relations with his colleagues having improved. From that point, in a decisive circumstance, Matiphous placed himself openly in an antagonistic position, and, in that way, completely repaid the amount of defiance and hateful feelings of which he had been the object. The tragic affair of Alexis Hulet has not been forgotten. Condemned to death by the in-house tribunal assembled when needed by the Secret Bureau, it will also be recalled that only one person on that tribunal had refused to vote for a condemnation and capital punishment. Only he accompanied the remains of his young and unfortunate colleague to his last resting place.

Now, it can be revealed that that charitable judge was Gregorio Matiphous. Neither the menacing reproaches of the other letter-openers, nor the stoic example of Hulet the elder, voting with the majority for the death of his son, could change the position of clemency the man from Malta had taken. Alluding to the dull cracking sounds of the Imperial throne, which, at that point, could be perceived, he responded as follows when they told him about the necessity of making a great example to establish forever the morality of the Secret Bureau:

"Come now! You want blood to cement the future. Who knows if you will even exist tomorrow."

These prophetic words were uttered on March 29, 1814. Two days later, on March 31, Paris had capitulated.[74]

X. Major Tomboff

If, the day of the battle for Paris, Matiphous had not taken up arms like the Hulets, but he had confronted dangers as great as theirs. Volunteering himself for the army's medical corps, he had seen his offer eagerly accepted, and all day, in

---

[74] The Battle of Paris was fought on March 30-31, 1814 between the Sixth Coalition—consisting of Russia, Austria, and Prussia—against the French Napoleonic Empire. After a day of fighting in the suburbs of Paris, the French surrendered on March 31, ending the War of the Sixth Coalition and forcing Napoleon to abdicate and go into exile. The emperor had been in retreat since his failed invasion of Russia in 1812. With the Russian armies following up victory, the Sixth Coalition was formed. Even though the French were victorious in the initial battles, the Coalition armies eventually joined together and defeated them at the Battle of Leipzig in the autumn of 1813. After the battle, the Pro-French German Confederation of the Rhine collapsed, thereby losing Napoleon's hold on Germany east of the Rhine. The supreme commander of the Coalition forces and the paramount monarch among the three main Coalition monarchs, Russian Tsar Alexander I, then ordered all Coalition forces in Germany to cross the Rhine and invade France.

the middle of shooting and fighting, he had worked to bandage the wounded.

The next day, after having rendered the last duties to the unfortunate Alexis Hulet, he had again presented himself as an auxiliary to various ambulances, but since it was no longer a matter of going out of the city to face bullets, it was among his colleagues that he was in the greatest hurry to second the military doctors. Then, another philanthropic idea came to him. Followed by Britannicus, who carried his instruments and a box of bandages, he left Paris and reached the Romainville woods and the Saint-Gervais fields, that is to say, the site of the battlefield, where, the evening before, the fighting had been the most intense. There, he gave himself the mission of looking for some of the unfortunate men that are too often neglected by the orderlies and left among dead. His effort found almost nothing. He was carrying for a poor conscript, for whom help had come too late, and who finally died in his arms, when, several steps from him, he saw Britannicus pick up a rock and start crushing the head of a Russian officer. That man had managed to get out from under a pile of cadavers beneath which he had remained unconscious.

"Are you mad?" Matiphous shouted, grabbing the black man's arm.

"I'm finishing him off because he's suffering too much," said Britannicus. "He won't come out of it."

And he again raised his arm to strike him. But the man from Malta pushed him aside roughly and, going to the wounded man, who, following the effort with which he proved his vitality, had fallen back unconscious, he felt his pulse and examined his facial characteristics, which could indicate his chances of life or death. After a short time, the constant attention that he gave to the wounded man produced a strange impression on him. He would have sworn that, in his features, he saw those of the equestrian artist who, in Florence, under the name of Tamerlane, had been suspected of the violence against Britannicus.

After that, although the Negro had said that he had separated from the horseman in excellent friendship, his attempt at murder had an explanation. Struck like his master by the resemblance of the wounded man to the man who had almost murdered him with a cudgel, he had just been motivated by a furious movement of vengeance.

Even if humanity hadn't been his first motivation, curiosity would have made Matiphous care for the wounded man. Having inspected his condition, he found on his head a wound from a pistol shot which, without being, in itself, very serious, must have caused prolonged unconsciousness by the trauma and a great loss of blood. After having administered immediate care, he had Britannicus help him transport the sick man to the closest ambulance; then, finding it was overloaded, he made a decisive decision, that of taking into his living quarters the man he had undertaken to fight death for. As a consequence, he ordered Britannicus to look for what we call today a *coupé* or a *citadine*, and what they called at the time our story took place, a *fiacre*, or more commonly still, a *sapin*.

The Negro had shown visible repugnance in lifting the wounded man in the place where he had been picked up, but he showed even more marked ill will when it was a question of taking him into his master's house.

"He shouldn't come in; better kill him now and spare him the suffering," he repeated with stubborn insistence.

Matiphous had to use the most commanding tone to make him obey his order to procure a method of transportation. When the vehicle was brought, Britannicus stubbornly refused to get into it, and when, without his assistance, the wounded man was finally put into a bed at Matiphous house, the man from Malta waited all day in vain for his servant's return. Not only did Britannicus not reappear, but the next day, one of his fellow countrymen came on his behalf carrying a note in which he reclaimed his belongings and whatever was due of his salary. He explained that kind of leave-taking given to his master by saying that, since peace had freed the seaways, he was returning to his own country.

Matiphous couldn't be duped by that sudden decision, and, in any case, nothing had taken place between him and the outgoing servant that made that way of communicating by letter and by representative natural. In addition, if the Russian had actually been the man from Florence, in the helpless state to which he had been reduced by his wound, how could the terror that he seemed to inspire in the victim of his former brutality be explained? What remained then that could be explained was that Britannicus was afraid that he might make certain revelations regarding the facts that had caused their quarrel. The Negro had never been precise about that subject. So, Matiphous promised himself that, as soon as the wounded man was able to hold a conversation, he would obtain from him all the truth about that affair. He had always instinctively felt that he had not been told the complete story.

However, as it was possible that the explanation might contain something unpleasant for the ego of his guest, in order to spare him an emotion which might compromise his convalescence, he resolved to wait to interrogate him until his recovery was completely satisfactory. It must be added that, in the meantime, the man from Malta had developed some doubts as to the infallibility of his initial assessment. Without considering the rank of Major that the stranger held in the Russian army, his exquisite politeness, his elegant manners, his constant worry about the disturbance his presence caused in his savior's house, and how he expressed his gratitude, at the same time both dignified and friendly, soon brought about the thought that he was a man who had received a distinguished upbringing rather than that of a lowly traveling equestrian entertainer.

Less and less confident of his first impression, Matiphous came to tell himself that the very salient characteristics of the Kabul type made all the individuals of that race look very much alike. Finally, one day, he had cleverly led the conversation to Italy and, upon hearing discussed a country which, for him, was so full of bad memories, the stranger showed no kind of embarrassment. From that, Matiphous drew the conclusion that he, as well as Britannicus, had been the plaything of an illusion.

Several days more having past, Major Tomboff—for such was the name of the Russian—found himself well enough to risk his first outing. With several officers among his friends, he rented a box at the opera to go to a play made exciting by the presence of sovereigns of the Allies. Invited to be one of the party, Matiphous didn't accept. The memory of the evening spent at the same theater with Mademoiselle de Lineuil didn't seem a pleasant one to relive. In addition, with his ardent Napoleonic convictions, he was too painfully impressed by the triumph of the foreign armies to agree to be seen in a public place in the company of the vanquishers who had just overthrown the Emperor.

The next day, the Major came to see his host.

"Doctor," he said, "I have a favor to ask of you."

"What's it about?" Matiphous responded.

"Yesterday at the opera," the Major continued, "we were seated across from a box occupied by a lively and dapper little gentleman who, although he had the wings of a pigeon, his face, wrinkled and saffron-colored, made him have the appearance of a young man over sixty. With him was a remarkably pretty woman who, by certain looks, let it be suspected that she was a kept woman. That woman looked at me several times with her opera glasses. It was evident that I had become the object of her particular attention. Naturally curious to know that caused that interest in my person, I went out at the intermission to show my face at the windowpane of the box that enthroned the provocative beauty..."

"A mistake, likely to provoke a quarrel!" Matiphous interrupted.

"Better than that," replied the Russian. "I hadn't been looking three seconds before the little gentleman, having seen me, came out like a fury and slapped his glove across my face, saying to me: 'Your Cossack upbringing should be entirely redone. I will gladly take charge of that.' "

"A duel with an old man," said the man from Malta. "That's an unfortunate combination, very disagreeable!"

"Wait," replied the Major. "That old man, his card told me he was a General, the Comte de Chandeville. According to the information that one of my comrades, who has contacts in Parisian society, could gather, he is a man of the very old nobility, who nevertheless served in Napoleon's armies. His rare bravery should have raised him to the highest rank, but he has never gone past the rank of Brigade General because he is a duelist, undisciplined, and he has had a thousand unpleasant affairs in the middle of the plebeian behavior of the troops, in putting on that veneer of casual aristocratic behavior that characterizes the military officers of the *ancien régime*. So, it's related that, during the retreat from Russia, on his bivouac and despite the most cruel privations, he retained an old valet who, like him, survived all the fatigues and all the misery. He didn't miss a single day having himself coiffed and powdered. No danger and no military duty could keep him from the daily cares for his toilette."[75]

"Considering that," Matiphous said, "he would be a very serious adversary."

"Without a doubt," answered the Major. "But here is what preoccupies me the most. A man with that character can't be an Othello. It wasn't jealousy, then, that incited him to violence. What's probable is that the injury he made to me was meant less to my person than to my uniform. The quarrel that he used as a pretext was an affair of national hatred. Tomorrow, he will, without a doubt, come to the terrain with two military officers, as hungry as he is, to *eat the Russian*. On my side, if I have my friends as seconds, it will truly be two armies confronting each other, and the conflict can then take on incalculable proportions."

---

[75] Note from the Author: "This is without doubt the same general officer about whom Monsieur Ségur wrote in his book about the Russian campaign. Volume 2, Book X, page 355."

"I couldn't deny that; but after all, you are not the one who provoked the duel."

"Ah!" exclaimed the Russian. "You don't know General Sacken![76] In turning over to him the governance of your capital, the Tsar expressly recommended to him that he maintain at any price the harmony between the Allies and the Parisian population. When this terrible man, who is discipline incarnate, learns what has happened, he will hold me responsible for everything, and God know what treatment will be in store for me!"

"Why the Devil," said the man from Malta, "did you go and look through that window? That's a new variation of that famous saying, *Mais qu'allait-il faire dans cette galère?*"[77]

"The only way," replied the Major, "that I have to get out of that predicament is in making the duel a purely personal matter by being accompanied by seconds who are neither military men, nor Russians like myself. In that situation, my dear doctor, I had to think of you. In your position as a surgeon, you could be useful there in more than one way. But that's not all; I don't know a soul in Paris, and you would have to extend your kindness by being willing to requisition some *bourgeois* among your friends who would consent to serve as a second witness. That's what it also means to save people's lives. After that, there is nothing they won't think they are allowed to ask."

---

[76] Prince Fabian Gottlieb von der Osten-Sacken (1752-1837), Baltic-German Field Marshal who led the Russian army against the Duchy of Warsaw and later governed Paris during the city's brief occupation by the anti-French coalition.

[77] Lit. "But what was he doing in that galley?" Famous line from Molière's 1671 comedy, *Scapin the Schemer*, in which to revenge himself on Géronte, his master, the valet, Scapin, tells Géronte that his son has been kidnapped and is on board a Turkish galley being held for ransom—which is false. To free him, Géronte must reluctantly part with 500 *écus*, and repeats five times in the same scene the famous line above.

In the overture that had just been made to him, Matiphous had too beautiful an opportunity to seek a clarification, which he had for a long time wanted to obtain, seizing, as they say, the ball on the bounce.

"I don't absolutely refuse," he answered, "the delicate mission which you offer me, but you must understand that, in such a case, one would like to know exactly for whom I am coming forward. I dare then ask you this simple question: in the past, have you ever spent some time in Italy?"

"Me? Never," answered the Major without the least hesitation.

"Take Florence, for example; are you very sure that you have never resided there?"

"Never. But, why this insistence?" asked the Russian.

"Because I would swear that, six years ago, I met you in that city."

"And why would that be?"

"There," Matiphous continued, "you were guilty of a wickedly brutal attack, leaving for dead on the spot, the poor devil you had beaten."

"For all us Russians," said the Major, smiling, "beating a man is not something to be very much remembered. We are somewhat accustomed to doing it frequently to our peasants."

"But, again," Matiphous continued, "did I, or did I not, see you in Florence?"

"One more time, no," responded the Russian. "What's more, who was that man whom my lookalike would have almost killed with the cudgel?"

"A very remarkable man, remarkable by his color if not by his social position, a Negro..."

"With a rather bizarre name," continued the Russian officer, "which might be Britannicus?"

"Precisely," Matiphous answered.

"Ah! If it's that's the man you mean, then he deserved the treatment he got; I can confirm that to you."

"That man was, at that time, in my service," Matiphous continued. "He still was six weeks ago when I picked you up from the battlefield at of the Saint-Chaumont hills. He seemed to recognize you, as I did, and if I hadn't been quick in turning aside his blow, he would have crushed your head with a rock."

"That wouldn't have surprised me the least in the world; he wouldn't have wanted to leave alive a man who could tell you about the rascal who robbed you."

"So you're appointing yourself official executioner and in charge of policing my house?" said the man from Malta, ironically.

"Monsieur Matiphous," replied the Major, somewhat solemnly, "I owe you too much, and I understand too well what debt I am contracting toward you by the service I am asking of you, to maintain any longer any reticence that might lead you to doubt my complete honesty. The most honorable families are sometimes afflicted with deplorable wounds. I have a brother, older than I; and I can tell you that it must be he who, six years ago, struck your manservant. There has always been, between him and I, a great resemblance. After a great number of other mistakes, because of the fatal passion he had developed for a street entertainer, he followed her equestrian group to Italy. You might, in fact, have seen him in Florence in a situation that makes me ashamed, and, I say with gratitude, which you have had the delicacy not to bring up before, thus forcing me to recall that dismal story."

"I am very sorry," said Matiphous, "to have been obliged to go over that explanation with you, and only because I accepted the role you've asked me to undertake as a last resort. But since you're using my servant's facts and actions in defense of your brother, I would not, I think, be indiscreet in asking you to please make the circumstances of their encounter more precise."

"Not only will I tell you everything, but with the information I can give you, I have the means to give to you evidence of my complete truthfulness. Following what he did to your servant, my brother had to leave Florence. From the place where he took refuge in order to escape being found by the law, he wrote me a letter asking me for some monetary help. He told me in detail what had happened. He died shortly thereafter. I have kept his letter, the last remembrance of a brotherly friendship that that deplorable mistakes hadn't altered. I must have it in my campaign bag. It still has the postal stamp, which will exclude any idea that it was altered for the need of the moment."

"Major," said the man from Malta, "I haven't for a moment doubted the sincerity of your words. And if you see me ready to take advantage of the communication that you are pleased to offer me, it's now only in the interest of personal curiosity."

After having searched for some time in his bag, the Major took out a paper that looked time-worn. He folded it so as not to leave all of its contents visible and handed it to the man from Malta.

"See here," he said, "this is the passage you're interested in:

"*As for that Britannicus that I beat,* Tamerlane wrote, *and who is the reason why I am today without bread, I had met him in the past in Livorno when I was doing the work you've so much held against me. Knowing he was very dishonest and a total ruffian, I had the idea of using him for one of my love affairs. A marvelous English woman, dazzled by my equestrian talent, had fallen in love with me. She was a very great lady, and not knowing exactly how to meet her, I had chatted several times with that blackguard of misfortune about various ways that could be used to achieve my goal. One day the rascal came to tell me that he had found a way. The master he served had difficulties with my conquest and possessed a paper he could use to compromise her a great deal. As for Britannicus, despite posing as a model of fidelity, he had already been led astray by the Englishwoman's chambermaid in order to steal that paper from his master. And in fact, he did steal it...*"

Here Matiphous interrupted his reading and ran to a piece of furniture where he kept his secret papers. He hurriedly verified if Kitty's Act of Marriage, which he hadn't looked at for a long time, had really disappeared. The verification confirmed what Tamerlane had written!

"You are right, Major," the man from Malta said, "it would appear that Britannicus did, in fact, rob me."

And he again picked up the horseman's letter, which continued this way:

"But instead of giving the paper directly to the English-woman, here's what the rascal thought about doing. He would go find her, tell her that the paper troubling her had fallen into my hands, and if on the day of Mid-Lent, she would come masked to the Pergola box, I would be there myself, hidden under a domino mask, and ready to deliver the document in question to her. The plot seemed to me well arranged; once a woman is interested, she doesn't ask anything better than to have a pretext to be forced to give herself. The day agreed on, the scoundrel gave me a paper about which I understood noth-ing. That was what I was supposed to give to the Englishwom-an. I stayed two hours sitting around, moping in a box where, at any moment, I expected to see my beauty enter. During that time, in another box, where the rendezvous with the hapless woman had in fact been set up in my name, with the aid of a domino costume and a mask, that infernal Negro succeeded in passing himself as me!!!"

Here, with several exclamation points, Tamerlane em-phasized the action that he had just described in words.

"That deception was indeed infamous," said the man from Malta, returning the letter to the Major, "but I can't tell if it wasn't deserved. In all honesty, if that bit of trickery hadn't involved me, I believe I would find the matter rather amus-ing."

"Understood," said the Russian, "but you can now un-derstand the reasons for my brother's anger."

"Let's leave all that villainous past behind us," said Matiphous, "and return to the present, which is a great deal more serious. What must I do?"

"You will go the General's residence in order to set up the conditions of the duel. Here is his card. As the offender, I would prefer to choose the sword, but the age of my adversary gives me some scruples. As for the rest, I'm sure that what you will decide will be well done."

A half-hour later, Matiphous had himself announced at the residence of the Count de Chandeville on behalf of Major Tomboff.

XI. Who Georgiana Was

If our readers will please refer to the contents of their memory, which we urged them to use to store the numerous details of this vast story,[78] they will remember that, in the night when that modern-day Sardanapalus,[79] François-Honoré Dubignon had let himself be consumed by a fire that he himself had lit in one of his townhouses, Georgiana, that fatal woman he had stolen from Alexis Hulet, was saved from the flames, in which Dubignon had intended for her to die, by a young Colonel with whom she was having an affair.

That situation had precipitated the denouement and, almost immediately, the easy favors of the former favorite of

---

[78] See the *Avant-Propos* in Volume 1.

[79] Sardanapalus was, according to the Greek writer Ctesias, the last king of Assyria, although in actuality Ashuruballit II (612-605 BC) holds that distinction. Ctesias' book *Persica* is lost, but we know of its contents by later compilations and from the work of Diodorus. In this account, Sardanapalus, supposed to have lived in the 7th century BC, is portrayed as a decadent figure who spent his life in self-indulgence and died in an orgy of destruction. The legendary decadence of Sardanapalus later became a theme in literature and art, especially in the Romantic era. The name Sardanapalus is probably a corruption of Ashurbanipal, an emperor-king of the Assyrian Empire, but Sardanapalus as described by Diodorus bears little relationship with what is known of that king, who in fact was a militarily powerful, highly efficient and scholarly ruler, presiding over the largest empire the world had yet seen.

Askar-Khan were granted to her heroic rescuer.[80] Her new lover was in full honeymoon the day of the Battle for Paris. When she replaced her rich and lavish provider with that skinny Colonel, whose because of his age and outstanding bravado had the ridiculous pretention of being loved for himself, Georgiana would have lacked all the natural instincts of a true courtesan, if, in accepting that conquest, she hadn't gained the outstanding pleasure of taking her lover away from a great lady, whom, she thought, was no longer attractive. But at the moment she brought about that pleasing dish of feminine malice, it must also be remembered that she counted somewhat on Russian bullets to relieve her of the boredom of that rather empty new liaison. The course of events had fully justified her charitable calculation. The next day of the battle outside Paris, with the death of the second successor of Alex Hulet, her third widowhood had begun.

The publicity of so many funerals, reflected by her charms, couldn't help shining a bright light on them. The Comte de Chandeville, who, in his youth had frequented *la Dervieux, la Duthé* [81] and other famous *impure* persons before '89, had been curious to compare.

"So let's see," he had said to himself, "what this little *petite,* who is so much talked about, is like."

And he soon put himself in the running after the succession of the three generations of lovers already harvested.

A former *émigré,* and by the generosity of the Imperial Administration, restored to his considerable estate, the old suitor had a fortune and was of an age to see himself eagerly accepted. The bargain immediately agreed on, the representa-

---

[80] In *The Brothers of Death*, Rabou had created the character of Mirza Babba, an entirely fictional Persian ambassador sent to Paris; the real ambassador was Askar Khan Afshar who arrived in July 1808. Rabou appears here to have forgotten about Mirza Babba and instead uses the name of the real ambassador.

[81] Two famous courtesans.

171

tion given that evening at the Opera, was an opportunity for him to display his good fortune. Georgiana's beauty, displayed in an open box, had made a sensation, and it was by trying to admire her too closely that Major Tomboff had earned the duel, the formalities of which Matiphous was now going to set up.

When, with an insignificant person chosen among his acquaintances, the man from Malta was introduced into the Comte's drawing room, the nobleman was in the hands of his old valet hairdresser, being made up with the gallant *oeil de poudre* [82] that the famous historian of the Russian Campaign did not disdain to mention into his narration as a contrast with the terrible deprivations endured by the men of the *Grande Armée*. In addition, all the most professional and fashionable refinements were spread out around the coquettish old man.

"With your permission, Monsieur," the Comte said to Matiphous, after the latter had declined his position as plenipotentiary. "I will finish with my *toilette*." Then, shortly afterwards, he removed his dressing gown gracefully, and showing himself clothed underneath in a delightful lemon yellow short housecoat with full sleeves, he continued: "Messieurs, the only thing to do in order to respond to your visit is, I think, to give you the address of my own seconds."

Although the duel had been set up in a way that, in fact, did not allow for any chances of reconciliation, Matiphous thought himself obliged to insert a statement, the sense of which was that it was very regrettable to see two honorable men about to risk their lives for nothing more than the more or less casual direction in which a woman had glanced. The Comte didn't deign to answer. He had gone to an elegant citrus wood writing desk and, without sitting down, had scrawled two names on a piece of paper.

---

[82] Fine white powder made of rice or pulverized starch that was used in make up on wigs and faces before the French revolution.

"Here are the name and address of my seconds," he said, presenting the paper to Matiphous. "These gentlemen have been told to expect you."

Then, without any other word being exchanged, but with all the outward show of the most courteous deference, he accompanied his visitors back to the door of his apartment.

The witnesses that Matiphous went to meet without delay, were not, as the Major had supposed, officers of the Imperial Army. As soon as the Restoration was complete, the Comte de Chandeville had returned to the bosom of the *Ancien Régime.* One was a Navy officer, who had escaped the disaster of Quiberon;[83] the other a Lieutenant from the guards of the city gates. No reconciliation was admitted as possible, but everything occurred with exquisite politeness. When Matiphous mentioned a scruple expressed by the Major relative to the choice of weapons, the Navy officer replied:

"Monsieur de Chandeville fights very well with the sword, and his age has not made him lose any of his dexterity. As for the pistol, let's forget about that; he would have too much of an advantage. Everyone knows that he is an almost infallible shot."

It was then decided that the duel would be with swords, the true weapon of gentlemen. Then, since the evening before, at the theater, the altercation had created some excitement, foreseeing a possible intervention of the police, and the unstable political situation, they set up the rendezvous for a little later in the Vincennes woods, near the former convent of the Minimes.[84]

---

[83] The Battle of Quiberon Bay (known as Bataille des Cardinaux in French), was a decisive naval engagement fought on November 20, 1759 during the Seven Years' War between the British Royal Navy and the French Navy. It was fought in Quiberon Bay, off the coast of France near St. Nazaire.

[84] Catholic religious order of monks founded in the 15th century by Saint Francis of Paola. Today there are only two locations of the order left, both in Italy.

At the location of the duel, the choice of weapons was again discussed, each of the combatants declining, out of chivalry, anything favoring his side. The sword was definitely agreed on; the combatants took off their coats and they were at the point of crossing swords, when, speaking to Matiphous, the Comte said:"

"Monsieur, you seemed to believe this morning that a reputation for lightness in the woman I was accompanying had brought about the quarrel we are going to settle in a moment. I must rectify your ideas on that subject. If that woman seemed to pay some attention to Monsieur," he said, pointing to the Major, "it was because she had recognized the man who was the accomplice of an odious attack upon her person."

"Me?" exclaimed the Russian.

"Yes, you, Monsieur, in 1799, in Livorno, you were engaged in a business that our relationship at the moment doesn't allow me to describe. Seeming, as it appears, that you provided women for the harems of several countries in the Orient, you were, at that time, in business with a scoundrel named Prince de Bevillacqua, who sold you a young girl. She must have been struck by the personality of the man to whom he delivered her, for she never forgot his features. She recognized you yesterday evening. That's why, Monsieur, I slapped you in the face, and why I also decided, by the honorable uniform you are wearing, to test myself with you. In a moment, with your permission, I will do you the honor of killing you."

"General," Matiphous said quickly before the Major had time to speak, "there is a deplorable mistake here. Major Tomboff is not the man whom you thought the lady recognized. A fatal resemblance for which he can furnish an explanation and the proof..."

"Allow me, Monsieur," said the Major, interrupting, "if the injury I received was one of those that could be washed away in some other manner than by blood, I would perhaps consent to demonstrate to Monsieur le Comte that he has completely misunderstood the situation. But in the manner things are now, any explanation is now useless."

"I am not of your opinion," responded the man from Malta. "Even if Monsieur le Comte died in this duel, you would nevertheless remain, *vis-à-vis* his witnesses and yours, under an accusation which belongs to a different tribunal than that of honor. You owe to everyone and to yourself the justification that I know is in your hands. When the error is recognized, the Comte is a man of honor; he has proved that. Certainly he would not be embarrassed to give you, more surely than by use of weapons, the satisfaction you are entitled to claim."

"That's fair," said one of the Comte's seconds. "This affair would have a terrible effect on the public. And when an opening for reconciliation presents itself, it must be taken."

"What these gentlemen have decided, I will do," said the Comte.

"But, my dear Monsieur," said the Major to Matiphous, "it is very cruel that these same explanations that I gave to you alone, I am now obliged to share with just about everyone."

"That's indeed unfortunate," replied the man from Malta, "but you could kill the Comte ten times without cleansing yourself of an accusation made in good faith, one that, with a single word, you could make drop at your feet. What's more, I am your witness, and in virtue of the mandate with which you have entrusted me, I declare that I am opposed to a duel that no longer has a reason to exist. In case you want to go ahead with this, you will have to choose other seconds."

Seeing that the Russian still resisted to back down, the Comte declared:

"Listen, Major, take some time to think about it. If the explanation that your witness asks you to provide is absolutely too painful for you, you know very well that I will still be available to you."

That *mezzo termine* [85] settled everything. It was decided that the duel would be at least adjourned. In leaving the Comte de Chandeville and his witnesses, Matiphous said:

---

[85] Lit. middle term; compromise resolution.

"It seems that I will have the honor to see you this evening."

"Exactly, Monsieur," said the General. "I am dining with these gentlemen and you will find us at home."

I will dine with those gentlemen was said quickly. It remained to be seen if Fate would lend its hand to that arrangement, as simple as it might appear.

XII. The Bloodied Girl

The Comte had brought with him his old *valet de chambre*. Putting his General uniform back on and, most of all, retying his *cravate*, took some time after the departure of the Major and his witnesses, when, out of the bushes in the clearing where the duel had been supposed to take place, emerged two persons, not less expected by the readers than by the group in the middle of which they appeared, seemingly having fallen from the skies.

One of them was the man from Genoa, the manager of the Imperial Lottery, who, under the name Prince de Bevillacqua, had been imprisoned in Vincennes, after the discovery of the secret association called the *Grand Firmament.* The other man, known to us under the name Colqhoum, under the alias of Marquis de Samaniego, and more recently under that of Salvador Arbib, was at the moment, the Marquis de Saint-Faust, former privateer and founder of the abominable association of the *Brothers of Death.* The Emperor, after having him brought before him, had sent him to Charenton.[86]

In that asylum, where his active and energetic intelligence made him too inconvenient and too unlikely a guest, his stay hadn't been long. Shortly afterwards, he had been sent to rejoin the man from Genoa in the dungeons of Vincennes. There, the two men, so well made to understand each other, developed a close friendship. Returned to freedom by the Restoration, which had opened the doors of the State prisons, they

---

[86] See note 11. Also refer to Volume 2.

had temporarily stopped in Paris. There, they were waiting for a new set of adventures to be thrown into their life, that would make a career of the satanic imaginations in which they excelled, and for which, we have seen, they had a ever-present instinct.

One morning, the Prince de Bevillacqua had said to the Marquis:

"A propos of nothing, the other day, I encountered that Negro that, in the past, had been in my service. He told me something strange. On the field of the battle for Paris, he had found, half-dead and disguised as a Russian officer, that merchant of human flesh who, in Livorno, took Lorenza Feliciani's daughter off my hands.[87] The funny thing is that his wounds have been cared for by one of our former acquaintances, that man from Malta whom you had branded in London, and whom I, in Paris, almost killed with the torture of Ugolino."[88]

"Eh!" answered the Marquis, "that information is important, and something can be built on it."

"Do you think so? Even if we have the skin of this Matiphous, what will that bring us?"

---

[87] See Volume 2, page 225.

[88] Count Ugolino della Gherardesca (c.1220-1289), Count of Donoratico, was an Italian nobleman, politician and naval commander. He was frequently accused of treason and features prominently in Dante's *Divine Comedy*. Dante places him and his betrayer, Archbishop Ruggieri, who left him to starve to death, in the ice of the second ring of the lowest circle of the Inferno, which is reserved for betrayers of kin, country, guests, and benefactors. Ugolino's punishment involves his being entrapped in ice up to his neck in the same hole with Ruggieri. Ugolino is constantly gnawing at Ruggieri's skull. The reference is to Matiphous having been walled up after discovering the role of the Prince de Bevillacqua in the *Grand Firmament* secret society dedicated to overthrowing all governments.

"It's not a question of that," answered Saint-Faust. "I no longer have the least rancor against that poor devil."

"Is it then the slave merchant Britannicus that you would judge it proper to do something to? As for me, I don't have any great inclination for that, although my former servant, tried to persuade me that his presence in Paris should worry me a great deal."

"Far from annoying you, I believe, on the contrary, that he could be useful to you, if, through him, what happened to the child could be learned!"

To that insight, Bevillacqua answered:

"I don't see the great benefit..."

"If we could really get in touch with Lorenza Feliciani, your wife, don't you think that, in our hands, such a fortune-teller could become an instrument of value? As I've told you, you didn't know how to deal with that woman, the widow of Cagliostro, the confidant of all his secrets. With a gentler hand than yours, she would have sounded less empty."

"Let's go see her then," answered the man from Genoa, who, in every situation, always deferred to the Marquis. "Britannicus knows that she entered a religious order. He gave me the address."

"Yes, we will go see her, bringing her good news. Between you and her, the past wasn't exactly rosy. I repeat, we can do something if, by means of the man from Livorno, we could give her news of the girl you kidnapped for him."

The same day, the two friends went to Matiphous' house. His address had been carefully pointed out by the Britannicus, the former servant of the Prince of Bevillacqua. Major Tomboff had just left for his rendezvous with his witnesses and a whole arsenal. Curious, like most of his colleagues, Matiphous' concierge had seen the swords, a box of pistols, and, suspecting a duel, he had arranged to overhear the address given to the carriage driver: *the Minimes, in the Vincennes woods.*

After that, two well-dressed gentlemen had come to inquire about a Russian Major who lived with the surgeon. What would have been the point for a man who took so much trouble to find out a secret to not sell it when such a convenient opportunity presented itself?

"The Devil!" shouted Saint-Faust, after learning the truth "what if he's the one who is going to duel and someone else's going to kill him for us?"

Our men immediately had themselves driven to Vincennes, a rather frequent theater for duels. Six men who arrive at a thicket at the same time and whose hands hold dueling weapons are always bound to be noticed by someone, and, what's more, that person will easily guess why they have assembled. Closer and closer, asking successively a road worker, a little boy throwing rocks at birds' nests, and a hunter having good luck, the two accomplices followed the traces of the men they were looking for. Rummaging around a little in the bushes, they came right to the place chosen for the duel.

Approaching one of the Comte's witnesses politely and already warned by Bevillacqua that their man, Matiphous, wasn't present, the Marquis asked:

"Could I please ask you if you are expecting here a Russian Major?"

"What business is that of yours?" responded the Comte, taking charge of the response.

"We have learned," replied Saint-Faust, "that he was today discharging an affair of honor in the Vincennes woods. He has information that is important to us and we would like to talk to him before the duel in case something happens to him."

"Go away with your subtleties!" answered the Comte. "Don't you think I can't see through you?"

"I don't know that there were any subtleties in my question."

"That good! That's good!" said the Comte with the greatest disdain.

"But, Monsieur," Saint-Faust then asked, "who do you think we are?"

"People always ready to get involved in something they know nothing about. You can very well see that there is no

179

Russian Major here. I am General Comte de Chandeville. And if Monsieur the Prefect of Police, has something to take up with me, he can call on me at my residence, which is not hard to find. As for you, amusing fellows, be off and leave us in peace."

"Police agents! Us? Coming to interrupt your duel!" exclaimed Saint-Faust, preventing the man from Genoa from talking. "You are not, my dear Comte, a good reader of faces. Far from being part of that nefarious administration, we are, on the contrary, one of its victims. Only a few days ago, we left a dungeon near here where we were being held prisoners of the State by Imperial tyranny. You will, I think, regret your unwelcome attitude when you find out that you are speaking to Prince of Bevillacqua and to Marquis de Saint-Faust."

"Bevillacqua," retorted the Comte brutally, "that's a very honorable name you are pronouncing!"

"What do you mean?" exclaimed the man from Genoa.

"Wait, my dear fellow," the Marquis continued, "the conversation is with me. I know how to answer for both of us, and to continue in a tone which seems better suited to the Comte's temperament, I will have the honor to tell him that he is an out-and-out insolent!"

"Gentlemen, gentlemen!"' shouted the Comte's witnesses, trying to get between them.

"No," continued the Marquis, "but the youth of today think everything is permitted them. That adolescent seems to me to need a lesson I am very willing to give to him."

Angered beyond control by that cutting irony addressed to his pretentions of youth, apparent in all his person, the Comte de Chandeville, if he hadn't been held back, would have been led to the utmost violence, even more so because the frail appearance of the Marquis was an encouragement to lay hands on him. Seeing that threatening movement, Saint-Faust grabbed one of the combat swords that lay on the ground near a box of pistols, and taking the *en garde* position, said

"At your pleasure, my little child," he shouted ironically.

"I am at your service, my dear fellow," the Comte responded, motioning to his old *valet de chambre* to pass him the other sword. And he also took the *en garde* position. Then, as the Comte's witnesses appeared to want to come between them, Bevillacqua said:

"Messieurs, let them continue. There is perfect justification for this duel."

"Absolutely," said the Comte. "Besides, don't you see that it was written that I was supposed to kill a man today?"

The two opponents crossed swords for a rather long time without there being a strike, before having to suspend the duel to take a breather. At the second resumption, no one had any longer any thoughts of interfering. As impromptu as the encounter had been, it had finally taken a normal look. On both sides, the marvelous ability of the two combatants seemed to put away any idea of serious danger. In that way, the duel became nothing more than a show of the use of weapons. The second engagement having produced no more result than the first, the Marquis said:

"We won't do anything to each other with swords; we are equal in strength. But there are pistols over there. Would you like to use that more incisive method?"

"With all my heart," answered the Comte.

At that point, there was a new attempt by his witnesses to put an end to that affair, where, one of the two said it really seemed to want to tempt God. After that, there was another complication. The Prince de Bevillacqua wanted to take the Marquis' place, since he was the one who had been insulted.

"Then load the weapons," said Saint-Faust, without paying any attention to the Prince's claim.

The weapons were ready; the two adversaries, that nothing could turn from their murderous intentions, let themselves, as the only concession, be positioned at a distance of thirty paces from each other. That precaution hardly bothered them. They were confident in their shooting skills. At a signal that the Prince de Bevillacqua was charged with giving, clapping his hands three times, the two weapons were fired. '

Struck in the lower stomach, the Comte de Chandeville collapsed, following forward. As for the Marquis, without touching him, the bullet had merely blown off his hat. But behind him, in the bushes, they heard a cry of distress as if the projectile had found another victim. While the winner hurried toward the Comte, Bevillacqua entered the thick woods to find out what kind of misfortune had happened.

"Lorenza Feliciani!" he said to the Marquis, when he returned to the group of which the Comte de Chandeville was now the center. "She was killed by the pistol shot meant for you!"

"But who could have brought her here?" Saint-Faust asked.

"Probably that miserable Britannicus!" responded the man from Genoa. "I thought I saw him in the distance running away on foot."

"Messieurs," Saint-Faust said to the Comte's witnesses, "with the help of his valet, you can carry the wounded man to his carriage. As for us, other cares now require our attention."

And followed by Bevillacqua, the Marquis walked into the bushes. The man from Genoa hadn't been mistaken. The deplorable end of Lorenza Feliciani could really be attributed to the actions of Britannicus. Not finding in his former master any enthusiasm for doing away with the supposed trafficker in human flesh, he had had the idea of taking Georgiana's mother out of the convent where she had retired, in order to throw her like a lioness onto her daughter's ravisher.

Matiphous had led the Negro right to his door. More than anyone, Britannicus had the opportunity to be informed by the concierge, since he was one of his acquaintances. The unhappy mother had immediately wanted to go to Vincennes. Following almost the same path as Saint-Faust and his friend, she was near reaching the place of the duel, just as the shot fired by the Count de Chandeville hit her.

That evening, when Matiphous arrived at the Comte's residence, he found the nobleman had died of his wound, which he has survived by only a few hours.

"What is most terrible, Monsieur," said the old valet, overwhelming him with surprise at all the details he recounted, telling him about the encounter in which his master had succumbed, "is that that miserable woman, while Monsieur le Comte was getting himself killed for her, has followed an English Lord back to London, almost as if she knew that my master, like all of previous lovers, wouldn't come back alive from that duel."

Returning to his lodgings, Matiphous was greeted by very different news. Major Tomboff had just shot himself with a pistol. The stigma that his brother's actions had cast on their name, coming to be known everywhere, had, without a doubt, as the newspapers say, carried him to that ultimate expression of despair.

That day, Georgiana had not been outdone in her fatality. A few hours later, while she was running away with her new lover, three victims, one of them her mother, were added to her necrology! An admirable purveyor of death, she was, to quote La Fontaine: "*Capable, en un jour, d'enrichir l'Achéron.*"[89]

XIII. The Strongbox

"And you, dark-skinned fellow, why are you here?"

It was in a sad residence, in the Rochefort prison, that that question was addressed to Britannicus, about six months after the events narrated in the preceding chapter. And we must add that the involuntary murder of Lorenza Feliciani, Madame de Bevillacqua, had absolutely nothing to do with the sad change with which the life of the miserable man had just been complicated.

---

[89] *Capable in one day of enriching the Acheron.* Quoting Jean de La Fontaine (1621-1695), *Fables* VII, 1, writing about the plague. The Acheron, in Greek Mythology, is a river which flowed into Hades.

Despite the care he had taken to hide all explanations, in selfishly leaving the victim even before knowing if all life in her was completely extinguished, in a moment, he saw himself in the hands of the law, which naturally asked him to account for that woman who had come with him. Afterward, his account of the incident, confirmed by the Comte de Chandeville's witnesses, had him soon released from official suspicion. Perhaps it wouldn't have been the same for the Marquis de Saint-Faust and the Prince de Bevillacqua, who were also wanted by the authorities. But, like prudent men who knew that their past was more than suspicious, our two gentlemen, after having made sure that Lorenza Feliciani was indeed dead, hadn't stayed long in Paris. We will leave them to their nomadic existence for the moment, and we won't have to wait long for them to reappear soon in our narrative.

As for Britannicus, he himself is going to tell us how he was conducted into the dismal place where we now encounter him. But first of all, we must place under the eyes of the reader a character only seen in the earlier portions of our story. An audacious criminal, that man, under the ignoble pseudonym of Rempailleux, had been introduced to us as the chief of the famous gang of the *Chauffeurs,*[90], stationed in the Orgères forest, and in London when, about to deliver him to his peculiar brand of justice, the Marquis de Samaniego, had unfolded his biography before the somber clients of the *Sleepers' Club.*

Having escaped from the terrible claws of the Marquis, Dulac, a.k.a. Rempailleux, had returned to France, where he had again declared war on society. He had conducted that war with so much ability and good luck that, right to the end of the Empire, he had gone totally unpunished. But in an encounter less fortunate, that will be told in a moment, his lucky star had abandoned him, and he had finally become acquainted with

---

[90] See Volume 1, page 149. The *Chauffeurs* received their name from their method of torturing their victims; they put the victim's feet to the fire to force from them information about their hidden wealth.

the living hell of prison where he had been condemned to serve a sentence of twenty years.

There, by his good behavior, by the superiority of his background, by his intelligence, by the money with which he was always abundantly supplied, without the jailers ever being able to find out how he procured it, and finally by the never-ending elegance and comfort with which he surrounded himself, despite the rigor of the rules, he had gained such consideration from his companions in shackles that he had tacitly constructed for himself a kind of prison royalty status.

At the arrival of those newly incarcerated, surrounded by what he called his "court" and "high dignitaries," he had the habit of passing his new subjects in review. Making them appear one by one before him, he interrogated them about their earlier life and the reasons for their condemnation. It was he who had asked Britannicus:

"And you, dark-skinned fellow, why are you here?"

"I?" responded the Negro. "I'm not here for what I did, I'm here for what I didn't do."

That answer didn't seem very clear to Rempailleux, but his *Minister of the Navy,* an old *Négrier*[91] who was there for having sold "Black flesh" by the pound, and was more up to date than he was about the Creole jargon, explained to him that the new arrival claimed to be the victim of a judicial error. Britannicus had been punished for a crime he hadn't committed, while an act for which he had admitted his guilt had received no punishment from the law.

"Lady Justice," Rempailleux then said, "often has similar distractions, but in that circumstance, what caused this blunder?"

"I didn't steal; I wanted to kill, but couldn't."

"Eh!" said the criminal king, "I like his complacency. Monsieur disdains being a thief and aspires to murder! Would it be indiscreet, my good man, to ask what was that failed murder?"

---

[91] A Negro who sold other Negroes into slavery.

185

"It happened in Florence," Britannicus responded, arranging the truth in variations almost like Bazile[92] did with the Proverbs, "I was much loved by an English woman, a great Lady. She birthed a little Negro child; her husband was very mad and had me beaten."

"You're looking at a fellow," Rempailleux said to his court, laughing, "who's allowed himself to hunt in white territory! Then what happened? You wanted to kill her husband?"

"Old husband got very dead all by himself, alone in Scotland, so the English woman went to Paris and found me, Britannicus, one day when I was pulling teeth at Saint-Sulpice."

"Are you saying you were a dentist in the out-of-doors?"

"Yes. I have a strong hand and big muscles; I also treat corns on the feet '"

"I understand; you're a dentist-pedicurist, and then the beautiful lady found you where you were practicing your trade?"

"She asked me to kill a man she wanted to revenge herself from, and if I did, she'd give me my child back, with lots of money for me to return to my country"'

"And you, being a good father, accepted her offer?"

"Yes, because I'm crazy about the child, so I found the man she wanted me to kill; he was an old master of mine, and I knew that he went out every morning, before daylight, to go to his surgery."

"What do you mean, 'his surgery?' "

"Yes," said the Negro, with a grotesque pantomime, "where he cuts off arms, legs, but never a head."

"I see. So he's a surgeon."

"Yes. I prepared to knife him in the back, but as I followed him, I realized he wasn't going to the surgery, but to

---

[92] From *The Barber of Seville*, by Pierre-Augustin Caron de Beaumarchais, Act IV, Scene I, Bazile, speaking to Bartholo begins the proverb, "One good turn deserves..." and before Bartholo can finish, he quickly adds, "...that I make use of it."

post some letters at the office on Rue Verdelet, and there I see a sentry box so I hide, but there's no soldier there, and when I looked again, my man had disappeared."

"Wait," said Rempailleux, "let me figure this out. You followed your man to the Post Office on Rue Verdelet, where you saw a sentry box fitted into the wall in which there was no guard on duty; your man entered it and disappeared. Is that correct?'

"Yes," said Britannicus.

"That's clever," remarked one of the listeners. "There must be a secret door; otherwise you'd have to believe in witchcraft."

"I," Britannicus said in a firm tone, "do not believe in witches. So I go inside the sentry box to look for a secret passage."

"And did you find it?" asked Rempailleux, adding for those assembled, "these devilish Negroes; they're born tinkerers; there's nothing cleverer than their hands."

"I did!" answered Britannicus with confidence "and place behind it was rather dark."

"And then?'" asked the questioner, seeming to take an interest in the story.

"Then, I saw a door that I pushed, and I found a very long corridor with another door at the end."

"Three doors then. And I assumed you pushed that one like the others"'

"Yes, but when I did, I heard some kind of loud music, ding, dong, ding, dong! Then the lights went on. Several men ran towards me, ten or twelve. They were stronger than I and took me to a room which was dark, and until the evening, I was given nothing to eat."

"Well, well, my boy, your story is becoming very dramatic. Finally, when the evening came, did they bring you some food to chew on?'

"Nothing at all! A man with lantern and a mask on his face eventually showed and ordered me in a booming voice to follow him!'

"That sounds worse than the Counsel of the Ten[93] or the Holy Inquisition," remarked an erudite man in the group.

"Yes, something like that," said Rempailleux, seeming to consider an idea, "but do go on, my dark-skinned friend."

"I obeyed and followed him. We traversed many passages. Finally, the man opened a door and I saw another big room. He gave me a small lantern and a little key and said to me: 'You can get out by that door over there, no another time, don't be so curious.' And then he left."

"Well! And what did you do then?" asked Rempailleux.

"I didn't know what to do. What if he'd only been playing with me?"

"There's one smart n***," said the king of the convicts, speaking to those around him. "He smelled the trap that very certainly they had laid for him. And so?"

"And so, after a while, when I don't try the key, three men came in; two had pistols and the third a candle, and the last man said to me: 'Your goose is cooked.' And he picked up a little chisel and a big iron tool that were lying on the ground, and he showed to the others the key and the lantern that ere in my hands, and pointed to an open strongbox that had been cracked open."

"Ah!" said one of the listeners, "there was a strongbox?"

"Yes. On it, it said: *money transfers.*"

"What a set-up! How well managed!" Rempailleux remarked. "Especially with an innocent like him. Then I suppose they arrested you, took you to jail where they gave you something to eat, and from there, a few days later, you were dragged before a magistrate?"

"Before a magistrate, yes," Britannicus repeated.

"There, you told him your story, without saying, of course, that you were trying to kill your former master. You saw that particular entrance in the wall and naturally that made you curious."

---

[93] One of the governing bodies of the Republic of Venice from 1310-1797. Their meetings were often very secret.

"No, I didn't say that; I said that my master went out at nights, and I was curious to know where he went."

"That's an even better story; but I bet they didn't really believe you."

"The magistrate said I was lying."

"Then you were brought to the Assizes Court and those good gentlemen that had arrested you testified on their honor and conscience that you had forced open the strongbox. How much time did they hit you with?"

"Five years," Britannicus answered.

"Breaking and entering, at night, with a false key, into an inhabited house, that should have deserved more than that. But they were cautious to apply only the minimum, one more proof that it was a trap. And I think I know what hand did it to you."

"If you will say, I'm curious to know."

"Later, my boy," Rempailleux answered. "I have to ruminate a little on your case, but the story is not any less pleasant. That doesn't happen every day, Messieurs," he added, addressing the assembly, I recommend our new comrade to you. He deserves all your esteem and all your help."

"The story is rather nice," said an old galley slave, puffing on his pipe, "but it's not the same as your own business with the strongbox. Tell us a little about that strongbox, for these gentlemen just arrived. Even so, we will contribute our part."

"But, my dear old fellow,"' said Rempailleux, defending himself, "I've made you listen to that story so many times."

"Oh, no, you haven't; oh, no, you haven't," they shouted from every direction.

"All right, my men," said the king of the criminals, "if that's all that amuses you..."

And he began thus:

"At the time when we were *chauffeurs* in the Orgères forest, one evening at night fall, being hidden in a clump of bushes, an American and his wife in a pretty carriage drawn by post horses passed by. As I was waiting to give the signal to attack until the travelers were a little further under the big trees, it happened that an imbecile in the area, a man named Vandel, whom I had overwhelmed with my benefits by not dropping him ten times when I had him in my carbine's sights, came to tell them that the forest wasn't safe, especially since a storm was about to break out, and offered to let them spend the night in their house.

"In the morning, in a well-chosen spot in the forest, I again picked up the ones I had missed. But they had nothing worth taking; just twenty-five silver Louis and some clothes. Being distrustful, the people had sent their baggage on ahead and I was feeling myself robbed when the American said to me:

" 'There's great profit for you here. You might be able to earn fifteen thousand pounds if you would take on yourself the job of stealing the last little boy from the man named Vandel, that man who took us in last night. Only the business must remain between you and me, and no one must ever know what happened to the child. That's a gift I want to pass on to my wife.'

"No sooner said than done. The child was stolen as vengeance for Vandel's having kept me from my clientele. The American took delivery of it at Vendôme, where he had set up a rendezvous with me, and put fifteen thousand pounds in my hand.

"Shortly thereafter, my band was turned upside down and I was forced to clear out for foreign lands, where I spent quite a bit of time. Finally, back in France, and probably about fifteen years later, I met my American again in these circumstances:

"One evening, I was in a bar with Virginie Leturc, my former mistress, a good woman whom I've had the misfortune to lose since then. Reading a newspaper, I saw an article that read: *Wealthy American has just bought a strongbox that re-*

portedly can't be broken into from the famous safe-maker Fichet.[94]"

"There is no strongbox that can't be broken into," said one of the convicts in a hoarse voice.

"That's well known," he was answered from several sides, "but safe makers like to advertize that."

"This famous strongbox that can't be broken into," Rempailleux continued, *"costs seven thousand francs and is a work of art that can't be opened except with an ingenious combinations of letters. It is built in such a way as to kill on the spot anyone who tries to force it open."*

"That would make me sweat!" exclaimed the convict who had already interrupted Rempailleux. "As if there weren't enough difficulties!"

"Let him tell the story," shouted the rest impatiently.

"Further, the man who has acquired it," Rempailleux continued, *"has the wherewithal to fill it. He is the terror of gambling houses and no later than the day before yesterday, he broke the bank at 129.*[95]

"The Leturc girl, on reading that article, said:

" 'That's an object that would be good to have, filled with its contents, but you're not gallant enough to acquire it and come place it at my feet.'

" 'We'll have to see about that,' I answered.

"Three days later, having studied the layout, with my pal Chenu, nicknamed called *Classic,* I found myself at the Place Royale in the American's bedroom, having gotten in through the chimney. I was already making off with the strongbox under my arm when I heard someone coming into the room

---

[94] Alexandre Fichet (1799-1862) began building safes in 1825 and, in 1840, produced the first fire-resistant safe. His company continued its operation until it merged with the Bauche Company in 1967. It continues its operations worldwide today.

[95] A variation of *piquet,* an early 16th-century trick-taking card game.

next door. There was no time to get up the chimney by which I had come in, so, in order to not to raise the alarm, I put the strongbox back on the table from which I had removed it and I hid myself behind the curtains. I reasoned that, if it came to it, I could *refrigerate* the unwelcome visitor, although it would be better for me not to put *raisiné* [96] on my bread.

"The inopportune man was none other than the American, not too much changed, although a little more grey.

" 'Well!' I said to myself when I recognized him, 'It's still part of my game to rob that man here!'

"His first movement when he entered was to upset me by putting a pair of pistols, which he took out of his pockets, on the table near the strongbox, the unwelcome fellow! I had only a *twenty-two* [97] to fight with. I thought that the man wasn't very happy, because he kept pacing back and forth, while talking to himself.

" 'This can't go on,' he said, 'that woman is beautiful and young, and close to her is a real good-for-nothing, cold as marble. What's life like then?'

" 'Ah! Bah!' I thought to myself. 'Is he thinking of killing himself? Kill yourself, my fine fellow, if that's your pleasure. It's certainly not me who will stop you.'

"After that, the sad man took a little key and opened the strongbox, which was glistening with gold, jewels, and banknotes, to which he added more gold and more notes that filled his pockets. My hand grasping my knife was itching.

" 'Must be smart, however, and see what's coming,' I said to myself.

"His nice job done, the worthy man began to write and then he turned in my direction. If he had turned his back away, I would have been able to come out of my hiding place without being seen; I wouldn't have risked getting caught.

---

[96] *Raisiné*: lit. grape juice, but used here to mean blood; from time to time, Rabou uses criminals' slang which he translate it into ordinary French within the text.

[97] A knife.

"His letter written, the American placed it in the box and took out the key. Next, he began another epistle. Having sealed it, he called his servant and, giving him the key and the letter, he said:

" 'For the Magistrate.'

"Then, he locked the door, poured himself a large glass of rum, and began walking up and down again.

"All those *postures* took a long time and annoyed me.

" 'Would he never finish?' I asked myself. 'Let him make his decision or I'm going to make mine!'

"Suddenly, I saw him pick up one of the pistols, examined the gun, make another turn or two with the pistol, then, gently putting the barrel in his mouth, *Bang*! My fellow rolled to the floor. Me, in the middle of the fumes, I rushed for the treasure, took it lightly under my arm, although it was rather heavy, and began to climb up the chimney, with the thought of how much time I had before they broke down the door and saw that the bird had flown the coop.

"Reaching the roof, that was not all. I had to go down on the other side. The discharge of the pistol had been loud, and had drawn imbeciles to the windows from one side and the other. If even my shadow was detected, they would sound the alarm, surround the house, and even the adjacent streets. The first thing to do, then, was to hide. Not far from me, in a house adjacent to that of the American, I saw an attic window open. No light. Coming near it, I heard no sound. What a stroke of luck! I decided to edge myself in there.

"After a moment, my eyes having adjusted to the obscurity, I recognized that I was in a painter's studio. While snooping about, a brick fell into my hand. I had the nerve to light a candle that made it easy for me to see a space between the wall and the wood framework, because that lodging was a real loft. That space was a black and deep nook where the strongbox could be stored like a jewel. To leave it there and come back to pick it up later at my leisure, seemed to me the most competent thing to do.

193

"I had hardly finished my little gambling den, when I heard footsteps on the stairway. I grabbed a letter that had fallen in a corner. It carried the name and address of the person whose attic I was in: *Monsieur Levillain, Artist, Rue Royale-Saint-Antoine.*

"I took care to extinguish the candle with my fingers, wet with saliva, so that it wouldn't give off fumes or odor. I went back to where I had started, which was now only a short walk since I was no longer weighed down and had my arms free. Without any trouble, I came to a house which was in the process of being upgraded, went down on the mason's scaffolding that I had already used to come up. That worked so well that, an instant later, I was walking away, strolling, my hands in my pockets, on the pavement."

"Well played!" said the old criminal who had asked for the story.

Rempailleux himself seemed to have authorized the interruption by instinctively stopping, as a storyteller, teasingly at the culminating point of his narration.

"The next day," the King of the Criminals continued, "my pal Chenu, a.k.a. *Classique*, who had done nothing but procure the information, while I did all the work, came to learn the news. He began strongly criticizing me, telling me it was badly managed, that the strongbox would be taken out by the painter. And finally suggesting that I let him see my find so that he could take out his share, he got me so hot that I hit him and threw him down my stairs.

"After that, he went to denounce me to the *rousse,*[98] which it wasn't too hard to do. Out of friendship, I had told him the name and address of the artist. He had said nothing about that to them, and, while I was being questioned, his idea was to go and take out the box. His way of sharing would have been to keep everything. But the thing didn't go exactly his way. Given his history, the police put their hands on him at the same time as they did me. And two days later, my good fellow

---

[98] The police.

was found dead in his bed of apoplexy. His well-known liking for absinthe had caused that unpleasant fact.

"At this juncture, the interrogations continued. I behaved as if I didn't know what they wanted to talk to me about: no proof, seen by no one, no body, I was on my way to being released, when one of the policemen recognized me as Rempailleux, the notorious *chauffeur* condemned to death in '96. I was handed to the Criminal Court to serve my sentence, mandated *in absentia*, but the members of my gang hadn't testified against me; I was like a god to them; most of the witnesses had died or disappeared. My affairs were like smells which, with time, evaporate. In short, instead of being condemned to death, I was only condemned to twenty years of hard labor, and here I am!

"After a short time, I sent a letter to the Leturc girl, in which I gave her all the clues, knowing that she was well situated to get the strongbox out of its hiding place, and with the cash that she would find inside, she could easily arrange to help me escape.

"Virginie answered me that she had gone to the studio, but that there was nothing there, neither the painter, nor my strongbox. I got to my little informant, and found that the Artist who'd stayed there had moved out just at the time I had visited him. Being down and out at that time, he has since then become rich. There was no more doubt; my *fourgat* [99] had appropriated the contents of my strongbox. But he shouldn't have played that game with me for one instant. Not intending to take root here, the few extra years more that would be given to me were not such as to bother me very much. So I denounced myself as having pinched the strongbox, but at the same time, I also reported the behavior of the artist Levillain. Given the letter that I had taken and put in a safe place, and which proved by its post office stamp mark the date of the affair, said artist was implicated with me as having knowingly received a stolen object, since all of Paris had known about the

---

[99] Fence.

American's suicide and theft, and that gave him a nice little case of complicity.

Sur la planche à pain,[100] I charged my man with having played a major role in the affair. He defended himself like an old shoe. Being asked why he had moved at that time, how he had suddenly come into so much money, he began by saying that a great foreign lord had come to order a painting from him and had paid in advance. As for the great lord, he couldn't name him, and he hadn't delivered the painting. When the *curieux* [101] get hold of a man, they strip off more than his shirt. They learned then that, at the time of the theft, several times a week, the young artist left his dwelling between two and three o'clock in the morning. Where did he go? What was his purpose in roaming around at night? It was suspicious; but they were never able to get an explanation from him.

"He was then condemned and returned to jail with me as his companion. I have since studied him closely, and I don't mind admitting that, in denouncing him, I now very much believe that I made a mistake. From time to time, he receives letters that the comrades of the first division, where he is locked up, have been charged with procuring me. The writing is that of a woman; he is told to be patient and that, one day or another, she will get him out of prison. This is proof that his nightly escapades were about a *girofle* [102] whom he didn't want to compromise. Here, nothing to complain about; a superb conduct! Because of his talents, he could have been employed in the offices of the administration; but he refused. He could have been made *Barberot* or *Paryot*.[103] Instead, he answered:

---

[100] In the law court.

[101] Judges.

[102] A beloved woman.

[103] Author's note: Barber or bookkeeper, two jobs very much sought after because they are lucrative and enable one to avoid the hardest drudgery.

" 'I will go like the others to the fatigue. To accept a favor would be to recognize that they had a right to condemn me.'

"What's more, doesn't bother anyone with his innocence; he's not happy, but he doesn't complain. He's not at all proud; he's helpful to everyone and, having painted the portrait of several men to send to their women, he has never been willing to accept money. Me, in the time he was part of my division, I wanted once to explain myself to him. But he said in a tone that didn't make me comfortable:

" 'Don't talk to me,. You have destroyed my life. If you believe I have done what you accused me of, how can you speak to me? If, on the contrary, your denunciation didn't come from the depth of your conscience, for me, you are the worst of miscreants.'

"That didn't keep him, one day when I had drunk too much and fallen into the water, from bravely jumping in and saving my life. So, I feel myself a little indebted to him and there is nothing I am not ready to do to make up for my blunder, because I'm now very sure that he's not the type of man to have appropriated my strongbox."

"But then, where did that satanic strongbox go?" exclaimed the old criminal who never got tired of hearing the story.

"I know," said Britannicus.

"You scoundrel, you know who stole it?" asked Rempailleux, taking the Negro by the arm and holding him in a convulsive grip.

"My Master, the one I wanted to kill, hid it from me, but I knew he had that box, but couldn't open it; I saw everything through the keyhole."

"So you saw your master try to open that box and he hid it from you?"

"Yes, he hid it, but I saw it,"

"How was that box made?"

Britannicus first gave a rather nebulous description, but by means of detailed questioning, Rempailleux managed to eventually get a close to accurate description.

"That's certainly it," said the king of the prisoners, "and what's the name of that mean bastard?"

"He called himself Deschamps, but I know that his real name is Matiphous."

"Matiphous!" exclaimed Rempailleux. "I know him! I found myself in London with him when he was *brancheur* [104]there. They even wanted to hang me, but he turned the job down. Ah, well, it's even worse for him than for someone else to act that way toward an old friend. But we'll settle that," he added, rubbing his hands together, "and we'll laugh!"

A hyena, licking his lips in front of a prey, if hyenas could speak, wouldn't have said that "we'll laugh" in any other tone.

XIV. A Gentleman with Several Decorations

At about the same time than the scene we've just recounted took place in Rochefort, a letter bearing the superscription: *Extremely Confidential* was addressed to the Director General of the Police in Paris. That functionary had replaced the minister of the same department, who had been dismissed by the Restoration Government.

Monsieur le Directeur General, someone had written, *A great judicial error has been committed. Condemned through conventional propriety to remain for a long time an accomplice, I would not forgive myself today, when I can speak, and would not delay by even one hour the reparations that must be offered.*

My first thought was to ask you for an audience; but in addition to the fact that your multiple duties might make me wait for days, forced to make a public confession, I feel myself

---

[104] Hangman.

to have more courage in writing rather than speaking. Beside, in voluntarily giving up a revelation when it was possible for me to remain silent, it seems to me that this exhibits from my part a lack of reservation and a confidence in the loyalty of your character which, perhaps, will recommend me to you.

In 1809, I was barely seventeen years-old when I was married to the Baron de Pringy, the famous member of the Academy of Sciences. Wealthy, a Counselor of State, surrounded with immense respect, M. de Pringy, despite his age, would have appeared to be an enviable bridegroom if his preoccupation with his scientific work had not so distracted him; he was like La Bruyère's Menalque,[105] whose absent mindedness and strange behavior all Paris society knew about.

Outside his mathematics, a veritable child with gray hair, M. de Pringy, when he married me, was doing less a considered act than making a thoughtless concession to the influence to one of the matchmakers of society that make it a kind of profession to constantly attack the liberty of old bachelors. A detail that I can very well tell here, after the ridiculous rumors, will sum up all the strange behavior which that reunion reserved for me. M. de Pringy spent his wedding night in his study, occupied with a problem which had come into his mind right at the doorway of our nuptial bedchamber.

Apart from the fact that he too often forgot having married me, M. de Pringy, in the eyes of society, could be considered as an adorable husband. Good, affectionate, when differential and integral calculus left him some free time, not limiting either my expenses or those of the household, which I was free to administer. Even giving me, in my contacts and in my actions, a liberty pushed right to the verge of incaution, for a man who saw nothing, who understood nothing, who took part in nothing, vis à vis a woman who had not fallen in love with him—wouldn't that have been, for me, the realization of an

---

[105] See Remark VI, Chapter XI of Jean de La Bruyère (1645-1696)'s *Characters* for a portrait of the absent-minded Menalque.

ideal situation? Nevertheless, the full possession of conjugal dictatorship didn't leave me any less without sadness and a sense of enormous emptiness.

There were, however, not opportunities lacking for me to fill that emptiness. Constantly faced with audacious activities that the blindness and lack of concern of M. de Pringy seemed to encourage, I spent my life denying myself my own desires and avoiding the incessant traps placed under my feet. Finally, the eternal widowhood of my heart threw me into a fantasy for which the saddest denouement was reserved. At Charany, near Claye-en-Brie, we had a house where we went to spend the summer season every year, not because it was a pleasant property, but because it was close. We entertained almost no one there. Given my nature, gay and laughing, that solitude often weighed heavily on me. To ward off boredom, I took refuge at a neighborhood farm, the only neighbor in that country of wolves. The mistress of the farm was a woman who had received some education and who warmly sympathized with my sadness. One day she had the bizarre idea of taking me, disguised as a farm girl, to a festival in a village in the area where no one knew me. She was going to pass me off as her niece and promised me a prodigious success with the Tircis [106] of the place.

There, to my misfortune, I encountered a young Parisian who, despite my disguise, or perhaps because of it, fell suddenly in love with me. He danced only with me, showered me with compliments and thoughtfulness and, thanks to the realism I put into my role, he remained persuaded that he had given all that attention to a mere country flirt. As we were separating, his insistence on seeing me again was so pressing and so warm that it created in me the unfortunate idea of giving a follow-up to my masked ball.

Without consenting to fix a day for him, I told him that, from time to time, I accompanied my aunt when she went to

---

[106] Name of a shepherd in *Tircis & Amarande*, Book VIII, #13, in Jean de la Fontaine's *Fables*.

Paris to sell her produce, and looking carefully, he would find me on the tiled floors of Les Halles. A week later, seated on the farm mistress' cart, among her cabbages and green peas. I made at night a foolish excursion to Paris. The poor man in love must have come to lie in wait every night for the opportunity, because immediately, in the middle of that ocean of vegetables and country people, he picked me out. Seated on a basket, at the foot of a mountain of asparagus, I spent two or three hours listening to assurances of the most ardent, and at the same time, the most respectful of loves.

Always under the same conditions, two more encounters followed. During one of them, my young painter—because I had an artist as a suitor—with unbelievable joy, told me that the most unhoped-for stroke of luck had just come into his life. Until then, he had had to fight against obscurity and poverty, but his talent was beginning to be recognized. A great lord, having noticed some of his works at the last exposition, had written him, ordering a painting for which he had paid him the most generous sum in the world, and, without giving his name, had sent him the price in advance. I laughed to myself upon receiving the confidence of that honor because it was I who had arranged to pay him from my little savings. But to my pretty adventure, Monsieur, followed a terrible awakening!

One night, my protégé didn't come to the accustomed rendezvous. I thought that he was sick; then, having no news of him, I wondered if the embellishment that I had made to his artist's life might not have egotistically distracted him from his great passion. In short, dominated by worry, I sent the farm woman, my confident, to find out. At the less poverty-stricken domicile that his new comfortable situation had allowed him to exchange for his attic, my emissary was greeted with horrible news. The man she was seeking information about had been arrested a few weeks before, accused of theft, and no one had seen him since.

Soon, a newspaper report of a criminal trial made me understand the whole extent of his misfortune. He was accused of having appropriated a valuable strongbox that a thief, after having stolen it, had come by way of the roofs to hide in the attic room that he had just left, the window of which was open. The only precise accusation was the testimony of the criminal who, from the jail where he was incarcerated for numerous other crimes, had denounced him. But alas! My fatal kindness was going to add to the arguments in favor of the accusation. The fact that the accused man had moved just at the time the robbery had been committed, his economic status having become better—for me, nothing that couldn't be explained—but for the judges, who couldn't guess my romantic imagination, those facts must, on the contrary, take on a most unfortunate aspect, especially when, with his artist's carelessness, the unfortunate man found he had mislaid the letter which would have established the reality of the order for the painting.

I was not to be only partly disastrous for him. Following the debates of the trial, I acquired the certainty that my unhappy suitor was most of all compromised by his habit of nightly outings which I had made necessary for him. And fearing that the investigation would come to me, confronted with a charge that he could have set aside with a word, and which would produce the most decisive effect in the minds of the judges, he had the courage not to speak and to refuse to give any explanation. For my part, condemned by the respect that I owe to the name of my husband to remain an impassive spectator of that terrible judicial drama, you can understand, Monsieur, my remorse and my heartbreak.

Free today by the death of M. de Pringy to restore to the facts their true character, I would like to think that the spontaneity of a confession so harsh to my ego will carry some weight toward the rehabilitation of the condemned man. The judgments of society, I foresee, will be cruel. I go forward, nevertheless, to my duty that is the manifestation of the truth at any price. Better than anyone, Monsieur le Directeur General, with the discretionary power invested in your office, you seemed to me the best positioned in order to lend me effective help. And this help, you will accord to my repentance, and *most of all, to the chivalrous devotion which, to protect the honor of a woman, did not recoil from prison and his infamy!*

As of yesterday, I am back from Rochefort, where I first went to make myself available to my victim, who has given me his most generous pardon. His innocence, if for a moment it had been in doubt, is henceforth clearer than day for me. Ask the authorities of Rochefort; they will answer that, for everyone, Adolphe Levillain is a martyr. The man who denounced him, and with whom I didn't hesitate to have an interview, has come himself to be convinced that he made a thoughtless accusation. He even says he knows the real guilty man. He didn't wish to give me his name, claiming with that boastfulness of people of his type, that only he is capable of repairing the evil he did. I dare, therefore, Monsieur le Directeur General, to ask you to have that man come, question him, and learn from him the true author of the crime. Efforts to protect my reputation, my social position, I do not insist on any, especially if they must have the effect of retarding by even only one day the deliverance of that unhappy man who is in prison. To return him to honor, to liberty, that is the first interest that comes before all others, and I am appealing to your humanity, as well as to your sense of justice.

Please accept, Monsieur le Directeur General, etc., etc,

By delicacy, which is understandable, the author of that letter had not wanted to write her name as a widow; instead, she had signed her maiden name, *Esther de Vaugeois.*

Already very interested by reading that confession, the highly-placed administrator had been even more so by the conversation with the pretty penitent that he had had brought to his office. He had immediately expedited to Rochefort the order to bring to Paris the prisoner named Dulac, a.k.a. Rempailleux, and, some days later, that man was to appear before him. One morning, in the interval, the orderly in his office came to tell him that a well-dressed gentleman wearing decorations of several orders, was in the waiting room, asking for an interview. He hadn't wanted to give his name, but he claimed to have a communication of the highest importance to give to the Director General. With the Director of the Police, that method of announcing oneself is almost infallible. Order was therefore given to show in the unknown man.

Presenting himself with self-assurance and ease, after taking a seat in the chair brought forward for him the man said:

"Monsieur le Directeur, you didn't occupy the functions, I believe, that you occupy today with so much distinction at the time of the affair I wish to discuss with you. It's a question of the suicide of a rich American, from whom there was taken a strongbox containing things of considerable value."

"Excuse me," replied the Director General, "but I am very up to date on that case, which has had some repercussions, and I haven't lost sight of it."

"Very well. Monsieur, I think I am in a position to throw some further light on this matter First of all, I will tell you that, on this occasion, the law, in the case of the man who was found guilty of having received the stolen goods, strangely went astray."

"Yet there were conclusive proofs."

"Circumstantial proofs, at best," replied the unknown man. "The evidence was given by the snitch, a criminal known as Rempailleux, who testified with extraordinary fierceness. What's more, that can be explained. He was a thief whose loot had been stolen, which infuriated him to want revenge on the man he thought had absconded with said loot. Which is sad, because otherwise he isn't a bad man, and, most of all, he's a very intelligent boy who shouldn't have let himself be taken thus by appearances."

"The notes gathered from the judicial summaries," the Director General replied, "show him in fact to be a very dangerous criminal and very clever, but they don't say anything about that good fellowship that you credit him with."

"All I can say is that I saw him in prison, where I went to get information, because that case has weighed a great deal on my mind, and he seemed to me to be in despair about that blunder that he wanted to repair at any price."

"Is it in the interest of the American's family that you have become interested in this case?"

"Not at all! In the interest of the young painter, whose innocence is for me so much less in doubt since I have very precise information about the true criminal, and with your help, Monsieur, I will be very able very shortly to place him in the hands of the law."

"I thank you for the help you want to offer me, but, before we engage in some kind of reciprocal action, to whom do I have the honor of speaking?"

"To someone, my goodness, who is somewhat guilty of the same misfortune that happened to the poor devil that the decision of the jury sent to prison. You perhaps recall that a highly placed man was supposed to have commissioned a painting from this boy?"

"That's at least what he claimed."

"They were wrong not to believe him. That patron of the arts—that was me."

"You astonish me. I now believe that that person was entirely imaginary, and, in any case, according to my information, that patron of the arts would have been a woman."

"I see," said the unknown man, "that you have seen *that woman.*"

"What woman?"

"A person who, like me, and I believe even a little more than me, is interested in the young inmate."

"In fact," said the Director General, seeming to become somewhat annoyed by the visitor's delay in announcing his name, "I did see a woman who came to visit me about the same case, asking me for my goodwill in regard to her protégé. She behaved in the way that always succeeds the best with me, that is total candor and perfect frankness."

As the Director General finished that sentence, his usher entered and gave him an envelope closed with a bulky red seal. It said:

From the Director of the Telegraph - Urgent.

"If you don't mind, Monsieur," the Director General said, and he then read and gazed a long time at the unknown man.

"I'll bet," the latter said, laughing, "that they are informing you of a prison break?"

"Yes, and a prison break will frustrate you as much as I. The Maritime Prefect is informing me that this Rempailleux, whom I had ordered sent to Paris, and from whom we could expect valuable information, disappeared three days ago."

"Well, Monsieur le Directeur General, in order not to keep you worried any longer, I must tell you that I already knew that. He had the condemnation of that young man on his conscience; he had learned that his rehabilitation was going to be looked into. Your thoughts and his were in agreement about the usefulness of his presence here. He wanted to spare you and the administration the expense of his transportation..."

"Let me guess... You're Rempailleux!" said the Director General, suddenly getting to the bottom of the situation.

"In the flesh," answered the convict with burlesque self-importance. "*I come like Themistocles,*[107] *to sit down confidently at the hearth of the British people.*"

The Director General was too ardent a Royalists not to find amusing that parody of the words uttered by *Buonaparte*, as he was now called, when he had surrendered to the British.

"You are, my dear fellow," he said, smiling, "rather amusing, but your *mascarade*, with which I wasn't duped for very long, is not a fortunate invention. If the information you claim you have really has some value, it would have contrib-

---

[107] (c.524-459 BC), Athenian politician and general. During the second Persian invasion, he exercised command of the Greek navy at the battles of Artemisium and Salamis in 480 BC. Due to a subterfuge on his part, the Greeks lured the Persian fleet into the Straits of Salamis, and won a decisive victory. This line of dialogue is a quote from Napoleon surrendering to the British.

uted toward getting you either a commutation of your sentence, or even a pardon, instead of now having added prison evasion to your record..."

"A pardon? Have I asked for one? Do I need that formality? When I remain in prison, Monsieur, that's because I am bored; that's because I feel I have nothing better to do. But when something more gripping calls me elsewhere, you'll see if I can be restrained."

"Come now, enough of your boasting; you say you know the name of the man who stole the strongbox?"

"Yes, Monsieur le Directeur General, and I regret to tell you that it is a civil servant."

"A public employee?"

"Public, no; I should have said instead, hidden, because I have never seen the names of the employees of the Secret Bureau listed in the *Royal Almanach.*"

"The Secret Bureau? What's that?" asked the Director General in an affected tone of the most naïve ignorance.

"Monsieur le Directeur General knows very well that it is the place where the government has the letters that interest them read."

"Come on, my dear fellow! You're repeating here one of those ridiculous rumors totally invented to amuse lazy men in the prison."

"Well! Monsieur, here are my sources..."

And Rempailleux recounted Britannicus' adventure, and all the deductions by which he had been led to persuade himself that Matiphous was in possession of the strongbox.

Not finding anything to answer, the Director General, like all persons of authority lacking in good judgment, wanted to use force.

"Supposing," he therefore said, "that your story is true, do you know that, especially for a man in your position, it's not wise to compromise yourself with state secrets? A man like you could disappear in a minute, and what would that matter?"

"Oh! Monsieur le Directeur General, not under the paternal government of the descendents of Saint Louis and Henry IV! Besides, I'm like Gribouille,[108] decided to throw myself into the water to avoid getting wet."

"What do you mean by that?"

"I'm saying that I'm beginning to get tired of always opposing society, and that, with a little encouragement, I would be very willing to become part of it. You see, Monsieur le Directeur General, I'm not a fool, and just like anyone else, I know how to wear a morning coat, even ornamented with a few decorations. In prison, that's different; I speak slang, and you can check it out. They will tell you that I'm popular! Well! That popularity has made me the depository of all the secrets, even those that honest people hide among themselves, which could be used to make me a very useful instrument of repression. In any case, I ask for the opportunity to put my knowledge of how to uncover secrets to the test. I warn you, Monsieur, that business is very hard. Before taking the advantage of coming to see to you, aided by the information given to me by his former servant, Britannicus, I made a descent into Matiphous's residence. After having examined everything and turned everything over with as much care as if I intended to have a clean house, I became sure that the strongbox is not in his lodgings."

"And you don't suspect where it might be?"

"At this moment, no, but if you commissioned me, I would take on the charge of finding its hiding place. I know an influence to use against our fellow... a woman... You understand, Monsieur, what weight can be lifted with that sort of leverage!"

"All right! Go ahead, but slowly! I desire, as soon as possible, to see clearly into that mysterious melodrama."

---

[108] Name for a popular gaffe-prone, foolish character dating back to the early 16th century, likely to throw himself in a river to keep from getting wet in the rain.

"The first thing to do, in order for your orders to be carried out," said Rempailleux gently, "is to see that, two steps away from your office, some agent doesn't come zealously to arrest me. I'm a delicious morsel and as soon as my escape is known, a lot of ambitious people will take to the field."

"Go on, I will give orders to that effect, and if you succeed in this first enterprise, we will talk again about the good intentions you manifested."

"Monsieur le Directeur General," Rempailleux exclaimed, "men like you are served in life and death!"

Next, he bowed respectfully and left.

XV. The Leverage

Rempailleux was a forty-nine-year-old man, very well preserved despite his adventurous life. The Director of the Police, and his usher, duped by his good appearance and by his decorations, had taken him for someone important. Two hours later, after leaving that interview, he was accepted on the same footing at a charming townhouse in the Champs-Elysees area where he presented himself. That townhouse was the dwelling of Lady Stuart. Britannicus' story had already told us of her presence in Paris. On seeing her aristocratic installation, the reader would perhaps be curious to know how, following the terrible adventure at the Pergola, she had been able to bring her ship right to the port where we find her so pleasantly moored.

Nothing else but the fact of her marriage already indicated that the old Laird had a great aptitude to believe a great deal and to accept a great deal. The evening of the famous masked ball, which Kitty attended to meet the equestrian artist Tamerlane, Lord Stuart, liking a good night's sleep, had indulged for a long time in the sweetness of slumber, including when his wife had furtively left the conjugal domicile. Although having caused a certain scandal, the discovery of the virtuous lady had only compromised the actors of that imbroglio. Only they had had the last say, and, in any case, the husband would have been able to get wind of it, at the earliest the next day by hearing the gossip in the city, since the guilty woman's leaving and returning had been known only by her roommate, a girl whom she trusted, and on whose discretion she could count absolutely. Now, during the night, Kitty had taken care to arrange everything, and coming to find her husband when he awoke:

"I certainly see that you have been dying of boredom in Florence for a while," she said. "Last night, the Mid-Lent ceremonies definitely closed the carnival. I won't take you away from a future of great pleasures in suggesting that we start on the road tomorrow morning for your dear Island of Mainland."

Then, when the good Scotsman, as disposed as he was to agree to that arrangement, made a few objections to the suddenness of their departure, his clever companion replied:

"Oh, take me at my word, you know, when the balls are over, the concert season begins. If we announce our departure, I will be pressed to stay from every direction. I will perhaps want to myself, and you are so good to me, that you will again decide against what you desire. The horses will be at our door in a quarter of an hour. Believe me, the safest thing is to take me away."

"You are certainly pretty enough for that," the old Laird answered gallantly, and they had immediately taken the road to Scotland.

At Edinburgh, where they had made a sojourn to rest from the fatigues of the journey, Lady Stuart wasn't slow in noticing in herself what the English call "*an interesting state.*" But to prepare her husband for the dark paternity which was threatening him, she put no less cleverness than she had for the departure from Florence.

In the furnished hotel where they were staying, there was a Negro who worked there. The first time that she saw that *monster,* as she called him, she had simulated a violent attack of nerves that the sight of that man was supposed to have produced in her. Later, when the denouement arrived, the apocryphal product was explained by means of a *glance of the moth-*

er, an expression by which the popular idea attributed to the impressions that such an unusual indirect contact on a pregnant woman might have on the fruit she carried in her womb.

On seeing a mulatto enfant brought to birth, that Kitty, during all the time of her pregnancy, had never stopped seeming to doubt its source, Lord Stuart had foolishly taken for a caprice and an error of nature, what was, on the contrary, one of its most regular and logical consequences. Far then, from his tenderness and his confidence being altered the least in the world, he had redoubled his care and affectionate feelings for the poor mother. He did that so well that, dying some years later, by a will in due form, he left her everything he possessed.

That's how Lady Stuart, whose interest in leaving Scotland was easy to understand, had been able to follow the kind of emigration movement at the moment of peace, that had impelled half of England to beat a path to France. That was how she was able to lead the elegant existence in Paris which could be supposed, just by looking at where she lived; how, finally, accusing Matiphous thanks to the hellish imagination of his black servant, she had been able to exert onto him a vengeance *à l'italienne*, appealing to Britannicus with the bait of a large sum of money. Afterward, the sentiment of paternity in the servant had turned into a kind of furious madness.

Introduced into a pretty boudoir as soon as he was announced, the Comte de Saint-Rambert, the new pseudonym of the convict Rempailleux, was impressed with the striking beauty of Lady Stuart, but at the same time, he seemed to have an idea that this wasn't the first time they had met. In that, he wasn't mistaken. Like everybody, in London, where we know he had lived, he had known Kitty Ketch, who, about 1790, was very popular there. What confused his memory was the amount of weight the white lady had gained after her thirtieth year. But it must be added that, for her, that weight gain had been very conservative, and that for the instincts of Rempailleux, a man with sensual appetites, a little stoutness in her figure was just one more merit.

Immediately, therefore, a double goal took place in the negotiations that he had come to initiate. First of all, to turn Lady Stuart into an instrument of perdition for the one who had stolen his strongbox, and next, to install himself in her good graces. That ambition, after all, was it asking too much? Carefully interrogated on all the details of his adventure, Britannicus had persisted, right to the end, in letting it be believed that the attractive lady had been attracted to him. Now, the Comte de Saint-Rambert was sitting right in front of a mirror. He judged himself, and, despite his fifty-years about to sound, a man of his physique and his intelligence could hope for something, after the burlesque character of Britannicus, that a scarcely likely caprice had been able, for a moment, to turn into a serious affair?

At the moment Rempailleux was dreaming this way, one hadn't yet imagined the existence of philanthropists, saintly people who strived to create a gentle and well regulated life for the young prisoners in the penitentiary systems, and to improve the regime of the prisons which had not yet been built. Presenting himself to Kitty as a man profoundly concerned with humanitarian questions in general, and the rehabilitation of convicts in particular, the Comte de Saint-Rambert preceded, therefore, all the Saint-Vincent-de-Pauls[109] that appeared in the government of the Restoration, and especially in that of Louis-Philippe.[110] The former criminal could

---

[109] St. Vincent de Paul (1581-1660) was a French Roman Catholic priest who dedicated himself to serving the poor. He is venerated as a saint in the Catholic Church and the Anglican Communion. He was canonized in 1737. He was renowned for his compassion, humility and generosity and is known as the Great Apostle of Charity.

[110] Louis Philippe (1773-1850) was King of the French from 1830 to 1848 as the leader of the Orléanist party. He spent 21 years in exile after he left France in 1793. He was proclaimed king in 1830 after his cousin Charles X was forced to abdicate in the wake of the events of the July Revolution of that year.

be considered the inventor of that profession, and never, since him, has the role been better filled.

"Madame," he said to Lady Stuart, taking on a rather solemn tone, "these unfortunate men, that human justice installs in desolate places that are called prisons, have always been objects of pity for me. I almost said of profound pity. These unfortunate ones, me, I visit them, I console them, I study their needs. And those who can be brought back to become useful members of society, after having been its shame and its terror, are more numerous than is commonly thought. In short, I consecrate to their betterment, physical as well as moral, all my cares and all the resources of an independent fortune. Therefore, I am not without some popularity among these men and a great number of them do not hesitate to make me the confident of all their secrets."

"You can only be lauded for that charitable work," Kitty responded. "Is it a question of counting on me for a contribution?"

"No, my Lady, you can do something better for them… or at least for one of them, whose release you would perhaps be in a position to secure by confirming a revelation that he is ready to make to the police. Lately, I met him in the Rochefort prison, where, as you probably know, he is being detained?"

"I, Monsieur? I don't know that I am acquainted with any of your protégés."

"His name will perhaps help you to remember: He is Britannicus, an African from Madagascar."

"I truly don't know what you mean."

"You astonish me. It is through him that I obtained your address. He especially asked me to remember him to you, and

His government, known as the July Monarchy, was dominated by members of a wealthy French elite and numerous former Napoleonic officials. His popularity faded as economic conditions in France deteriorated in 1847, and he was forced to abdicate after the outbreak of the French Revolution of 1848. He lived out his life in exile in Great Britain.

a while ago, a charming child that I saw in your antechamber made me believe in the existence of a pleasant past that he didn't hesitate to recount to me."

"That man," shouted Lady Stuart, violently coming out of the reserve in which she had, at first, heard his deductions, "has dared to claim that he was something to me?"

"*Something*, Madame, would be saying very little. The products of his race have the advantage, or the inconvenience, as one might say, to carry with them their own seal of evidence!"

"Monsieur, if I am the mother of that child, it's by a crime; did the miserable man also tell you that?"

"Certainly not," Rempailleux answered.

Noticing the convincing tone of the beautiful lady, thinking he was on the wrong track, he added:

"I must admit to you that, from the first moment that I saw you, I could hardly comprehend how so much beauty had been able to stray into such hands."

"And that crime," Lady Stuart continued with the same vehemence, "he wasn't the one who had the inspiration. An obedient machine, he committed it for the profit of the hatred of a scoundrel whose valet he was."

"Oh! Then that explains to me why you wanted to take this Matiphous' life, because it was he, isn't that true, who inspired Britannicus with that vengeance?"

"He escaped that time," said Lady Stuart, without quibbling about her thought of murder, "but I will know how to find a surer hand than the clumsy one that I haven't seen or heard from."

Then she added pleasantly:

"Certainly they did well to send him to prison."

"Life," Rempailleux continued sententiously, "is filled with strange encounters. It is exactly against that man that you have so much to complain about, that I have come to solicit your help. My stupid approach in recommending myself to you by means of that conceited Britannicus had no other object than to arrange a defensive and offensive alliance against that devil, Matiphous! Madame, I have something less dependent on luck to get to him than a stab from a knife. And if I could count on your valuable cooperation..."

"Count on it, Monsieur. All the harm that I could do to that scoundrel, I will do."

"Well, first of all, a question, and I dare hope that you will answer, because its purpose is to determine the role that it would be the most useful for you to play in the drama I am putting together. Between this Matiphous and you, how, please, did that hatred, that from both sides shows itself in such violent acts, begin? I can see only love that could turn to bitterness to bring about such extremes."

"Love? On his side, perhaps," Lady Stuart replied disdainfully. "The truth is that, in the past, he wanted to marry me. But as for me, I never thought about him."

"The scene," Rempailleux asked cleverly, "didn't that take place in London, where I met you in the past?"

"Yes, I believe it was in London," Kitty answered, showing a little embarrassment.

"Then," continued the supposed Comte de Saint-Rambert, "he was the collaborator of your father?"

A dark red spread over Lady Stuart's face. Forced to torture her memory, with the circumstances of Matiphous' matrimonial claims helping him, Rempailleux had finally managed to recognize Jack Ketch's daughter, and to let her know that he had done so in a rather transparent way. However, with people he wanted to lure into his schemes, it was necessary to not take his advantage too far.

"But what am I saying about your father," he continued, trying to put a bandage on the wound he had just opened. "Certain privileged beings, Madame, begin only with themselves. Their beauty, their mind, their talents, those are their ancestors, their nobility, and Lord Stuart must have had a great heart to have understood this."

"Lord Stuart," Kitty answered, "in fact, corrected many of the caprices of fate for me. And even after having had the misfortune to lose him, I find myself, through his goodness, with a pleasant existence. It took that man, whose name I cannot bring myself to pronounce without horror, to bring desolation and sorrow."

Thus brought back to the topic, the so-called Comte de Saint-Rambert asked:

"Here's how we're going to get the upper hand of that fellow. In the prison at Rochefort, there is a very remarkable man, who, it must be said, has never been understood. For the law, he's a criminal of whom we should be afraid, even when he is being held in chains.

"For me, who has studied him and who understands him in depth, he has the temperament of a conqueror, or of a pirate, if you prefer that. He has one of those energetic natures which need a great deal of air and space, who take their place violently in the sun of civilization, and who, for lack of having been helped by circumstances, turn into a Fra Diavolo [111] or a Schinderhanes [112] instead of becoming a Jean Bart [113] or a Napoleon."

---

[111] Fra Diavolo (lit. Brother Devil) (1771-1806), the popular nickname of Michele Pezza, a famous Neapolitan guerrilla leader who resisted the French occupation of Naples, proving an "inspirational practitioner of popular insurrection". Fra Diavolo figures prominently in folk lore and fiction. He appears in Alexandre Dumas' The Last Cavalier (published post. 2007), Washington Irving's short story *The Inn at Terracina* (1824), Daniel François Auber's eponymous 1830 opera and was the inspiration for Paul Féval's Colonel Bozzo-Corona, the allegedly immortal leader of the *Habits Noirs* [Black Coats] criminal brotherhood.

[112] Johannes Bückler (c.1778-1803), nicknamed Schinderhannes, was a German outlaw who orchestrated one of the most famous crime sprees in German history. On 21 November 1803 he was guillotined before the gates of Mainz. He remains Germany's most famous outlaw. His legend still attracts a great deal of tourism to the region wherein his gang operated.

"Well! Monsieur, who is that man?" Kitty asked, to hasten the exposé of Rempailleux, who speaking about himself in veiled terms, was letting it become long and drawn out.

"That man, Madame, who deals only with great things, appropriated a strongbox containing considerable valuable articles, and it must be added that he didn't steal it from anyone, since the owner had just committed suicide under his eyes. Caution had forced him to deposit that box momentarily in a spot where he thought it would be was safe. But it was later stolen by Matiphous, who, cowardly, without running any danger, and with actions, the depth of which take the proportion of a State secret, didn't hesitate to appropriate it."

"He must be arrested," said Lady Stuart, with a vivacity that can be imagined.

"No, that would be a mistake. First of all, we must be certain that the strongbox is in his hands. Britannicus saw it there, because the first information came from him. And notice, Madame, the march of Providence. Matiphous used that same black man to set up an infamous trap for you. That man, in your turn, you used to punish that crime. The attempt failed; Britannicus was taken to prison, where he made public the misdeed of your enemy. Now, it's he we will put on his trail."

"Yes," said Lady Stuart, "the ways of Providence are often admirable. But if there are only clues…"

"Not clues! There are proofs," Rempailleux continued. "Just the description of the stolen strongbox given by Britannicus would already be conclusive; but in addition. deductions made from several other factors, which would be pointless for me to recount to you, establish the theft in other irrefutable ways. However, in the eye of the Law, those still

---

[113] Jean Bart (1650-1702) French naval commander and privateer. Many anecdotes tell of the courage of this sailor, who became a popular hero of the French Navy. He captured a total of 386 ships and also sank or burned a great number more. The town of Dunkirk has honored his memory by erecting a statue and by naming a public square after him.

remain only circumstantial proofs. At present what the legal experts call the *corpus delicti* is necessary."

"Trying to find that, I don't really see how I can be of any use to you."

"Let me continue, and you will understand. A secret visit to the guilty man was made, and I'm now certain that the strongbox has been moved and that Matiphous has hidden it somewhere outside his domicile. Now there are two possibilities which require your intervention. In the first, you will ask Matiphous to come to your house, telling him that you have something serious to communicate to him. He won't fail to answer your appeal. Then, armed with your charms, which according to me, are both very fascinating and very dangerous, you will tell him that, tired of your mutual enmity, you have decided to end it. And as proof of your friendly dispositions, you will reveal to him the danger he runs by Britannicus' revelations."

"But if he's warned," the petulant lady interrupted, "everything will be compromised."

"Let me finish," said Rempailleux. "After having given him that proof of the sincerity of your desired reconciliation, you will go further. You will go as far as the thought of again taking up the idea of marriage that existed between you, and proposing to leave France with him in order to avoid the possibility of being followed, with which he is menaced. If he accepts, you will leave with him..."

"Me!" shouted Lady Stuart, "travel with that man! Never!"

"Calm yourself, Madame. You won't go with him past the frontier. The police will be alerted, your vehicle stopped, and as your loving suitor, leaving without thinking of returning, will not have failed to take the strongbox with him, he will be arrested and his crime will become as clear as day."

"But, Monsieur, if he plots to take the valuables with him but has destroyed the box they were in, how can that compromise him?"

"Impossible, Madame, the strong box has a secret, and it was made in such a way as to kill the one who tries to force it open. Britannicus saw him trying vainly to open it for months. Besides, he will have some trouble accounting for the valuables he's carrying."

"In any case, Monsieur, I don't feel I have either the courage or the ability necessary to play the comedy of repentance and goodwill towards that man I despise that you expect of me."

"Don't you believe, Madame, that the love you don't feel is the one you can simulate the best? You have a number of ways to turn a head, and I know that, in Matiphous' place, I would be sure to succumb."

"You have some illusions about my skills," answered Lady Stuart, "and I am not disposed to undertake a seduction that I feel incapable of bringing to a successful end. My hatred would be stronger than my will to deceive, and I would betray myself."

"So be it!" said Rempailleux. "Then we'll have to rely my second possibility. You will not see our thief. You will only write to him, telling him what will seem the truth that you obtained from Britannicus..."

"Oh, no, Monsieur, that will not be credible at all. He doesn't know that I looked up his servant and that I set him on his tracks."

"There, you see! The first plan is the best, and if I were given the role you are declining, I would go even as far as confessing to him that I tried to have him murdered. Your idea of reconciliation would only be more easily believed. You would seem to be a woman who, after that grand attempt had failed, tired of hating, came to ask for mercy."

"I understand that," said Kitty, getting used to the idea, little by little, of once again deceiving her former suitor, "but, truly, I don't feel myself up to that role."

"Come, now!" said Rempailleux, in his most gallant tone, "if you write just to deceive your enemy to get him on the road, we have some chance of success, because fear will still be rather strong on his heels. But if you are there, with your eyes, your lily and rose complexion, your blonde hair, with your adorable figure, the fascination that you believe will be so difficult will accomplish itself."

"All right, I'll think about it," said Lady Stuart.

That idea had now gone to her head, since success in this matter was so important to her.

"Of course! But you don't know the full consequences of your success. Matiphous' crime, Madame, made another victim. Accused of having stolen the strongbox, a young artist, very talented, entirely innocent, is shivering at this moment in prison. A woman, almost as attractive as you, is working to have this man whom she adores released. It was in order not to compromise her that he didn't use all his means of defending himself. I have sworn to her that the innocence of her young friend would triumph, and that could never be better recognized than the day the truly guilty man is arrested. Hers is a very romantic story and very touching, that I will recount to you at another time, since I have already greatly abused your patience in listening to me."

At that, Rempailleux rose to leave.

"Well, Monsieur," said Lady Stuart, "please come and see me tomorrow. From now until then, I will have thought about your proposal. Perhaps the good action that will result from it will give me more courage than the ardor of revenge."

"Adorable!" said Rempailleux, taking Kitty's hand and daring to place a kiss on it.

That audacity was not badly received. Lady Stuart found that Rempailleux was an intelligent man and good company, Only, as sometimes happens to clever people, he talked a little too much.

XVI. Matiphous' Difficult Position

Needless to say, Lady Stuart finally accepted the role that had been destined for her. And she played it with superlatively well, so much more energetically, since at the beginning of the interview accepted by Matiphous, she believed she saw in him a great inclination to walk blindly into the trap into which she had been charged with leading him.

Even with people for whom one has little esteem, one does not like to be misjudged. Therefore, Matiphous' first words were to justify himself with respect to the affair in Florence, and to emphasize Britannicus' responsibility for the entire invention. Kitty didn't believe a word of his explanations, even though they were made very believable by all the details he gave her. Besides, they were given with a great air of good faith and sincerity. But on seeing Matiphous' eagerness to cleanse himself, she thought he had, at the back of his mind, a plan to renew the project of marriage that had formerly existed between them, from the advantageous position where he would put her.

For a moment, therefore, believing to have achieved success, she put into her comedy such cleverness and verisimilitude so enthusiastic that very few could have resisted it. However, she came up against two obstacles, of which one, at least to her, was completely unexpected. To be the successor to Broughton, and in some way, to be a second edition to Lord Stuart, that could be overlooked, but to come after Britannicus, when that fellow had left a living testimony of their affair after him—could he accept that?

In any case, being the involuntary, but very real, cause of the death of Madame Limeuil, Kitty Ketch, just for that reason, had become for Matiphous an impossible woman to love. He thanked her for the interest that she had been willing to show him. And, although, according to him, he had nothing to fear in being pursued by the law, he declared himself no less obliged to his beautiful enemy. He guaranteed her the absolute and indefinite suspension of all hostilities in the future. Their meeting could have thus been able to end, at least relatively, in terms of pleasantness and cordiality.

But Kitty's ego couldn't settle for that conclusion. When she saw that all her enticements had ended in such a cold and formal separation, she took off her mask, and, considering that the essence of her mission was, either by seduction or by fear, to throw her enemy into some trap, she told him that he was very presumptuous to believe in her forgetfulness of the past between them and in the seriousness of her intentions to make up with him.

"It's useless for you to deny it," she finished. "I am certain of the information that your Britannicus transmitted to me. And before twenty-four hours have elapsed, the law, that I am going to inform, will know how to convict you."

That threat was an allusion to the profession of the Honorable Monsieur Ketch, but Matiphous limited himself to answering:

"Blood will tell."

If, on leaving Lady Stuart, the man from Malta had made the least move, as it would have been reasonable to believe, to change the location of his "treasure," or bury it deeper, his precautions would have betrayed him. Rempailleux, having received *carte blanche*, had organized around the smallest acts of Matiphous' life an active and hidden surveillance that would infallibly have caught him in its snares. But apparently, having prepared for such an event for a long time, the man from Malta didn't budge. And, for several weeks, his behavior and manner of conducting himself didn't give room for any actions that could be taken advantage of against him. He must have thought about leaving Paris and France, because, as we already know, the disgust with his functions and the bad rapport in which he lived with his colleagues, had been, most of all, his reason for his bad action. If, therefore, he had been able to open the impenetrable strongbox, he would have been able before that time to send across the frontier the riches contained inside it. Probably Britannicus' revelation would have arrived too late, and he would have been found, a long time before, sheltered from all searches. But counter to the steps taken by Rempailleux, despite the apprehensions that his interview with Lady Stuart must have raised, Matiphous found it neither prudent nor useful to disappear, telling himself that, everything considered, without that piece of evidence, action against him wasn't possible, and that, in addition, the way in which the Secret Bureau was mixed up in all that affair made it rather difficult to bring a legal action against him out in the open.

Rempailleux, however, was dying of impatience, since the official position for which he had shown ambition seemed to depend on the success he had obtained in that encounter. On the other hand, Madame de Pringy was moving heaven and earth in order to aid the work of the police, which she was being kept abreast of by the Director General. Seeing they were making no progress, in her fervor to help the "guest" at Rochefort, finally, the beautiful widow, prompted by the inspiration of a rather unusual step, without consulting anyone, immediately set her plan in motion.

One day, Matiphous saw her enter his establishment.

"Monsieur," she said to him, "I don't have the honor to know you, but I need for you to listen to me with great indulgence. The conversation that I would like to have with you, whatever the subject might be, is testimony of the good idea I have formed of your character. One doesn't come to ask a man to willingly set straight a misfortune of which he has involuntarily been the cause, without supposing that he has noble and high sentiments. What I dare expect of you is a sacrifice to that instinct for justice that is always sure of being encountered in well placed hearts. What's more," she added, "to have the right to speak to you in this way, which could seem offensive to you, I, myself, am going to begin by blushing before you, and confessing to you my wrongs and my weaknesses."

And she recounted her relations with the young painter almost in the same way as he had recounted it to the Director General of the Police. When she had finished her story, she said:

"If, Monsieur, as it's claimed, that strongbox is in your possession, please believe that I don't judge you severely for that. I would think, as you did also, that you had given way to an impulse, that you had seen it as a sort of property fallen into the public domain, and that it might be piquant and meritorious to intercept it, preventing it from falling into unworthy hands that would keep it. But once you were told about the terrible consequences that this good turn would have, you would make it your duty, I'm sure, to neglect nothing in order to give an unfortunate man freedom."

"Madame," Matiphous replied, "a scheming woman asked me, a while ago, to come see her, and there, like you, she talked to me about a strongbox that I was supposed to have stolen, and about information on that subject given by a scoundrel who was formerly in my service. At this moment, that man is in the prison at Rochefort. I told her that I didn't understand a word of what she wanted me to say, that the police could continue its investigations, which didn't seem to me to have their point of departure in a very pure source, and if I was officially attacked, I would defend myself. To find today the same insinuations in a mouth as honorable as yours, must assuredly hurt me. However, I am no more worried than when they came from a less pure mouth. I certainly have interest and sympathy for the unhappy man you have wanted to speak to me about, but, really, what can I do? Go put myself in the hands of the law to state that the young man should not be there, where he has been sent. That helpfulness, you can understand, would be going a little far, and the heroism that you seem me capable of wouldn't, however, go that far."

"If you were," Madame de Pringy said in her turn, "the admitted author of the theft you are accused of, I wouldn't be so foolish as to claim the absolute devotion that you think me capable of. In that case, I would be content to point out to you that, for a long time, you have had no chance, without running the danger of being discovered, of again taking possession of that object. Secret searches of your house have not been able to find it despite the minutest investigations."

"Meaning," Matiphous quickly interjected, "that the less I can be found to have the *corpus delicti,* the more I should be declared guilty?"

"I would have added," Madame de Pringy continued, "because I am speaking hypothetically, that the persistent and prolonged attention with which the irritated ego of the police seems to have decided to surround you, must be a permanent danger, despite ever more clever ways to throw them off the scent. In that kind of duel, you seem destined, sooner or later, to get the worst of it. Faced with such a situation, I would have asked you if you don't think that, at least a moment's absence…"

"Advice," said Matiphous, interrupting again, "already given to me by the scheming woman I told you about a moment ago, in the hope that I would be arrested in possession of the famous strongbox at the first border crossing."

"Me, Monsieur, I would have advised you in a different way. I would have said to you: *Go abroad; let the storm pass; but carry with you only the sum that you would carry for a simple trip.* Only then, when you have made sure of your safety, I would have asked of your good heart that, admitting the truth, you finish what is possible to free the victim from his odious torture. Then, also, I would have expected something more of your generosity. I am rich, and whatever amount of money that, while waiting for better times, seems to you necessary, following a change of residence, I would have the presumption to offer it to you and have you accept it."

"It would be impossible, Madame, to present that chalice more graciously. I believe, however, that I can tell you I have refused better offers. The charming siren, who also thought of deporting me, was like you, beautiful and rich, and she carried the passion to make me decide as far as the offer of her fortune and her hand."

The not very kind comparison the man from Malta had just allowed himself to make, and the markedly ironic tone of his words, let Madame de Pringy understand that she could expect nothing more from him. Consequently, she took her leave and Matiphous accompanied her with a great show of courtesy to the door of his apartment.

However, her visit had had more effect than she figured. In revealing the intensity of the suspicion and the surveillance of which he was the object, she had achieved removing the sense of security that the officious intervention of Lady Stuart had only troubled. It would have taken a great deal for Matiphous to have remained insensitive to the misfortune of which he had become the cause. He hadn't known about that sad event. The artist's trial had received very little publicity and, like three-quarters of the citizens of the Empire, except for the Bulletins of the *grande armée,* he seldom read the newspapers. But from the moment that he learned the deplorable error which he had brought about, his conscience had begun to speak loudly to him, and it was pushing him to adopt the action pointed out by Madame de Pringy: to go across the border, from where he would confess to the law, mocking them a little, and then find the way to again get his hands on his strongbox, that in the meantime he knew how to hide so as to be able to foil all the searches.

One consideration made him hesitate, however. If he couldn't hide his departure from the Argus whose eyes were always open on all his actions, to give by that attempted evasion a new weapon to his accusers, from the point of view of his employment with the Secret Bureau, wouldn't that constitute flagrant desertion?

He continued, therefore, being very perplexed when, some days later, when he was busy with his work opening letters, the Director, Monsieur Hulet, approached him and asked that he not leave their ordinary work place before becoming aware of something he had to tell him.

Matiphous immediately thought that the terrible judge had been told about the suspicions hanging over one of the employees of his secret administration. It wasn't without a certain emotion that, after having seen all his colleagues leave, he found himself alone with a man whose habitual severity, proofs of which he had seen on more than one occasion, without counting a particular feeling of ill-will, had against him.

"Monsieur," Hulet said to him, "at a time of sad remembrance, when, in the interest of the morality and the dignity of our institution, a terrible sentence was passed against my unfortunate son, there was disagreement between your sense of justice and mine. The father more than the magistrate assessed your clemency, and, as it was to my benefit, I tried to find only honorable motives for it. Events today prove that I was wrong."

How's that?" Matiphous asked quickly.

"Several days ago, I was ordered to the office of the Director General of the Police. He told me of the serious suspicions which are weighing against you. And from that, I explained your indulgence. Looking into yourself, you must not have felt the courage to condemn guilt a great deal less venial than yours."

"Suspicions," Matiphous answered. "Everyone can be exposed to that, but right up until the time they are established proofs, I have the right instead, Director, to your protection rather than your severity."

"What for others," Hulet responded, "may be the object of a doubt, for us is evidence itself. The letter from which you drew the information, that you must have so unworthily abused, naturally keeping the one to whom it was addressed, was communicated with no one. Who then could have known its contents? You, Monsieur, using the functions which are entrusted to you here."

"Your deduction has so little accuracy that the law found someone else guilty."

"But you know very well that undisputable proofs have since then come to prove his innocence; an unfortunate man is suffering in your place!"

"That is, at least, what it is convenient for you to believe."

"That is what our family tribunal has deliberated and judged, pronouncing themselves this time unanimous."

"And it is you, no doubt," Matiphous said ironically, "who have been charged with executing the sentence?"

"Your past," Hulet responded, "has taken from us the care of designating an arm. Several years ago, the British Admiralty, that also has a charge against you, demanded your extradition. The relationship existing between the Cabinet in

227

London and our new government makes it natural that you be no longer protected against their demand. If, therefore, you have some taste for ending at the hand of your former father-in-law, you are absolutely on the road to that satisfaction."

"Executioner for executioner, Matiphous then said, "it's better the one whose duty is that sad office, than the man who looks for the refined pleasure of parricide."

"You are mistaken, Monsieur," the ex-member of the Convention[114] replied without emotion. "Whatever stoicism that the sentiment of duty permitted me to carry to the terrible task that the cruelty of fate had seemed to want to invest in me, I was not put to that harsh test. The hand of God struck just at the moment when I believed I was to decline my bloody mission. And it is because I have remembered that you piously accompanied the victim to his last dwelling that today I have come to render you a supreme service in warning you of the deplorable fate reserved for you."

"To help me avoid it?" Matiphous asked less aggressively.

"Your evasion," Hulet answered, "I have not the means either facilitate it or stand in its way. I only know that you would in vain try to escape the network of official surveillance which surrounds us in every direction. At the first step that you would risk out of its circle, you would see the sort of loose rope captivity, with which the police now hold you, exchanged for a true prison."

"For more than ten years," Matiphous then said, "buried in the boxes of files of the Foreign Affairs, that demand for my extradition had very little chance of being known by the functionaries of the new regime. Be frank, Monsieur, and admit that its exhumation must be laid to your implacable cruelty."

"Why would I hide it? When you came to take your place among us, for you as for all your colleagues, I had care-

---

[114] Hulet was a member of the Convention that voted for the execution of Louis XVI.

fully informed myself about your background. It didn't offer, it has to be admitted, great guarantees, and if you will remember, I exhorted you strongly to walk always in the narrow path, not letting you be ignorant of the fact that our punishments were terrible. It pleased you to encounter them, and whatever you may say of my bloody tastes, I do not enjoy myself in applying them. I have at hand a method of turning over to another justice the care of dealing with you. I have so much less hesitation in using it when, at the same time, I could tell you of the danger you face, and make available to you the resources to escape it that a man of heart always has."

"Is it my life that you are asking me for, to serve as a burnt offering on the altar of your holy cavern?"

"My unfortunate son was less guilty than you are, and that was the refuge that he had chosen. I warn you: in two days, everything will be arranged for you to be deported to London. And I repeat, you won't able to make the least successful attempt to avoid that destiny."

"All right, Monsieur, I will take the warning," Matiphous said.

One can estimate his gratitude on considering the service that the one he was leaving had claimed to render him.

XVII. Two Men Who Can't Agree

Great historic events have, at first, a natural inclination; that is to say, first, a vast and extended action modifying human destinies on a large surface; then, after that, in an isolated and indirect way, showing consequences in the life of individuals. It was thus that Napoleon's return from the Island of Elba came suddenly to offer Matiphous the appearance of a way out of the impasse where he had been thought to be driven into a corner.[115]

---

[115] The so-called "Hundred Days" marked the period between Napoleon's return from his exile on the island of Elba to Paris

He judged that, deserting every other interest, the police would straight away turn passionate, exclusive, attention to that very threatening attempt. And, in fact, the term that Hulet had set for him that was supposed to bring a denouement, had already been passed for several days, without anyone seeming to have any intentions to seize him. That forgetfulness, joined to the disarray of the measures undertaken by the Restoration Government to stop the progress of the new Napoleonic enterprise, was more and more apparent; and it made him hope that, in the middle of the panic of the Royalists, who were beginning to emigrate in every direction, he would find a way to slip away unnoticed.

Events fully supported that calculation, and about mid-March 1815, managing without any encumbrance to cross the Belgian frontier, he could believe himself safe in Bruges, from where he wrote the following letter to Madame de Pringy:

Bruges, 14 March, 1815.
Madame,

I was very late in becoming aware of the judicial error of which Monsieur Adolphe Levillain, that young artist in whom you have so great an interest, found himself the victim. I, better than anyone, can testify as to his innocence, since that strongbox he is accused of appropriating, it was I who collected it from a lodging where he had, for a long time, ceased to be a lodger.

My aim was to keep that rich prey from the greed of a criminal who, after having gotten hold of it, had secretly deposited it in Monsieur Levillain's attic. I was about to write to America to the heirs of the man from whom it had been stolen, when it was surreptitiously removed from my domicile. My first suspicions accurately involved a Negro that I had, at that time, in my service, and who, after having given me several proofs of infidelity, had suddenly left. The denunciation that

on 20 March 1815 and the second restoration of King Louis XVIII on 8 July 1815.

this scoundrel dared bring against me from the prison where he was sent for another crime, and the circumstantial description that he has given of the object, can today no longer leave me in doubt.

Knowing how some badly intentioned persons count on using that ridiculous accusation against me, following the advice of that legal authority who recommended that every accused person begin by saving himself from the accusation of having stolen the Notre-Dame towers, I had to protect myself from an all too apparent malicious intent. But from the place where I am momentarily, I can very well defend myself and report the one who is rightfully responsible for the theft laid to my charge. While waiting, Madame, I authorize you to make whatever use of this letter appears useful and proper to you in the interest of liberating your young friend.

Please believe me, Madame, with respectful eagerness, to be,

Your very humble and obedient servant,

Deschamps
Ex-surgeon in the Stables of
the Grand Duchess of Tuscany

As can be seen, while doing all that was necessary to re-habilitate the young painter, Matiphous tried to give an honest turn to his bad case, and when he turned against Britannicus the indiscrete revelation the servant had made, he was using a maneuver that found, in addition, its justification in all the procedure of that man against him.

Six days later, the 20th of March, Napoleon was back in the Tuileries, and Louis XVIII was hiding in Ghent. That great change, and soon afterward, the news of the nomination of Fouché [116] to the post of Minister of Police, made Matiphous

---

[116] Joseph Fouché, 1st Duc d'Otrante (Otranto in English) (1759-1820), French statesman and Minister of Police under the Directory, the Consulate, and the Empire. In 1814, Fouché joined the invading allies. However, he switched sides and

believe that his affair was opening in a new horizon. Thinking to himself of the unusual goodwill with which that great minister, as he called him, had honored him at another time, he had no doubt that a letter explaining and apologizing for his situation would be taken into particular consideration by his former protector. To insure that that letter would go only to him, he took care to address it in an envelope to Madame de Limeuil, asking her to place it in the right hands, implying that the communication which he was entrusting to the ex-lady of the Palace, would concern the service of the Emperor. His reentry into France thus prepared, despite his first intention, he continued to reside in Bruges until he received a response.

That response was not immediate, which was explained by the immense occupations of the man to whom he had written. Finally, after two weeks, it arrived, going beyond his hopes. Not only was he told to return to Paris, but he was asked to make the trip in all haste, in expectation of an important mission that they intended to give him.

Putting himself on the road, Matiphous wasn't yet very sure of the action he wanted to take. Should he present himself, as he had been invited, to the Duc d'Otrante to receive his orders, or, instead, hidden under a disguise, after having taken his precious strongbox from where he had left it, having in his pocket the Ministerial letter which everywhere on his route should prove be an excellent passport, should he go definitely and without hope of return to shelter his loot abroad?

Matiphous was traveling in business class. He counted on reentering France by way of Menin and Lille. Having just past Ostend, a little town not far from Bruges, when, in the middle of a plain on which the first shadows of night were beginning to fall, the gallop of several horses, which seem to

---

was Napoleon's police minister again during the Hundred Days. After Napoléon's defeat at Waterloo, Fouché headed the provisional government and tried to negotiate with the allies. In 1816, the royalists dispensed with his services. He died in exile in Trieste in 1820.

be following him, suddenly drew his attention. They soon caught up and he saw his carriage surrounded by five armed men, while he himself had no method of defense. How could an attack of robbers be supposed to take place on one of the beautiful and tranquil roads of Flanders, which he was at the moment traveling!

"Coachman, my friend, you have taken the wrong road," shouted the most visible member of the troop. "You were told to go by way of the Ostend Canal, and you have passed it."

"The Ostend Canal?" repeated the coachman with an astonished look.

"Yes, the canal which leads from Bruges to Ostend; don't you know it?"

"Oh, yes, I do, very well, Monsieur."

"All right, turn your horses around, and make good speed!"

"But, Monsieur," Matiphous then said, intervening, "why are you interfering? That direction is not the one I want to follow."

"Monsieur, I greet you," said the officious guide, "but it's not you that I have business with. If this rascal doesn't obey me, I'm going to blow his head off. Let's go, then," he added, turning the heads of the horses in the direction he wanted to take them, threatening the driver with a pistol.

Matiphous protested in vain against the violence done to him. The vehicle was turned in the direction indicated and three-quarters of an hour later, still escorted by the men who had turned him away from his original route, they stopped on the border of the canal, a few steps from a small boat moored there. Coming to the window, the man who had first spoken asked Matiphous said:

"Monsieur, that boat is lacking nothing but you to set sail. Will you please get aboard? My men will be careful in transporting your baggage."

"But what's all this about?" replied Matiphous with animation. "What does someone want with me? Where am I being taken?"

"I have already had the honor of telling you that. The boat that you see is at your orders. My mission is to conduct you to Ostend, dead or alive. I think that of those two choices the second is the one that would agree with you the most."

"Mission from whom?" Matiphous shouted, not seeming disposed to give in.

"Mission from my superiors, and I warn you, we don't have any time to waste. Get out therefore with good grace; otherwise I have four strong fellows who will do away with your resistance. But you won't force me to resort to methods of force. To tie down a man is a proof of bad taste, which shouldn't take place between well educated people."

After having still demurred for some time without seeing any clearer into his adventure, Matiphous gave in to the threat of violence which evidently must have been imminent, and let himself be put into the boat. Then, as he seemed to intend to stay on the bridge, the commander of the expedition said to him:

"No, into the cabin, please, where we can talk better. He who has done the greater can do the lesser."

Matiphous ceded rather easily to that injunction. After that, he was left by his questioner, who, he said, was going to oversee his effects being loaded aboard, begging him, just in case some other boat should come past, not to call in any way for help, unless he wanted to be exposed to the extreme humiliation of a gag already prepared that he showed him.

A few moments later, two trunks and some other parcels were brought into the place where Matiphous was being held as a private charter. He was politely asked to check that everything had been carefully brought on board.

When the task was over, the newcomer, who remained alone with his prisoner, said:

"It appears that you didn't find it convenient to bring with you the most precious of your belongings. I regret that because, if I had found what I was looking for, I would have been able to spare you the trip to Ostend, where, I must warn you, a ship awaits to transport you to England. And there, you know, you will have to chat with the Lords of the Admiralty."

"What valuable object are you talking about?" Matiphous demanded.

"Come now, dear Monsieur," he was answered, "let's not play a battle of wits this way. Clarity and frankness in explanations shorten and usually simplify things. Look at me closely. You don't recognize me?"

"No," said Matiphous, with disdain little disguised.

"Nevertheless, we saw each other in London some fifteen years ago, and in one of those circumstances which don't easily slip from one's memory. Both of us were in the hands of the dreaded Marquis de Samaniego at the time, and you had the graciousness not to want to be the executioner of the sentence of death that he had condemned me to."

"You must admit," Matiphous said, "that with you, a good deed is never lost."

"You will allow me," continued Rempailleux (for the reader has certainly recognized him), "to state that it was you yourself, dear Monsieur, who began to strike down the good rapports that would not have ceased between us. What the Devil! I took the trouble to discover a gold mine in the shape of a strongbox. You snatched it away from me! Two charming women, each in turn, took the trouble to go see you, in order to bring you back to better sentiments. Instead of recognizing your mistake, you skipped out abroad, and from there, to defy us, you wrote to her, giving us your address."

"Since Madame de Pringy," Matiphous responded "had the honor to be in contact with you, and she communicated to you the letter that I had really wanted to write to her, you must know that the strongbox you are looking for has passed into the hands of the Negro Britannicus, my former servant."

"First of all, my dear Monsieur," Rempailleux responded, "I don't like the way you stress the phrase, *had the honor* to be in contact with me. You can certainly believe that we are alike. Equal as to that strongbox that we both stole, I have this superiority over you: having been in prison, I'm happily not there anymore, and you, having dodged Rochefort, are now on the high road to the gallows. As for Madame de Pringy, she didn't tell me anything. It was to the Director of the Police that she gave the letter you addressed to her, apparently for her to use as she pleased, and if, in his turn, the Director of the Police made me aware of it, it was because I have the honor, in order that you know it, to be one of his principal agents."

"You will admit," said Matiphous, "that it was difficult for me to guess that."

"You know it now, and a little at your expense, I imagine. To that, I would add that it isn't a man of my intelligence that you can make believe fancy tales like that of Britannicus, becoming the holder of the strongbox that is being demanded from you. If he was the third thief, nothing forced him to reveal himself. The strongbox, when he mentioned it to me, was in your possession, and no one doubts that it is still there. Now, today, please listen to me, I am going to lay my cards on the table, and you will have to see if you judge it proper to use the same procedure."

"So be it!" Matiphous said, "I'm listening."

"Today," Rempailleux continued, "I have before me two open roads. Because of your case, I came into contact with the man who directs the Police of the Kingdom..."

"Who was directing it, you mean to say," Matiphous remarked, interrupting.

"Who is directing it, my dear Monsieur, because Ghent has its police as Paris has its own. Being then in contact with this high official, I gave him a rather advantageous idea of my ability so that he would judge it proper to attach me to him. I have since been rather fortunate in being able to render some services to the government of His Majesty Louis XVIII in exile. I have welded myself to his fortune. Before three months, we will have finished with Bonaparte. It's then only up to me to move forward into a career begun with such good fortune. The motto of Colbert *Que non ascendum!* [117] can very well be that of the existence that is beginning for me."

Probably waiting for some sign of agreement or disagreement, Rempailleux stopped with that pompous insight. Seeing that Matiphous had not said anything, he continued:

"However, in the place of an existence to create, I had in that strongbox that it pleased you to take from me, an existence already made, and well made. With its contents, going to establish myself abroad, I could lead an honorable, pleasant, independent life. And if I have to admit my inclination to you, it is still on that side that I would lean most willingly. You see then that you yourself must make a decision on this matter: in giving me back my property, you make me give up my ambitious career and I make you free, which will be the equivalent, I think, of the service that you rendered me in the past. If, on the contrary, you obstinately refuse to return what you stole from me, in a few hours, you will be on the road to London. Each step will bring you closer to the scaffold, and you will become one of my steps to my political fortune. Louis XVIII, an intelligent man who likes capable people, knows of our duel. Through Madame de Pringy, whose passion for young Levillain has made her approach him, he knows of our history, and has given orders for you to be deported to England. In this moment, most of all, when he has great need of that power, he wouldn't mind making a gift of your head, formerly refused by the Imperial Government. And certainly, there would be favors for the man who put him in the position to turn you over. Therefore, give me back what you took from me, or go get yourself hanged in England. These are the alternatives that I offer you and between which you must make a choice."

"But there is something else," Matiphous replied. "What you're asking me for, I no longer have."

---

[117] To what height can I not ascend!" Jean-Baptiste Colbert (1619-1683) was Minister of Finances from 1665 to 1683 under the rule of King Louis XIV.

"Let's not equivocate," replied Rempailleux. "I see very well that you don't have the object we are debating about with you. But you must have left it somewhere in France, and when I arrested you, you were probably going to fish for it in the troubled waters that have been made in our beautiful homeland by the return of the usurper."

"And when that happens, would I be more in a position to fulfill the condition that you place for my freedom?"

"It would be necessary to see," Rempailleux said. "We could come to an understanding. What would keep us from making the trip together? In order to cross the frontier, you must have made sure of some method giving you total security."

"Me? No," the man from Malta said casually. "With the change in government, I thought I would not be bothered."

"You are not telling me the truth; a man with as much cleverness as you have shown in all this business doesn't go to place himself thoughtlessly before all the possible eventualities. Will you please show me your papers?"

"My papers?" Matiphous said, in a show of bad temper. "I don't have any papers."

"Pardon me, but you always have papers, and when I left Rochefort Prison, I didn't have one passport, I had three of them, and all of them perfectly in order. Come now, show me your wallet."

Seeing the embarrassment that requirement seemed to cause his prisoner, Rempailleux clapped his hands three times. Two strong deck hands appeared at that signal.

"Search Monsieur," said the former convict in a short and imperative tone.

The resistance that Matiphous tried to impose to the execution of that order couldn't last very long. At the end of several minutes, the letter of the Duc d'Otrante was in Rempailleux' hands.

"Well well," said Rempailleux, "I have myself a fine boy. If I started on my way with you, at the first French outpost, we would reverse roles and you would have me apprehended. So, decidedly, there is nothing to be done with you. You are too solidly armed. You will keep what you stole from me, and I will become a great policeman. I'm your servant, my dear Monsieur," he said, going through the cabin door, which he double-locked behind him.

A minute later, Matiphous noticed that the boat was in movement and making its way toward Ostend, according to the announced itinerary.

Rempailleux hadn't said anything that was beyond the truth. Although Matiphous had slipped through his hands, the Director General of the Police had found in him a man very suited to the functions for which he had presented himself. Carrying to politics the intelligence and energy that the man from Malta had thwarted during the agony of the first Restoration, the former guest of the Rochefort prison had been employed for the surveillance of the Bonapartist Party, which, from moment to moment, showed itself to be enterprising and more threatening.

In a time of revolution, the instruments that are at hand aren't looked at too closely. And after all, Rempailleux wasn't the first prison escapee, masquerading in a uniform or a political job, to embody the type that, during violent times, never fails to rise to the surface of the new society. By the services he had rendered, he had recommended himself so well to the high functionary, whose conquest he had begun, that when said functionary went to Ghent to rejoin Louis XVIII, he had wanted that clever agent to accompany him.

In Ghent, Rempailleux knew he was close to Matiphous, who had acted with bravado in revealing his place of residence. After the first cares given to the organization of the emigration police, he had taken up the affair of the strongbox again. For the reasons earlier given, it had finally interested the deposed King, and, with money and the most extensive powers, Rempailleux had left for Bruges.

Matiphous, without having the least idea of what was happening, wasn't slow in again becoming the object of a surveillance as tight as that he had known he was under in Paris.

This time, however, he hadn't been able to make preparations for his departure, without Rempailleux, who, for some days, had been ready to arrange for his enemy's kidnapping, having been apprised of the road that he was going to take. In order not to create diplomatic difficulties in stopping a refugee on foreign soil, when, in addition, it was known that the King of the Low Countries was coldly disposed towards the Bourbon cause, the former *chauffeur* had been authorized to proceed in almost the same fashion as the one he had used when he had operated in the Orgères Forest. In that way, he didn't have an official mandate, and if he had been able to put his hands on the fortune Matiphous had stolen from him, he wouldn't have had the slightest scruple in parting company with the service of the Very Christian King. But he didn't make the mistake of carrying that infidelity beyond what he hoped to be a firm result.

When he saw things arranged so that he had again to rely on the good faith of his prisoner, either for finding where the strongbox was hidden, or accomplishing the hard task of going to retrieve it by himself, or being taken there by Matiphous himself, he judged that there were too many chances to run. At that point, no longer bargaining with his mission as a policeman, resigning himself to do without his loot, he decided that, as is commonly said, that Matiphous would carry the secret he was going to deliver with him in his tomb. Without any more explanations, he took the man from Malta to Ostend, accosted an English ship which, for some days, had been navigating about the port waiting to pick up his prisoner. After having put poor Matiphous on board, he abandoned him to his fate.

XVIII. How Matiphous Fended for Himself

On arriving in London, Matiphous was incarcerated in Newgate Prison. His situation was far from seeming to him as desperate as Rempailleux had described it. He felt there was before him more than one way to ward off the catastrophe that had been arranged for him. A great illusion, which very few minds escape, is to believe that, when we return, after the passage of some years, the places we have left, men and things, are going to be found in the same state and the same place, as if perpetual change was not the law of life.

Thus, the prisoner's first action was to write to Sir Sydney Smith, who, fifteen years before, after the false execution of Broughton, after having gotten him out of the hands of the sheriffs, had procured him the situation as guardian of the Bell Rock lighthouse. Supposing him still influential, to have his help, he thought he had only to tell him how things had occurred after his departure from Bell Rock. But, first of all, Sir Sydney was not at the moment in London. He had gone to the Congress of Vienna to solicit the abolition of the Slave Trade and the repressive measures against the Barbary States. Besides, the time had passed when the conqueror of Saint-Jean-d'Acre enjoyed from the King and his Ministers a favor which made anything possible. The attentions that he had received from the famous Queen, Caroline of Brunswick, the wife separated from George IV, had thrown him into complete disgrace, and his intervention in favor of his former protégé, would been less than efficacious.[118]

---

[118] Caroline Amelia Elizabeth of Brunswick-Wolfenbüttel (1768-1821), Queen of the United and wife of King George IV from 29 January 1820 until her death in 1821. In 1794, she was engaged to her first-cousin and George III's eldest son and heir George, Prince of Wales, despite the two of them never having met and George already being illegally married. They married the following year, and nine months later Caroline had a child, Princess Charlotte of Wales. Shortly after Charlotte's birth, George and Caroline separated. By 1806, rumors that Caroline had taken lovers and had an illegitimate child led to an investigation into her private life. In 1814, Caroline moved to Italy. In 1820, George became king of the United Kingdom and Hanover. He vowed she would never be the queen, and insisted on a divorce, which she refused. Caroline returned to Britain to assert her position as queen. She

Lacking that help, the prisoner thought about the Chaplain of Newgate, that original free-spirited man with whom he had dinner the evening of Broughton's execution and who had such unusual insights into human infirmities. Having good health being in the eyes of that man the first of virtues, Matiphous, despite a certain foretaste of *Hemp fever*, as English thieves call hanging, felt himself in good enough shape to interest that fanatic admirer of good health. By his functions, as well as by the great esteem in which he was held by the magistrates, despite his bizarre characteristics, that maniac, if he wanted to act, could become a very useful protector. As a consequence, Matiphous hastened to see him.

But after having spoken ill so often of valetudinarians,[119] the poor man had finally seen his own robust and impertinent constitution also altered. At the time when one of his duties called for his ministry, gout, for which we have seen him so cruelly reproach the Director of Newgate, held him nailed to his chair in his turn, forcing him to recognize that, if it was an evil, it was not a crime.

Thus deprived of the support on which he had counted, Matiphous had to think of a more complicated scheme, which actually suited him better, perhaps, since Mistress Aston, the tavern keeper, and Broughton, the boxer, with whom he still had an old account to settle, would be called on to pay the price for it. But first of all, the question was to know if the two honest characters were up to what he intended to have in store for them. During the first and short sojourn that he had made in Newgate, everybody there knew Mistress Aston, the sister-in-law of Jack Ketch. But since 1799, when her famous tavern,

---

was wildly popular with the British populace. On the basis of loose evidence collected against her, George attempted to divorce her, but failed. In July 1821, Caroline was barred from the coronation on the orders of her husband. She fell ill in London and died three weeks later.

[119] One unduly concerned about one's health and given to discussing it.

The Bottle and Magpie, had been closed, and she had left the business, the prison personnel had almost been renewed. The clerk Matiphous spoke to, not knowing that the London hangman had a sister-in-law, was even less able to say under what name she was married and where she lived. Several of his comrades from whom he also inquired, showed themselves just as ignorant. At that point, the man from Malta had only one resource, that of asking Jack Ketch himself for the information he needed.

Given the ulterior and forced relations that he could have with that person, to put himself spontaneously in his presence, was nothing to be happy about. However, overlooking that consideration, Matiphous nevertheless asked the executioner to come see him in prison. Asking for that interview was no surprise to anyone. The condemned in England, either to sell their cadaver, or to stipulate the method of strangulation, more or less expeditiously, were in the habit of dealing directly and over the counter with the hangman.

"You have asked for me?" said Jack Ketch, on entering the rather clean room where, by means of a good price paid in advance, the prisoner had been installed with all his baggage, "What can I do for you?"

Judging it useful to pique his curiosity with some preparatory talk, the man from Malta responded:

"My dear Mister Ketch, we have almost been close to seeing ourselves united by ties of blood, for me not to have forgotten your lovely family. In the impossibility of seeing myself able to go offer my homages to Mistress Ketch, I wanted your visit in order to have news of all of you, and also to ask you of those of Lady Stuart."

"Lady Stuart?" said Jack Ketch. "Don't know her."

"What? You don't yet know that your daughter, my former fiancée, married a Lord who died, leaving her all his fortune? But Mistress Aston, your sister, knew about all that good fortune. It's very astonishing that she didn't make you aware of it."

243

"My sister-in-law only told us that we didn't have to worry about Kitty anymore, that she was happy, but she didn't enter into any more details. Those two ladies have always had their little secrets together."

"Who are you telling that to! Nobody knows it better than I."

"Without a doubt, they were a little in league against you, but that was justice. You were no more frank with me about the collar. To think of saving that Broughton! And to think that you had shown talent for the job, and that in you, without your prejudices, I could have had as worthy a successor as I might have hoped for."

"But, Papa Ketch, if I'm not mistaken, you have two heirs?"

"Certainly. There is even one of them who's beginning to fly with his own wings. Lately, he has been commissioned by the authorities of New South Wales, and the other one continues to study under me, but he's not a subject who shows your talent. That's what it is to have flouted a profession where you could have succeeded! You see how it's turned out! Instead of holding the right end of the rope..."

"...I now have the luck to see it around my neck," said Matiphous, bravely completing the thought. "Your remark, Mister Ketch, is particularly just. But what do you expect? You have to defend yourself. But that good Mistress Ketch, you're not telling me about her?"

"As for her health, excellent; for her disposition, you know, still a little rough."

"And your sister- in- law, that dear Mistress Aston?"

" Oh! Mistress Aston, she's like her niece. She's had good fortune. She is today the wife of a rich owner of a bar in the market town of Southwark, where there are the strongest industrial establishments in all of London."

"Ah! Broughton is dead, then? Matiphous exclaimed eagerly.

"Broughton? Who knows what's become of him? But I don't see what his death has to do with Mistress Aston's marriage."

"Well! They have something in common, since Mistress Aston had married him in a first marriage."

"And when was that, if you please?" asked Jack Ketch.

"It was about six years ago, while Lady Stuart and I were in Italy."

"It was exactly six years ago that Mistress Aston married John Sedley, who at that time was speculating on public bonds. Since then, he has become the owner of a bar. At the time, Mistress Aston made his acquaintance, he was enormously fat, and since then, his corpulence has only increased. You can imagine how that resembles the portrait of Broughton, who was slim, sinewy and all muscle!"

"I was misinformed," replied Matiphous, who, having gotten his information, didn't find it useful to insist. "But," he continued, "great lady that she has become, the former hostess of *The Bottle and Magpie,* wouldn't she also have the charity to pay me a visit? You could tell her that I have a great many things to tell her about her niece, whom I encountered in Paris and in Florence. Florence! You understand, Mister Ketch, that's the city where the two ladies wrote to each other often, a fact which your sister-in-law will surely remember."

"I will convey your message," said Jack Ketch, "and Mistress Sedley will have a good laugh when I tell her you think she has become the wife of that miserable Broughton. As for me," he added in a significant way, "you have nothing else to tell me? No little arrangements to make with me?"

"Oh! Dear Mister Ketch, we aren't there yet, thank God!"

"Hum! A frigate and two schooners lost through your negligence; the case is serious, my friend, and I would be wrong to let you have any illusion."

"But what do you know? In case of a misfortune, I have my little bag of tricks."

"Oh! With me," said the conscientious operator, "these little tricks don't work, and if in making me come here, you had counted on some connivance, erase that hope from your mind. You see, even if it were my very own wife whom the sheriff ordered me to launch into eternity, I would spring the trap without hesitation, and without trickery, because, for me, duty comes before everything else."

"That's good, worthy Mister Ketch. Your incorruptibility is known and respected by all. But I have been charmed, nevertheless, to have seen you, just as I will be to greet Mistress Sedley. That's right, isn't that her name, Sedley?"

"Yes, Mistress John Sedley. You can rest easy; from the moment you have something to tell her about *Milady,* her niece, you can be sure of seeing her come running. Now, I don't know if I should tell you good-bye."

"By the Devil! These gentlemen of the Admiralty haven't yet let me know the day when my trial will take place."

"It's already taken place, your trial," thought the good Mister Ketch, "and you would have done well to have chosen from the assortment of ropes that I brought along, the one that you found the most suitable."

"That old scoundrel," Matiphous said to himself, "he believes that he has already launched me into space without having any idea of the stains that I can cast on his noble family."

That didn't keep the two from separating with every appearance of the most perfect cordiality.

Several days went by and Matiphous received a formal notification that fixed the day of his appearance before the Admiralty Court without Mistress Sedley having given any sign of her existence. The prisoner became impatient. He wrote a letter to her, a rather strong letter in which he said that the conversation asked in his name by Jack Ketch could prove as interesting as it could be for her as well as for himself, and he was astonished at a negligence that she would later regret.

An hour after receiving that letter, the former Mistress Aston entered Matiphous' cell and began by telling him that her brother-in- law hadn't fulfilled the commission which he had been given.

"What's more," she said, "I can explain to myself why he didn't do so. Without having exactly quarreled with them, we no longer see either my sister or her husband, who has been received rather coldly several times. After that, Ketch saw things in the wrong way, and, according to him, you are probably a finished man, for whom he would have found it useless to bother me."

"But, for you, Mistress Sedley," asked Matiphous, "am I therefore lost, without resources?"

"Goodness me! My dear, your case is not one of the best. When it comes to their navy, the English are nothing less than difficult. That bad situation took place ten years ago and it's still remembered as if it happened yesterday. As soon as you arrived in London, all the newspapers reported your arrival and I can believe you can count on there being some curious to see you judged."

"The curious interest me very little," remarked Matiphous, "but during my trial, I'm also counting on the people who, having put me in this predicament, would certainly, I hope, take in this affair the part that is rightfully theirs. These people, Mistress Sedley, you are acquainted with them."

"That's possible, but if I am, it's without my knowing it."

"Has Broughton never told you what happened at Bell Rock?"

"Broughton?" responded the former tavern keeper with embarrassment. "Do you believe that he even thought about putting his feet back in London?"

"He has done better than that; he has married here, and he is today the head of a very important establishment, a bar where he earns much coinage, I understand."

The pretended Mistress Sedley turned purple red, but understood that it was time to confess when the evidence was grasping her by the throat.

"You foreigners are astonishing," she said, "for knowing so much more than the natives who live here."

"So," the man from Malta continued, "you don't know anything about Broughton since the day when, by your intervention, he so pleasantly supplanted me with your niece, nor do you know about his marriage with her at Gretna Green, or his trip to Bell Rock with Fauntleroy, or the subtlety of the former hostess of *The Bottle and Magpie* spying on them when they embarked and forcing him into marriage later? You don't know, either, that he wanted to be married under the name of MacLeod, and, in order to better to hold him in check, his tender spouse required that the Chaplain of Newgate enter his real name of Broughton into the marriage register? Then, however, as the name of a hanged man isn't of too much use in social situations, you also don't know that the couple has registered their marriage and their bar under the name of Sedley?"

During that long recital, the former tavern-keeper had had time enough to regain a little composure.

"And when did all that happen?" she asked in a rather resolute voice.

"If all that happened, the man who knows so many things that you seem to ignore, would have, it seems to me, the right to make some demands?

"At least, it's necessary to know them," said Mistress Sedley, appearing to be ready to negotiate while still without admitting anything.

"Since Broughton," the man from Malta continued, "didn't tell you anything about his nice conduct at Bell Rock, I'm going to tell you."

And he recounted the murder of Ephraim in all its details, such as he had gathered them from the ex-boxer's correspondence with Fauntleroy.

"And you, at Bell Rock," Mistress Sedley then said, attempting to throw a diversion in the enemy camp, "you conducted yourself gallantly toward Kitty, whom you threw from the top of the lighthouse into the sea!"

"That's a lie," Matiphous quickly replied. "I was satisfied with putting fear into a miserable woman who had callously deceived me. Someone else inflicted the punishment I had threatened her with. And yes, everything for her ended in a bath in the sea, but it turned out for the best. But, in any case, that's not the issue here. The issue is that I left a colleague at the lighthouse to illuminate the beacon. Broughton killed him with a blow of his fist. Broughton is therefore the only and true cause of the loss of ships by the Royal Navy, and that has to be made known."

The former Mistress Aston, having naturally an insolent character, had, little by little, regained all her self-assurance, so she answered ironically:

"There is therefore only one thing to be done. That's for Mister Sedley to come, take your room here, and following that plot, to be hanged in your place."

"No, Mistress Broughton," the man from Malta replied, "I am far less demanding. If I don't denounce the secret of his identity, Broughton will not be hanged for giving a knock-out blow, like that to a bull, to a man who had nothing but his breath. To tell the truth, that fool Ephraim was threatening him with a knife. Broughton was afraid, and it was a case of self-defense, which makes his action excusable and leaves him, at most, a chance of being admonished. What I am asking, therefore, and it's not a great sacrifice, is that when I have him called as a witness, that Broughton come to tell things the way they happened, and that, finally, he help me to get out of the bad situation where I have been cast because of him."

"And if you don't get what you want?" Mistress Sedley asked in a smugly ironic tone.

"Oh! Then the account is easy to balance. Broughton is a murderer escaped from the scaffold, and I will say so. Broughton is a bigamist, since he married you while his first wife, Kitty, was, and still is, alive and I will say so. Broughton is not named John Sedley, and I will say so. Finally, Broughton, and his worthy friend Fauntleroy for a long time counterfeited currency from the Bank of England, helped in that task by the virtuous Mistress Aston, and you can really believe that I will also say so."

"By the Devil! That's quite a litany; but that's not all, my boy. To say those things when you're on the bench of the accused, you must also prove their veracity."

Then, taking out of his wallet a letter that he was very careful not to let it get into Mistress Sedley's hands, Matiphous replied:

"Quite right. My dear Mistress Broughton, come and look at this. Do you recognize your handwriting?"

On seeing the letter she had written to Kitty during her stay in Florence, and that Matiphous had intercepted, Mistress Sedley remained, you might say, frozen as if she had been turned to stone by Medusa herself. She finally shouted:

"Thief! You stole Kitty's correspondence!"

"Stolen or not, it's in my hands, and it proves in your own hand that Broughton and you were counterfeiters; that you, Mistress Aston, have stolen a page from the Gretna Green marriage register, and as for usurping the name of Sedley, that will be established by the Newgate Chaplain. He's an honest man, and he won't refuse to testify to that in Court."

"You've got us, that's sure," the former tavern-owner then said, going back to her familiar behavior of another time. "It will really be necessary for my husband to help you out. But are all these threats needed? Couldn't you obtain the same thing by kindness? We aren't stubborn as Turks and we could have come to an understanding."

"All right! Let's understand each other. Do you promise that Broughton will appear before the Court and that he will tell the truth?"

"How would you, my cherub, want him to do otherwise?" answered Mistress Sedley, caressingly. "But if, however, his testimony doesn't save you and they condemn him anyway?"

"Then he'll get out of it as best as he can. It's not necessary to foresee misfortune; it comes soon enough."

"Send your story to John Sedley so that I can drum it into him as much as necessary."

"Very well! Good-bye, Mistress Sedley, you see that your visit wasn't useless."

"You filthy Maltese," said the ex-tavern keeper, giving him a friendly push. "If you can con people like this! Get your neck out of the friendly hands of my brother-in-law, if you can, and then come and see us. We're easy to find, and then, as for the remainder of your stay, there may be some way to come to an understanding."

Having said this, Mistress Sedley took her leave and that type of overture said upon leaving, pertaining to a piece of compromising evidence that remained in his hands, made Matiphous believe that the woman, on whom he had counted the most for his defense, wouldn't let him down.

Two days later, an immense crowd gathered at the Admiralty Court, brought together by the First Lord, assisted by twelve jurors, because of the importance of the affair. To the accusation lodged against him, Matiphous replied by announcing that there would be a witness for the defense, who, when called, would shed full light on his innocence. But the clerk called the name of John Sedley in vain. The vaunted witness didn't appear.

Not believing that Broughton and his worthy half wanted to confront the terrible accusations that he could make against them, and not keep their word to him, the accused man begged the judge to suspend the hearing and to send someone to the domicile of John Sedley, who had perhaps been delayed by some unforeseen circumstance. One of the jurors then asked to speak. He observed that the delay would be useless and the action demanded by the accused man seemed unnecessary to him, because, to his knowledge, one of his friends has signed a contract the evening before with John Sedley to buy the bar. He had been given a large reduction in its price if it was paid in cash immediately. Sedley and his wife had then embarked precipitously for Holland, where Sedley had said he was called on the most pressing business, and, at that hour, they should have arrived there, unless the strong winds of the past few days had made his crossing difficult.

In the presence of a desertion so well stated by the juror, Matiphous had to recount the facts himself, such as they would have been attested to by the man who had clearly broke his word to him. Evidently, the good faith, indignation and conviction that he put into his account had a great effect on the jury. They marveled at the fact that John Sedley was none other than the famous Broughton, hanged in the view of, and known by, all in London, and miraculously resuscitated by the hands of the one who, at that moment, refused so inhumanely his help.

In England, criminal debates are not conducted as they are here in our High Courts. Among our British neighbors, effectively, and not in virtue of a fiction too often badly observed, the accused man is considered innocent, right up until the time his crime is recognized by a declaration of the jury. The judge never asks him any incriminating questions by which he might show that he has already formulated an opinion about the putative guilt of the accused, which remains to be proven. On the contrary, if the accused man directs his defense badly, taking the road to condemn himself, the judge warns him against it.[120] In certain cases where there is a magistrate, whose functions are equivalent to those of our own Public Prosecutor, who, in principle, doesn't exist in the United Kingdom, parting from the idea that he is the accusation incarnate, as the lawyer for the accused man is the defense in flesh and blood, if that magistrate permitted himself to use against the man he is charged with prosecuting, those violent words, those vehement apostrophes, in a word, those forms of language that presume guilt, by which our own young prosecutors often seem "to sell the bear's skin before they have

---

[120] Rabou, in a roundabout way, is informing his readers that, in British common law, a person may not be forced to testify against himself and that he is presumed innocent until proven guilty.

felled the bear,"[121] he could be strongly admonished by the Presiding Judge and by the murmurs of those listening. The Judge, in England, is, technically speaking, charged only with pronouncing the sentence in virtue of the jury's verdict. He is a sort of referee in that duel between the accused and his accuser. He tries not to be in favor of one or the other, neither partial nor complaisant. He gives weight only where he sees justice and truth. It was thus that the Lord of the Admiralty was quick to notice that the desertion of Broughton, known as Sedley, given the information that he had just received, gave great verisimilitude to the role Matiphous had attributed to him, and found that the death of Ephraim must be attributed to him

But, unfortunately for the accused, another custom of English justice was to hold to the express letter of the law in the application of punishment. What was the law here? It was the regulation that at all times the Bell Rock lighthouse must be tended by three guardians charged with caring for it. Two must constantly be at their post. Now, what did Matiphous do? He had left his post, leaving only one of his colleagues to take his place. If Broughton had not intervened, and the beacon had been lit, the absent guardian would not have been less at fault. But his irregular absence having brought about the loss of three vessels of the State, his act took on the character of high treason! That was the way the question was put to the jury and, in that sense, it was resolved by its verdict.

From there, contradictorily, as he had been judged *in absentia,* Matiphous ran the risk of the death penalty. It was, in fact, that penalty to which he was condemned.

It will be noticed that, in his defense, the man from Malta had not at all used the devastating knowledge that he had of the past of the boxer and Mistress Aston. In that, he had shown proof of a very strong intellect, since it would have been of no value before the court judging him. To blacken the

---

[121] French idiomatic expression equivalent to "count their chickens before they're hatched."

people who were not part of the trial, except by the testimony which convicted them, would not have made himself any whiter, and it would have lessened the value of information that, in case of some misfortune, a recommendation had to be made to the authorities. In fact, in denouncing all the misdeeds that were on the conscience of the so-called Sedley spouses, would have given the law a pretty bouquet of crimes, and that gift could inspire some indulgence toward him. Often victim of the audacity and multiplicity of counterfeiters who falsified its currency, the Bank of England was especially replete with examples that could be used against them. The promise to tell them the source of a clandestine operation that had bothered them for a long time, might easily bring some kind of offer, and, with it, a condemned man could very reasonably hope for a commutation of his sentence.

Matiphous had to search less for his salvation in that way, since the people destined to become his substitutes for the gallows seemed to have put themselves beyond pursuit, and therefore could be executed only in effigy. As a consequence, he was already busy drawing up a memoir to the Governor of the Bank of England, when he was told he had a visitor. That visitor was the Chaplain of Newgate. His gout attack had lessened its violence since the time Matiphous had asked for him. On learning that he had a condemned man to console, he had drawn from the sentiment of Christian Charity enough moral strength to supplement a kind of convalescence that he had immediately used in the service of one of the most imperative duties of his ministry.

As much sympathy as that the worthy Chaplain had seemed to feel for him, just so much repulsion he had always felt for Broughton, and he had agreed to marry him clandestinely to Mistress Aston only with great dislike. However, his former friendly relationship with the Ketch family made him overlook his repugnance and be part of that affair. But when he learned that Kitty was still alive, and that her aunt had deliberately taken her place, he became violently angry against the former tavern-keeper who had thus misused his religion.

He told the condemned man not to take the trouble to draw up a memoir.

"Trust me with the evidence that you have against the odious household," he said. "I will take charge of all the necessary steps. I will have more authority and more chance of success than you."

The result was almost immediate. The very next day, the death penalty pronounced against Matiphous was commuted to twenty years deportation to the penal colony of Botany Bay.[122]

The English police function with great ability. Having gotten wind that Broughton and his worthy other half, in view of retaining some part of the fortune that they counted on taking with them, had only *pretended* to embark for Holland, they became very active in their search. They were not long in finding them hidden in a little village with the counterfeit plates of the bills created in Florence by the engraver Hans Krafft. In Fauntleroy's hand, when he was found in the unusual place of rest that Salvador Arbib had organized before his departure from Livorno, that counterfeit plate, that it was almost impossible to distinguish from the original plate, had not been destroyed. Following negotiations with Ferdinand III, Grand Duke of Tuscany, it was returned to the English government. Today it is on display in the British Museum as an object of curiosity.[123]

---

[122] Botany Bay is located in Sydney, New South Wales, Australia. On 29 April 1770, it was the site of James Cook's first landing. In 1788, the British planned to use the site for a penal colony. Although the penal settlement was almost immediately shifted to Sydney Cove, for some time in Britain, transportation to Botany Bay was synonym for transportation to any of the Australian penal settlements.

[123] Rabou may have been inspired by the real-life William Booth of South Staffordshire (b. c.1778), a notable forger of English banknotes, who was hanged for the crime in 1812.

Several of his forgeries and printing plates are today in the collection of Birmingham Museum and Art Gallery

PART II. COMMANDANT LEFEBVRE[124]

I. The Fortune that Rempailleux Made

Times of revolution are marvelous for those who, having lived a damaged existence, try to get themselves rebranded. The heat and the all the fierce energies striving for the possession of power being carried to their highest degree, people hardly concern themselves with the morality of the passions they engender, and are only concerned with their ardor and their zeal. Before the Ghent trip, Rempailleux had begun to make himself useful to the Bourbons. During the three months that the interregnum lasted, he continued to show himself devoted, active, ready to undertake any mission, because his conscience never bothered his diligence, and the adventurous audacity of which he had given so much proof was equal to all the challenges.

Each time he had a task to carry out, it was accomplished cleverly and easily, as had the kidnapping of Matiphous been

---

[124] According to Rabou's outline from Volume I, this section should have been Part III, and there should have been another Part II entitled "Botany Bay," likely about the further adventures of Gregorio Matiphous in Australia, but there is no trace of it in this volume While Matiphous returns in the next volume, the details of his Australian adventures remain mostly untold. As was the custom of the times, it is entirely possible that this was the result of editorial interference, Rabou being asked to cut short this plot thread that might have proved unpopular with the readers. In any event, Rabou, who had probably researched the subject already, didn't let go of it, and Botany Bay plays an important part in the last chapters of the fourth and final volume.

effected. The care he took for the business he had been charged with, on that occasion, did not let him neglect his own interests.

As the catastrophe of March 20 unfolded,[125] Lady Stuart, like all of her compatriots, saw herself obliged to leave France and flee before the cruelest enemy of England. Not daring to return to her country, and having but few relations in the one she was forced to leave so suddenly, she would have been somewhat hampered socially by her displacement if, cleverly seizing the opportunity to follow up on the tender projects that he had for her, Rempailleux hadn't come to put himself gallantly at her service to take her to Belgium, where he himself had gone. In making her profit by the official position that he had already gained for himself, he simplified all the difficulties that, for a woman most of all, always complicated such a hurried departure.

Once in Ghent, Lady Stuart became the object of her guide's frantic attentions. He used every method to seduce her. Since he had found Jack Ketch's daughter amiable during their first interview, and since he was privy to almost all the secrets of her life, she could hardly show herself indifferent to his overtures. In that situation, in any case, it was certainly necessary that she acknowledge her humble servant.

But chance willed that, by doing a good action, a truly moral act that broke with the stupidity of the rest of his life, Rempailleux had found a way to recommend himself in the most decisive way to the goodwill of the one whose conquest he had undertaken. Without knowing it, he had encountered her weak side, and given himself a halo of unusual merit that, as we have seen, always appealed with a sort of fascination to that strange woman. One evening, when he was visiting that beautiful woman, a fire broke out in a neighboring house. The fire had spread so quickly that an elderly woman in an upper floor found it impossible to escape and seemed to be facing

---

[125] March 20, 1815, date of Napoleon's return from Elba, leading to the Hundred Days.

inevitable death. The sinister Rempailleux, full of pity, taking advantage of the scaling lessons that are always part of the studies of a consummate thief, using a knotted rope and some ladders, lifted himself to the apartment threatened by the fire and managed to bring down safe and sound the poor woman that everyone had thought lost.

Watching that dedication from her windows, the woman who had formerly admired Broughton and Tamerlane was most of all impressed with the agility and the truly audacious acrobatics that her suitor had just shown, and, from that day, the actions of his gallant enterprise took such an upward flight that he could broach the question of marriage and be favorably heard. Without a doubt, Kitty Ketch didn't have the right to be very demanding in the choice of a new husband. It is not very probable, however, that if she had known the kind of work her intended husband did, she would have accepted to bear his name. But that was exactly why, apropos of that name, that he, always the clever negotiator, imagined an ingenious comedy of frankness and delicacy, to hide the antecedents of the famous Dulac, also known as Rempailleux. Everything was there to win over the last hesitations of the pretty widow, supposing that she experienced some scruples in marrying a man of whom she knew neither his occupation or his means of existence, and whom she knew only by his row of medals, by his verbose passion for reforming the prisons, and his way of hauling himself up to the highest peak of a sheer wall by the method of painters.

"Dear beautiful one," Rempailleux said to her some days before the celebration of their marriage, "I owe you a confession. The name of Saint-Rambert is certainly mine; however, the title of Count that I am in the habit of adding to it could very well be contested. It has always been worn in our family, but, I must be forced to admit, without our genealogy supporting it. At a time when the nobility is becoming all powerful again, it could be possible that this might become a touchy subject, and I am not without some fear that there could be a squabble about it. If you will agree then, you will call yourself just Madame de Saint-Rambert, without any other qualification."

Kitty Ketch answered him that it was very easy to agree with such scruples, when so many people, who were not even gentlemen, didn't hesitate to deck themselves out with a coat of arms and give themselves titles by their own authority.

For a marriage celebrated in a foreign country to be valid in France, it has to be preceded by being published in that country. Either because, in light o0f his his unusual position, Rempailleux saw some difficulties too great in accomplishing that formality, or he didn't absolutely intend to build the edifice of his conjugal felicity for eternity, he didn't take the trouble to conform to that prescription of the Civil Code, and by marrying in Ghent a few days before the battle of Waterloo,[126] he managed to escape a formality with which a French Civil Officer would have asked him to comply.

Immediately after, the two spouses crossed the frontier back into France, in the wake of the Bourbon contingent, and concerned themselves with fixing a detail that, for the future of their union, was an incontestable problem. It was a question of arranging the fate of the interesting by-product left in Lady Stuart's hands by the villain, Britannicus. To get rid of it, the father had to be set free, and that condition was arranged during the general discharge of the affair of Madame de Pringy. Not being able to be heard in the middle of all the grave preoccupations requiring all the attention of the Imperial Government, the poor lady had again brought up the matter as soon as a calmer political situation had arisen and, given her ardent activities, had met with some success.

We have already seen that Louis XVIII had been made aware of that judicial error which was in need of repair. Although the previous Director General of the Police had been replaced during The Hundred Days by the Duc d'Otrante, the former functionary had kept enough of the King's ear to remind him of the fate of the unfortunate man in whom he had

---

[126] 18 June 1815.

seemed to take an interest. Gregorio Matiphous, now recognized as being the real thief of the strongbox, the young painter, who did not meet the conditions required by the Code of Criminal Prosecution to be rehabilitated, was nevertheless granted a pardon in the most reparatory and honorable terms. In addition, what was a more pleasant and just as conclusive a justification as one that might have been handed down by a royal court, he was to become, just as soon as the legal waiting period for widowhood had expired, the happy successor of the late Monsieur de Pringy.

In this way, thrown into the bargain because their revelations had paved the way for that happy denouement, Rempailleux and Britannicus saw themselves included in a sort of friendly general amnesty, and their respective pardons were also granted, on the condition that the Negro immediately leave France, where it was feared that his indiscretions relative to the existence of the Secret Bureau might be revealed.

As soon as the formalities necessary to give the royal pardon time to take effect were completed, the child, whose presence in her household Kitty had, until then, explained as a kindly caprice that had caused her to adopt him, was turned over to Britannicus with an adequate sum of money. For more security, Rempailleux himself conveyed the happy father to Le Havre. There, he saw him aboard a ship which would take him back to Madagascar. In that way, it was hoped he would never be heard from again.

Then remained for the former host of the Rochefort prison to his other an ambition, that of securing in the police the fixed and definitive position that, until then, had only been an unofficial attribution. The moment to satisfy that desire wasn't very favorable. Fouché, by a strange combination, after having been the Minister of the Police during the Hundred Days, was showing signs of staying on the job during the Second Restoration, and he sought to protect, to the extent it was still possible, the dignity of his administration. He probably wasn't so naïve as to want angels or prizes of virtue as agents, but a pardoned convict seemed to him too scandalous an instrument.

He didn't therefore want to employ the former leader of the *Chauffeurs,* and Rempailleux saw himself halted in the first steps of his career, where he had promised himself the most shining success. Fortunately for him, in that passionate period of 1815, independent and separate from the official police, two or three other parasitic police entities were, at the same time, recruiting their own personnel.

It's known that, parallel to Louis XVIII's government, the Comte d'Artois,[127] taken by the *Ultras* [128] to be a Jacobin[129], had organized a counter-direction of affairs. The police of that occult government, that had a certain allure of a conspiracy, had naturally to show itself less demanding than that which operated openly. Presented to one of the intimate advisors of *Monsieur*, the King's Brother, by the former Director General of the Police that Fouché had replaced, Rempailleux was very appreciated and became one of the most active agents of the Marsan Pavilion,[130] thanks to another influence which, from time immemorial, has played an enormous role in the affairs of this world. He didn't wait long to see his dream

---

[127] The future King Charles X (1757-1836), who reigned from 16 September 1824 until 2 August 1830. The younger brother of Louis XVI and Louis XVIII, he supported the latter in exile and eventually succeeded him. His rule ended in the July Revolution of 1830, which resulted in his abdication and the election of Louis Philippe I. Exiled once again, he died in 1836 in Gorizia, then part of the Austrian Empire. He was the last of the French rulers from the senior branch of the House of Bourbon.

[128] French political label used from 1815 to 1830 under the Bourbon Restoration. An *Ultra* was usually a member of the nobility of high society who strongly supported Bourbon's monarchy and traditional hierarchy between classes.

[129] A member of the Jacobin Club, a revolutionary political movement that was the most famous political club during the French Revolution.

[130] Part of the Louvre that temporarily housed the police.

of political fortune largely accomplished and realized. It must be revealed that the new patron of Rempailleux was a middle-aged Duke very fond of success and women, and that, in his courtly existence, that great Lord had found the means to make politics, gallantry, and religion live together in passable harmony. Decided to advance himself at any cost, the former criminal found the way, without saying so, to let his protector know that he was the husband of a very agreeable woman. Then, by a transcendent hypocritical inspiration, he let the great lord who honored him with his patronage, know confidentially about the domestic wound that was supposed to be the torment of his life.

That poor man! He had married a Protestant! And that difference in religion, although not bringing any exterior trouble into his marriage, was nonetheless, for him, the saddest and most constant preoccupation. Thereupon, the gallant Duke offered himself to approach the pretty heretic about a change of religion, a subject that Rempailleux declared that he had never dared to bring up with her. Then, under that pious pretext, the missionary multiplied his visits to the wife of his agent. Besides, that was not a relationship where one could surround oneself in mystery, since the woman in question was living in a townhouse in the Faubourg St. Honoré where everything breathes elegance, so that, if her husband followed a police career, it could be believed that it was as an amateur, as is sometimes seen, with an unusual taste for intrigue and political secrets.

Kitty Ketch had never been very devout in her religious practices. So, when the converting zeal of a charming Duke and Peer of the Realm, often seeming to be preaching about himself when speaking to her about the love of God, was supplemented by that of two dowagers from the Faubourg St. Germain, one Father of the Faith[131] and that of the Bishop *in*

---

[131] The Society of the Faith of Jesus, whose members were commonly called Fathers of the Faith, was a religious congregation created in 1797 in Italy by Nicolas Paccanari. After

partibus of Persepolis,[132] her already weakened religious convictions were shaken, and she saw no reasons to refuse to give her spiritual patrons the consoling spectacle of an abjuration.[133]

The ceremony took place at the Foreign Missions Church, surrounded by an immense crowd of that aristocracy, often testy in its relationships with an honest bourgeois man who doesn't try to overstate his origin, and so tenderly welcomed by intriguers who plot to dupe him. It wasn't only Rempailleux's terrible past that advised him to be cautious. Suddenly, thanks to his wife, that society had begun to be mad about him, and he could have been able to obtain his admissions to the salons of the noble elegant neighborhood. But he didn't try to take his beautiful convert there, and she couldn't properly take advantage of the access given to her, leaving her husband at the door as one does his cane or his umbrella. The admission of the usurpation of a title that had preceded their union still served Rempailleux as an explanation for his repugnance to be introduced into the world of Dukes and Marquis. And besides, since Kitty's father was still living and exercising his profession, Kitty Ketch was the first to comprehend that, always at the mercy of some unexpected revelation, she could not introduce into her life a too bright light for some jealous or curious person. What was possible for her, however, with the help of the great lord who had evangelized her, and who continued to be her passionate admirer, was to have a

---

having merged with the Society of the Sacred Heart in 1799, it established itself in several countries of Europe and existed until the re-establishment of the Society of Jesus in 1814 that it had prepared.

[132] *In partibus infidelium:* In the lands of the unbelievers; used in a bishop's title after the name of a diocese conquered by a power of another faith.

[133] The solemn repudiation, abandonment, or renunciation by or upon oath. The term comes from the Latin *abjurare*, to forswear.

salon where there was no woman from the world of high society, but where her beautiful contralto voice attracted men with
the proudest names. Artists, pretty middle-class women, jour-
nalists, excellent music, quadrilles when they wanted to dance,
and an absolute lack of restraint and etiquette, made those
meetings at Madame de Saint-Rambert's so much more attractive, especially since her husband had the prudence to be
scarcely visible, to the point that his very existence eventually
came to be questioned.

But while Rempailleux held himself prudently to one
side, his wife's credit with all the noble *habitués* of her house
put down rather deep roots, and an opportunity presenting
itself, she found herself in a position to push the worthy companion of her life into a position that was for him of unparalleled value since, surrounded with impenetrable mystery, it
could never expose him to the world of the press, or, on seeing
him then clothed with public functions, no one could think of
looking into his past.

That position was that of Director of the Secret Bureau,
in other words, the very same job that, since the Consulate,[134]
had been filled by Hulet. In mounting the throne of his fathers,
Louis XVIII, having in mind the will of the Martyr King,[135]
had pardoned the regicide members of the Convention, and,
after the Hundred Days, they did not think they needed to worry. But, on the occasion passing this law of amnesty the
Chambre Introuvable [136]voted for the banishment of those
among them who had accepted functions after the return of

---

[134] The Consulate was the government of France from the fall
of the Directory in the coup of Brumaire in 1799 until the start
of the Napoleonic Empire in 1804.

[135] Louis XVI.

[136] The so-called Unobtainable Chamber was the first Chamber of Deputies elected after the Second Bourbon Restoration
in 1815. It was dominated by the Ultras who refused to accept
the results of the French Revolution. That nickname was
coined by Louis XVIII.

Bonaparte from the Island of Elba. Despite his long and constant opposition to that rigorous measure, Louis XVIII, who was at heart a constitutionalist, was forced to bow before the will expressed by the majority of the national representatives.

After that, a question had been raised: would the law be applied to Hulet, a regicide member of the Convention who, during the second reign of Napoleon, had continued to direct the Secret Bureau? Without a doubt, he materially fell under the purview of that new law, but it seemed that more than one objection could be made to the idea of applying it to him. His functions being of an essentially occult nature, could it be said that he had accepted *public functions* under the reign of the usurper? In addition, didn't his mandate have the character of an overriding and fatal duty? Riveted in infamy, almost like the public executioner, he was obliged to work for all governments. Finally, holder of many a state and private secrets, should he, by revocation and exile, be in some way freed from his oath of absolute silence, or even if he was considered to be still tied to it after the State having so violently separated itself from him, was there a way to be sure of his silence, abroad or at home, and could he be required to give an account for having spoken if he didn't keep his vows?

Of course, with all those considerations in play, there was enough evidence to justify keeping Hulet as head of the Secret Bureau, which he had administered with intelligence and integrity, remaining carefully free of all political passion. But we have seen that his claim to keep his management away from any other control but that of the Head of State, had made him many enemies. So he was not only a regicide, but a married priest, and in a government surrounded in every way by clerical influence, the consequences of that situation could well be imagined. No one better than Madame de Saint-Rambert, the new convert, was in a better position to exploit a situation that became decisive in the matter of his replacement.

The Marsan Pavilion also very much wanted to have a man of its own in charge of a department as important as that of the Secret Bureau, and they employed a great deal of activity to obtain that result. In short, the replacement of Hulet by the ignoble Rempailleux was decided. The former member of the Convention received a rather high indemnity, and at the beginning of 1816, was ordered to leave France.

At that time, under the auspices of the Lallemand brothers, former Generals of the Empire, there began to be a question of the establishment of some French refugees in Texas. An effort publicized by the newspapers, known since under the name *Champ d'Asile*, that colony, finally sadly abandoned, attracted Hulet and, with his wife and daughter, he embarked for America.[137]

---

[137] François Antoine Charles Lallemand (1774-1839). French general who served under Napoleon. After the Emperor was defeated and exiled the first time, he joined the army of Louis XVIII. In 1815, he and his brother Henri tried to lead a rebellion against the Bourbons, but were arrested. When Napoleon returned from Elba, he released them and gave them both commands in the Imperial Guard. After the Battle of Waterloo, Lallemand accompanied Napoleon to Rochefort, where Napoleon surrendered. Lallemand tried to follow Napoleon into exile but the British refused that and imprisoned him in Malta for two months before he escaped. Lallemand and other Bonapartist officers were condemned to death in absentia. The brothers were not included in the later amnesties. Lallemand then went to the United States and tried to found a colony in Texas. After Louis-Philippe restored the old imperial military grades after the July Revolution of 1830, Lallemand returned to France and was asked to serve as governor of Corsica. The *Champ d'Asile* (Field of Asylum) colony was a short-lived settlement founded in Texas by the Lallemand brothers in January 1818 by 20 Bonapartist veterans. Land was offered to the settlers on March 3, 1817, after a vote by Congress. The colony was to bring some military men for protection, but concentrate on agricultural work, cultivating grapes and olives. On December 17, 1817, the settlers, included about a hundred

If he had known that Rempailleux had kidnapped his younger son to give him to his guest at Orgères,[138] the hope of finding that dear and cherished regretted child would have been a stronger reason for him going to the United States. But he didn't know then the exploit of the criminal and his determination to enter the New World seemed to have been the result of no specific interest; it was simply an instinct.

II. Commandant Lefebvre

Former Battalion Chief of the 122nd line, Commandant Lefebvre was a short, stocky little man with an athletic build which is ordinarily the result of a marked preference for the material life over the moral life. His hair was deep silver; his thick neck, between the tie and the back of the head, turned into a roll of fat. And most of all, his abdomen, that, in walking with a studied stiffness, he tried to hide by making it flow back into the thorax, would have been enough to show that he was approaching the half-century. But he wouldn't have given himself that age. He rarely missed an opportunity to recall that, joining the army at twenty-three as a volunteer in 1799, he had had the honor to be part of all the campaigns of the Republic and of the Empire.

For a man who had fought so much, especially for the Empire, where, thanks the massive periodical killings, to advance in rank was almost synonym with a spirit of survival, having only achieved the rank of Battalion Chief, was a rather

---

veterans from the *Grande armée*, sailed from Philadelphia for Galveston, where they arrived on January 14. Lallemand and the other colonists convened in New Orleans, and on March 10 left for Galveston. They sailed up the Trinity River to Atascosito where they built two small forts. Mexican governor Antonio María Martínez, having heard about this expedition, sent his own troops to San Marcos, wary of an attack. The colony was abandoned shortly afterwards.

[138] See Volume 1.

mediocre result. But despite his bravado and some other military attributes, Lefebvre had seen his advancement curtailed and his military career weighed down by his limited intelligence, a deplorably neglected education, the misfortune of often having served in a corps that fought far from the eye of the Emperor, and, most of all, to use the language of the barracks, by displaying a frenetic mania for chasing after skirts.

In Illyria, at the beginning of his career, he had disastrously complicated matters by having an affair with a kind of Canteen Venus, who, in inflaming his desires with unexpected resistance, had exalted them right up to the point of marriage. That folly having eventually come to an end, he had nonetheless continued to be at the mercy of the first provocative pretty face passing by. For him to commit some stupid act, he had only to encounter a woman in his path. To say that his political opinions had prevented him from serving under the Bourbons, would be to misunderstand an idea a great deal too complex, that is to say that most of the people like him, at that time, could be summed up in a single characteristic: their fanatic and exclusive admiration for Napoleon. Beyond that man, who, to them, was the God of War, there was still a military career, promotions to win, and glory to acquire, but it really meant nothing to them. As for the nature of the regime under which they would have to live, as for liberty, as for political guarantees, in the absence of their idol, they found those good questions only worthy of occupying lawyers and bureaucrats. And for them, it said everything about government that, from the moment that the King was no longer able to mount a horse, he had the gout and wore gaiters like the pot-bellied Englishmen who were then flooding Paris.

For Commandant Lefebvre in particular, it must be added that, if he had shown little enthusiasm to be employed by the Restoration, on the other hand, no effort had been used by the Restoration to keep him in the ranks of the army. The notes in his dossier offered nothing outstanding. To give and receive blows, that was almost all the ability attributed to him. If, to a hardly distinguished exterior were added his notoriety

269

for scandalous behavior, and a habitual look of rebellion showing his intemperance in the use of gross and dirty language, the little amount of enthusiasm shown by the War Bureau to keep him in the ranks they had to fill can be understood. Toward the first days of the month of March 1816, Commandant Lefebvre was therefore in that limited and sorrowful position that the jokers of the time called *the demitasse,*[139] and, unfortunately for him, outside of that reduced and precarious treatment, his resources, that he had almost never saved, were as insufficient as can be imagined.

The father of two children, a son who, by means of a scholarship, had attended a lycée, and a daughter, that his position as a legionnaire had allowed to obtain a place at the Imperial School of Ecouen,[140] Lefebvre had, for reasons of economy, set up house in Belleville. There, his wife, aided by her daughter, languished in doing a little business in lingerie. As for him, he went down every morning to Paris, always in the hope, forever postponed, of being named to a position of inspector in an insurance company that insured against hail. These steps taken, he then went to the Café Lemblin [141] to join

---

[139] Half-cup, i.e.: half-pay.

[140] The *maisons d'éducation de la Légion d'honneur* were the French secondary schools set up by Napoleon originally meant for the education of girls whose father, grandfather or great-grandfather had been awarded the Légion d'honneur. Napoleon appointed Jeanne-Louise-Henriette Campan, former readers of the daughters of Louis XV and lady of the bedchamber of Marie-Antoinette, headmistress of the first *Maison*. She had wanted Napoleon to set the school in Saint Germain, but he chose instead the Château d'Écouen, near Paris, which had been a property of the Légion since July 6, 1806.

[141] Famous Parisian coffee shop founded in 1805 (the year of the Battle of Austerlitz) by a former coffee boy of La Rotonde named Lemblin. At that time, it was located at No. 103 of the gallery of Chartres, nowadays gallery Beaujolais, of the Palais-Royal. It was from 1815 a center of opposition for the

some friends who, until dinner time, occupied themselves with defaming the present and regretting the past. Then he made his way toward the Temple neighborhood with a very lukewarm eagerness to see his family, since, almost daily, he was await-ed there by a jealous scene, sometimes stormy, sometimes wet with tears. His wife, despite her having passed her forty-fifth year, and because of her completely vanished beauty, had nev-er become accustomed to the fact that, as she said, he was running to Paris every day, and that his applications, which she seemed mere pretexts, were never crowned with any suc-cess.

One day, crossing the gardens of the Palais-Royal, Lefebvre was not a little surprised to see coming toward him a man that his memory should have given him every reason to avoid. The one approaching him under those unexpected cir-cumstances was one Laverenette, a former major of his regi-ment. Following some crooked manipulation of military pay-roll, he had been lucky to avoid being court-martialed by re resigning instead. Before that disguised discharge, the Major had had rather violent confrontation with Lefebvre on the sub-ject of the various acts of embezzlement that had compro-mised him. Without the difference of rank, an affair of honor between them would have become almost inevitable. We are saying "almost" because events proved that it was not easy to cross swords with Laverenette. As soon as he had returned to civilian life, strongly provoked by the Commandant, he had done what the military call a "total dive: and failed to resur-face; since then there had been no occasion for contact be-tween the two adversaries.

While in Lefebvre, dressed in a blue redingote buttoned right up to the throat in order to hide his linen, everything in-dicated negligence and poverty, the former Major presented himself in attractive morning dress that seemed not to leave any doubt as to the excellent state of his affairs. Perhaps he

Bonapartists. The half-pay of the army came to recount their recollections of the Spanish War and the Russian campaign.

found in that contrast, but most of all in the impudence that is natural to people of his kind, the courage to accost, a smile on his lips, the man from whom he could expect only the most contemptuous greeting.

"Ah! It's that dear Commandant Lefebvre," he shouted, in a very pronounced Marseille accent. "How are you since we've last seen each other, and the world, you might say, has become new?"

"I find it amusing," Lefebvre answered, "that you feel the need to speak to me."

"What! Still harboring some resentment?" Laverenette continued, "and for something as silly as a peccadillo in the service. Come now! *Unite and forget*, that's the word of the wise monarch who governs us, and what he says for parties can very well also be said to heal civil discords between two former comrades."

Lefebvre had never thought about politics while he was in the service; but since he frequented the Lemblin Café, it had become too ardent a preoccupation for him not to react bitterly to the praise Laverenette had just lavished on the conciliatory intentions of their monarch. He let himself be drawn into continuing a conversation that he had, at first, wanted to close with only two words, so he replied:

"Ah! Ah! So Monsieur, it appears, is for the white flag?"

"Upon my word, my friend, I've done the same as Europe and most of our Marshalls; I had enough of that furious madman, who would have killed us all! And, what the Devil! we didn't make the Revolution of '89 to end up being governed by an iron scepter."

"As for me," said Lefebvre, "I prefer a scepter of iron to a scepter of sh**!"

"Ah! I felt it coming!" exclaimed, Laverenette, laughing, who didn't disdain a pun on the occasion. "Good old Lefebvre! Always a vulgar word, but basically amusing and witty."

What kind of bad temper could resist a flattery that picks up every word out of one's mouth and polishes it like a gem?

"Come on," Lefebvre said, finally accepting to converse with Laverenette, "with your hand on your conscience, can you say that this is a good time, the one we're living in?"

"My friend," said the ex-Major, "that depends on the way of looking at it. For you, who are pouting, there could have been pleasanter times; but, after all, you've kept your arms and legs and have the leisure to be love's young dream when, as Commandant Lefebvre, you had a taste for it and were cut out for that exercise."

Ce tron de l'air [142] of Laverenette was decidedly clever and ingratiating because he had just touched a chord that was never without an echo in the Commandant's ardent nature.

"Ah! Yes! Love! Let's talk about that," said Lefebvre. "There's always time to talk about that when there's nothing to eat."

"À propos," said the Major, "that Polish woman that you lost your head over during the siege of Dresden, did you know that she's in Paris?"

"No," said Lefebvre, becoming animated. "Have you run into her by any chance?"

"Oh! better than that," said the Major. "I've seen her very often at her place, where she's very nicely set up, thanks to an old Peer of France. We've chatted about you very often."

"Really? She remembers me?"

"Ah! Jesus! Does she remember! She's goes on and on about 'that dear Commandant,' 'that excellent Commandant.' You're still warm in her memory."

"Is there a way to know her address?"

"Your address, my dear fellow? But that wouldn't be of any use to you. The first thing to do, if I gave it to you, would be to not go there. The old protector is as jealous as all the devils, and doesn't leave her for a moment. It would be some-

---

[142] Since Laverenette is from Marseille, Rabou throws in a bit of Provençal slang used to describe a bright, cheerful, energetic person.

thing to see if he met a Hercules like you with his mistress. He would make a great racket about that with her."

"But you certainly go there, don't you?"

"I go there because I was acquainted with her gentleman at a former time, and he himself introduced me. But when I want to a private conversation with the beautiful girl, we have to make a rendezvous and go out."

"What! You scoundrel!" Lefebvre said cheerfully, "you would cuckold a Peer of France?"

"No, my dear fellow, you haven't gotten it right. I already have a little affair on the side in the Saint-Germain neighborhood, a Marquise. I would be her husband tomorrow if I weren't more than anything else in love with my freedom. But you know, a young and pretty woman chained to an old, fragile lover with rheumatism isn't doing that for her pleasure. The old man is not hard to get along with, and the household is kept in a condition where she has nothing to complain about, but the woman, who is young today, knows that she won't be tomorrow. So, thinking about her future, she has an idea about arranging something for herself. We are plotting between ourselves to do something about that, because I have the man's ear. Parbleu! Not later than this morning, we were holding a conference about that in a private salon at Véry's.[143] Ah! Here's an idea! What if I say you're one of us? That would be a surprise for her, and she wouldn't be embarrassed to chat with you and me about her little projects."

"No, thank you," said Lefebvre. "Tell her, if you will, that you have seen me."

"Oh! To do that, no," responded the Major. "I won't let her be worried sick about a man who refuses to see her when the opportunity presents itself, because that means that, probably, the gentleman finds his pleasure somewhere else."

---

[143] During the Napoleonic era, the Very, located near the Palais-Royal, the colonnaded, tree-lined area adjacent the Louvre, was one of the city's finest restaurants.

"Eh? No, no, my dear fellow. I am good behavior personified. Tied down as I am, as you can surely see, I'm not a man who's enjoying that good fortune."

"Well! Then, is the reason why you won't take me up on my offer that you're still holding a grudge against me? Surely, my offer was straightforward and, with the added attraction of a former mistress who has never been more charming, if you didn't still have something in your heart against me, you wouldn't refuse to meet me for a meal out of friendship."

"Let's me think about it," said Lefebvre, who was reluctant to have any kind of complicity, as the people of the law say, with Laverenette. "Tell me where I can find you. I will run my errand, and I will come join you at dessert."

"No, not at all," said the Major. "It's either one or the other. Either you go slumming with this scoundrel, this droll fellow Laverenette, or I won't say a word to you. You can always go and try to look around Paris for a woman like her, especially when she goes out only in a carriage and lives in a secluded area."

"But, you joker of a Major, what if I stood guard outside the restaurant and pretended to accidentally meet you as you leave?"

"To take care of that, there are two exits from the restaurant. What if I tell the waiter that he watch to see if there is outside a particular man with a moustache wearing a blue redingote, so that I can slip out the other door?"

"All right!" said Lefebvre, "it's fated that these devilish women will always make me do stupid things. This rendezvous, however, is important and it could lead to a change in my position."

"Of course! We will improve your position," said the Major, taking the arm of the man he had just tamed.

They began walking toward the Véry. Instead of taking the front door, Laverenette entered from a side door opening onto the garden side. Walking with his host across the main dining room to reach the mezzanine, the location of the private salons, Lefebvre was immediately troubled with the ease with which he could be linked intimately with a man he despised. Dining at a table that he would have to walk in front of, and be seen in the unfortunate company, was a colonel of his former regiment. In order not to be spotted, the Commandant had recourse to a rather naïve method, instinctive in such a case, that consists of not looking at the person one by whom doesn't want to be seen. But if the thing had to be done over, Laverenette wouldn't have abandoned his resistance so easily.

Showing that he was a habitué of the place, Laverenette said to a waiter who had come to greet them:

"Alexandre, has a lady in a rose hood and a green paisley pattern cashmere come to ask for me?"

"Not yet, Major, but Monsieur de Saint-Rambert is here in salon number 6."

"Well, watch for that lady's arrival and when she gets out of her carriage, be kind enough to take her to our salon."

That said, he opened the door that had been pointed out to him, and, seeing that Lefebvre hesitated to enter, said:

"Come on, are you afraid of one of my friends?"

"You know very well," the Commandant answered, "that I'm not afraid of anyone. However, you spoke to me of having lunch with a woman."

"Whom you see very well I'm waiting for. But Saint-Rambert is a charming man whom you will be delighted to know. He's a fellow who has a very long arm, and who knows what he might not be able to do for you?"

Lefebvre, who felt himself badly involved, could probably have been able to insist on leaving, but Saint-Rambert, who had heard the discussion, appeared at the door, and said to Laverenette:

"My dear Laverenette, if the gentleman had counted on dining alone with you, I wouldn't want to impose myself. Everyone isn't as eager as you seem to be for my company. Also, you're expecting a lady..."

"Please, Monsieur! You know the woman: she's the little Polish woman of our old Marquis. She's coming here to discuss that rental agreement that you know about, and you wouldn't be intruding to give her some advice about it."

"Very well, but I don't have the honor to know this gentleman?"

Dominated by human respect that, to tell the truth, is still king of the world, whatever instinct Lefebvre had about the trap he had been led into, he didn't dare insult a man who had shown him exquisite politeness by refusing to sit at the same table with him.

"After all, they won't eat me," he thought, without counting the fact that he had not lost the hope of seeing arrive the bait that had drawn him.

"Monsieur," he said, addressing Saint-Rambert, "I apologize for my lack of proper dress, but I went out this morning very early without being aware that I was to dine in company, and I am not dressed so as to dare present myself."

"Come now, Monsieur, between men," said the new Director of the Secret Bureau, "does anyone pay attention to dress?"

Then, as the Commandant, followed by Laverenette, had decided to enter the private salon, Rempailleux added:

"Besides, if I'm not mistaken, your dress indicates that you're one of the remains of the honorable Imperial phalanges composed of those men who carried the flag of France so high and so far, and as a result, are always sure of being welcomed everywhere."

"Commandant Lefebvre," said Laverenette, making the formal presentation, "ex-chief of the 122nd line Battalion, where we served together."

"But why ex-chief? The gentleman isn't old enough to have taken retirement?"

"Everyone, Monsieur, is not of your opinion concerning the soldiers of the Empire."

"Do you eat oysters, Lefebvre?" asked Laverenette, who was busy consulting the menu.

"Yes, gladly."

"What about you, Saint-Rambert?"

"Oh! Me, a dozen, no more; that's all my capacity."

Taking up then the conversation begun with Lefebvre, Rempailleux continued:

"What you've just said there, Commandant, is unfortunately true. And there are some fools who sell our national glory cheap, feigning indifference to the mistreatment of those who earned it with the purest of their blood. But let's also acknowledge the fact that there are a great many prejudices in the other camp. Peace was made, and I think that you, like me, hold it as a good thing, because people can't eternally spend their lives killing each other."

"That's true," said Lefebvre. "The Emperor loved war too much."

"Well! I was saying then that once peace was made, the government could not keep the military in the state it had been at another time. The Emperor himself, if he had disarmed, would have had to discharge a great number of officers."

"I don't say he wouldn't, but he would have done that in a restrained way, taking care to be sure that his old companions in arms had bread."

"That is to say that the results would have been almost the same, because the main question is this: Can an officer who is not on active duty be paid the same salary as one on active duty? The difference is that there would have been a few more forms."

"Well, Monsieur, form, that's everything."

"That's everything, that's easy to say," said Laverenette, intervening after having returned the menu to the waiter. "Just go and see a little if that kind of currency can be used in restaurants."

"The French soldier," Lefebvre said, "has shown that he can endure privations. In Poland, before the battle of Eylau, we spent a wretched winter, and there was never a murmur heard. In Russia, I believe there were hard blows, and that was still swallowed. But humiliation, that's what can never be endured."

"Well! Gentlemen, let's eat," said Laverenette, seeing the oysters he had ordered arrive. "And you can believe me if you will, but I much prefer to be here than sitting in front of a slice of horse meat at the Berezina." [144]

"Where you never were, you joker," said Lefebvre.

"Fortunately," said the Major, "because if I had been, I probably wouldn't have the pleasure right now of pouring you a glass of this excellent Chablis. There were only old dogs like you, my dear Commandant, to survive such battles. He was of all the campaigns of the Republic and the wars of the Empire," he added, enumerating for Saint-Rambert Lefebvre's service records, "seven wounds, three high feats of bravery, and despite all that, still a simple legionnaire and head of a battalion in 1814. That's a well-compensated man who can afford to shed regrets about the overthrown regime."

"It's certain," said Saint-Rambert, "that, compared to so many others whose promotions were far less-merited, Monsieur is an unusual example of modesty. But everything can still be repaired, supposing that too absolute ideas of military fidelity prevent him from again taking his rank in the army, civilian life offers more than one position in which his honorable services could open up a new and fortuitous path for him."

"Undoubtedly," said Laverenette, "for example, in the administration that you direct."

"Yes," answered Saint-Rambert. "It's probable that I will have some positions available, since, as we had foreseen, the

---

[144] The Battle of Berezina took place from 26 to 29 November 1812, between the French army of Napoleon, retreating after his invasion of Russia and crossing the Berezina river near Borisov, Belarus, and the Russian armies under Mikhail Kutuzov, Peter Wittgenstein and Admiral Pavel Chichagov. The battle ended with a mixed outcome. The French suffered very heavy losses but managed to cross the river and avoid being trapped. Since then Berezina has been used in French as a synonym for disaster.

insurrection is now out in the open. Yesterday, there were mass resignations and there were petitions to the Minister."

"Ah! Ah!" exclaimed Laverenette, "and what did the Minister say?"

"The Minister refused to accept them. You know that he already has enough to do to maintain himself against the influence of the Marsan Pavilion not to want to start a fight against it about ancillary matters. He had some trouble appointing me, but the more he thinks about it, the less he is now disposed to change his mind."

"That's unimaginable," said Laverenette, "those people are living in clover and are prepared to throw away a salary of twelve thousand francs!"

Lefebvre was all ears and he wondered what that administration could be where there were distributing positions of twelve thousand francs. But here, the conversation was interrupted by the entry of a waiter who brought two bottles of cold champagne and the rest of the lunch.

"Ah, we're progressing very quickly" Saint-Rambert then said. "What about the pretty guest that you were waiting for?"

"Oh! She's not coming now," Laverenette answered. "She can't go out; you know how the old man watches her. And, on my word, his instinct serves him very well, because I present to you a hearty fellow who has former rights to exploit, and the Marquis had better watch out!"

"Ah! Monsieur knew her? I compliment him. She's a charming woman, and if I were a bachelor like him!"

"What do you mean, bachelor? He isn't that the least in the world. He's been married for all eternity, and it's exactly for that reason that the scoundrel does all kinds of things that would upset his respectable wife."

"My dear Monsieur," said Lefebvre, "you're painting there a hardly flattering picture of my virtue."

"Come now, Lovelace [145] that you are!" said the Major, pouring him champagne. "In Spain, Italy, Germany, in Poland, God knows how many women you made unhappy!"

"Well, in Paris," said Saint-Rambert, "Monsieur must find a different way to conquer. Women here are expensive, especially the ones who don't cost anything."

"But look at this fellow, my friend! His chest, his shoulders," Laverenette answered.

"Very fine, but young women don't pay attention to those qualities in men like us who are no longer twenty-five-years-old."

And as means of consolation, Saint-Rambert lifted his glass in a toast to Lefebvre.

"As for those who are mature and understand us, my experience is that they can't be had for nothing. Because of that, I would permit myself, perhaps rather stupidly, to underestimate the monetary appeal of Monsieur."

"Not at all," replied Lefebvre. "I am not at all a capitalist and I don't drink champagne every day. It's not with two children, a wife, and half-salary that one can think about having a good time."

"Then, Monsieur, I'm sorry for you," Saint-Rambert said, "because of all the passions, the one that Laverenette attributes to you is certainly the strongest. There's gambling, ambition, alcohol, avarice, hunting, the rage for building, fishing; all that is nothing compared to the passion for women."

And throwing himself whole-heartedly into that common subject, the former *Chauffeur*, who loved to hear himself talk, held forth on the different occupations to which the human will could fall prey, an interminable dissertation which bored Lefebvre considerably. Into that thesis, Laverenette gave a few passing replies, but for the Commandant, who, got in a word

---

[145] The villain in Samuel Richardson's *Clarissa* (1748) in which the virtuous eighteen-year-old heroine, Clarissa Harlow, is seduced and raped by the debonair but villainous Robert Lovelace.

edgewise very occasionally, and with great trouble, he had nothing to distract him but the resource of absorbing several glasses of champagne. When the waiter brought coffee, it was time, in his opinion, that Saint-Rambert bring up another subject.

As a transition, calculated perhaps to come back to the one that might interest Lefebvre the best, the new Director of the Secret Bureau said:

"Another passion that I was forgetting is that of vanity. For example, there are people who, having what are truly sinecures, are paid handsomely, sheltered from all political revolutions, and who, by not accepting orders which displease them, manage stupidly to destroy their careers."

"Don't worry about that," said Laverenette, "they will be only too happy to withdraw their resignations."

"Oh! Excuse me," Saint-Rambert responded, "it's a fight where someone will certainly remain on the canvas. You don't try to disorganize a service without some form of punishment. It's a true coalition of workers, something made punishable by law. And certainly, as it happens in such a situation, an example will be made of the leaders. These gentlemen thought they were putting me in a difficult spot, but I will have forty times more applications than I will have places to fill. This morning, at seven o'clock, one of the aides-de-camp of Monsieur, the brother of the King, sent me a Chevalier de Saint-Louis, a man with a great name, who would be delighted to be employed."

"And I, who isn't just everybody, was very happy to be accepted by you; and without going very far, here is one of the glories of the Empire, a man having merit right up to his fingertips, who would also be happy to work for you if you were to offer him a position..."

"I would be happy to do so," said Saint-Rambert, "but I'm a little suspicious of the rigidity of the men of the Empire. Having seen Napoleon govern despotically, with only the halo of glory, they aren't very able to comprehend certain precautions regarding liberty and freedom of speech that are forced on governments only seeking to protect themselves."

"My word, gentlemen, I will admit to you," said Lefebvre," that for the last half-hour, I have been racking my brain to guess what these functions so well paid are, and which I wouldn't fill very well. In fact, as it seems to appear, if it's a question of police functions, I agree with you. I wouldn't fit there at all, and I won't have anything to do with that job."

"Your supposition, Monsieur, is helpful," retorted Saint-Rambert, in an annoyed voice.

"Good Lord! An administration that can't be named and which pays salaries like those of the heads of divisions!..."

"...Could only be that of the police, that's evident by employing, in general, only tarnished men, and having, as many as it wants of agents at twelve, fifteen and eighteen hundred francs salary, they must be very eager to give them positions of twelve thousand francs!"

"But then, without offending you, can't that administration that you direct be named? I didn't come to look into your secrets. I was invited to lunch to visit with a woman who is not coming. There is talk of a position that I could fill with my services, but for which I don't think myself fit because I am a Bonapartist. At the end, I can very well ask the key to the enigma."

"Ask for it, yes, but not guess at it in a haphazard way. The administration that I direct, Monsieur, employs only people with exemplary integrity, absolute discretion, perfect incorruptibility, and they must, in addition, show great independence of character and a complete absence of prejudice. It's in this last matter that I don't have blind confidence in you. When someone has an ardently declared political opinion, such as you have, he can't see things in a wider perspective. For the additional requirements, to speak like the former Kings of France, Laverenette, my Chancellor, will tell you the rest, but only if, however, he deems it proper. With that, I must take my leave, because I am expected for an appointment with Monsieur, the Brother of the King."

With that superb apostrophe thrown out, Saint-Rambert picked up his hat and left.

"Well," Laverenette said to the Commandant as soon as they were alone, "what beautiful work you did there. You're placed on the road to a fortune, and that's how you second me!"

"He's unusual, your friend," Lefebvre answered. "He can't be asked what he does?"

"Well, no, you don't ask people 'What do you do?' You phrase that in a little more sophisticated way, but, above all, you don't tell them they are in the police. With your devilish opinions, you see policemen everywhere. And then, don't you think your dear Emperor succeeded without the police?"

"Well, then, in what regiment do you intend to enroll me?"

"In a regiment, my dear fellow, where they pay a whole salary, and a nice one. Now, as for telling you anything more, I won't take that on myself; I'll have to talk to Saint-Rambert again. If, one of these days, you would be good enough to come by my place, here's my card. You will find me almost always at Number 6, Rue Lepelletier, from ten to noon."

"Would you like to know my idea," said Lefebvre to his Amphitryon[146] when, on leaving the restaurant, they were on the point of separating rather coldly. "You were expecting the Polish woman as much as I was expecting a dance."

"You've guessed it, my dear fellow," said the Major, laughing. "It was all a plot, a Saint-Barthelemy's massacre,[147]

---

[146] In Greek mythology, the wife of Amphitryon, who was away in battle, was deceived by Zeus who impersonated her husband. He slept with her; she became pregnant and gave birth Hercules. Amphitryon has come to be used in the sense of a generous entertainer, a good host.

[147] The St. Bartholomew's Day massacre on 24 August 1572 was a targeted group of assassinations and a wave of Catholic mob violence, directed against the Huguenots (French Calvinist Protestants) during the French Wars of Religion.

against the officers of the former army. The lunch that we've just had was just an ambush having for its goal the preparation for that terrible drama."

III. The Gentle Slope

The reader has understood that the nomination of Rempailleux, a.k.a. Saint-Rambert, to be Director of the Secret Bureau, had raised a kind of storm. All the employees, as in the affair of Matiphous, were able to know what kind of man was being put as their head, and since there is no profession, however little honorable it may be, that doesn't have its sense of honor, those men, profoundly humiliated to have a pardoned criminal as their new boss, had given their resignations en masse.

Probably forced to recruit a new staff, Rempailleux, who knew Laverenette, since he had in the past done some dirty business with him, had made him his aide-de-camp, and put him in charge of recruiting. Meeting Commandant Lefebvre in his path, the ex-major, with a feeling that had nothing in it of goodwill, had immediately thought of making him an affiliate. He felt that that man had the right to feel contempt for him, and, after having been crushed in the past by his integrity, he had seen in recruiting him a way to bring him down to his level. The poverty, the libertine appetites of the man whose downfall he was undertaking, had seemed to him to add so many more chances for the success of his seduction. His meridional imagination had immediately brought to birth the story of the Polish woman, which hadn't had the shadow of foundation. It had served to bring the game he had just flushed out under the eye of Rempailleux, with whom he had a luncheon meeting at the Véry restaurant.

Given what he knew of the character and the background of Laverenette, Lefebvre should have been led to greet with suspicion the overtures of which he was the object. And although he hadn't exactly put his finger on the wound threatening his honor, having a good instinct about the presence of the

285

police being mixed up in the brilliant position painted in glowing colors that had been offered him, he hadn't found himself very far from the truth. The two procurers were too clever not to have stopped short before the somewhat brutal rejection shown by Lefebvre and, evidently, before renewing their effort or abandoning it all together, they wanted to confer. By not going any further than they had, they still had a chance to succeed. They believed that, once on the road to the trap, their prey, coming to sniff at it out of curiosity, without any new provocation, would be drawn to fall into it by himself.

That foresight was only reasonable because, when he was alone, Lefebvre had never stopping feeling himself rather beaten. Those men that he had left, in arousing his desire to know, had strongly installed their insinuations in his mind despite his every precaution. It was not impossible that, in the period of strong social fermentation where one then lived, among those mushrooms of fortune that grew so thick on the bed of revolutions, Laverenette and his friend had, in fact, slid into some honorable situation, where it would be possible, without compromising oneself, to take a place at their side.

If that was the way it was in fact, was it not remarkably clumsy to have shown himself so little accommodating, when his situation forced him every day to cling to that miserable possibility of employment in insurance, without even any certainty of arriving at that meager result?

While he was walking, thus absorbed in thought, Lefebvre had just met, in the person of a creditor, the full measure of the humiliations to which one is exposed by a narrow and descending financial situation. The man with whom he found himself face to face was a German boot-maker who had advanced him some shoes. The debt, it's true, was ancient, since it went back to the departure of the Commandant for the campaign in Russia. At that time, however, the tradesman wouldn't have been wise to be haughty toward a client who was a superior officer in Napoleon's army. He would have been afraid that impertinence would put his ears in danger. But times had changed. The old lions had neither claws, nor teeth, and they could be approached, hat on your head, to insolently remind them of the date of the bills they had not paid.

The scandal was great; Lefebvre, antagonistically called to account, made the mistake of lacking moderation. There was loud talk; a crowd gathered. And finally, having learned that it was a worker who was demanding payment, the public was not rooting for the Commandant. He was obliged to leave in the middle of boos, and not without having run some risk of being taken to the nearest police station.

He had barely escaped, somehow, that bad situation. Still irritated, walking straight ahead, without being too much aware of where he was going, and turning his feet more and more toward the Lemblin café, where he at first intended to go, he ended up walked down the entire Rue de Richelieu. He came out onto the boulevards and had reached that portion that was then called the Grands Boulevards, when, seated in a chair, blossoming in the rays of a beautiful winter sun, there appeared a woman who immediately became the prey of some strange fascination for him.

There is no one who, in his life, who has not experienced that sort of magnetism, which can be explained neither by the beauty of her face, nor by the perfection of her shape, or by her figure, because a woman even without all those advantages is still capable of casting that spell. From the woman by whom we are thus affected, there seems to emanate a current of warm exhalations, a ray of intoxicating corpuscles that have a natural affinity with our particular temperament. Working from a distance, without any other instrument of communication but a look, that type of physical sympathy is like real electricity that still lacks its Franklin.[148]

Lefebvre, better than anyone, was susceptible to that conquering invasion, and when he was submitted to it, he immediately forgot everything else. Neither the still warm affront

---

[148] Allusion to Benjamin Franklin, who, in 1752, successfully tested his theory that electricity could be harnessed from lightning.

he had endured, nor the serious questions about his future that, a moment before, had agitated his brain, nor his good genie that counseled rigorous abstention of all gallant enterprises, remained present in his head. Absorbed in the discovery he had just made, he maneuvered himself in a way so as to be observed by the coveted object of his desire. The attention he gave, not lacking to be given back to him in a certain proportion, his ardor grew more intense.

The woman who occupied him in that way was not remarkably beautiful. Her face, bearing deep traces of small pox, would have been displeasing to some, but she was dressed with taste; her waist, although slightly high, lacked neither suppleness nor grace; her lower members were thin and elegant; her complexion was of extreme paleness and something, chastely lascivious, combining with an intelligent expression and a great air of distinction, managed to achieve a very attractive whole that was in reality quite stunning.

Going to sit down near her, Lefebvre, who was accustomed to those sorts of approaches, wasn't slow to bring about the opportunity to speak to her. She answered without prudishness, but also without marked encouragement. Nevertheless, conversation began, and shortly thereafter, the unknown woman, having looked at her watch, seemed to want to end the conversation. The Commandant asked her if she lived in the area.

"I live two steps from here, Rue de Provence," he was answered without hesitation.

"Well," said Lefebvre, "I have business with the banker Martin Lambert, whose townhouse is in that street. Will you allow me, Madame, to offer my arm to your house?"

A very dry and very decisive "No" accompanied that proposition—a clear rejection at least for the moment.

"But you won't forbid me to take the same path?"

"I wouldn't know how to keep you from going about your business."

Lefebvre began then to walk beside his new acquaintance, without being worried about making a spectacle of himself in the way he carried on an animated conversation.

Nothing is easier to recognize than a man who is courting in the open air, and who is being simply tolerated near a woman he has not been authorized to accompany. Arriving at an entry door, that, preceding a well-lit alley, was elevated one step above the pavement, the unknown woman left him in the middle of one of his sentences, and quickly parted company with him.

The Commandant was for a moment surprised, but, when he saw that the reluctant woman stopped at a door that opened onto a corridor, he concluded that she lived on the ground floor. He rushed after her. While she was turning her key in the lock, which again raised the probability that no one was waiting for her, he had time to reach her and, with a sort of respectful and entreating violence, blocked the door to prevent her access. There he was, in the apartment of the enchantress. Probably fearing a scandal, she hadn't made a desperate resistance. Lefebvre himself then closed the door!

"I hope, Monsieur," said the owner of the apartment, that had just been entered by assault, "that you are going to leave at once. Such audacity has never been heard of!"

"Madame, please!" answered the Commandant, "don't see in my daring anything but the impression your charms made on me."

"My charms? I will soon be thirty and have a face disfigured by smallpox."

"That must have been the way you appealed to me," exclaimed Lefebvre, "since you pleased me right from the start! Thirty! The age at which one begins to understand the meaning of love!"

It was obvious that Commandant Lefebvre was a great deal ahead of Balzac.[149]

---

[149] A reference to Balzac's novel *La Femme de Trente Ans* ("A Woman of Thirty") (1842).

"Come now, Monsieur, leave! I consent to consider all this as a joke, but the shorter ones, as you know, are the best ones."

"Yes, Madame, I'm going," said Lefebvre, taking a seat. "but, first, give me permission to return. Women aren't mistaken about the feelings they inspire; you see very well that I am moved and even disturbed by you. Tell me when I may come again."

Before answering, the unknown woman went to close a window that opened onto the street and through which passers-by could see what was happening inside the apartment. Then, opening a door that led to a small salon furnished with some elegance, she said:

"Since you absolutely want to stay, come this way. Everything that is said in this room can be heard from the corridor. I am going to explain myself to you frankly in order to cut short your fantasy before it becomes more serious."

"How good you are!" said the Commandant, passing into the little salon.

"You are mistaken; I am not good," the unknown woman responded, taking off her shawl and hat, "but I am frank, and I like to solve problems quickly. Everything will be settled between us with this statement: I am madly in love with someone else. You can see, then, that your insistence would be useless."

"You're saying that to get rid of me."

"I'm saying that because that is true. Besides, is there something in what I said that is very unlikely? Did my heart, by chance, have to wait for yours to give itself?"

"Well, the one who has your attention, I'm sure, doesn't love you as I would love you."

"That's a different question, and you even mean to say that he doesn't love me in any fashion, because he doesn't know me, doesn't pay me the least attention, and probably when he sees me, he wouldn't be in the least enthusiastic to accept the love that I would be happy to throw at his feet."

"Then I am not discouraged, and I will take it upon myself to make you forget that straw lover."

"Neither you nor anyone else could manage to do that; I love him passionately. Besides, you are too delicate a man to still think of me after such an admission. Who then would wish to slip shamefully into the little part of a heart that another occupies completely?"

"When you love as madly as I am capable of doing, you know how to be content. In the army, when I couldn't sleep in a good bed, I still arranged myself very well in a little place at a bivouac fire."

"That's true; you do have a military appearance. Are you a general?"

"No, less than that."

"Colonel?"

"Still less than that."

"Captain then?"

"Something more: Head of a Battalion."

"That's a nice rank. Are you on active duty?"

"No, on half-pay."

"And you are married."

"How did you know that?"

"Don't I see a wedding ring on your finger?"

"That's true. I'm married, but so little! My wife is almost sixty years-old."

"Then we're equal. Neither you, nor I, are free, so in no way are we suitable for each other."

"We are so right for each other that you will be mine. I swear it! It must be so, at any price."

"At any price, that's a lot! A woman who puts her beauty up for auction doesn't set her price at less than a figure of five millions."

"If I had five millions, don't you believe that I wouldn't offer them to you?"

"Yes, because you don't have them. I knew a man who had ten, fifteen, twenty million perhaps. I was young and beautiful then. Well, that terrible malady, the traces of which you see on my face, he sent me to have it cured in the hospital."

"He was a scoundrel and if I had known...!"

"Oh! All of Paris knew him. He was François-Honoré Dubignon, supplier to the army![150] He finally went mad and roasted himself in one of his buildings, which he had set on fire. That was my revenge, since I had contributed more than a little to bring about that denouement. It would have been talked about a great deal if it had not happened a few days before the Allies' battle for Paris."

"And it was after him that you began to love that shadow that you can't have?"

"No, I promised myself never to love anyone. As I was not rich, I tried to take advantage of the passable education I had received. For some time I was Assistant Headmistress at several boarding schools. Then I lived with a friend, whose fortune I had contributed to making. But it was exactly at the moment when a heavy responsibility for me arose that she left for England, without even letting me know her intention."

"Then you found someone to help you out of your difficulty?"

"Left an orphan at the age of eighteen, by the death of both of my parents, I had a very young brother whom an aunt took charge of. Suddenly, I learned that she had died without having done anything to provide for the fate of her nephew. I was then going to have to bring up that child, for whom I needed money, and there remained no one at my side to support me."

"Poor woman," said Lefebvre, with more or less real emotion that he took advantage of to take the hands of the woman.

"He lacked for nothing, Monsieur," she said with pride. "I didn't want to turn him into a laborer. He's in a secondary school, at the College Henri IV, where he is always the first in

---

[150] See volume 2, page 182.

his class. But the trimesters come around so quickly that I had to let myself be helped by a friend."

"Well, what about that friend?" Lefebvre asked with curiosity.

"He seemed happy to help me with something. Our only quarrels were that he wanted to give me a less modest position, and I didn't want to endure that. When my good little Jules' food and lodgings were paid, and the money for his tuition was deposited with the school registrar, what more did I need for myself? I don't have a taste for noisy pleasures or showy dresses. A nice apartment, very clean, for which I don't want even a cleaning woman, some books to charm my solitude and some candy for my child's free days, are all I need. I couldn't want anything more than that."

"Then your friend," exclaimed the Commandant, "had a treasure in you!"

"Yes, only the treasure fell in love with a sylph.[151] The friend saw that I was becoming sad and dreamy. He had a jealous character. He pressed me with questions and I admitted everything to him."

"Everything? What was that, since the one you were in love with had never even spoken to you?"

"Yes, that's true, but if good luck decreed that I found myself in his path and he noticed me, oh! how I would soon consent to be guilty for him!"

"What! You would even consent to sacrifice your brother's future?"

"Without a doubt. I was only asked one thing, to no longer think of my adored one. I didn't want to promise him that."

"Funny woman that you are," said Lefebvre. "If I were rich, I wouldn't care about the sylph."

"Yes, but you aren't, and you're married."

"But your brother's school, how will you take care of that?"

---

[151] In mythology, a spirit of the air.

"Up until now, I've been able to pay for it. And don't think that I'm telling you tales! Look at this!"

The bizarre creature, going to open her secretary, gave Lefebvre a packet of receipts.

The Commandant read aloud:

COLLEGE HENRY IV.
Received from Mademoiselle Herminie Daliron
the sum of two hundred fifty francs due for the trimester, etc.
Cashier: Letermilier.

"There you are," said the Commandant, stamping his feet. "Under the other government, there were relations; you could have tried to get a scholarship for that child. But today, we are outcasts, thieves of the Loire."[152]

"I am grateful to you for your kind words, but now you should leave."

"Of course, I shall. What else can a good-for-nothing like me do? But please, allow me to return. I love you more now than when I entered this apartment. That is to say, I love you differently, because I now see that you have a heart, candor, and any man with you would be very happy."

"Not at all; it is not reasonable to even think about it."

"On the contrary, it's very reasonable, because in a few days, my life may have a lot of new things in it."

---

[152] At the Restoration, the remains of Napoleon's Imperial Guard retreated behind the Loire river. They were disbanded in August, 1815, and the soldiers who were faithful to the Emperor were sent back home. Marshall MacDonald (1765-1840) was put in charge of this operation. The appellation *brigands de la Loire* was an expression used by the partisans of Louis XVIII to tarnish the image of these soldiers. It was the reverse of the expression used by the Republicans during the Revolution against the *brigands de la Vendée* who supported the king.

"May it please God, my poor Monsieur, that it might be happiness!"

"Happiness!" exclaimed Lefebvre excitedly, "but that's you, my beautiful one; that's to possess you; to press you in my arms!"

"Monsieur!" Herminie (for it was she![153]) said, offended.

"Forgive me! I'm an old fool, but it's you who made me lose my head."

That said, he quickly left like a man for whom, in order to whom to stay master of his will, felt the need to rush along.

IV. Herminie Daliron

Everything that strange girl had recounted was true, and only recalling the refinement that she had put into making Georgiana the instrument of her revenge against Dubignon, will lead to the recognition that, by her intelligence and the energy of her character, she had escaped that rather vulgar uniform and ordinary mold into which kept women were thrown. But what, most of all, gave her her exceptional character was that romantic, idealistic, unreciprocated passion by which, however, she was dominated, to the point that she wasn't able keep it a secret for her *useful* lovers, making it almost a law of her submission that they be indulgent toward it.

It was not love that her first seducer, François-Honoré Dubignon, had made her feel, no more than another man with money whose assistance, in the middle of the destitution in which Georgiana's sudden departure had left her, she had been forced to accept in order to continue her young brother's education. It could be said that, at past twenty-nine years of age, Herminie Daliron had a virgin heart, and as her double physical and moral makeup showed, her feelings were too energetic and too strongly developed for that inflammable nature not to explode at the least contact.

---

[153] Georgiana's lesbian lover; see Volume 2, page 156 seq.

Almost every day, at the hour the fortunate of the day came to ride on horseback on the Champs-Elysées, from her windows, Herminie saw by a young man on horseback with an elegant look pass by. Unknown to him, and without ever having glanced at her, he had just made himself the master of all her thoughts—the poor fool!—so much that she often ran from the other end of Paris in order to not miss being at home at the hour when her god-like passer-by usually showed himself. It was to be on time for that unreciprocated rendezvous that she had looked at her watch and gotten up and had told Lefebvre that he should not prolong his visit.

The man who occupied her thoughts in that fashion, as much as she had been able discreetly to ascertain, was the private secretary of Monsieur Martin Lambert, a rich banker and an influential member of the Chamber of Deputies. Being with the opposition, like almost all the banks of that period, Martin Lambert, by means of some written speeches, had gained some popularity at the tribune, and acquired a rather influential position in the parliament. Since from the orator to the man the difference in social class and education remained very wide, gossip had spread among the public that the distribution of roles between the great financier and his private secretary was completely new, the first writing while the second dictated, precisely the contrary of what usually happened with all private secretaries.

The probability of that arrangement, independent of the very apparent ignorance of the banker, was first established by the outstanding intellectual value that distinguished the collaborator he was paying. A laureate of the *Concours Général*[154] almost as soon as he left the Lycée, the future private secretary had distinguished himself by one or two remarkable publications, notably a political brochure that drew

---

[154] In France, the *Concours Général* is the most prestigious academic competition held every year between students of the final grades in almost every subjects taught in both general, technological and professional high schools.

some attention. Next, because of the manner in which the young man was treated by his employer who, while paying him rather stingily, it's true, let him ride his horses, lodged him nicely, asked him to do almost no apparent work, and devotedly took his opinion on every occasion, it became almost impossible not to suspect the existence of one of those secret complicities, where, as the *Barber of Seville*[155] said, brought distances together and turned all hierarchies upside down.

Another more conclusive indication: Martin Lambert had an only daughter around whom glittered an enormous dowry, which can perhaps explain why her father was not in relative haste to get her married. Ardently sought after, even by great names of the aristocracy, among the chosen group of her suitors, Mademoiselle Lambert, one fine day, had audaciously inserted the candidature of the young private secretary. And as a favorite sure of his ground, that extraordinary suitor had taken almost no care to hide his ambitious aim from the dishonest and greedy prince of finance.

Madame Martin Lambert, noticing the tender aspirations of Monsieur the Private Secretary, was, herself, full of believable indignation, and if she had been listened to, the insolent man would not, that very same evening, have slept in the house. But the Deputy of the Opposition, probably finding that it was in the logic of his democratic opinions to allow every kind of candidate to try for marriage to his daughter, only laughed at the great anger he witnessed. And despite the ardent hostility, dating from that moment, which his wife had declared against the young man, he had nonetheless been maintained in favor and in his functions.

As for the beautiful heiress, her attitude was difficult to define. Young, handsome, witty, sentimental, as one always is at twenty-two years-old, taking care to direct his flame at the girl's beautiful eyes, and not at all at the treasure she represented, the private secretary, by means of common habitation

---

[155] See note 64.

and being constantly together, couldn't miss possessing a great advantage that he knew how to use cleverly. He hadn't stopped seeing the diamond that he undertook to polish to his profit. But that was all he had received. Capricious, having, like a lover, two poles, one attracting, the other repelling, one day happy, friendly, welcoming; the next, taciturn, bitter, and almost disdainful, Mademoiselle Lambert had made her poor suitor pass through the most stormy alternatives, his skiff sometimes at the crest of the wave, sometimes rolling right into the depths.

Herminie Daliron knew all these details that she had easily found from the domestic staff of the Lambert townhouse. They did not have the effect of discouraging her in her foolish pursuit as an *amoureuse courtisane*. On the contrary, if Monsieur Alfred—that was the only name she knew for the young private secretary, and she found that name charming and it was enough for her to think about him—if then, as we said, Monsieur Alfred seemed somehow accessible to her, it was because that of the unhappy and capricious love of which he was the victim, because of the interminable rigors and caprices of Mademoiselle Lambert. Herminie had laid out a complete plan. Before exposing the details of that wise feminine scheme, we must return to Commandant Lefebvre, whom we left leaving the Rue de Provence. It must be added that, as he had said, he did have serious business at the banker's townhouse, but he didn't go there, and also decided not to spend the rest of his day at Café Lemblin café. In his tormented mental state, how could he remember anything?

Even if he had believed in the existence of that platonic passion that Herminie Daliron had disclosed and placed in the way of his ardor, the Commandant didn't treat things of the heart with so much refinement and delicacy that the shadow of a vaporous rival could bother him very much. In the confidence made to him, he had, in reality, seen only one of the thousand and one ways in which bought women try to raise the venal value of their charms. And one single thing had appeared positive to him in the difficulties that he had encountered on the path to his fantasy: that was that he would have to provide for the young brother, whose studies must continue, without counting the personal needs of the sister who, it goes without saying, for which he would also have to provide.

Now, as modestly as he wanted to estimate those two expenses, Lefebvre was a hundred leagues away from being able to afford them. In his own household, he could hardly afford the required necessities, and his appointment to the putative position as insurance investigator, in the event that it was finally obtained, could only, more or less, bring his own humble budget into alignment. The *Eldorado*, or, as we say today, the *California*,[156] to which Laverenette held the key, was then the only gold mine that he could think of dipping into. But he was reviewing all sorts of good luck in store for him before yielding to that temptation. Instinctively distrustful, his mental framework was that of a man to whom the Devil had made honeyed advances, and who couldn't keep himself from thinking about them, while being decided not to give in at all.

On arriving in Belleville, he began by colliding with a horrible household quarrel. His wife had never been bitterer and less contained in the expression of her jealousy. It was as if she had had a secret revelation of the projects of infidelity with which her husband had to reproach himself. The wounds her tongue made that day were so much more penetrating because Lefebvre received them with a guilty conscience, because he had already sinned in word and in thought, if he wasn't yet guilty in deeds. That storm was calmed by the helpful habit that he had developed for such occasions, to let her say everything without answering it. H

is daughter, Amanda—that was a name popular during the Empire—then took him aside to let him know that the butcher, not wanting to let a bill on which he had received only rare and insignificant payments, get any larger, had re-

---

[156] Allusion to the California Gold Rush which had begun on January 24, 1848, when gold was found by James W. Marshall at Sutter's Mill in Coloma, California.

fused to give them any more credit. Then she added that her mother, out of their puny sale of lingerie, had the mania to charge things that she was always sure of paying easily, and that morning, someone had come to collect seventy-five francs that they hadn't been able to pay. They could then expect the next day another visit and more bills.

After a night cruelly agitated by all these disastrous news, while the gracious image of Herminie Daliron floated over that domestic fog, Lefebvre went out to go to Belleville to look up a former regimental comrade. He was counting on borrowing from him the miserable sum necessary to settle the outstanding bills. To bring back that money would be a great diplomatic triumph; first of all, the bills would be paid; then, he would be armed to give Madame Lefebvre a lesson about her imprudent commercial transactions. In the shaky position she would be in, she must, for at least two weeks, call a truce to her shouting and her conjugal temper tantrums.

Sadly, the friend to whom Lefebvre had to ask for a loan, wasn't in a position to render him the service he was expecting. Far from it, he was himself reduced to extreme distress and that situation must have subdued him a great deal, because he began to badmouth the Emperor, whose foolish ambition had ruined them all. Tired of fighting, that blasphemer admitted that he had surrendered. He had been offered a position of secretary to the Police Commissioner, and, tired of poverty, he had accepted it.

"But that's a police job!" Lefebvre said in astonishment.

"Not secret police," his friend responded, "and it means bread!"

Lefebvre left him with a downcast soul, and the first thing he found on his return from that excursion, from which he brought nothing back but the feeling of degradation which had just been confided to him, was a bailiff who had come to follow up on the butcher's protest. He had only to fill out a small document known and drawn up in advance. Like most of those of his kind, that *Monsieur Loyal* [157] had a gentle and annoying politeness which totally got on the nerves. The more the bailiff sweetened his words, the more the Commandant became animated in his discussion. The outcome was a return to that time when the *pékins,* [158] and out of all the *pékins*, especially the bailiffs, were treated in a cavalier fashion. As a result, a ticket for failure to comply and for injuries crowned his useless intervention and his intemperate expense of eloquence.

That beautiful campaign finished, Lefebvre could no longer remain at his house, and, after having gone down to Paris and after having taken a turn at Café Lemblin, he was drawn toward the Rue de Provence like straw into a whirlwind. There, he received only another disappointment: the curtains over Herminie's window closed quickly as soon as he came in sight. Without knowing it, he had come at a sacrosanct hour, when they assuredly would not be opened for him. Taking a chance to knock at that door that, the evening before, he had so audaciously gone through, he received no answer, and a prolonged and insistent knocking only earned him another lesson that the concierge of the building gave him:

"You see very well that there's no one there, or someone who doesn't want to let you in," said that woman sharply, tired of hearing him knock.

That humiliation should have made him wise; on the contrary, it raised the level of his desire to its highest paroxysm. The next day, after a night still filled with more anxiety than the preceding one, he presented himself at Laverenette's apartment at the time the Major had indicated he would be sure to be at home. Using very transparent finesse to avoid

---

[157] Traditional French name given to a circus' ringmaster.

[158] Military slang referring to civilians; it was used by soldiers during the Revolution as a label for those who didn't wear a *colback* (military headgear consisting of a wicker frame covered with skin and bear hair similar to the fur cap worn by the grenadiers of the Imperial Guard).

bring up immediately the real object of his visit, the Commandant said:

"Well! That beautiful Polish lady, have you seen her?"

"What beautiful lady?" Laverenette asked.

"The Polish woman."

"But you told me that she was a dream of my imagination, and that I was expecting her as much as you dance?"

"My dear fellow, I could think that in a moment of bad humor. But today, I'm in a better mood. I've come to ask you if you have told her that you ran into me."

"These women, they are *bagasse*.[159] When I told her that we had expected her for lunch, didn't she make a scene! She said she didn't want to see you. Did I want to compromise her? She didn't like men on half-pay, that you might try to borrow money from her."

"Who does she take me for?" Lefebvre said, wounded to the quick.

"What do you expect, my dear fellow; it's not good to be poor. Just anybody will try to humiliate you."

"You are damn well right. Is that great position you talked to me about still open?"

"Well, there are an extremely large number of applications."

"But did you confer with Monsieur de Saint-Rambert as you indicated was your intention?"

"Of course I conferred with him! He's thinking about it."

"The best way to change my opinion would be, it seems to me, to tell me frankly what the job entails."

---

[159] Lit. the fibrous matter that remains after sugarcane or sorghum stalks are crushed to extract their juice. It is an out-dated Marseille slang, meaning "crazy," often ill-used by French writers to add characterization to their provençal characters, although Marcel Pagnol pointed out in *Fanny* that no one in Marseille actually used the word.

"Your opinion, my dear fellow, do you really think that Saint-Rambert cares anything about that? He can do you a great deal of good, and you can't do him any harm."

"Since you put it that way," Lefebvre said vehemently, "let's not talk any more about anything. He himself had ordered his *Chancellor* to tell me the rest, but if what is left are impertinences, I thank you. You know that I don't endure them well."

"You're right," said Laverenette, returning to a friendly tone, "but it's only because I hesitate to speak openly to you. A state secret is not a small thing, and you can very easily burn your fingers if you don't handle it with precautions."

"But do you then believe me to be so stupid as to play with that gun powder?"

"I didn't say that, but it's your damned opinions. You allow everything to your Emperor. He could whip your back with his riding crop and you would say, 'Oh! what gentle caresses!' However, the method of government I'm talking about, he made use of it, and I will prove it to you whenever you like."

"I can't contradict you, because I don't know what it's all about."

"It's a question of your believing us to be now in the best terms with all the rest of Europe, right?"

"Good Lord! It seems to me that if all of Europe hadn't been against us, the *Other One* wouldn't be at Sainte-Helena today."

"Well! That's what makes me sweat, to hear you talk like that. It's as if you thought His Majesty Louis XVIII had won the Battle of Leipzig."[160]

---

[160] The Battle of Leipzig was fought from 16 to 19 October 1813, at Leipzig, Saxony. The coalition armies of Russia, Prussia, Austria, and Sweden, led by Tsar Alexander I and Karl Philipp, Prince of Schwarzenberg, decisively defeated the French army of Napoleon. The battle was the culmination of the 1813 German campaign and involved nearly 600,000 sol-

"Ah! That, no! He can't be reproached with that."

"So if he didn't ask Europe to kick that Corsican trouble-maker out, he mustn't trust all those foreigners that came in behind him and which he didn't call. Do you thing England, for example, will be happy to see France become great and glorious again under the Bourbons?"

"The English are our eternal enemy," exclaimed Lefebvre, "and to think that that genius of a man delivered himself into their hands like a June bug!"

"What they did to Napoleon, I guarantee you, they will do tomorrow to Louis XVIII if they are not closely watched."

"Ah! Well! If it's a question of spying on the English, that could suit me well, although I would prefer to fight with them."

"Spying, my dear fellow, is one of those words that is used when one isn't very familiar with things. And if the English, the Russians, the Prussians are plotting something against France, and you find a letter laying out its secret, would you keep it in your pocket and not carry it to the Kings's prosecutor?"

"No, but I would go to someone among the former generals under whom I served and I would say to him, 'Here's what's being plotted. See what you can do with this discovery.'"

"Well, since the foreigners don't leave their letters lying about, and since it's not bad, however, to know what they're up to, don't you know, my dear fellow, that from all eternity, since Louis XIV, Napoleon, and others, there has been a place where they can examine letters which will entrap those fellows, and that they, on their side, don't worry about putting their nose in ours? That's what's always been done, and it's a farce called diplomacy."

---

diers. Decisively defeated for the first time in battle, Napoleon was compelled to return to France while the Allies hurried to invade France early the next year. Napoleon was forced to abdicate and was exiled to Elba in May 1814.

"The fact is that the diplomats couldn't give a rat's ass about what methods are used."

"That doesn't keep the lowest positions in that organization from being paid twelve, fifteen, thirty, and even up to three hundred thousand francs, and being decorated and dining with all the sovereigns."

"That's true. Diplomats, me, I've never had much use for them. However, when we yelled enough, they were the ones who came to finish the dance, and my military career having gone to the Devil, I'll resign myself to going into diplomacy."

"You see then, my dear fellow, that you aren't so far from agreeing with that excellent Monsieur de Saint-Rambert."

"But, let's be more precise. Exactly what is that position? Me, I don't know any English, Russian, or German. I know a little Italian because my wife is Illyrian."

"Bah!" said Laverenette. "Italy! There's not very much to watch there. It's a lot of little princes you could put in your pocket. But," he added, "after some reflection, the Foreign Office is not really the best place where you might be employed."

"Goodness! You can see that I'm open to suggestions."

Arrived at the heart of the difficulty, Laverenette, as it could be seen, had already used a fair number of circumlocutions. He didn't find that the moment had come to walk more deeply. It wasn't astonishing to see him putting off the question of homeland surveillance as far as possible. So, instead, he asked Lefebvre if he was a Republican.

"Republican?" answered the Commandant. "I was that, like everyone else at one time, like the little Caporal.[161] But it was soon seen that their Councils and their Directory[162] were stupidities. France can only be France under the Empire."

---

[161] Napoleon.

[162] The Directory was a group of five men who held the executive power in France according to the constitution of the year III (1795). They were chosen by the new legislature, by the

"Then you're not a Republican and you are a Bonapartist. But, after all, you are for the Monarchy rather than the Guillotine of '93?"

"That's evident. The guillotine and the lawyers,[163] no, thank you!"

"Now, Napoleon, do you think he really is in Saint-Helena?"

"Good lord! You have to believe so."

"And do you think that he is coming back from it, as he did from Elba, which was only a small step across our Mediterranean?"

"I admit, that's more difficult and the chances are that that exploit can't be done twice."

"It's so much better if the English keep him under their control! You understand me…"

"Ah! The scoundrels! They're capable of anything!" said Lefebvre.

"So you do agree with me that his reign is finished—absolutely finished?"

"But, my dear fellow, there's always his son."[164]

Council of Five Hundred and the Council of Ancients; each year one director, chosen by lot, was to be replaced.

[163] Several leaders of the Reign of Terror, such as Maximilien Robespierre, had been lawyers.

[164] Napoléon François Charles Joseph Bonaparte (1811-1832), King of Rome, known in the Austrian court as Franz, Duke of Reichstadt from 1818. He was the son of Napoleon and his second wife, Marie Louise of Austria. By Title III, article 9 of the French Constitution of the time, he was Prince Imperial. When Napoleon abdicated on 4 April 1814, he named his son as Emperor. However, the Allies refused to acknowledge him as successor. Although Napoleon II never actually ruled, he was briefly the titular Emperor in 1815 after the fall of his father. When his cousin Louis-Napoléon Bonaparte became the next emperor in 1852, he called himself Napoleon III to acknowledge Napoleon II's brief reign.

"His son, my friend, is tubercular[165] and in the claws of Austria and his mother! Let's not talk about her. I say then that the Empire has sunk to the bottom. And if we don't want to see anarchy again, the worst, the money and the inflation of the Revolution, and the guillotine, the best thing is to keep what we have. Almost all our Marshalls are for the present government that, on my word, doesn't treat them too badly."

"Finally, what are you getting at?"

"I'm coming to the fact that if the government watches our enemies abroad, it must also watch its enemies inside the country, seeing that they are a great deal nearer and also more enterprising."

"That, my dear fellow, is the job of the police."

"The Devil take the police!" exclaimed Laverenette. "I can't say a word to you without you bringing them up again!"

"You bet! It seems to me that they're the ones in charge of discovering plots."

"Precisely—but they don't discover any. They are a pile of do-nothings, agents provocateur, and they don't even know how to sweep the streets. Those who can find out something are a few members of the gendarmerie, the King's informants, the public prosecutors, and the prefects at the head of each *départements*.[166] But surely you don't consider any of them to be mere snitches? You wouldn't refuse to be Head of the Po-

---

[165] In 1832, Franz caught pneumonia and was bedridden for several months. His poor health eventually overtook him and on July 22, 1832, he died of tuberculosis at Schönbrunn Palace in Vienna.

[166] The *départements* were created in 1790 as a rational replacement of *Ancien Régime* provinces with a view to strengthen national unity; the name was used to mean a part of a larger whole. Almost all of them were named after physical geographical features rather than historical or cultural territories which could have had their own loyalties.

lice? Savary,[167] who didn't get on too poorly with the Emperor, certainly was."

"That's for sure. There needs to be police, if only because of the thieves."

"And the conspirators, those people who turn a country upside down, who steal thrones and crowns like others steal watches and scarves, don't you think they need being watched too? And what if they write letters, shouldn't we be able to find out what they're plotting in those letters? Not only in France, but very often abroad, because you certainly remember Pichegru[168] and Georges Cadoudal[169] and all the correspondence between *émigrés* that tormented the First Consul for such a long time."

"But to look at these letters," said Lefebvre, coming back to the subject, "someone must have forgotten to seal them?"

"Just as to open a door without its key, it would have been necessary for someone to have forgotten to close it. But if one had a duplicate key, or, without it being apparent, someone carefully jimmied the lock?"

"So," said the Commandant, finally understanding, "twelve thousand francs to unseal letters, that is what you are offering me?"

"Me, I'm not offering you anything. You're the one who has been turning me any way but loose to know how the gov-

---

[167] Anne-Jean-Marie-René Savary (1774-1833). Confidant of Napoleon and Minister of Police from 1810 to 1814.

[168] Jean-Charles Pichegru (1761-1804). French general who plotted with the Monarchist in 1795. Suspected of treason, he was forced to resign in 1796.

[169] Georges Cadoudal (1771-1804). The author of multiple plots aiming to return the Bourbons to the French throne, he led an unsuccessful revolt in 1798 and again in 1799. In 1800, he tried to assassinate Napoleon with a bomb placed in a carriage in the path of Napoleon as the Emperor was on his way to the Opera. He fled to England, but returned to France, and was guillotined in 1804.

ernment can discover so many of the wicked projects that are plotted against them! My dear fellow, that's how, and it's not so wicked as all that."

"What you've just confided to me, my dear Major, merits some reflection."

"You go reflect, my friend, you have time. The positions in the interval will be filled without you. And then, if you come too late, mind you, I'm sure that Polish woman will hold her purse at your disposition."

"Will you give me at least until tomorrow to give you an answer?"

"Answer to what? I'm not offering you anything. I talked in general terms about you to Saint-Rambert. He wasn't too impressed with you. If you decide to join us, I will talk to him again and see if I can set aside his hesitation. I don't need to tell you that these things shouldn't be talked about. It can be dangerous for you to know about them when you are not part of this protected group."

"I am not a child," Lefebvre said, rising, "I know how to keep secrets that are entrusted to me."

"On your honor, then!" said Laverenette, after he had taken his visitor back to the door.

He opened the door again to shout:

"Remember that tomorrow, it may already be too late. Don't beat around the bush too long."

V. The Day of a Stroller

On leaving the Rue Lepelletier, where Laverenette lived, Lefebvre found himself on the boulevard, almost at the place where, two days earlier, he had encountered Herminie Daliron. The weather was superb and he thought it possible that he might find her at the same place. Both thinking about her and the conversation that he had just had with the Major, he made several turns in front of the café without seeing the one he was looking for.

Then, as it was Sunday, and since he was in that nervous irritable mood in which strong preoccupations puts you, he became tired of being shouldered by the crowd of strollers. He decided to sit down, in addition believing himself surer of not missing the amiable apparition that he still hoped would be produced.

He had been on the look-out for more than an hour; he had gotten up; he had sat down, and was about to stand up again when an old comrade came up and sat down beside him. They began to talk about that friend in Belleville whom Lefebvre had gone to see in his difficulty the evening before. The newcomer also knew the desperate condition that had made the poor devil decide to accept the insignificant position of secretary to the Police Commissioner. However, he saw that decision from a different point of view than Lefebvre had.

"He made a good decision," said the man. "In that position, he can render us a lot of great services. If one of us is compromised in some political affair, as that can hardly miss happening, he could warn us and perhaps help us get out of trouble. That's the game to play: to insinuate ourselves into all the public functions that we can, in order to take advantage of the new government. We will have more information in that position, and soon the siege will be over."

That theory was an illumination for Lefebvre, and, applying it immediately to his particular situation, he thought that, in the job that he had been offered, he might be very much in a position to be useful to his party. The thought of evil, especially when it is advised by a passion, always shows itself prodigiously clever to seize on any pretext. Lefebvre was probably going to be imprudent and consult his friend about the question of his possible affiliation with the Secret Bureau, certain that he would be strongly encouraged to make that *sacrifice*, but at that moment, as he returned to examining the passersby, a task from which his interest in the conversation had, for a moment, distracted him, he believed he recognized the hat and shawl that Herminie Daliron had worn in the evening two days before.

310

That was not all. As she had gone rather far ahead of the spot where he was seated, and he could only glimpse her amid the crowd, it seemed to him that she was not alone and that a man had given her his arm.

"Good-bye," he said, rising up immediately. "I see passing over there a gentleman I was waiting for. I absolutely believe that you are right, and that our old comrade did well to accept that job."

That said, without waiting for a response to his sentence, he rushed after the path of the lady of his thoughts. And, in the speed of his pursuit, after having shoved aside some of those he found in his way, he soon confirmed that neither his eyes nor his heart had been mistaken. As for the cavalier who had so strongly contributed to double his emotion, there was nothing disturbing about him: he was was a young student whose height and physique was that of a boy ten to twelve years-old, evidently Herminie's young brother, who was on an outing with his sister on his free day.

After having looked behind him to be sure that the man he had dashed away from so suddenly was not on his heels, the Commandant walked for some time very near the woman he had resolved to approach. Then, moving forward some more, and approaching her in the most eager and most respectful way, he asked:

"How is Madame Herminie today?"

Called to in that way, Herminie Daliron quickened her steps and answered:

"You must be mistaken, Monsieur, as I do not have the honor of knowing you."

"But..."

"I repeat, Monsieur, that I don't know you," said Herminie.

At the same time she looked expressively from Lefebvre to her young brother, a look that could be interpreted by the famous maxim from antiquity: *maxima debetur puere*

311

reverentia.[170]Almost happy not to have been repulsed, except by what could have been called an end to seeing her, the Commandant didn't insist.

"Pardon, Madame," he said, his hat in his hand. "I was in fact mistaken."

But after having let his dear, beautiful one get somewhat ahead of him, he believed he should make her notice his happiness in being near her by continuing to follow her at a distance, respectfully enough so that no one could suspect that he was stalking her, but only that he was continuing his walk along the same path. To walk slowly with a woman who is strolling is not an easy maneuver. He had to measure his steps with hers, not pass her, nor let her get too far ahead of him and possibly lose her from sight. The problem became complicated if, as Herminie did to please her young companion, she stopped frequently in front of stores; most of all if she entered them, and he took his eyes off her for one second, he could let her escape. That's what happened to Lefebvre. Suddenly, he no longer saw anyone in front of him. He walked faster, thinking that he had been left a great distance behind. Then when he had gone far enough to be sure they were not in front of him, he retraced his steps with the agitation and emotion of a dog looking for its master. He finally discovered the object of his feverish search in a pastry shop, the student gorging himself. Then, as standing there at the door seemed to him eternal, talking aloud to himself, he said:

"He's eating the whole pastry shop. What a horrible child! The Devil! Just in meringues and tarts alone, that student is ruinous."

The student stuffed, the walk continued down the boulevard without any other encumbrance, past the former Rue Napoleon, since then renamed Rue de la Paix, to the great scan-

---

[170] Author's translation: "We owe the greatest respect to a child." From Juvenal's *Satire* XIV, line 47: People should keep the strictest guard over their words and actions, in the presence of boys.

dal of Lefebvre, then to the Place Vendôme, and finally to the Tuileries. It's known that, since time immemorial, the fashion on Sunday for the Bourgeois is to go and sit from two o'clock until five o'clock to look at each other, and, as La Bruyère[171] said, to disapprove of each other.

Mademoiselle Daliron, having sat down with her brother, it was impossible for Lefebvre to go and sit beside her as he would have done in a café on the boulevard. Behind her, he wouldn't have been able to see her; in front of her, she would have been hidden from his sight by the tight ranks of the strollers. The only resource the would-be suitor then had was to walk up and down the alley where his divine one was seated endlessly, throwing her each time he passed a supplicating glance which she never returned.

To that long torture, that any other man in love would also have had the stupidity to impose on himself, there was soon added another torture. Mademoiselle Daliron was approached by a man with white hair and gold-framed glasses, but who hadn't yet reached old age, and seemed to greet him enthusiastically. More than that, she invited him to sit down next to her. While her young brother went to look for some comrades to play with, the old Celadon[172] started a *tête-a-tête* with the sister. The conversation was most animated and apparently most delightful, because Mademoiselle Daliron was constantly laughing, and that was also an opportunity for her to show off the whitest and straightest teeth.

To paint the jealous fury, to tell the violent and devastating ideas that, during his long martyrdom Lefebvre felt, would be impossible. However, he was able to control himself, fearing that a scandal in such a public place would chase him away from paradise forever. Three-fourth of an hour was thus

---

[171] See Note 105.

[172] A shepherd who is also a tender lover in the 1627 pastoral romance *L'Astrée* by Honoré d'Urfe (1568-1625). The term was first used to designate a color in the 17th century because Celadon wore pale green ribbons.

spent this way. The brother returned, his face warm and flushed. His sister wiped his ruddy jaws in a motherly way with a fine batiste handkerchief. They then stood, and Lefebvre thought that the annoying man was undoubtedly going to take his leave. But no! The Commandant was not at the end of his misery! The annoying man offered his arm, that was taken without hesitation. The duo, which had become a trio, went back the same way by which Lefebvre had been led.

At each corner of the street, the Commandant hoped that the *scoundrel,* as he was calling him, would separate from his prey. Every street corner was successively passed, and the awaited separation had not yet taken place. The cup was going to be overflowing. Arrived at a jewelry-clock shop, the abominable trio stopped at the shop window, then entered. And then, staring into the shop to discover the wicked mystery that was taking place there, Lefebvre saw the merchant spread out an assortment of silver watches. Evidently, it was a gift that the man with the gold-rimmed glasses, decidedly a dangerous rival, wanted to give to the student, a maneuver definitely cleverer than if he had addressed his munificence directly to the sister. And how could it be doubted that the seducer was the one to pay, since the watchmaker was addressing all his eloquence, all his enthusiasm, all his explanations, all his smiles, to him? Actually, no one paid, and it appeared that no watch had been bought.

"Old miser!" Lefebvre then shouted to himself, in a pleasant contradiction and completely illogical manner, indicating his derangement as a lover. "To bargain for an hour for a silver piece of junk!"

His rival's supposed avarice did the Commandant's heart good and brought some consolation to the end of his sad Odyssey. Arrived at the angle of the Rue de Provence and the Rue de Monsieur, as the Rue Lafayette was then called, Lefebvre walked faster, hoping, with some appearance of logic, that the separation would take place there.

From a distance, it seemed to him that Mademoiselle Daliron made some effort not to be taken any further, and in addition, the way in which they were parting seemed decisive. But, after a short time, the trio, without separating, began walking again. Lefebvre's fury was limitless.

"If he enters after her," he said to himself, "I'm going to knock at the door after them and they had certainly better open it to me, or I'll break it down!"

He wasn't reduced to that extremity. Arrived in front of her domicile, Mademoiselle Daliron dropped the arm that had brought her that far, and, after having gallantly said goodbye to her cavalier, quickly entered her apartment, followed by her brother. Placed in ambush some distance away, Lefebvre carefully watched the behavior of his rival. He didn't see him wander around the house, look furtively at the windows, express fugitive regrets, as a poet wrote about the Seine, [173]go through all the actions of a man who is only at the first chapter of the novel. On the contrary, his goodbyes said, he left straightforwardly and even with a certain haste, which seemed to indicate he was only an acquaintance of Mademoiselle Daliron, having no claim on her.

But Lefebvre had suffered too much to accept that peaceful explanation. He saw instead in the calm indifference of that white-haired Lovelace the appearance if a conqueror who, for a long time, hadn't waited in the antechamber. He decided, whatever the authority of his rights, to trouble him in their tranquil enjoyment. He advanced resolutely to that nightmare and said to him:

"It seems, Monsieur, that you are acquainted with Mademoiselle Herminie Daliron?"

"Yes, Monsieur, I have that advantage," responded the gentleman with gold-rimmed glasses, who, in order to better see the person speaking to him, brought the eyeglass frame closer to his eyes, in a gesture habitual with short-sighted people. "But why your question?"

---

[173] In *Epître sur un Mariage* [Epistle on a Marriage], a poem by Jean-Baptiste Gresset (1709-1777).

'That's because I, too, have the honor to be acquainted with her."

"Well, Monsieur, I give you my sincere compliments. She's a perfectly exemplary person."

"Then why then are you trying to ruin her reputation?"

"Me, compromise Mademoiselle Daliron?" the object of that strange accusation exclaimed. "In what way did I do this, if you would please explain yourself?"

"By holding on to her arm for hours, and going into jewelry stores where it seems you were going to buy all the necklaces and bracelets in the establishment."

"It seems, Monsieur, that you have taken the trouble to follow us. May I ask by what right?"

"By the right that pleases me, if you're not happy with that!"

"No, Monsieur, I am not happy; I'm far from being happy, in fact, and I find the way in which you are acting quite extraordinary and rather petty."

"It's like that, and if that doesn't suit you, my name is Lefebvre, ex-Chief of line battalion no. 122, and I live in Belleville, Rue de Paris, No. 37."

"And I, Monsieur, am Simonnet, Professor of the fifth form at the Collège Henri IV, living at Rue Clovis, No. 21, and don't think you frighten me with your moustaches and your boorish airs. I don't fight, Monsieur, because the University doesn't tolerate any scandals, but we're perfectly aware of those who keep dragging their sabers around. Their reign is over, those dragging around sabers, and understand this very well, Monsieur, ordinary *pékins*[174] will no longer be trampled underfoot by the Mamluks of terror."[175]

Monsieur Simonnet's voice was naturally very strong and resounding. He had pronounced that phrase with anima-

---

[174] See Note 158.

[175] Mamluk is an Arabic designation for slaves. The term is most commonly used to refer to Muslim slave soldiers and Muslim rulers of slave origin.

tion, and accompanied it with a very animated pantomime, so that several passersby began to stop. Lefebvre, who remembered the scene that he had experienced two days before with the German boot-maker, didn't want to undergo a similar embarrassment. Besides, he was wrong and the rivalry that he thought he had seen looked now less and less probable.

"Monsieur," he said, taking a more softened tone, "I believe there's a misunderstanding. Let's walk on, if you will, so as not to draw a crowd. I'm going to explain my error to you in a few words."

"Speak, Monsieur, I'm listening," said Monsieur Simonnet, testifying to his calmness by the way in which he inhaled a pinch of tobacco, and then brushed the stray grains off his coat.

"I have the honor," the Commandant continued, "to be a relative of Mademoiselle Daliron. She is alone in Paris, and some disturbing reports about her frequentations and her conduct having come to her family, they have charged me to find out about it. That was the cause of the spying that I admit I was doing a moment ago."

"So that you saw in me a seducer?" said Simonnet, smiling.

"But, Monsieur, you are neither of an age nor of a physique to not credibly arouse such notions."

"I appreciate the compliment, but I don't seduce anyone. I'm married and a grandfather. In that double position, I am incapable of any straying. I have the honor to know Mademoiselle Daliron by being the professor of her young brother, to whom I know she gives the most motherly care. And without taking on myself the right to look after her conduct, I must add that I believe her to be on a very straight path. The proof is that she asked me, just a few minutes ago, how best to use the talents she has for education, talents, I don't hesitate to say, about which, based on the pleasure and erudition of a conversation as substantial as varied, I have the most advantageous opinion."

317

"In fact," Lefebvre said, "since I have known her, she has worked in several secondary schools."

"Now," Simonnet continued, "to establish my relationship with that young lady even further, and dispel even the shadow of the slightest doubt, I will explain why, in fact, I did stop, a short while ago, in her company in a jewelry-watchmaker shop. The young Daliron, Monsieur, I'm pleased to say, is one of the most distinguished students in my class. During the last three weeks, he has been first of his class three times. And I can only approve of Mademoiselle, his sister, when appraised of his truly extraordinary success, she decided to award him one of those recompenses that, for boys, are constantly the object of the strongest and the most impatient ambition. The first watch, Monsieur, I don't know if that joy doesn't surpass even that of the first pair of boots or the first mistress. Mademoiselle Daliron communicated to me her desire to fulfill that hope with a gift of that kind. At the same time, she let me know that she was perfectly ignorant about watches, a fact that concerned her. A little more experienced than she, because I have lived longer, I then offered to assist her in her acquisition. Under my auspices, she has just bought a watch for twenty-eight francs fifty. The watchmaker is keeping it to check and regulate its time. The day after tomorrow, he promised to have it sent to the student Daliron at the Collège Henri IV without fail. These are the bracelets and necklaces with which I was occupied at the moment you were watching us, busy becoming a troublesome seducer into the thoughts of Mademoiselle, your relative."

"Monsieur, please accept my profuse thanks and my excuses," the Commandant said effusively.

"I do accept them," Monsieur Simonnet said, on leaving him, "but, in your turn, may it please you to accept some advice from my white hairs: that is, to be less prompt to suspect wickedness, and not believe that in spying on women, you would ever find yourself more informed."

Monsieur Simonnet had already gone several steps and he was saying to himself that he had certainly put that man in his place when he heard quick steps behind him and turned around. He found himself again face to face with Lefebvre.

"Monsieur," the Commandant said to him, "I ask you to please not tell Mademoiselle Daliron about our encounter."

"Monsieur," the professor responded, "I don't see Mademoiselle Daliron twice in six months and I don't make a habit of getting involved in family affairs. It will be as you wish."

This time, the parting was definitive. Broken by fatigue, and most of all by emotion, Lefebvre returned slowly to Belleville. The sad campaign that he had just completed had raised to a serious sentiment the violent movement of sensuality that had at first attracted him to Herminie Daliron. The woman who was for one moment suspected, once the injustice of that suspicion had been demonstrated, gained by that test a sort of halo. He was so relieved by the lifting of that weight oppressing his breast, that there was an ineffable rush of gratitude and of tenderness towards the same woman who, from an abyss of anger and despair, now transported him into the heaven of loving sentiments and faith. This didn't affect only the particular sentiment which preoccupied him; the benefit of the declaration of innocence that she had just obtained extended over the entire life of the accused. So, from that moment on, for Lefebvre, Herminie Daliron was no longer that available, seductive woman, whom he had not hesitated to approach. She was a noble woman who, through hard work—since she had asked Monsieur Simonnet to find her lessons to give—was trying to reform her life which, in addition, she was honoring by her marvelous devotion to the young brother confided to her care. Begun as a rather vulgar adventure, the Commandant's encounter with that girl, had been changed into one of those invasive, dominating passions, for the satisfaction of which he felt ready for every sacrifice and which could have the most decisive influence over his entire life.

Returning home, Lefebvre said to his wife:

"I believe that I have decided to take that position, and it's better paid than I was expecting. Come now, old girl, cheer up. In the future, your signature will be honored."

319

VI. Double Entry Bookkeeping

Two days after the great little events we just recounted, Alfred, the young secretary of the banker Martin Lambert rode past Herminie's windows on his way to make his usual ride in the Bois de Boulogne. Needless to say, behind a discreetly opened curtain, Mademoiselle Daliron was watching. Suddenly she let out a frightened cry, and, throwing circumspect behavior to the winds, she rapidly opened the window. A moment later, her head bare and showing an indescribable emotion, she began suddenly running down the street.

"Take him into my apartment over there, across the street, on the first floor," she said to two passing officials who had lifted the young man, unconscious, from the pavement.

A pile up of carriages had frightened the horse Alfred was riding, and he had been thrown off by its violent rearing. Taking the victim of that accident to his domicile, the home of the banker whose townhouse was very near in the same street, would have undoubtedly been the simplest thing to do. But Mademoiselle Daliron, thought only of immediate care for the condition his wound required. Providentially, in Paris, a doctor rarely misses appearing at the theatre of an accident; he found that initiative appropriate, and followed his new patient into the lodging that offered itself to be transformed into a surgery. After several efforts to bring his patient out of his swoon, seeing that he remained unconscious, the doctor thought that he should bleed him at that moment and on that spot.

Nothing could have been more opportune. The trauma caused by the fall had started a concussion, which was thus averted. As soon as the blood had stopped flowing, the sick man opened his eyes and seemed astonished to find himself in an unknown apartment, lying on a divan, in the hands of a doctor who was applying a ligature to his arm. Shortly thereafter, he recalled what had happened to him, and, making sure by examining himself that it had caused no fracture or internal lesion, finally, once again totally himself, he addressed his strongest gratitude to the gracious hostess whom he saw standing beside him. He soon found himself recovered enough, leaning on the arm of the doctor, to return to the townhouse where he lived.

The next day, his misadventure having had no repercussions, he went to Mademoiselle Daliron's apartment to pay his thanks. Just imagine the delight of the poor woman, distraught by the most sudden and the most unexpected event, to possess, all to herself, seated on her divan, the man whom, the evening before, she was still happy to view from behind the fold of a curtain, without even daring to hope that her passionate attention would be returned. It wasn't that, on receiving the warm thanks of her guest the evening before, she hadn't somewhat counted on that stroke of good luck. The truth is that, preparing for any eventuality, after having sent the next morning to the Martin Lambert townhouse for news, that was completely reassuring, she had immediately begun to prepare for action. Running to a florist in the neighborhood, at a price that at any other time she would have thought outrageous, she had bought enough flowers to fill a small garden. When she returned, she arranged her apartment with the minutest and most attractive small attentions; then she got busy with herself. For two hours, she worked to create a simple toilette where everything had been weighed, calculated, planned in a way that nothing seemed artificial, but also where everything showed off her type of beauty.

Nevertheless, everything foreseen and arranged for her happiness, she still not did not appear calm. When she was in the presence of the dream of her heart, she was emotional and breathless, and couldn't answer the kind and graceful sentences by which the man in her debt was trying to express his gratitude. Finally, however, she soon recovered her self-possession, and the man who had already experienced the goodness of her heart could, on hearing her, take away an opinion not less favorable of the distinction of her mind.

That first visit, however, didn't last long, and the unusual thing was that it wasn't discretion but a kind of discomfort that

Alfred experienced that made him cut short his visit. A more adroit woman, perhaps less in love, would have been better able to manage the fervor of her reception, and by not coming on too strong, she wouldn't have made her pigeon take wing. Not naturally conceited, not being able to guess the prodigious impact he had made in the feelings of his amiable improvised nurse, Alfred couldn't understand anything about the truly immoderate impression he seemed to produce on her. Her eyes plunged with excitement into his, then were suddenly lowered; her voice seemed at moments to be altered; she felt a kind of galvanic skin response to her whole body by only accidentally brushing his hand. All that, it must be admitted, resembled the maneuvers of a coquette who had decided to ensnare him. On the other hand, he had to tell himself that rarely a comedy so close to the truth had been played out. Challenged by where he stood as to his good fortune, he thought he would see clearer in a second encounter, and when he asked permission to return, gallantly noting that his gratitude was far from having been sufficiently expressed, one didn't wonder if that permission would be quick to be granted.

In life, bad and good luck come in waves. Mademoiselle Daliron had no sooner seen hope emerge in hers than she received a note from Monsieur Simonnet in which he told her to go without delay to see a family he had told about her. There she could probably be hired to give lessons to two young students. The remuneration, the old professor added, seemed to be very honorable. Carefree, as one is when there is a breath of happiness in his sails, Herminie ran there, where she was expected. Immediately hired and having accepted the arrangements, the generosity surpassing all her expectations, she returned home gaily, and like the Perrette[176] of La Fontaine,

---

[176] Perrette is the milkmaid in one of Jean de La Fontaine's *Fables* who, on the way to the fair to sell the jug of milk she is carrying on her head, daydreams of what she will do with the money. She mentally turns her milk into cash, the cash into a

started counting her expectations. Just with the money from teaching, she could pay all the costs of her brother's education. As for her personal needs, she should also be able to pay for them if, as she had been led to hope, in case they were satisfied with her services, they would procure her additional students.

The night had already fallen. Totally occupied with her budget, Herminie Daliron had arrived at the door of her house when she suddenly found herself facing Lefebvre who had probably been loitering there for some time waiting for her. She wanted to avoid being accosted by that man, since at that moment, she felt not at all disposed to listen to him, but he blocked the door.

"Ah! Mademoiselle, today you are alone," the Commandant said to her. "You can be talked to."

"No, Monsieur," Herminie answered drily. "Please let me enter my house."

"Certainly, if you will let me step inside with you, because I have a million things to say to you."

"But, Monsieur, I have nothing to hear."

"Please," said Lefebvre, "it's not a matter of insignificant things to tell you; it's a very serious subject I have to take up with you."

"There can be nothing serious between us. I don't know you. You imposed on me on that one time, but I will not permit your insistence to become an obsession."

"You are wicked and you would regret the harshness of your treatment of me if you knew what I have decided to do for you."

"I don't know that I have asked you to do anything for me, and will you please, I repeat, not keep me standing in the street this way."

"It seems," said Lefebvre, annoyed by the dry tone with which he had been answered, "that since me, you have made

---

calf, the calf into a cow, the cow into a pig, the pig into chickens; but trips and breaks her jug of milk. Also see Note 89.

some richer conquest? That's to be seen, however, because I have become a rich man, Mademoiselle. It's good for you to know that."

"So much the better for you, Monsieur, and I'm sure there is no shortage of women to whom that news should appear interesting. Will you, please, let me pass?"

"Or perhaps," Lefebvre continued, with that kind of premonition that men in love are sometime gifted with, "Monsieur the sylph has descended from the skies?"

"That's possible," said Herminie, in a tone in which pride of happiness had made her put more affirmation than prudence advised.

"Well!" Lefebvre shouted in a threatening accent, "if I find him anywhere near you, that handsome cherubim, I'll take care of him."

Frightened by that statement where all the possible consequences came immediately to mind, and seeing that she was dealing with a man definitely and brutally in love, Mademoiselle Daliron said:

"If you believe you will be listened to with that kind of violent argument, you are very much mistaken. I could perhaps not remain insensitive to a love that spoke the language of the heart, but I shall not put up with threats and domineering behavior, when you have no right over me!"

"You are right! I'm a fool," said Lefebvre, "but I have gone through so many worried thoughts since I met you. I have thought about you so much! And when I came completely happy to place at your feet the new existence that I have made for myself, It is painful to see myself treated with this cruelty!"

There was in Lefebvre's voice an emotion so real that it would have been communicated to Herminie even if, by the clarity of a street lamp several feet from them, she had not been surprised to see a large tear roll down the ruddy and suntanned face of the old soldier.

"Come now," she said, "dear Monsieur, I have yet to know your name, and you want me to be in love with you!"

"My name is Lefebvre," said the Commandant, "and I know that neither my name nor my person are such as to turn the head of a charming woman like you. But why, when, the first time that we saw each other, you were kind and talkative, and today, you won't even allow me to talk to you?"

"Because I have social propriety to consider, because you have already compromised me once by entering by force in my apartment where I never invite anyone, and you next come to knock impolitely on my door as if I were a prostitute."

"But, Mademoiselle, you know very well—I told you so—that I didn't leave your apartment with the same ideas I came in with. Would have I become as passionate about enriching myself as I have done for a prostitute?"

At that moment, someone who rented an apartment in the same house knocked at the door and interrupted the conversation taking place there. Herminie tried to take advantage of this opportunity to part company with the amorous Commandant, but he seized her arm and held it in a tight grip. Fearing a scandal, she let the neighbor enter and closed the door after him.

"This is terrible, Monsieur," she said when they were alone, "to make a spectacle of me like this, to use violence against me!"

"Well," said Lefebvre, with the stupid obstinacy of a man in love, "let me come in. I repeat, I have a million things to tell you and you would be less compromised than to talk to me here in the street."

"No, Monsieur, you will not come into my apartment where I never invite anyone, and most of all at such an hour. If it's absolutely necessary that I listen to you, let's do it here."

"Take my arm then," said Lefebvre. "That will draw less attention."

"All right," Herminie said, and she walked rapidly until they had come to the entry of a street less frequented than the Rue de Provence and the Chaussée-d'Antin, which, at that time, was the end of busy Paris traffic.

"Well, then, Mademoiselle," the Commandant began again, when he believed they were in a place where they would not be interrupted. "I was telling you that I have thought a great deal of the precarious position that you have confided to me, and above all, of that young brother whose education you are supporting with a devotion that touched me."

"I appreciate the care you want to take of me, but you are concerning yourself uselessly. I am not in the desperate situation that you seem to believe. With the ability I have for teaching, I will always be able to earn my living honorably. I am not the least in the world embarrassed to find lessons."

"I don't mean that, but especially when there are responsibilities, from one day to the next, you could fall sick and in addition, at some point, there might not be any lessons available, and it seems to me..."

"That a kept woman," Herminie interrupted quickly, seeing the poor Commandant searching for his words, "is accommodated in a much better way?"

"What you are saying is horrible," Lefebvre responded. "A woman isn't kept when a trusted friend, who is better able than she to share his good fortune, dips into his purse."

Lefebvre wasn't clever enough to phrase his thought better. Mademoiselle Daliron also somewhat embarrassed him by answering:

"Friendships which agree to accept such services are not formed from one day to the next. They must, on the contrary, be of long duration and robust, in order to withstand such favors."

"But everything must have a beginning."

"Without a doubt; but a beginning is not the end."

"All that," said Lefebvre, "is the argument of a woman who isn't in love."

"Did I, by any chance, tell you that I was in love with you?"

"No, but me, I love you, like a fool, and passions such as these always end up being shared..."

"What you are saying, my dear Monsieur, doesn't make a shadow of sense. Is anyone master of his own heart? Can't someone be sensitive to a man's devotion, be sorry for him, without, for all that, giving herself to him?"

"Well, that's all I'm asking of you. Be sorry for me; but to have sympathy for me, you must see me. Time will do the rest."

"On the contrary, time will cure you if, just by talking with me for a quarter of an hour, you were able to fall into one of those loves which torment a life."

"Then you won't allow me to visit you?"

"No, in your own interest"

"Because you are in love with someone else."

"No, Monsieur, I don't love anyone. I told you about an imaginary love, thinking that would be enough to turn your thoughts. But how could I love someone who wouldn't recognize me, and by whom I would never hope to be noticed. If I loved someone, it would be to make him a husband, but I am not thinking of any such thing. I'm thinking of earning my living by teaching children; I'm thinking of the future of my brother; and just for him, I would decline any other engagement. I don't want him, one day, after I have managed to help him to an honorable existence, to be ashamed of his sister."

"That future, Mademoiselle, we will work for it together. I will be like a father to him. A woman cannot bring up a boy alone. Besides, you talk about lessons; you don't have any, I know. The proof is that you yourself told me that. At another time, you were obliged to listen to a person who helped you."

"I told you that, Monsieur, because I wanted to disgust you with me in every way."

"You did not succeed! Since we have seen each other, I have not had any other thought but of you. Be whatever you are, what does that matter to me? I love you, and my blood boils. The fire that you have lit, beautiful Herminie, only you can extinguish."

Putting his arm around the waist of the poor girl, the amorous Commandant tried roughly to steal a kiss. But Herminie

327

broke away with a gesture of disgust, which made the Commandant beside himself.

"After all," he said, "do you believe I'm your dupe? A woman who earns her living honestly doesn't have time to sit on the boulevard, as you did when I saw you."

"Very well, Monsieur, insult me now with your words! I'm only a woman and I can't avenge myself. It has to be said that you have a very seductive way of paying court to people!"

"Forgive me, Herminie. I lost my head. I'm saying hurtful things, but you know that I don't mean a word of. Tell me that you will allow me in your apartment."

That kind of refrain to which Lefebvre came back incessantly, if it wasn't witty or conclusive, testified at least to a man who was seriously obsessed by a single idea. Only an imperious and dominating love could make him proceed with that stupid insistence and turbulent lack of reason.

"That's impossible," responded Mademoiselle Daliron. "In a position like mine, I must take the greatest care. A man who came frequently to see me would soon be noticed, and I cannot, by an appearance of flighty behavior, expose myself to losing the confidence of the families where I will earn my bread."

"Then you swear to me that you don't receive men in your apartment?"

"Obviously, and I am astonished that you can think the contrary."

"That's good! I'll find out!" said the Commandant, that Herminie had brought back to the entry of the Rue de Provence. And bowing to her with a resolution and coldness that frightened her, he let her return to her apartment alone.

VII. Desperate Times, Desperate Measures

Herminie Daliron, couldn't hide the fact from herself; a terrible worry had just entered her life. She was dealing with a madman dominated by a kind of bestial passion whose violence was equaled only by its tenacity. For herself, she would have to endure a tiring obsession that, sooner or later, might have ended. It was only a question of time. But if Alfred, entering or leaving her apartment, was seen by that madman who was going to set up watch outside her house, what misfortune might then occur? To deprive herself of the visits of the man she loved would have been a cruel sacrifice, but would that lessen the danger? Unless she confided the entire situation to the young secretary, wasn't it to be feared that, seizing on the most insignificant sign of recognition, a bow, for example, from him that Lefebvre caught in passing, couldn't that madman seize on that to justify a quarrel? Besides, to make such a confession to a man whom she had met only so recently might either discourage him from continuing a relationship that had scarcely begun, or on the contrary accelerate the danger she was trying to avoid. If she'd be in a better financial state, Mademoiselle Daliron would have soon decided what to do: to move, hoping that her persecutor would soon lost her trace. But moving would have entailed expenses that she didn't feel she was in a position to shoulder. The flowers she'd bought that morning had left its mark on her poor budget, and now how could its balance be maintained if she had to support a new extraordinary expense because of that unexpected necessity?

Herminie thought of another way: to go and lodge a complaint with the Commissioner of Police of her neighborhood, and to place herself under the protection of that magistrate. But not only was that violent extremity repugnant to her, it didn't remove the possibility of a collision between the two men who had entered her life in such different manner. And, again, to bring public scrutiny into her life, one should have a completely pure and irreproachable conduct. After François-Honoré Dubignon, Mademoiselle Daliron, as she herself had admitted to Lefebvre, had had another paid liaison, and nothing proved that the day the Commandant had found her on the boulevard, she was not becoming ripe for a third grape-picker that her limited resources and financial difficulties had advised her to meet.

After a night spent going over all those thoughts, Herminie remained greatly perplexed, when her good star brought to her the excellent Monsieur Simonnet. He came with the very natural curiosity of knowing the success of his recommendation. He was happy to learn its fortunate result. That subject exhausted, keeping poorly the promise of absolute discretion he had made to Lefebvre, for whom he had very little respect, the old professor asked Herminie:

"Do you have a relative in Paris?"

"Me? Not that I'm aware of," she answered.

"Don't you know a military man to whom your family gave the care of watching your behavior?"

"No. I don't have any family. An aunt who took charge of the education of my young brother, and who, dying, left me the care of the poor child, was the last surviving member of my family."

"Then this gentleman told me a fabricated story, and it was only for himself that he took the care of watching you."

"Ah!" Herminie then said, "Now, I know who you are talking about. A man who took it into his head to fall in love with me, and who is tiring me with his obsession."

"That's charming!" said Monsieur Simonnet, bursting out laughing. "Did he then think he should be jealous of me because he saw you on my arm?"

"What! He dared to approach you?"

"Certainly! But you have to see how I rebuked him. What was even more comic was that he challenged me to a duel."

"But that's inconceivable," said Herminie. "And you perhaps thought that he had some rights to me?"

"As far as that, no. Also, I believe that if you decided to take a lover, you wouldn't choose one of that type."

"It's impossible to imagine, Monsieur, the persecutions he has made me endure. But how can we get rid of this madman? I say we, because I'm looking to you for advice. What more should I do? I no longer dare see my friends. Just imagine, for example, if you had been younger when he challenged you to a duel!"

"Good Lord! My dear young lady, those sorts of troublesome people are to be dealt with by the Police."

"I've already thought about that; but a woman alone has so little support! People are always ready to believe that she has, to a certain point, authorized the persecution she has come to complain about."

"Well! Move. The Rue des Postes, where your two students live, is not very near the rue de Provence, and you would avoid a long trip."

"My intention had really been, in fact, to be closer to my students, and what has happened with that monomaniac is one more reason to make me decide to move. But when you are not rich, you can't do what you want when you want it."

"Is that all?" the old professor replied. "Leave your furniture here and rent your apartment furnished. In this elegant neighborhood, you will get a good price, and come to the Latin Quarter, where your students reside. I know a very quiet hotel, Place de l'Estrapade, where you can get cheap rooms. With my recommendation, you will be enthusiastically welcomed and you can pay at the end of the month. After that, you will have very nice neighbors, thanks to your gentlemen students."

"Ah! Monsieur, you don't think that a woman of my age…"

"No, I was joking," answered Monsieur Simonnet, "but if don't like with my solution..."

"No, I do, completely. Would you be kind enough to be my agent in this matter and get my new lodgings ready?"

"In two hours, that will be arranged, and you can move into our neighborhood. However, I suggest that you should not give your concierge your new address. That devil of a man might find a way to make her talk."

"Ah! Certainly, I will take care not to do that."

"If renters are found for the apartment you are leaving, I will come to collect the rent during my walk."

"In truth, Monsieur, you overwhelm me with your kindness!"

"No, and you should understand that I'm doing it for the sake of morality. Further, I am delighted to be able to obstruct the projects of that ugly and stupid seducer. Besides, it amuses me to take a stand against one of those janissaries [177] who have oppressed our beautiful country for such a long time."

"That means," Herminie said gaily, "that I can even dispense with gratitude! That being so, Monsieur, I accept your kind offer and in two hours, my bags packed, I will be at the hotel you mentioned."

"It's the *Hôtel de Londres,* Place de l'Estrapade," Simonnet answered and immediately got on his way to do his good deed.

Mademoiselle Daliron's first care, as soon as she had taken possession of a neat and tidy bedroom in the hotel where she had been recommended, was to write the following note:

Monsieur,

Obliged by unforeseen circumstances to leave my lodging on the Rue de Provence, I thought, in case you took a notion to visit your former neighbor, that I should inform you of my new address. It seems polite for me to do that. To take advantage of this information would be heroic of you, because it's a matter of a trip to the end of the world.

Please accept, etc.

Herminie Daliron

In adding the address of her hotel on her note, Herminie regretted not having the family name, which she had never thought to learn, of her flame. So she merely addressed it to *Monsieur Alfred, c/o Monsieur Lambert, Rue de Provence.*

---

[177] The Janissaries were elite infantry units that formed the Ottoman Sultan's household troops, bodyguards and the first modern standing army in Europe. Like *Mamluk* before, the word is being used here as a pejorative equivalent of soldier.

She then said to herself:

"I seem to be writing to a valet. That doesn't matter. If he comes, I'll explain that.'"

Then, she no longer lived for anything but his visit for which she had just set up the opportunity.

A week passed without her having received any news from Alfred, and she was beginning to see her beautiful dream vanish when, one afternoon, when her soul was sad to the point of tears, she heard a soft tap on the door, which brought back all her illusions.

Having rushed to open it, she found herself face to face with Alfred. She became pale; and had to put her hand over her heart to slow its beating. Feeling her legs give way beneath her, she fell into a chair which, fortunately, was near her.

In that situation, it couldn't be a question of being coquettish. Such an expression of emotion couldn't be acted out without a little preparation, and the face can't turn red on command. Alfred then could be sure that he was awaited with an impatience full of anxiety, and he had to be even more certain of it when Herminie said to him with very badly feigned surprise:

"What, Monsieur, you've had the courage to come into this far-flung neighborhood?"

"But it was a duty," the young secretary answered. "And it's not very often one find among duties those very pleasant to fulfill. I should, perhaps, have done that somewhat earlier, but some pressing business kept me."

"As I dared to send you my address at a moment's notice, you were sure of being received with gratitude."

"But," said Alfred, smiling, "you intend to study law, since you have come to lodge so near the Pantheon?"[178]

---

[178] Located near the Sorbonne, the historical house of the University of Paris, founded in 1257, and still home to one of France's most prestigious Law School today.

"No, I'm not a student. On the contrary, I make people study and I have moved closer to several students I have in his neighborhood."

"Music lessons?"

"No, Monsieur, something much more prosaic: lessons in French, history, geography…"

"Really? But then we are colleagues, because I work in literature."

"I know that. And I even know that, despite your young age, your success has been brilliant. As for our being colleagues, it resembles a little like the Dictionary resembles an epic poem; they are both books."

"Good Lord! Who knows if, in intellectual careers, you haven't chosen the better path! Me, I have just started, and I already I find the profession very demanding."

"However, you're still young, and your talent has already earned you an enviable position. You have come to be indispensable to a man who is on his way to becoming a Minister…"

"You should say, secretary to a bag of silver."

"Perhaps. But for a father-in-law, a wealthy financier isn't something to be disdained!"

"A father-in-law?" Alfred answered with astonishment, "Who told you that?"

"Neighborhood gossip. Paris, despite all its districts, is like a little town where everything is known."

"When one seeks to inform oneself," Alfred remarked.

"Oh! Obviously. If one doesn't seek to inform oneself about things, one has very little chance of learning them."

"But how have I merited that you take so much interest in me?"

"I saw you ride on horseback every day past my windows; you then became one of my neighbors, and neighbors, you know, are always a little interesting."

"Yes, but you gathered much false gossip, such as the tale of this impending marriage."

"Ah! I know that it's not true! The mother formally opposes it; the father is neutral; as for the girl, she's a coquette who does and doesn't want it, and one dies with the pain of trying to find out her real truth."

"Enough! You're confusing me with all these details."

"Are they accurate?"

"Not the least in the world."

"Then, they shouldn't confuse you. There is nothing easier than to be misinformed. However, I believe that I obtained some good reports, and I am often astonished at your patience. To endure something like this, someone keeping you suspended between a yes and a no! In your place, I would force that young lady to make a decision."

"Then how would you think to go about doing that?"

"Why would you tax my imagination for a mere hypothesis?"

"But let's say it isn't one."

"Well! Nothing is simpler; I would make that *Belle Arsène* crazy with jealously."[179]

"Then she must be given a rival?"

"Without a doubt she should have a rival, and she should know that."

"But to love two persons—can that be?"

"Oh, no! Men, most of all, are incapable of that; everyone knows that. Nothing is so rare as to see their heart endowed with the gift of ubiquity, to be in two places at one time."

"You would at least allow that it would be necessary that the woman with whom one is plotting an odd affair, have the means to deliver her secret to the coquette, for whom it would be like a form of torture!"

---

[179] *La belle Arsène* (1773) is a French *opéra comique* by Pierre-Alexandre Monsigny to a libretto by Charles-Simon Favart.

"Dear Monsieur, do you have yet to learn that women, just for the pleasure of striking down a rival, are prepared to do anything?"

"In addition, be aware then, Mademoiselle, that, in order to be efficacious, love as a weapon cannot be used beyond a certain reality."

"But to be sure, to play a role well, it must be entered into completely."

"Well! Where can there be found a woman who would consent to a temporary liaison that would have no other goal but to install eternity into the life of someone else?"

"Search and you will find."

"Yes, you, dear Mademoiselle, you would be that person, because you are all grace and all charm."

And saying that, Alfred took Mademoiselle Daliron's hand. She made no answer; her breast rose, making her respiration so short that saying a word would have been impossible. At the same time, she lowered her eyes and made no effort to take back her hand. Alfred, for his part, was no less moved. He slowly drew his lips near a dazzlingly white shoulder. Instead of making a gesture of distaste, as she had during the indiscretion of Commandant Lefebvre, Herminie seemed like a woman who felt she was dying.

Two hours later, when Alfred left the Hôtel de Londres, Mademoiselle Martin Lambert was going to have something to react to!

VIII. Lefebvre's Rival

Commandant Lefebvre had some ability in organizing the surveillance with which he had threatened Herminie Daliron. In the first three days that followed his meeting with the young woman, he was occupied with getting installed into his new functions, and, therefore, he didn't go wandering around town, so that all the arrangements to countermand his disquieting projects could be undertaken in complete freedom.

336

In the morning of the fourth day, as he was passing in front of the lodgings of the cruel object of his unreciprocated love, judge his stupefaction on seeing behind the opened curtains a shaving mirror hung from one of the windows, and in front of that mirror, a gentleman of a respectable age busy shaving himself!

"That's too much!" he shouted to himself, "a rival scandalously living in her apartment."

Getting immediately to the bottom of the situation, he ran to the doorbell that he rang violently, and then almost without a pause, he continued to pound on the door with his fist.

His razor in his hand and his face covered with soap, Mademoiselle Daliron's tenant came to open the door, saying:

"My word, Monsieur, you're in a big hurry."

"Where is Mademoiselle Daliron?"

"Don't know her."

And the man with the razor closed the door.

Lefebvre, not considering himself beaten, was going to begin knocking again, when the concierge, with whom he had already had a brush, intervening, said to him:

"So, what do you want again? Mademoiselle Daliron is not here. She has left Paris, and you can see that her lodgings are now rented to someone else."

"But where has she gone?"

"To China," the concierge answered.

"Come now, Madame," the Commandant continued, "don't joke. You know where Mademoiselle Daliron has gone..."

And he tried to slide a hundred *sou* coin into her hand.

"I don't want to steal your money," she then said, somewhat mollified. "Mademoiselle Daliron left here three days ago without confiding to me where she was going and charging me with sub-letting her place furnished. The apartment is well taken care of and nicely furnished. I therefore immediately found a respectable gentleman, whose cleaning I will do, and I beg you not to disturb his tranquility."

"And you don't know where she has gone, if she has left Paris, or only changed neighborhoods?"

"That might be, and that might not be. Mademoiselle Daliron wasn't very talkative and didn't tell me anything even in confidence."

"But then, did she have many visitors in her apartment? The day she left, did you see anyone?"

"I heard something. That day, I saw an old gentleman with gold-rimmed glasses that she later told me would come to collect the rent if the apartment was rented."

"And when are the rents paid?"

"Furnished apartments are paid by the month, and I ask that the first month be paid in advance."

"So that, from one moment to the next, you may see that gentleman arrive, coming to collect her money?"

"It may be like that, or it may not be. That depends on whether the man is more or less in a hurry. He doesn't have to worry that I will give him an exact accounting. I can say that I am known in the neighborhood, where, for seventeen years, tending the same door, no one has ever said a word about my integrity, nor that of my husband."

"Well! When this gentleman comes back, try to learn a little from him if Mademoiselle Daliron is still in Paris. I have some things of major interest to tell her."

And another hundred *sou* coin came into play. This time the concierge accepted it and Lefebvre was thus authorized to return for information. He could have worn himself out a long time in vain quests if, at the end of two weeks, fate, which, from time to time, takes a pleasure in being the greatest of romanticists, and also because of his perseverance in frequenting the Rue de Provence, hadn't finally thrown him onto the steps of Monsieur Simonnet, who had come to Herminie's former lodgings to get news of the rent.

Lefebvre didn't make the mistake of approaching him, or wasting time by going to see the concierge to collect the information that she might have been able to procure. Following the steps of the old professor at a distance, so as not to run any risk of being discovered, he went across all of Paris with him, and finally saw him enter the Hôtel de Londres, Place de l'Estrapade, where he stayed only for a moment.

Lefebvre's first thought was to go into the hotel and to ask for Herminie. But he thought that she may not be registered there under her own name, and without being able to get to her, in taking that useless action, he would have exposed himself to arousing her attention by the report that would be given about him: *a gentleman came to ask for you.*

The best thing for the Commandant in love to do was to assure himself with his own eyes of the fugitive's presence in the hotel. But that surveillance was not without difficulty. The Place de l'Estrapade, where she must go about, was an open and moderately frequented square, and any man stationed or walking up and down there couldn't miss being noticed.

Lefebvre now had money. Laverenette had carried away his last indecisions by promising to have the first month of his salary paid in advance. Taking possession immediately had become a determining consideration. His ardent passion for Herminie made him believe she would give in by the offer of a monthly subsidy. He could then, like lovers in comedies, pay a scrap metal dealer who kept a shop across from the Hôtel de Londres, a moderately fair price to let him set up an observation post there. He passed himself off to that man as a police agent working on a political surveillance, which didn't harm him in any way to be considered. Ordinary citizens didn't feel the repugnance for the police that they caused the upper classes; they saw them only as men clothed with a certain portion of power.

To give himself every chance of success, Lefebvre, still playing a role, judged a disguise necessary. He changed his outer coat for a workman's shirt and put on a laborer's cap. Thus decked out, in the shop to which he had gained entrance, placed so as nothing that happened in the hotel escaped him, he waited.

After two hours of feverish surveillance, he saw Herminie leave the hotel to go and give her lessons. If he had followed his inclination, he would have immediately dashed after her; but he recalled that his previous street encounters had gone badly. Then, as the saying goes: "Appetite comes with eating." Not content with having picked up the trail of the fugitive, he wanted to know what people she saw and to solve the problem of the rivalry that was his obstacle, if such a thing existed. He remained then at his observation post and continued his surveillance.

That first day was hard; it gave him nothing beyond what has just been said. Once she had left, Mademoiselle Daliron did not return until very late in the evening. She had dined in the house where she gave her lessons.

The scrap metal dealer closed his shop at nightfall. Chased from his post, Lefebvre tried for some time to continue his surveillance standing outside. But at that time, there was a veterans' barracks near the Hôtel de Londres; the sentry standing guard at the door, seeing a man dressed in the same uniform as he, seemingly lying in wait, found that competition suspicious. He threatened to arrest him if he didn't leave. In addition, Lefebvre was half-dead with hunger; he therefore went to have supper, promising himself that, the next day, he would break into Herminie's room, even if he had made no new discovery.

The next day Mademoiselle Daliron didn't go out; she gave only one lesson every other day. But in the morning, Lefebvre, who was at his post early, having seen her at a window on the third floor, had good hopes of resolving his problem. About three o'clock Herminie came to her window. Her looking constantly in the same direction seemed to indicate that she was expecting someone. Ten minutes later, a carriage stopped at the door of the hotel. A man with a young physique got out, holding a bouquet, and, at the same time, Herminie closed the window and left it. Lefebvre had neither the time nor the opportunity to see the face of the man he immediately took to be a rival.

"It's the sylph," he said to himself with the clairvoyance that jealousy gives, and he immediately took off his disguise.

He went across the square, resolutely entered the hotel and asked for Mademoiselle Daliron.

"On the third floor front, number 12," answered the bell-hop he had addressed.

When he arrived at the door of the room he intended to invade, Lefebvre listened carefully and heard nothing. He knocked; no answer. He knocked again, louder; still the same silence. Becoming more and more violent, his insistence threatened to create a scandal, to the extent that the owner of the hotel who, in a neighboring room, was overseeing some arrangements, came out into the corridor, saying to the turbulent person:

"Why are you making that noise at that door, Monsieur? If no one comes to the door, that's because there's no one there."

"I beg your pardon, Madame, but before entering, I saw the lodger at her window."

"Well! Then that's because no one wants to open the door. With the noise you're making, there is no doubt that someone heard you."

"Yes, but I want someone to open the door."

"What's that? You *want* someone to open the door."

"Yes, Madame, I have the right to want that. The person who is hiding under the name of Mademoiselle Daliron is my wife, and if she is still obstinate and won't open the door, I'm going to have the Commissioner of Police called to lend me the force of the law."

"What! Monsieur, a scandal like that in my house!"

"Avoid it, Madame, by intervening yourself. Call out that stubborn woman. Tell her that you know she is in her room and that someone needs absolutely to speak to her."

Deciding that doing that would prevent the danger of seeing her house compromised, the woman approached the door, and after having knocked rather discretely:

"Mademoiselle Daliron," she said, "open the door! It's me; I have something urgent to tell you."

Since there was a small room before Herminie's bed-room, she hadn't been able to hear the exchange that had taken place between the hostess and her persecutor. She therefore came to open the door without a great deal of mistrust. She attributed the preceding noise at her door to some badly trained domestic sent by the proprietor, after which she had decided to come up herself. When the door was opened, Herminie immediately saw Lefebvre.

"Madame," she cried out, speaking to the owner, "have that man thrown out."

And she tried to close her door, but the Commandant had already rushed into the apartment. The owner, who, without the recommendation of Monsieur Simonnet, would never have accepted Herminie as a lodger, saw in the present situation something to think about. She saw in Lefebvre a mature and decorated man, a very plausible husband. She therefore didn't call for the help as Herminie asked, simply saying, before she left:

"Monsieur, I beg of you, no scene! Because you know that I will be the one then to go and get the police. It is, as you know, just two steps from here."

With a rapid glance, the Commandant had noticed the door of a closed cabinet, the bouquet placed in a vase on the dresser, but not the rival he was looking for.

"Well, Monsieur," said Herminie, "what do you mean by this persecution? Seeing me here, doesn't it prove to you that my decision not to listen to you was definite?"

"Yes, I begin to see that my presence is not very pleasant to you, but that's not for you to tell me. There are people" he said, raising his voice affectedly, "who have the words to persuade me."

"What do you mean by that?" Mademoiselle Daliron asked quickly.

"I mean that bouquets don't walk all by themselves, and when I find them somewhere, they were brought by someone. This one is very pretty; it has a good odor. Couldn't the gallant

342

knight that you are hiding be asked the address of the florist who made it, so as to buy one when needed?"

"But, Monsieur, you are insane!" shouted Herminie.

"Insane, that's possible, but at least, I'm not a coward!"

Mademoiselle Daliron feared nothing so much as seeing the cabinet opened. However, at that last word, she was somewhat astonished to see it remain closed.

"Monsieur," she said to Lefebvre, "will you please leave, otherwise I'm going to ring and the threat the proprietor made to you, I will carry out myself."

"Leave!" said Lefebvre, shrugging, "It's the *other one,* dear young lady, that has to be told that. I also see that he must be helped..."

And he impetuously advanced toward the cabinet. Herminie, for her part, had thrown herself in front of him to bar the way.

At that moment, the door of the cabinet opened:

"Father," said Alfred, coming out, "without a doubt, you think, as I do, that it's time to put an end to this scene, where the Lefebvres aren't playing a role very worthy of them."

"My son!" exclaimed the Commandant, stunned.

And he dashed out of the apartment as if he had seen a bombshell about to explode near him.

TO BE CONCLUDED IN
THE MARQUIS DE LUPIANO

MYSTERIES & THRILLERS

M. Allain & P. Souvestre. *The Daughter of Fantômas; The Death of Fantômas*

A. Anicet-Bourgeois & Lucien Dabril. *Rocambole* (stage plays)

Guy d'Armen. *Doc Ardan: The City of Gold and Lepers; The Troglodytes of Mount Everest/The Giants of Black Lake; The Abominable Snowman*

A. Bernède. *Belphegor*; *Judex* (w/Louis Feuillade); *The Return of Judex* (w/Louis Feuillade); *The Shadow of Judex* (anthology)

A. Bisson & G. Livet. *Nick Carter vs. Fantômas* (stage play)

André Caroff. *The Terror of Madame Atomos; Miss Atomos; The Return of Madame Atomos; The Mistake of Madame Atomos; The Monsters of Madame Atomos; The Revenge of Madame Atomos; The Resurrection of Madame Atomos; The Mark of Madame Atomos; The Spheres of Madame Atomos; The Wrath of Madame Atomos* (w/M. & Sylvie Stéphan); *The Sins of Madame Atomos* (w/M. & Sylvie Stéphan)

Félicien Champsaur. *Homo-Deus; Nora, The Ape-Woman; Ouha, King of the Apes*

Jules Clarétie. *Obsession*

V. Darlay & H. de Gorsse. *Arsène Lupin vs. Sherlock Holmes: The Stage Play* (stage play)

Harry Dickson. *Harry Dickson: The Heir of Dracula; Harry Dickson vs. The Spider*

Séamas Duffy. *Sherlock Holmes in Paris*

Paul Féval. *The Black Coats (The Parisian Jungle; Heart of Steel; The Sword-Swallower; 'Salem Street; The Invisible Weapon; The Companions of the Treasure; The Cadet Gang); Gentlemen of the Night; John Devil*

Paul Féval, *fils. Felifax, the Tiger-Man*

Louis Forest. *Someone is Stealing Children in Paris*

Fortuné du Boisgobey: *Two Crimes*

Émile Gaboriau. *Monsieur Lecoq; The Casebook of Monsieur Lecoq*

Arnould Galopin: *Harry Dickson: The Man in Grey; Tenebras*

Goron & Émile Gautier. *Spawn of the Penitentiary*

G.L. Gick. *Harry Dickson: The Werewolf of Rutherford Grange*

Léon Gozlan. *The Vampire of the Val-de-Grâce*

Georges Grison. *The Heads that fell in Paris* (non-fiction)

Paul d'Ivoi. *Around the World on Five Sous* (w/Henri Chabrillat)

Paul Lacroix. *Danse Macabre*

Jean de La Hire. *Enter the Nyctalope; The Nyctalope on Mars; The Nyctalope vs. Lucifer; The Nyctalope Steps In; Night of the Nyctalope; Return of the Nyctalope*

Rick Lai. *Shadows of the Opera: Retribution in Blood; Sisters of the Shadows: The Curse of Cagliostro*

Etienne-Léon de Lamothe-Langon. *The Virgin Vampire*

Steve Leadley. *Sherlock Holmes and The Circle of Blood*

Maurice Leblanc. *Arsène Lupin vs. Countess Cagliostro; Arsène Lupin vs. Sherlock Holmes: 1. The Blonde Phantom; 2. The Hollow Needle; The Island of the Thirty Coffin; 813; The Many Faces of Arsène Lupin* (anthology)

Gustave Lerouge: *The Mysterious Doctor Cornelius* (3 vols.)

Gaston Leroux. *Chéri-Bibi* (stage play)*; The Phantom of the Opera; Rouletabille & the Mystery of the Yellow Room; Rouletabille at Krupp's*

Maurice Limat. *Mephista*

Jean-Marc & Randy Lofficier. *The Katrina Protocol;* (anthologists) *Tales of the Shadowmen 1-13; The Vampire Almanac* (2 vols.)

Charles Malato. *Lost!*

Richard Marsh. *The Complete Adventures of Judith Lee*

William Patrick Maynard. *The Terror of Fu Manchu; The Destiny of Fu Manchu*

Frank J. Morlok. *Sherlock Holmes: The Grand Horizontals* (stage play)*; Sherlock Holmes vs Jack the Ripper* (stage play);

Sherlock Holmes, Fantômas, Lupin, Raffles and More: The Spanish Plays (stage plays)

Jean Petithuguenin. *The Adventures of Ethel King, The Female Nick Carter*

P.-A. Ponson du Terrail. *The Immortal Woman; The Vampire and the Devil's Son; The Police Agent*

Georges Price. *The Missing Men of the* Sirius

Charles Rabou: *The Secret Bureau: The Secret Bureau: The Brothers of Death*

Antonin Reschal. *The Adventures of Miss Boston, The First Female Detective*

Henri de Saint-Georges. *The Green Eyes*

Norbert Sevestre. *Sâr Dubnotal: Jack the Ripper; The Astral Trail*

Eugène Thébault. *Radio-Terror*

P. de Wattyne & Y. Walter. *Sherlock Holmes vs. Fantômas* (stage play)

David White. *Fantômas in America*

Pierre Yrondy. *The Adventures of Thérèse Arnaud of the French Secret Service; The Adventures of Marius Pégomas, Marseille Detective*